A *Queen*
AND A
ROOK

TESTAMENTS OF THE SILK ROADS

DREW GALLAGHER

BALBOA.PRESS
A DIVISION OF HAY HOUSE

Balboa Press books may be ordered through booksellers or by contacting:

Balboa Press
A Division of Hay House
1663 Liberty Drive
Bloomington, IN 47403
www.balboapress.co.uk
UK TFN: 0800 0148647 (Toll Free inside the UK)
UK Local: (02) 0369 56325 (+44 20 3695 6325 from outside the UK)

Print information available on the last page.

ISBN: 978-1-9822-8705-4 (sc)
ISBN: 978-1-9822-8706-1 (e)

Balboa Press rev. date: 03/30/2023

Prologue

Black Sea, February 493 BC

"The winds are definitely changing, my Lord. Not for the better, I would wager?" the captain noted breezily. He gazed warily at the ominous clouds on the distant horizon.

"In the event of a storm, will we return to Panticapaeum?" the young Prince asked uneasily.

The Jewel of Mamy'eva is a middling size merchant vessel which flew the Boar's Head insignia of the Orch'tai Royal House. It had departed the port of Panticapaeum on the eastern coast of the Crimean Peninsula in the late afternoon and was now several hours out to sea. They hoped to reach the port of Tepe on the south-east shoreline of the Black Sea early the next day. The journey had been uneventful thus far, unusual for the time of year, yet the sky had darkened ominously in the past hour, a sure presage of a rare storm to come. The captain was a seasoned adventurer named Naeasses, now aged in his early thirties. He had been born and raised in Tanais to an Orch'tai father and Cretan mother, both long gone, and had first journeyed to sea at the tender age of six. His loyalty to the Orch'tai Crown was unquestioned, and it was for this reason that he had been selected by the Kor'nai to undertake this delicate clandestine mission.

Naeasses grinned at his young companion, aged only a year or so past his majority. "I take it you are not comfortable entrusting your fate to the will of Poseidon, my Lord? It is nothing to be ashamed of. Many a seasoned mariner once lived in abject terror of the sea."

"Were you once terrified of the sea, Captain Naeasses?" Crown Prince Ach'ti asked shyly.

"I was, my Lord. Any man who proclaims otherwise is a liar. Sailing at this time of year is always plagued by fears of a storm. Whenever the winds from the north meet the balmy air of the south, we are destined for a rough night."

Prince Ach'ti shivered lightly. "It is not natural for a man to be at sea in such foul weather, I would venture?"

"I am a Sea Captain, my Lord. It is most disagreeable for me to be ashore in any weather" Naeasses mused glibly.

"You sure tease, Captain Naeasses?" Ach'ti smiled tightly.

The captain grinned. "Only a little, young prince, I assure you." Naeasses leaned in close to the young Prince. "I shall let you in to a little secret, young man. That is the surest means of settling a queasy belly in the face of an approaching storm."

"What would that be, Captain Naeasses?" Ach'ti smiled hopefully.

"A belly full of wine or wodki, of course!" the captain grinned. "There is no surer cure for sea-sickness! I shall instruct the young wench, Paessa, to provision a couple of flagons to your quarters with haste. Dinner will be served in my private galley in two hours. I would be honoured if you would join me, young Prince, for you are my esteemed guest?"

"You are certain that we shall arrive at Tepe a few hours after first light, just as we planned?" the prince pressed. "I do not think it wise to keep our welcoming Committee waiting, Naeasses?"

"Indeed, we shall, my Lord. You shall be safe in your cabin until we disembark. I will send the girl, Paessa, along to your quarters presently."

A short while later, Crown Prince Ach'ti, son to the Royal Prince Khai'duc, beloved nephew of His Royal Majesty King Tagar of the Orch'tai Royal House, and his chosen heir and successor, sat alone in his cabin reading an urgent correspondence when a knock came at his door. "Enter!" he commanded. The door opens and the young girl, Paessa, aged twelve-and-a-half, enters with a tray bearing two large flagons, one of wine, the other wodki. "Thank you", the prince smiled warmly at the girl, who nodded politely at the handsome young man and left, closing the door behind her. A short while later, Paessa returned to inform Prince Ach'ti that supper was being served in the Captain's Private Galley. Prince Ach'ti was by now dressed for supper, and he hastily gathered his correspondence in a security box, locked it with a key, and squirreled this inside a pocket within his tunic. He left the room, locked the door, and followed the girl down the narrow corridor to the Captain's Quarters at the rear of the vessel. Sometime later, a ghoulish figure, garbed in a heavy black cloak, its hood drawn tight to avoid recognition, unlocked the door to the prince's cabin and slipped inside. A brief time later, the spectre locked the door and vanished into the gloom of the cargo hold.

Supper was a luxurious affair, befitting the Royal status of the esteemed guest. The pair dined on roast pheasant, pan-fried squid in lemon-garlic butter, roast mutton, and fresh oranges, washed down with fine wine from the Bordeaux and generous measures of apricot wodki. At the end of the meal, two hours later, the sky is cast in ominous gloom and the wind howls like a tormented soul. The sea was increasingly choppy and, soon enough, a cacophony of thunder battered *The Jewel of Mamy'eva* as surely as the wind, rain, and waves. The young Prince Ach'ti, who was unaccustomed to heavy feasting, was unsteady on his feet as he made his way through the lower deck to his cabin, so much so that he almost slipped and fell heavily twice. He was relieved to eventually reach his quarters and, slipping out of his evening dress and into his sleeping attire, he poured himself a large restorative draught of wodki. It tasted wonderful, far sweeter than the liquor served at the Captain's Table. He drained the goblet in a single gulp and poured himself a generous refill. Soon enough, he fell fast asleep.

When he awoke, a few hours later, Ach'ti felt nauseous and was sweating profusely. His sleeping robe was damp and clammy. He had been awoken by a strange sound coming from just outside his cabin, almost as if an animal had been clawing desperately at the door. Now, there was silence. Ach'ti felt decidedly queasy and stifled an immediate urge to vomit. He glanced around the cabin for a chamber pot, yet this was nowhere in sight. Climbing gingerly out of bed, he reached for his light woollen cloak. Perhaps his chamber pot had been left outside the door? *The girl, sweet little Paessa, must have hoped to empty it before he rose in the morning?* He unlocked the door and stepped outside, blinking in the gloom of the hold. The chamber-pot was nowhere to be seen. "Hades below!" he hisses, blinking fast as his eyes adjust to the natural light from the stairwell to the upper deck, a dozen yards or so away.

"Excuse me?" a soft voice entreated. It sounded like a young girl.

"Who is that?" Ach'ti whispered hoarsely.

"My name is Neria? Are you feeling ill, my Lord?" the girl asked earnestly. The concern for his welfare was genuine and comforting.

"I feel terrible, Miss? I think I shall be sick!" the young Prince mumbled despairingly.

"Would you like me to help you on to the deck? I was not myself, a brief while ago. It is nothing to be ashamed of, my Lord?" the girl spoke comfortingly. "I went on deck for a brief stroll. The fresh air did me a world of good."

"That would be lovely, thank you, you are most kind, Miss" Ach'ti sighed.

"Please, let me help you? It is this way." The girl seemed to breeze across the timbers, her feet barely kissing the deck. She was a strikingly pretty child, aged on the cusp of her teens, fast flowering in to a rare and comely creature. She had pale skin, blonde hair, and piercing blue eyes. Her features were sharp and angular, her nose almost hawk-like. Neria smiled reassuringly at the young prince and took him by the hand, leading him toward the stairs. "The stairs are just here, my Lord. Can you see them?"

"I feel terrible!" Ach'ti winced miserably. "The sea is no place for a man, not in this weather."

"I have witnessed far worse storms during the past few years, my Lord," the girl lied smoothly. "The storm and the malady will pass soon enough. You just need fresh air, that is all."

The girl, who had surprising strength in her lithe limbs, helped him up the stairs to the deck. The wind still howled, yet the thunder and rain had now ceased. The vessel seemed to bob lightly on the cascade of waves which crash rhythmically against its sides. Ach'ti adjusts his eyes to the light of the moon and nodded to a seaman who was slumped against the mast. The man was either dead or ensconced in a drunken stupor. "Is he drunk?"

"I fear so, my Lord, for you know what sailors are like?" Neria mused glibly. "Then again, perhaps you do not?" she teased.

"What in Hades name do you mean by that?" Ach'ti replied testily.

"You do not strike me as a man accustomed to life at sea?" Neria chirped.

"I much prefer the land. Thank you, sweet child, this is most welcome" Ach'ti sighed morosely.

"Is this your first voyage?" the girl asked. The hood of her cloak remained drawn tightly around her face.

"It has been quite some time since I was last at sea" Ach'ti lied smoothly. "Hopefully, it will be some time again before I travel by sea" Ach'ti confessed.

"It is much calmer in the summer months. Perhaps you could delay your return journey until then?"

A wave crashed against the side of the ship, unsteadying the pair. "I think I need to be sick!" Ach'ti groaned weakly.

"Come this way, my Lord? You can be sick over the side. I will steady you, so you have nothing to fear" the girl spoke softly.

The pair strolled steadily toward the starboard side of the ship. When they reach the side, the girl snaked her right arm around Ach'ti's waist as he vomited violently into the sea below, comforting him with soft, gentle words. "By the Gods, I could do with a drink?" Ach'ti shivered in the chill of the night air.

"Stay right there, I will fetch a flagon." Neria twirled away to return almost immediately with a flagon she had taken from the slumbering sailor. "Have some of this, it will take away the taste and make you feel better?"

"You are most kind, sweet child. The captain shall hear of your charity this night, for it will not go unrecognised. I am at your service, now and forever."

"That is most gracious of you, my Lord, and I am humbled by your chivalry. Alas, my sweet, for you there is no forever. I am sorry for that, my Lord" the girl spoke softly, with no malice.

Neria expertly slid a six-inch iron hairpin under Ach'ti's ribcage and drove it deep into his lung, piercing the muscular wall of the heart. Ach'ti gapes at the girl in silent terror, unable to scream, as his soul slips into the next world and his legs buckle beneath him. The girl held him tightly, slipping the hairpin out of his lung and stashing it within her cloak. She heaved with all her considerable strength and vaulted the young prince's corpse over the side of to plunge into the murky depths below. They would never find his body, for the sea-daemons would surely make short work of him. The comely young assassin moves silently across the slick of the deck, past the sleeping sailor, to disappear down the steps and vanish once more into the gloom of the hold.

Captain Naeasses was aghast when he learned of Prince Ach'ti's disappearance soon after first light the next morning. He could scarcely credit the news, less entertain its dire consequences. *The poor fellow must have drowned. There was no simply other logical explanation for his disappearance? It was an accident, nothing more, and was surely nobody's fault!* Soon enough, *The Jewel of Mamy'eva* berths at the wharf in Tepe, where an armed escort of Argata Royal Guards awaited their arrival. Quite regardless of Captain Naeasses humble protestations, the Argata soldiers took the entirely necessary precaution of summarily beheading the unfortunate sailor who was drunk on duty the previous night and, in the interests of certainty, the young servant-girl, Paessa! A visibly ashen Captain Naeasses supervised the unloading of the cargo, including an ornate oak chest, secured by a key that was now entrusted to a merchant named Telomenes, once the chest was secured aboard a waiting wagon. In the interests of historical accuracy, the same chest was subsequently entrusted to a Captain Nekhamose of *The Sycamore* for its onward journey to Samos a few days thereafter. Nekhamose, an

Egyptian by birth, was now in the employ of a mysterious merchant from Knossos. This man was Thassalor, and he was no friend to the Persian King or his pledged allegiants, which included the Royal House of the Argata in Archaeopolis!

PART ONE

One

The Royal City of Archaeopolis, historic capital of the Argata, is situated in the fertile Colchian Plains some fifty miles east of the Black Sea port of Tepe. The northern margins of the plains are dominated by the breath-taking panorama of the Caucasus and the majestic, snow-capped peaks of Mount El'bru and Mount Ush'ba. To the south, lies the rugged, emerald massif, known locally as the *Ze'bat*. The Colchian Plains laid claim to some of the richest soils in Asia Minor, and this facilitated the rapid ascension of the Argata in the middle of the Sixth Century BC. The origins of the Royal City are ancient, predating the diaspora of the Argata from the north, yet the accepted date for its foundation is the late Seventh Century BC, in the immediate aftermath of the sack of Nineveh, which its founders, the mystical *Ai'khaiti*, may have played a significant role. Persian scholars have long accepted this as truth, and the great Cyrus had taken a keen interest in taming its threat forever. The Argata had waged three wars against Persia, two against Cyrus himself (546 BC – 535 BC), and one against his successor, Cambyses (529 BC – 527 BC), during which the present ruler, Queen Lezika, was born. All had ended in ignominious defeat. According to legend, scarcely a fitting topic for public discussion, the spectre of renewed conflict with Persia had haunted the Argata in the last decades of the Sixth Century, culminating in the death of its last two King's, Dai'ma and Cai'fais, the latter allegedly murdered by his sister, the Princess Lezika!

Archaeopolis was no rival to Athens or Susa, nor did it make pretence to be, yet it was a magnificent sight to behold. Its impressive fortifications,

1

which ran for a little over two miles, encompasses nearly one-third of a square mile, with the Royal Palace to the far north, sited on a small escarpment on the west bank of the Velia'khi River, which courses to the east of the city, just beyond its wall. The sky was an ominous grey, and a thick winter fog shrouded the city as a despatch rider gallops north to break news of the tragedy to his beloved Queen. The man had ridden hard for two hours, each footfall closer to his reckoning with Her Majesty's wrath. Yet, in truth, while Queen Lezika had been rattled by the news of Crown Prince Ach'ti's unexplained disappearance, she had maintained her composure throughout the audience in her Private Chambers. She immediately called an emergency session of her Royal Counsel.

The Queen, together with her Counsel, led by the Honourable Counsellor Miris'kar, Her Majesty's Chief Counsellor, or *Kor'nai*, convened in the Throne Room of the Central Wing of the Royal Palace and hour or so after the despatch rider had arrived. All were shocked by the news of Prince Ach'ti's presumed death aboard the charter from Panticapaeum, and there were ominous mutterings of dark deeds. "Is there any evidence to warrant a suspicion of foul play?" the Kor'nai addressed Queen.

"Not according to our sources. It seems the fool fell overboard in the middle of the night" the Queen mused brutally.

"Perhaps he was drugged, Your Majesty?" ventured Sam'zir, a young intelligence officer. "There is a trove of rumours alluding to a sinister ploy by renegade elements loyal to the Armenians in the Crimea to engage in some incendiary mischief?"

"You think the Armenians wilfully targeted the heir to the Orch'tai Crown? To what end, may I ask?" the irascible Kha'rin seemed doubtful. Fast approaching the twilight of his seventh decade, he was the oldest of the Queen's Counsellors,

"We advised the Orch'tai of this intelligence?" the Queen clipped.

"Indeed, we did, Your Majesty" Sam'zir replied earnestly. "They dismissed our reports as malicious rumour, for their own agents in Argishtikhinili could not corroborate any prescient threat to the life of the

Crown Prince. As we are aware, the Orch'tai maintain cordial relations with the historic Kingdom of Armenia."

"What do you think, Captain Sam'zir? Is it possible dissident elements in the Crimea, loyal to the Armenian cause, targeted the prince for death?" the Kor'nai eyed the young intelligence officer closely.

"It is possible, my Lord. Yet, it I cannot fathom what would they hope to accomplish by such brazen outrage? The Orch'tai will appoint a new Ambassador, possibly within the next moon?"

"What of the Ur'gai? Could they be involved?" Mer'chi bristled.

"Such an outrage would surely undermine the spirit of the *Accord Scythiac*, my Lord?" Sam'zir ventured. "Whilst there is a growing nest of Ur'gai sympathisers in the Crimea, it is difficult to conceive of them engaging in such an overtly hostile act."

"What of the betrothal of the Crown Prince Ach'ti to the Princess Cordicca? Could that be a motive for murder?" Mer'chi ventured.

"Now there is a motive for murder, if ever there was?" the Honourable Counsellor Hy'kalon mused airily. At the age of twenty-six, he was the youngest member of the Royal Counsel.

"You think the Ur'gai may have been stung by the prospective union of our two Royal Houses?" the Kor'nai directed his question directly to the Counsellor.

"If not they, then perhaps the Hellenics, for such a union would surely shift the regional balance of power firmly in our favour?" the young Counsellor smiled brightly.

"Whilst there is merit in the young Counsellor's proposition, Your Majesty, it is my opinion that the poor soul drowned. This was not an act of malice; it was simple misadventure" the Kor'nai sighed lamentably.

"I would be inclined to defer to the wisdom of the Chief Counsellor, Your Majesty" Mer'chi declared.

"Will the Orch'tai be so willing to accept this as mere tragedy?" Hy'kalon quipped.

"I think the Honourable Counsellor brings us readily to the point, does he not?" Kha'rin mused gloomily.

3

"The question of the succession is now cloaked with doubt" the Kor'nai mused sourly.

"Even the darkest cloud may shimmer with a lining of silver" Hy'kalon ventured breezily.

"You think we might play the King's grief to our advantage, Honourable Counsellor?" the Queen's hazel eyes twinkled with mischief.

"Have you devoted any further thought to the prospect of marriage between your eldest son and heir to the eldest child of the Royal Princess Sychoria, Your Majesty?" Hy'kalon enquired.

"I do not see how such a union, as desirable as it would be, resolves the dilemma of the Orch'tai succession?" the Queen smiled brightly.

"What of your youngest son, the Crown Prince Sea'gir? Would not the Princess Alicharia make a suitable future bride?" Hy'kalon pressed.

"What an intriguing proposition?" the Queen mused sourly. "If such a union were to be realised, it would surely advance the rightful claim of the Princess Sychoria?"

"She is last in the line of succession, Your Majesty. Whilst she is cherished far more than the Royal Princess Naemoria, her elder sister, the Royal Princess Miskal'ya, is held in equal devotion" the Kor'nai ventured. "She is the rightful heir. Her husband, the Prince Dhu'vai, is a renowned soldier, currently serving in the east. They could yet sire a son, Your Majesty?"

"As could the Princess Sychoria, I would venture?" Hy'kalon quipped. "This day's tragedy will strike hard at the King. He is no longer blessed with vitality and is prone to excessive bouts of melancholy" Hy'kalon shrugged ruefully.

"You think he may wither at the news of Ach'ti's death?" the Queen seemed unconvinced.

"His resolve may do so, Your Majesty!" Hy'kalon smiled brightly. "We may find His Majesty far more receptive to the virtues of an enhanced union of our two Royal Houses."

"These unions would surely serve to embellish the Princess Sychoria's claim to the crown. After all, she would have two daughters who are ready to assume their regal duties" Mer'chi added.

"I think it might be better if such a proposition came from someone with the ear of the King?" the Kor'nai ventured.

"If I were King Tagar, given the current climate, I would be wary. Nonetheless, if such proposal were to be broached by one whose devotion to preserving the Royal House is unimpeachable, it would surely merit consideration?" Lezika smiled thinly.

"It will be done, Your Majesty. Our agents in Mamy'eva shall be informed of this new initiative with haste" the Kor'nai stated emphatically. He shot Hy'kalon a glare of withering distaste.

⌒∕∂

Mamy'eva, February 493 BC

"You look drained, my love" the Crown Prince Voskar stroked his wife's hair tenderly.

The Princess Sychoria gazed sadly into the mirror. She looked every inch as sickly as she felt. Her eyes were raw and puffy, and her skin was a deathly pale. It was not yet light, but she had spent much of the previous day weeping disconsolately. "I don't suppose you love me anymore, do you? I look like an aged and wrinkled hag!" she sighed morosely.

"In spite of all the Argata have said, it appears this was nothing more than a tragic accident, my sweet. There is nothing to substantiate anything sinister in the death of your cousin. Poor Prince Ach'ti must have simply fallen overboard in the dead of night."

"He always hated the water, ever since we were children. I never thought I would see the day he would dare to venture out to sea."

"He was not one of life's natural sea-farers? It is a natural fear, for us all" Voskar remarked.

"Ach'ti was terrified of the water. He refused to even swim in lake at Gra'chi. He nearly drowned in the Wol'yi one summer when we were children. We were travelling by barge to Sar'kta and he somehow contrived to fall overboard. I cannot quite remember how, for he was barely more than

5

a toddler" Sychoria smiled ruefully at the memory. "It caused an ungodly furore among the Guards and the King."

"They obviously managed to save him. I suspect a lingering fear of the water was something he wished to face down as an adult" Voskar smiled wryly.

"I was astonished when he told me of his intention to take a charter from Panticapaeum, rather than the barge from Astrach'yi. The journey across the Kas'pa is shorter and less treacherous at any time of the year."

"Might his reluctance to face his fear all this time have been influenced by a sense of duty to his mother and sister, following the death of his father? With his appointment as Ambassador to the Argata Royal Court, it may have become a bane he felt he could no longer carry?"

"I think he feared for Laeschalla, with her condition, though she has not been afflicted with an episode in several years. Perhaps he did elect to travel by sea purely to confront his fears."

"Did the Argata have any involvement in arranging his transportation?" Voskar probed.

Sychoria was genuinely puzzled by the question. "The captain was handpicked by our agents in Panticapaeum. His loyalty is unimpeachable. The Argata could not guarantee security of passage overland from Bu'khu, given the current situation in northern Armenia. That is the reason Ach'ti boarded at Tanais. You think that is of importance?"

"No, my love, I do not" Voskar protested. "I was simply curious as to why he did not elect to take the barge. I do not think there are grounds for inferring anything sinister in your cousin's death."

"You cannot stop people gossiping, especially commoners. Ach'ti's death will be the talk of the city for quite some time, for it throws the succession into turmoil once more" Sychoria sighed sadly.

"It seems disrespectful, even dangerous, to opine on such matters" Voskar cautioned warily.

"My sisters have likely talked of nothing else since they learned the news. You may rest assured of that, my love." Sychoria said tartly.

"It is a matter for the King and Counsel. We should not get involved" Voskar beseeched.

"There will obviously be a Memorial, even though we have no body. I remember Grandfather's funeral, though not very well, for I was only a toddler. This will be more distressing, for obvious reasons" Sychoria looked genuinely distressed.

"You were close, when you were children, were you not?"

"I was more of a sister to him and Laeschalla, long before the death of father, and especially so afterwards. It was a great comfort to me, once I was old enough to acknowledge that I despise my elder sisters, and they I" Sychoria smiled ruefully.

"I would understand, as would the girls, if you wished to spend time with Laeschalla during this deeply upsetting time?"

The offer was genuine and unconditional. Sychoria gazed in adoration at the man she had fallen so helplessly in love with all those years before. "I sometimes wonder what I ever did to deserve you, my sweet. You were cursed by fate to marry into a most unfortunate family. Not even the wisest Counsel can alter the will of the fates. We are a cursed dynasty, now and forever. It is the will of Gods."

"You must not speak of such things, my love. The Gods have gifted us health, love, and two beautiful daughters as cherished embodiments of our union. We have been blessed, darling Sychoria, not cursed."

"The commoners think differently" Sychoria mused glibly. "I would wager heavily the gambling dens have done a roaring trade on the issue of the succession and the identity of the ferryman's next passenger" she muttered cynically.

"You must go and see the Princess Laeschalla, my love. She will need your love and support in the next few days, and many more to come" Voskar smiled sweetly at his wife.

"She is currently sedated by the King's personal physician, old Hy'kir, for he is the finest in the Kingdom. Poor Laeschalla! She will be devastated by the loss of her brother. She doted on him, as he did her."

"I could ask Sierna to pack some belongings for you to travel, if you would like me to? I could also speak to the girls, for they have been asking after you? Mikhouri is of an age to understand" Voskar took his wife's hands in his own and kissed them lightly.

"Thank you, my love. I could leave shortly after midday if that suits you. I think I ought to be there when Laeschalla wakes from her drugged slumber. Are you sure you will manage on your own, my love?"

"We are a short ride by carriage, are we not?" Voskar smiled resignedly. "The girls will wish to visit as often as they would be permitted, given the circumstances. It might be good for Laeschalla to get to know her little cousins? Perhaps she might find some solace in the duty of being a big sister to them, just as you were to them?"

"Laeschalla was no Alicharia, my sweet!" Sychoria grinned.

"Alicharia is one of a kind, is she not?"

"She most certainly is! I do often wonder what a future suitor will make of her?"

Rost'eya, February 493 BC

The Mistress Gol'aya, Chief Maid of the Royal Household at the Palace of Rost'eya, was surprised to find the young Handmaiden alone in the scullery, immersed in silent thought. A goblet of steaming mint tea is set to one side on the aged oak table. It was a bitterly cold winter's morning, yet the girl sat away from the brazier and was attired only in her nightclothes and thin wool shawl. "You will catch your death, young Lady! That tea alone will not sustain you in this cold" Gol'aya reproved the girl gently. "I thought you might have enjoyed the rare luxury of a late morning rise, given the rigours of the journey ahead?"

"I have been awake for hours. There didn't seem much point in staying in bed" the girl replied.

"How long have you been down here?"

"At least an hour, perhaps twice as long as that" the girl shrugged apologetically.

"Have you eaten yet?" Gol'aya smiled brightly. "You need to keep up your strength? It will be a long and hazardous journey to Mamy'eva at this time of the year."

"I really should be thinking about Her Majesty's breakfast" the child sighed.

"Her Majesty is well looked after, and don't you forget it? She has an entire detachment of Royal Guards engaged in packing her belongings" the woman mused cynically.

"She won't let them anywhere near her jewellery, will she? I have the responsibility for that" Yari quipped.

"What time are you due to depart? I was told it would be as soon as this wind dies down?"

"You know more than I do, that is for sure?" the girl seemed troubled.

Gol'aya eyed the girl shrewdly and knew instinctively that something was amiss. She pulled a chair and sat down, directly facing the girl. "Are you fretting over Corelya? It is only to be expected, what with her being away?" Gol'aya smiled sweetly. She was an extremely kindly woman, aged in her middling thirties, slim and attractive. Yari was now fast approaching her thirteenth birthday.

"I was thinking about Laeschalla. The poor baby! I don't even know what to say to her?" Yari looked genuinely pained.

The woman smiled at the girl affectionately. "I am sure you will know exactly what to say when you see the Princess next. You have a natural way with people, unlike others I could mention"

"Are you talking about Corelya?" Yari grinned.

Gol'aya frowned. "Now there is a young Lady who certainly has a way with people! And with her words! She caused an ungodly scene with one of the Royal Guards before she left. Corelya is as mad as a bald lamb if you care for my honest opinion?"

Yari giggled. "I heard about her row with Nar'ga. I would not be overly concerned. Corelya will likely kill him sooner rather than later."

9

"She should be careful what she wishes for!" Gol'aya frowned. "Nar'ga is a nasty piece of work, on that we can both agree. Would you like some bread and honey? There is wodki in the pantry if you care to grab a flagon."

Yari rose and made her way across the scullery to the pantry. She returned presently, with a flagon of wodki and two goblets. Gol'aya eyed the girl with mock severity. "What about the honey?"

"I don't have access to the honey cupboard, as well you know. You only made the mistake of leaving it out once, if you care to remember?" the girl chided.

"Don't I just! I remember having to clean your vomit from the floor. Nearly half a jar of honey you devoured that morning. You won't be in a hurry to repeat that, will you?"

"I was five years old! You should not have left me alone with such temptation" Yari grinned.

"I suppose I am now expected to rise earlier than usual, just to make sure your honeypot is safe from temptation?" Gol'aya raised an eyebrow mockingly.

Yari flushed hotly. Gol'aya giggled. "You know that more than a few of the stable boys fancy you, don't you?"

"I don't even notice them. I hear things, obviously?" Yari smiled shyly.

"Why on earth do you think we hide the honey, Yari? It is not just for spreading on bread. Not when you reach a certain age, it isn't!"

"Hades aflame, Gol'aya! Is that appropriate talk for the breakfast table?"

"Why don't you fill the kettle with fresh water, and I will fetch young Gar'vai from the chipping room? He can tend to the fire in the brazier, for we shall catch our death in here soon enough." the woman smiled. "You know where the mint leaves are, don't you?"

Yari eyed the woman with suspicion. "What are you up to, Gol'aya? I know how to make a fire. Gar'vai usually just brings the barrow in with the fuel, does he not?"

"I just thought you might be sweet enough to make him a cup of tea?" Gol'aya smiled tightly. A twinkle of mischief flashed in her eyes.

"He can make his own bloody tea! They have their own scullery, don't they?" Yari frowned.

"Ah! But they do not have access to the honey, do they? He may have more than a mouthful you can drizzle with honey!" Gol'aya giggled shrilly.

Yari scowled. "I can't believe you, Gol'aya. I knew I should have stayed in bed."

Or'vych, February 493 BC

Later that afternoon, an elegant carriage arrives at the gates of the Summer Palace of Or'vych, a little over two hours ride northwest of the Royal City of Mamy'eva. The grounds of the estate encompassed one-third of a square mile of lush greenery, nestled in the shadow of the Sugarloaf Mountain, which dominates its boundaries to the north. The Guards ushered the carriage through the gates and the driver whips a train of four thoroughbreds along a gravelled track that leads to the Palace. The track is graced by plum trees on either side, bare in winter, and the carriage soon reaches the west end of the track and the Summer Palace. On either side, the Palace is flanked by a series of minor lodges, built in wood and stone. The driver chided the train to a halt outside the lodge farthest to the north, nestling in the shadow of the Sugarloaf. This is the Morning Lodge. It is segregated from the other dwellings by a small lake and ornate garden. The driver climbs down from the cabin and opens the door to allow Princess Sychoria and her two young Handmaidens, Sierna and Gh'aena, to alight. A coterie of footmen, garbed in black, morph from the entrance to collect the luggage from the hold at the rear. Standing in the doorway is Guy'nim, formidable Chief Steward to the Dowager Princess Arialla, who appears pale and sombre. Sychoria steps forward to greet him and took his hand, gazing into his eyes. "I honestly don't know what to say, dearest Guy'nim" she spoke softly, as her eyes film with tears.

"It is devastating news, for everyone, Your Royal Highness. Please, come inside, the Dowager Princess Arialla has been expecting you?"

Sychoria and her Handmaidens are led through the Reception Hall, with its ornate staircase which leads to the second floor, and through a small door on the right to the Dowager Countess' Sitting Room. Here they found the formidable matriarch, garbed from head-to-toe in black silk, sitting on a cushioned chair as she sips a goblet of scalding mint tea. There was a plate of bread and jars of honey, plum, and apricot preserve, yet untouched. "I knew you would come as soon as you could" Arialla greeted the Royal Princess.

"Of course, I did, my Lady. I have been beset with grief ever since I heard the devastating news. I still cannot believe the truth of it. It is like a nightmare from which I cannot wake" Sychoria spoke softly.

"You were always an honest child, Sychoria, and you are a credit to your family. Unlike others I could mention, you have far too much of your mother in you, for all the good it did her." Grief had not disarmed the Dowager Countess of a single barb of armament.

"My husband sends his condolences, my Lady. An entire city is in mourning."

"I suspect your elder sisters are united in joy at news of the tragedy. It shall not be long before they hiss like feral cats over the matter of the succession" Arialla spoke with an acid contempt.

"That is unjust, Arialla!" Sychoria rebuked the woman lightly. "Have my sisters sent flowers?"

"The flowers arrived earlier, if you must know, as did yours" Arialla sipped her tea.

"I have a conscientious and dutiful husband, Arialla."

"Indeed, you do, my Lady. You should be eternally grateful for the blessing the Gods bestow on you?" the woman smiled tightly. With Arialla, even a compliment was edged with a barb.

"How is Laeschalla? She must be devastated at the news, the poor baby."

"My daughter is sleeping. She has been drugged, of course. Though she is no baby, Sychoria, you may rest assured of that."

Sychoria eyed the woman shrewdly. "Laeschalla is still a child, Arialla, and all of this is new to her" she admonished the older woman lightly. "Were you and I any different at that age? I had a monstrous crush on one of the stable boys when I was thirteen, if you remember? When mother discovered the truth of it, she threatened to whip me bloody if I did not quell my lustful urges. Yet, it did not stop me from acting upon them."

"Quite!" Arialla said simply.

"Can I see her? I will not wake her, if she is sleeping, I promise" Sychoria implored.

"Have some tea, Sychoria? You look drained" Arialla clipped tersely.

"Of course, my Lady, that would be lovely. Has the King sent a messenger?"

"Your father sent a messenger yesterday and another this morning. I have not the faintest idea what I have done to warrant such courtesy?" the woman raised an eyebrow mockingly.

"You think the King and Counsel should not have appointed Prince Ach'ti as our Ambassador to the Argata Royal Court?" Sychoria watched the woman's reaction closely.

"I never warmed to the idea, as well you know. I was even less enthused by the prospect of his betrothal to the Princess Cordicca, which is more than I can say for your father?" Arialla seemed bemused by the King's machinations.

"Cordicca is a sweet and comely girl, Arialla. She is not cut from the same cloth as her sister" Sychoria beseeched.

"Would you allow *your* children to marry into *that* family? They are nought more than savages! Little removed from the Cimmerian brute from whence they sprang!"

Sychoria blushed faintly. "My father's Court is a leaky bucket, is it not?"

"It was ever thus, sweet child. You have never shown an active interest in matters of state. Your elder sisters, on the other hand, have forever indulged in infantile intrigue!" Arialla smiled wryly.

Sychoria felt uncomfortable in the presence of this woman, as she always had. Arialla had a mind as sharp and as dangerous as her tongue, and her opinions of the King, Court, and the rest of the Royal Family ranked among the worst kept secrets in the realm. And yet, as was often the case, there was something left unsaid. Sychoria sipped her tea and locked eyes with a woman who was nobody's fool.

"What grounds do you have for suspecting foul play in the death of your son?" Sychoria asked.

"Wouldn't you like to know, sweet child?" Arialla smiled tightly.

The Great Steppe, February 493 BC

The Royal City of Rost'eya, historic capital of the Ur'gai, lies twelve miles south of the easterly course of the Donets River and nearly one hundred miles north of the central coast of the Azovi Sea. Nestled on the northern fringe of the Great Steppe, its historic eminence owed more to the wealth of its immediate environs, encompassing some of the most fertile soils in the entire Ur'gai Duchy, rather than any obvious strategic significance. In this respect, Rost'eya is a curious anomaly, for every other major centre in the region has strategic proximity to a major river. Trakhtemirov lies on a promontory on the west bank of the Dneiper, the Hellenic polis of Olbia commanded the estuary of the Bug, and the greatest conurbation in the Great Steppe, the Royal City of Mamy'eva, historic capital of the Orch'tai, lies to the south of a marked elbow in the Great Wol'yi, two-hundred-and-seventy miles further east. The origins of Rost'eya are obscure, yet it was likely founded in the late Eighth Century by migrants from the west, the mythical *Sy'takh*, ancestors of the present-day Scythia, but this remains a subject of controversy. What is not contended, at least by the Ur'gai themselves, is the baffling rationale for founding the Royal City in the first place. The answer, quite simply, is a long, cold, and cruel winter!

Not surprisingly, the Royal Train, accompanied by two-hundred elite members of Her Majesty's Royal Guard, did not leave Rost'eya as planned, due to an unforeseen snow blizzard that lasted several hours. The blizzard had now cleared, for it was mid-afternoon, and Yari gazed north out of the window of the covered wagon at the dense snug of forest which carpeted the horizon, almost as far as the eye could see. The forests, a source of unimagined bounty in the spring and summer, were the surest shield against the cruel and unforgiving winds of a Siberian Winter. A great many children had died this winter, as they had the last. It was the way of things, *the lore of the Steppe*! The wagon was led by a train of four superb thoroughbreds and now trotted east along a snow-covered track towards the Khy'rg of Yur'vyk. Queen Illir'ya had planned to lunch with the Count, before making firm ground eastwards until sunset. They now planned to spend the night at Yur'vyk. Yari wrinkled her nose for the umpteenth time, partly with distaste, mainly to ensure a healthy circulation of blood, for she was quite certain it was frozen!

At this rate, and in such foul weather, would they ever make it to Mamy'eva?

"I thought I might find you here?" a cultured voice, born to command, startled the girl from her solace.

Queen Illir'ya stands in the doorway of the scullery. She wore a dark blue gown, edged with silver, and a thin woollen shawl of the purest pearl, not entirely practical, given the season, yet a Queen must maintain appearances, must she not? Yari smiled brightly at her mistress. "It did not occur that you had need of me, Your Majesty. I thought you were at supper with Count Yur'vyk?" Yari replied.

"It had not occurred to me how deeply you despise me? Would you strip me bare and whip me from the gates this night?" the Queen raised an eyebrow mockingly.

"Am I to take it that Count Yur'vyk is not the most delightful of hosts?" Yari grinned.

"The insufferable fool kept harping on about the harvest! He is plainly aggrieved at the thought of provisioning our breakfast" Illir'ya said sourly. "He did bother to feed you, I hope?"

"The maids took care of me. They said it was fine to stay here, whilst they finished their duties."

"I don't suppose they revealed where they keep the wodki? A Queen must mind her manners, at least in public" the woman grinned.

Yari beckoned the Queen to sit beside her on the pew. "They keep it in the cellar. There should be a couple of flagons in the cupboard over there" she pointed to the far corner of the room. I will go and grab a flagon if it pleases you?"

"It would please me if you grabbed two!" Illir'ya quipped tartly. She watched the girl closely as she strolls across to the cupboard. "He makes his wodki from bramble fruit. What an indecent waste of blackberries!"

"I actually like it. The sweetness gives it an extra kick, for it is surely more potent than the plum we drink?" Yari mused.

"We might as well travel with a hangover, don't you think?" the Queen mused glumly.

Yari laid the flagons on the floor and padded across to the dresser. She plucked two goblets and returned, passing one to Illir'ya. She sat down on the pew and reached for a flagon, frowning as she did. "Shit!" she swore. "I don't have a dagger?"

The Queen smiled mischievously. "It is a good thing I came prepared!"

Illir'ya stood and turned around, raising her left leg, knee flexed, to rest her foot on the bench. She teased back the hemline on her gown and slid the dagger from its sheath, attached by a garter belt around the top of her thigh. Yari glanced away, for Illir'ya wore no underwear. The woman giggled. "I doubt you are bare downstairs anymore, my not so little Handmaiden?" she chided.

Yari quickly worked away at the seal of wax on the flagon and passed the dagger back to her Queen. This time, she did not blush at what she saw. "I haven't started bleeding yet, if that is what you mean?" She plucked the stopper from the flagon and filled the goblets.

Illir'ya slid the dagger back into its sheath and lowered her leg. The gown fell to her ankles. "I wasn't sure if you had? You have been rather pensive these few days past?"

"I have been thinking about Laeschalla" Yari sighed sadly. "The poor soul must be devastated, for she was devoted to her brother, as he was to her."

The Queen sipped her drink. "Of course, she must, the poor lamb! You must spend time alone with her in Mamy'eva. I insist upon it?" Illir'ya said emphatically.

"She may not even wish to see me, not with everything that has happened?" the girl sighed despondently.

The Queen was momentarily startled. "Why in Hades name would you think such a thing? You are not responsible for Ach'ti's tragic death."

Yari met the Queen's gaze, and then deliberately lowered her eyes to her goblet. *Something was clearly amiss.* "Do you think it likely the King will name Laeschalla as his successor?"

The Queen smiled sweetly at the plainly troubled girl. "His daughters have precedence, Yari. Ach'ti was the only male heir, though it is likely that Miskla'ya and her husband may yet sire one. The Orch'tai have a strange attitude to women, at least compared with us. You would never suspect that their Royal line was founded by a warrior Queen."

"Is it really true? That King Tagar and his daughters are descendants of Queen K'ouhr?"

"To them, she is Kh'our, or Khou'ri! A plain dishonesty, to be sure, yet there are few among them who can correctly pronounce her name. Not least, that illiterate cunt for a King!"

Yari was astounded by the outburst. Illir'ya eyed her sternly. Yari grinned. "Neither Corelya nor I have their names pronounced the way they once were, even by our own people. I am really Y'ayr, as Corelya is, K'rylya. Is it true that K'ouhr was an illegitimate daughter of the fabled Princess Y'strii, daughter of the warrior King Uh'dakh?"

Illir'ya drained her drink and reached for the flagon. "You must miss her, surely?"

"K'rylya? If truth be told, I am rather enjoying the peace!" Yari snickered. She drains her goblet. This was plucked from her hand and immediately replenished by Illir'ya.

17

"You and I must talk, Yari. Not tonight, but preferably before we reach Mamy'eva. I am quite sure these walls have ears."

Yari frowned. "Have I displeased you, Your Majesty?"

Illir'ya stood and plucked the unopened flagon. "No, sweet child, you have not. I fear this world of ours may soon disappoint your most cherished hopes."

With that, Queen Illir'ya stood and strode away without another word. If Yari were troubled before, she was certainly so now. She drained her goblet in a single gulp and refilled it almost to the brim.

Early the following morning, the Princess Laeschalla stirs from her drugged slumber. The girl moans softly, rubs her eyes, and gasped in startlement as the Royal Princess Sychoria morphs from a chair beside her bed. "I am sorry if I startled you, sweet child. There is a goblet of mint tea if you would like some?"

"I didn't even know you were here, Sychoria? When did you arrive?" Laeschalla spoke softly. She was pale and withdrawn, her hair dishevelled. "Tea would be lovely, thank you!"

Sychoria turned away and filled a goblet with warm tea. "I arrived yesterday, just after midday. I wanted to see you, of course I did, but you were sleeping, little dove. I didn't want to wake you" she smiled sadly at the girl.

"I cannot sleep forever, can I? The Surgeons would have me in a drugged slumber for the rest of my days" the girl mused cynically.

"The surgeons are worried for you, my love, and so are the rest of us. You have been getting better these past few years, have you not? I can't remember the last time you had an episode" Sychoria stroked the girl's lank blonde locks affectionately. "Drink your tea, sweet cherub, for I have laced it with wodki" Sychoria raised an eyebrow.

"Not poppy oil?" Laeschalla chirped mockingly.

"I think they have been giving you too much poppy oil if you care for my opinion. I have spoken to your mother, but she has deferred to the Surgeons."

"They claim it reduces the frequency of attacks, yet it induces sleep as deep as a winter snow. My mother would approve, of course, for she does not approve of my new friends" Laeschalla smiled shyly. She was approaching her fifteenth birthday and had flowered in to an attractive and comely girl, with long, flowing blonde locks and eyes of the palest blue.

"They are your friends, not hers? I think it is wonderful that you have finally come out of your shell. You are a most beautiful butterfly, Laeschalla, and you have been imprisoned far too long in your cocoon."

"My mother would rather I spent my time knitting and embroidering, for those are wholesome pursuits for a high-born girl? I wonder if she has even savoured the taste of forbidden fruits" Laeschalla smiled ruefully.

Sychoria smiled wryly at the girl. "I can assure you that she has, my sweet, and you should never delude yourself otherwise. Who is this fox who has bewitched your loins?"

"I am not telling! Mother would surely have him flayed alive?"

"Why do you think I would tell your mother? We girls must have our secrets, after all?"

"He is uncommonly sweet to me. He treats me like I am special. Like I am the only girl in the vale, though he surely cannot be starved of their affections" Laeschalla spoke with an unbridled passion, as her eyes twinkled like stars in a winter sky. "And, before you say anything, it is assuredly not because of my family or my title, for he seems to care nothing for them!"

"He cares for you, though? Not just for your virtues?" Sychoria smiled sweetly at the girl.

"My virtues, such as they are, are already his. As they have been for close to a year. Do I shock you?" the girl smiled proudly, almost as if she had hoped to do just that.

"No, Laeschalla, you do not, though I cannot speak for your mother."

"She would keep me in irons, would she not? Either that, or else imprisoned alone within my bed-sheets with only my dreams and my memories for comfort" the girl grinned slyly.

"Are you in love, Laeschalla?" Sychoria eyed the girl steadily.

"I am in lust, Sychoria, and it is all I have ever wanted. I do not wish to be a prisoner of my condition, or my House. I just want to be normal, like all the other girls" Laeschalla said emphatically. "Ach'ti knew the truth of it, for I told him so."

"And how did he take the news?" Sychoria was not in the least surprised the girl confided in her elder brother, for they had been devoted to one another.

"I don't think it came as a great shock to him, for he had already discovered the truth of it, or at least he suspected. I think mother knows, for it would be foolish to presume otherwise. She has a legion of spies throughout the vale, does she not?"

"There is little that escapes her notice, that much is true. You may rest assured, little rose, that your mother's eyes and ears go far beyond the realms of the rivers, meadows and forests of the vale."

"She harbours a suspicion that Ach'ti's death was not as some would have it cast." Laeschalla sipped her tea and smiled sadly.

"Has she intimated any such thoughts to you?"

"What do you think?" Laeschalla eyed the woman steadily.

Sychoria sipped her tea and placed the goblet on the small side table. She fixed her gaze on the girl. "I am not sure, my love. I cannot believe your brother had mortal enemies, for he was as sweet as you. He was terrified of the water, was he not? Perhaps it might have been wiser if he had waited until summer to venture across the great sea." Sychoria mused forlornly.

"He was not enthused by prospect of being King. You surely knew that?" Laeschalla looked suddenly troubled.

Sychoria was astounded by the revelation. "I did not. Was there anything specific underpinning his reservations? Did you talk with him often about this?"

"Perhaps we did, for he could scarcely confide in mother, could he?" Laeschalla spoke softly. "Ach'ti did not welcome the responsibility, especially in respect of the Royal Army. He considered it to be too large, too unwieldy, and potentially dangerous. Ach'ti was enthralled by the prospect of lasting peace with the Ur'gai and Nur'gat, for he felt they would be our closest allies in bringing a lasting peace to the east."

"Did he ever give the impression that he had spoken with others about this? Is it possible he may have confessed his reservations about the political power wielded by the army and the Generals to another confidante?" Sychoria ventured hesitantly.

"I cannot say, truly I cannot. I know he wished to reduce the size of our army in the east, over the duration of his reign, had such a thing been feasible. I also know he was steadfastly opposed to the new army being created, but you surely know of that?"

Sychoria was rattled by both the revelation, and by the question. "I know of the army, and the rationale for raising and training it."

"Ach'ti was not convinced of its necessity" Laeschalla drained her goblet and placed it down on the side-table. "He intimated there may be something sinister in its motive, and that it might be employed against defenceless Sauromatae communities, innocent women and children? This could destabilise the east and necessitate the creation of an even greater army whose sole purpose would be to increase the power of the Generals further. He also fretted about whether the King and Counsel were being entirely truthful in their dealings with the Ur'gai?"

"I see" Sychoria smiled tightly. In truth, she was both flabbergasted and bewildered.

"Do you think it possible that a sinister clique of recalcitrant Generals, serving and retired, or even elements on the King's Counsel, would have wanted my brother dead had they discovered the depths of his concerns?" Laeschalla gazed intently at the woman sat opposite, whom she adored as a sister.

"I do not know, Laeschalla. Your brother's suspicions would certainly have fermented hostility, even discontent, amongst the army and the Generals, serving and retired."

"So, who will take the Crown now? Has the King anointed a successor?"

"Not to my knowledge, little dove. Would you be Queen, Laeschalla, if it were offered to you?" Sychoria smiled wanly at the child.

"No, I would not! I do not wish to be Queen, not now, nor ever!" Laeschalla replied fervently.

"What do you wish for, my little rose?"

"To be far away from here and the prying eyes of mother, so I can roll naked in the clover from dawn till dusk" Laeschalla beamed proudly.

To those who knew him well, King Tagar appeared increasingly gaunt and jaded, far older to the eye than his fifty years would belie. He had been plagued by a restlessness of sleep these past seven years, ever since the death of his younger brother, the dashing Prince Khai'duc, killed in a bloody skirmish with the Sauromatae in the Central Plains of Kazakh'yi, a barren and unforgiving world, far to the east of the Signet. There were many in the Royal City of Mamy'eva who lamented that a part of the King himself died the day the fateful news was relayed, yet few would admit the uncomfortable truth, not even his closest friend, the Royal Counsellor Mes'khu. Without a *bona fide* male heir, a celebrated line of Kings would be condemned to an inglorious end. Banished with a whimper, rather than the heraldry of trumpets, a fitting end some might say, for this King was surely not his father. The obvious solution, unanimously accepted by the Royal Counsel, was for the Crown should pass to his beloved nephew, the Crown Prince Ach'ti. Yet, within a year, tragedy had fastened its talons around the heart of this unfortunate dynasty, cursed by its perennial plague of daughters.

Chief Counsellor Kol'cha, Kor'nai to His Royal Majesty, had devoted countless waking hours these past few weeks past to a resolution of the thorny issue of the succession. To his mind, as sharp as any razor ever honed, even in the twilight of his years, there was but one, and only one, solution. No matter the indelicacy, the King must be seduced by wisdom alone, for the future of the Duchy now lay imperilled. He must name his middle daughter, the Royal Princess Miskal'ya, as his rightful heir. The

King must then be persuaded to renounce the Crown to ensure a secure and timeous transition. Given the right incentives, perhaps even a novel tincture, Miskal'ya and her husband, the Prince Dhu'vai, may yet sire a son to secure the dynasty for the remainder of the Century. And yet, if there were truth to the recent despatches from his trusted agents in the Signet, the issue of the succession might be the least of his woes. The reports alluded to a massacre of innocents; an indiscriminate slaughter of entire villages in the Western Plains of Kazakh'yi, at the hands of hastily raised and poorly trained units, reputed to be little more than an ungovernable rabble, whose rapacious conduct had stung the Sauromatae to frenzy. There was darker allusion to an even graver threat, from the disillusioned upper echelons of the Royal Army itself, who might be tempted to exploit any current political paralysis and seize the throne for themselves! Such a thing would have been unthinkable in the days of King Mag'kar, yet his son had ascended to the throne a mere shadow of his father, neither warrior, nor statesman!

On this morning, the King had slept fitfully the previous night and was, predictably, tired, and irritable. He had risen in early, dressed hastily, and informed his Steward, Y'dryk, that he would take a flagon of wodki and kettle of mint tea in his private study. There he remained for the next few hours, engrossed in correspondence, until his Kor'nai found him. The King glanced up, squinting in the dim light of the windowless room, as his elderly Chief Counsellor closed the door and approached the desk. "I am besieged by poorly scribbled heralds of fealty, old friend!" the King grimaced. He turned to point to the pile of parchments at the far corner of the desk. "Am I expected to respond to all these people!" he growled.

"Of course not, Your Majesty! I shall take care of things on your behalf" the Kor'nai soothed.

"Thank you, old friend. Has that infernal bloody woman arrived yet?" the King scowled. He reached for his goblet and drained it.

"You refer to Her Royal Majesty, Queen Lezika of the Argata, I presume?" the Kor'nai raised an eyebrow in mock severity.

"I wasn't referring to that other mad bitch, was I?" the King replied testily.

"According to my sources, Queen Lezika and her party should arrive in later this morning. Her Royal Majesty, Queen Illir'ya of the Ur'gai is due to arrive later in the day, so far as we can tell" the Kor'nai replied evenly.

The King eyed his Chief Counsellor shrewdly. "Speaking of mad bitches, send word to the Dowager Countess Arialla that she might grace us with her indomitable presence. She may bring the Princess Laeschalla with her if the child feels up to it? Do we have further word from that incorrigible old bastard in Mus'kyv?" the King's eyes gleamed with suspicion.

"According to the latest despatch, His Royal Highness, King Ni'ghul of the Nur'gat remains dangerously ill. He may not survive the winter!" the Kor'nai sighed apologetically.

"We may live in hope!" the King mused brutally. He replenished his goblet and motioned for the Kor'nai to sit.

The Kor'nai acknowledged the King's command with a gracious nod and took a cushioned chair directly facing him. He could smell the alcohol on the King's breath. "Ambassador Gor'ych will attend the Memorial Service, on behalf of the Nur'gat, of course."

"What demands do you think that insufferable cow will make upon us? After all, she is now in the market for a husband for her youngest daughter?"

"There must surely be a suitable son in the realm? Count Vy'nyr's eldest boy would make a fine husband for the Princess Cordicca?"

"There is rumour she no longer resides in Archaeopolis?" the King's eyes gleam with suspicion.

"The Princess is enrolled at School in Corinth, is she not?" the Kor'nai smiled brightly.

"My agents say differently. That she has vanished completely and has not been seen since the Solstice" the King pressed.

"That may be so, my Liege, yet even if it were so, it would have little bearing upon our current dilemma?" the Kor'nai spoke evenly.

"You would have me name my daughter Miskal'ya and her oaf of a husband as my legitimate successors, is that it?"

"The Royal Princess is universally admired, Your Majesty. She has the makings of a fine future Queen?" the Kor'nai declared emphatically.

"She has the brains of a hen! That cow in Archaeopolis would dance rings round her!" the King spoke feelingly. "As for her husband, the man is thicker than pig-shit!"

"She will be guided by the wisdom of her Counsel, Your Majesty. The Crown Prince Dhu'vai is a celebrated Commander, adored and respected in equal measure" the Kor'nai reproved the King mildly.

"What of my youngest daughter, the Royal Princess Sychoria? Does she have the makings of a future Queen?" the King smiled thinly.

The Kor'nai was quite bewildered. "Are you serious, Your Majesty?" he gasped.

"You are not impressed by her, is that it?" the King eyed the older man closely.

"On the contrary, Your Majesty, my opinions of the Princess Sychoria are well known. It cannot be denied she is the brightest of your daughters, by a considerable stretch!" the Kor'nai replied softly.

"She may yet bear a son. She is both young and healthy?"

"The same could be said of the Princess Miskal'ya, Your Majesty?"

"She is a dolt and a dullard. Sadly, that is all she will ever be" the King hissed.

"There is the matter of the Royal Army, Your Majesty? They will surely rally to Miskal'ya's standard?" the Kor'nai ventured.

"They will rally to whomever I choose. We shall speak no more of this, not until after the Memorial."

"This is surely a matter for Counsel, my Liege?" the Kor'nai smiled tightly.

"And it shall be, I assure you. We may yet resolve this malaise with a deft sleight of hand" the King smiled wryly.

Yari had never visited the Royal Palace of Mamy'eva and was astounded by its size and opulence. In contrast with the Royal Palace of Rost'eya, which had been constructed in wood with external and internal walls of tempered mud brick and a layer of wattle-and-silt plaster, the Palace of King Tagar was largely fashioned from stone and marble, presumably at eye-watering expense. Peeking through the window slats of the covered wagon, she had gaped in awe at the Gor'ki Gate, commissioned in solid marble by King Mag'kar, and had been equally dumbstruck by the size of the Parade Square, commissioned for the annual Royal Parade of the His Majesty's Guard, numbering five thousand men! Even the stables were impressive, for she had never seen the like of such in all her life. "Stop gawking, Yari! It is quite unbecoming of Royalty!" Queen Illir'ya had hissed icily.

The Ur'gai Royal Party comprised the Queen, Her Royal Majesty's Consort, Crown Prince Mais'ki, the Kor'nai, other members of Her Majesty's Counsel and, much to her surprise, apparently herself. She was not in the least surprised to learn that she would be billeted on the opposite Wing of the Palace from Her Majesty, given that her every need would be catered for by a coterie of Orch'tai servants. She had even been assigned her own Handmaiden, a bright-eyed nine-year-old named Ny'vi, who dutifully gave her a tour of the entire perimeter of the Upper Tier ("Royal Tier") of the Palace before they reached her private chambers. Nothing could have prepared the Sauromatae orphan for the splendour of her new abode, no matter how temporary the duration of her stay. The young Handmaiden, Ny'vi had stifled a giggle as Yari gaped at the upholstery and décor of the Sitting Room; *her own Sitting Room!* The Orch'tai girl smiled sweetly and twirled away, a mischievous smile playing at her lips as she strolled along the vestibule to the door. Alone with her private thoughts, Yari stood in the centre of the room and gazed enchantedly at the room, even its ceiling. She resisted an urge to pinch herself, for she must surely be dreaming!

"It becomes more than a little boring, after a time" a bemused voice giggled.

Yari turned and gasped for pure joy. "Laeschalla!"

Laeschalla eyed the girl coldly. "You are supposed to tell me how deeply sorry you are? Have you completely taken leave of your senses?"

Yari was visibly chastened. "I forget myself, Your Royal Highness. Please forgive me, I humbly beseech you?"

"Come here and give me a hug, you silly moo! You really are a sight for sore eyes, do you know that?"

Yari skipped across to the older girl, a true friend, and an even truer Princess, and embraced her warmly. "I am sorry about your brother, Laeschalla, truly I am. I don't even know what to say?"

Laeschalla smiled sadly at the younger girl. "Thank you, Yari. Now, let me show you to your bedroom. You are definitely going to want a boyfriend after you see the bed!"

"Hades aflame! What is with everyone lately? Anyone would think I had suddenly sprouted tits!"

Laeschalla surveyed the younger girl, who had much changed physically this past seven months, with a mocking gleam. "I would say so, Yari-bear!"

Two

Mamy'eva, March 493 BC

The Royal City of Mamy'eva lay ten miles southwest of the elbow of the Great Wol'yi, two-hundred-and-twenty miles northwest of the port city of Astrach'yi, and almost twice that distance southwest of the Sama'zka Plain, the northern frontier of the Orch'tai realm. According to legend, it was founded by the celebrated "Warrior Queen" Kh'our, also known as Khou'ri or K'ouru, a humble farmers daughter born in the Sama'zka Plains in the mid-Seventh Century BC. Over a period of nearly two decades of bloody conflict, Kh'our conquered and assimilated a vast swathe of territory along the course of the great Wol'yi, which had been further expanded over the next century-and-a-half into the present frontiers of Orch'tai realm. She had also founded a celebrated and unbroken line of Warrior King's, including the present ruler, Tagar. Although it is rarely acknowledged publicly, the sentiment of the populace is that this line was cursed from its inception, possibly by the malevolent spirit of a maligned Sauromatae *Sha'mani*, for daughters outnumbered sons by a ratio of almost three to one. Kh'our had sired three sons who survived to adulthood, two of whom had fallen in battle with Sauromatae tribes east of the Uras'ka. The Royal City occupied an area a little under four-square miles and is enclosed by fortified walls that stretch for seven miles. Beyond the North Gate, towards the banks of the Wol'yi, the Mercantile District boasts a density of carpenters, bone carvers, metal workers, and potters to rival Hallstatt on the great Rhini. Mamy'eva dwarfs the Royal centres of the Argata and Ur'gai, and is rivalled only by Mus'kyv, the Royal City of the Nur'gat, in wealth and density of populace.

The Royal City was home to nearly forty thousand souls, many of whom lived in extreme poverty.

Queen Lezika and the Argata delegation had travelled from Astrach'yi by wagon, accompanied by detachment of two hundred of her finest warriors who were now billeted in a temporary camp in the plains, four-and-a-half miles southeast of Mamy'eva. Queen Illir'ya and the Ur'gai delegation had arrived the following day, for her journey had been undeniably more arduous, and her two hundred warriors from Rost'eya had been rewarded for their indefatigable efforts with a billet in the frozen and sparsely populated Udu'ya Plains, nine miles due southwest of the Royal City. The Ur'gai Queen had bristled at such naked discourtesy from a supposed ally, yet this succinctly contrived insult had greatly bemused the Argata Queen! Within hours of their arrival, the two Queens, both long-standing historic rivals, gathered with their advisors in the Gor'khi Hall, named in honour of the emphatic victory over the Nur'gat, the last great battle between the two regional rivals. Upon hearing the choice of venue for the welcoming reception, the irascible General Gor'ych, Nur'gat Ambassador to the Orch'tai Royal Court, exploded with rage and cursed like a common soldier. This was no great surprise, given he had joined the Nur'gat Royal Army as an Infantryman thirty years earlier in the aftermath of the crushing reversal at Gor'khi. "This is an outrage! A total fucking disgrace! I should torch this fucking city to a cinder!" the ruddy-faced General had beleaguered his visibly appalled staff.

The Ambassadors ill temper was unlikely to be soothed by the presence of the Argata Queen, a woman he openly detested and derogated publicly as *'The whore of Halys'*. His petrified staff elected to ply him with copious quantities of wodki in the forlorn hope it might moderate his temper. Queen Lezika elected to ignore the fool, yet the spectacle of his rapid descent into inebriation proved too delightful an opportunity to squander, and so she despatched her Kor'nai across the Hall to needle the cantankerous buffoon. "It is a pleasure to make your acquaintance again, Ambassador Gor'akh" the Honourable Counsellor Miris'kar greeted the Ambassador with a mocking smile. Gor'akh was a rustic dish of rye porridge, spiced with garlic, sage, and onion. It was the national dish of the Nur'gat, and a staple of the poorest families in the realm.

"My name is Gor'ych, Honourable Kor'nai!" the General spat indignantly. He plucked a flagon to replenish his goblet.

"Of course, it is, General Gor'akh. Her Royal Majesty sends her esteemed regards!"

"I am honoured, truly I am, Honourable Kur'nyk" the General mused irreverently. "I do hope the journey from Astrach'yi didn't prove too arduous to those turds, I mean Guards, from the Royal Palace of Archaeopolis!"

The Kor'nai bristled indignantly, for Kur'nyk was the Argata name for a privy pot. "You speak coarsely, Ambassador. Perhaps it is the drink that blackens your spirits?"

"I can remember who I am, you half-wit! My name is Gor'ych, as I have told you before. As for the drink, it is more than palatable, which is more than can be said for the company."

The Kor'nai smiled brightly at the incorrigible oaf. "I fear for the King's health, naturally?"

"I hope the bastard dies. No good will come from his recovery, you mark my words."

The Kor'nai raised an eyebrow in mock severity. "He is your King, dear fellow?"

"I thought you meant that other swine. Still, there is little to choose between them, is there?"

Queen Illir'ya had observed the interaction between the two men with growing alarm. Her own shabby treatment at the hand of the Orch'tai King still rankled, yet she now harboured a suspicion that it may have been the Argata Queen, that '*Scarlet Braid*', as the Ur'gai named her, that was the guiding light of the Orch'tai King's irreverence. She knew full well the mind of this Queen, and how best to counter it! She strolled across to the Refreshment Table and accosted the Nur'gat Ambassador, whilst completely ignoring the Argata Kor'nai. "It is always a delight to see you again, Ambassador Gor'ych" she smiled sweetly.

"Your Royal Highness. The pleasure is entirely mine. May I introduce the Orch'tai Finance Minister, the Honourable Counsellor what's-is-face?"

Illir'ya's eyes twinkled with mischief. "I had no idea Queen Lezika had been graced with such a bolt of ingenuity, Counsellor Miris'kar? I am certain you shall make a fine Treasury Minister, quite regardless of your advancing years."

The Kor'nai nearly choked on his wine. "Forgive me, Your Majesty, I am Her Royal Majesty's Chief Counsellor!"

The young Queen smiled wryly. "Of course, you are, dear fellow. How silly of me? I do hope you forgive me, Honourable Kor'nai, but I thought I might intrude on a moment of the Ambassador's valuable time, for we have the pressing matter of pig-fodder to discuss, do we not?"

The Ambassador fixed the young Queen with a sombre expression. "Indeed, we do, my Lady. As you can see, dear fellow, duty calls me from my liberty. It was a rare pleasure to meet you once more, Honourable Counsellor!"

The Kor'nai scowled and turned away without another word. "I thought you might strike the fool?" Illir'ya whispered conspiratorially, loud enough for the departing Kor'nai to hear.

"It had crossed my mind, my Lady" the Ambassador scowled. "Where is that insufferable cur?"

"I rather fear the King's intention is to humour himself at our expense" the Queen sighed sadly.

"I didn't come for that prick! I came to pay my respects to the young man's family. A terrible business, is it not, my Lady?"

"Such a lamentable tragedy, to be sure, and a cruel blow to both his family and the realm?" the Queen mused sadly.

"I fear the Argata may seek to exploit this to their advantage, my Lady?" Gor'ych mused sourly.

"I would wager heavily on it, dear fellow. And with Persian gold, no less" the Queen quipped.

Queen Lezika was perched on an elegant, cushioned chair, sipping a goblet of mint tea, surrounded by her Counsellor's, when a brief tattoo drummed the door. The door opened, and her visitor, the venerable Banassarias of Persepolis, Persian Ambassador to the Royal Court of King Tagar, was courteously ushered in. He bowed with a flourish and greeted Her Majesty with a doleful smile. "The King in Susa will be deeply saddened by the loss of such a fine future King and husband for the Princess Cordicca!" Banassarias exclaimed, with dutiful piety.

"We are all of us crushed by this tragedy, my dear fellow. Please, join us for a cup of tea, or wine, if you prefer?" said the Queen.

Banassarias took a vacant chair, facing her Majesty, flanked on either side by her Counsellors, and elected for a goblet of Hellenic red. "My heart weeps for King Tagar, Your Majesty. He is a mere shadow of the lion that once roared?"

"I hadn't noticed, venerable Banassarias" the Queen quipped slyly.

The Persian Ambassadors eyes gleamed with suspicion. "I forget myself, my Lady. The death of the Crown Prince was an equally cruel blow to your cherished hopes of a deeper union between you two great peoples?" he said silkily.

"The King in Susa will be bruised by our disappointment, is that it?" the Queen smiled thinly.

"The union was blessed by King Darius himself, was it not? As would any future initiatives, you have my solemn oath on this" Banassarias smiled brightly.

"What of the King's own son and heir, dear fellow? Is there no woman in Susa who may yet tame his mane?" Lezika's eyes twinkled with mischief.

Banassarias smiled ruefully. "It is true, my Lady, that Prince Xerxes has been hitherto reluctant to commit to a sacred union. He is young and has much to learn of the ways of this world."

"You surely did not entreat me with your presence to further the hopes of the King in Susa?" the Queen eyed the Persian Ambassador closely.

Banassarias shrugged ruefully. "It should come as no surprise to you, my Lady, but there are some in Mamy'eva, perhaps only a small number, yet they are not without influence, who opposed the marriage and a deeper alliance between your realms. And yet, we remain at one on the issue, as we are a great many things?"

"Are you intimating that Prince Ach'ti may have been murdered by dissidents and malcontents in Mamy'eva?" the Queen raised an eyebrow. Her eyes betrayed nothing.

"We have reason to suspect the involvement of Hellenics, Your Majesty. There are rumours swirling among our agents in the Crimea" the Ambassador confessed.

"The Orch'tai suspect the dark hand of the Armenians in this treachery?" said the Kor'nai, the Honourable Counsellor Miris'kar ventured.

Banassarias chuckled. "They have neither the wits, nor the funds, for such elaborate trickery. If there was foul play, and there is more than a whiff of treachery here, we must seek a higher purpose to its motive?"

"Do you believe the Crown Prince was murdered?" the Queen eyed the man closely.

"I am inclined to believe it was an accident, Your Majesty. And yet, this tragedy is a convenient blessing for our enemies, is it not? I am sure you have heard the rumours from the east?"

"You refer to the alleged atrocities committed by these new Orch'tai Divisions in the Eastern Plains?" the Kor'nai challenged.

"There is also the renewed spectre of a Sauromatae Confederacy. I cannot stress how poorly this news will be received at the Royal Court in Susa?" Banassarias sighed sadly.

"Will these units be ready for the summer, venerable Banassarias?" the Queen asked earnestly.

"We believe so, Your Majesty. Yet, for the present, the uncertainties of the succession cloud all judgement, do they not?"

"That is a matter for the King and his Counsel, is it not?" the Queen smiled brightly.

"Yet, we are allies, are we not? As such, we are duty bound to counsel and to assist a friend in their hour of need, are we not?" Banassarias spoke evenly.

"The King in Susa would support a union between my eldest son, the Crown Prince Disch'al, and the King's granddaughter, the Princess Mikhouri?" the Queen sipped her tea.

"As I have already said, the closer union of your two great Houses was blessed by King Darius himself" Banassarias smiled thinly. "And yet, such a union would not resolve the issue of who will succeed our noble King Tagar, when the time comes."

"I think we have an understanding, venerable Banassarias? There is the issue of my youngest son, the Crown Prince Sea'gir?"

"The Orch'tai King has several granddaughters who would make a fine future bride for your darling son, yet there is only one daughter fit to wear the crown?" the Ambassador ventured softly.

"And the King would be amenable to this novel proposition?" Lezika mused.

"The King is not himself, my Lady, for he is beset by woe. In such dangerous times, treachery always lurks in the shadows. If the death of poor Prince Ach'ti was no accident, we must pray the hand of malice, and of tragedy, do not strike the King's soul further?" Banassarias mused glumly.

Queen Lezika smiled tightly, for she understood perfectly what must now be done. "Then pray we must, venerable Banassarias, for our deliverance from such earthly fates."

The Honourable Counsellor Mes'khu nodded politely as the older man poured him a goblet of apricot wodki. His summons to the Kor'nai's private chamber had been expected, for it would have been an act of pure folly to imagine that his own efforts to resolve the plague of the succession would have eluded the attention of this wily old fox. The men sat on cushioned chairs, directly facing one another, across an ancient table furnished with silver flagons of wine, wodki, and mint tea. "The King's mood remains as bleak as a midwinter mist, does it not?" the younger man said evenly.

"The King was exceptionally fond of the young man, ever since he was a boy. Such a cruel blow, to all our hopes, and one which has left His Majesty distraught" the Kor'nai sighed bleakly.

"And yet, as His Majesty's Counsellors, we must set aside our personal grief for the greater good of the realm, is that not so?"

"A noble and virtuous course, Honourable Counsellor" the Kor'nai noted sourly.

The younger man smiled tightly. "We cannot ignore the issue any longer, old friend, for it will surely be the talk of the city within a mere few days?"

"The issue in question is the gravest matter of state in a Century. We should make haste in our Counsel to satiate the idle tongues of commoners?" the Kor'nai eyed the younger man icily.

"We cannot still the idle tongues of commoners, old friend. Nor can we silence the chatter of our esteemed guests. The grave matter of the succession cannot remain undecided for much longer?" Mes'khu sipped his wodki. "This is an exemplary batch, old friend. Brewed from the fruits of the orchards of your estates in Talosk'ye unless I am mistaken?"

"And whom would you Counsel, my young friend? You have something of an advantage over the rest of us, for you have been a confidante of His Majesty ever since you were children" the Kor'nai smiled tightly.

Mes'khu's eyes flashed angrily. "It would never have occurred to me that you held me in such ill grace, Honourable Kor'nai? You honestly think I would taint my Counsel to exploit our recent tragedy for personal gain?"

"Such duplicity would not be beyond the realms of possibility, you would agree?" the Kor'nai smiled brightly.

"You will forgive me, if I have given cause for offence, but I serve at His Majesty's grace, as you do. If the King commands my opinion, as lowly as it surely is, then my opinion he shall have."

"Which brings us readily to the point, does it not, Counsellor Mes'khu?" the Kor'nai eyed the younger man with icy distaste.

The younger man bristled at the pointed disavowal of the honorific. He reclined in his chair and gazed intently at the older man. "The King regaled me for my humble opinion upon the virtues of his two youngest daughters, nothing more than that."

"During which you ventured preference for the Royal Princess Sychoria, is that not so?"

"The King's opinions of his daughter's virtues are a matter of common knowledge, are they not?" Mes'khu's eyes twinkled with mischief.

"Did you express a preference for Princess Sychoria?" the Kor'nai's eyes flashed dangerously.

"No, old friend, I did not! As I am sure you are aware, the matter of the succession is but one issue that presently plagues the Duchy?" Mes'khu replied silkily.

"I am aware of that fact, Honourable Counsellor? As I am equally aware of His Majesty's desire to further deepen our relations with the Argata Royal House?"

"I thought you were in favour of the betrothal of the Princess Mikhouri to Prince Disch'al?" Mes'khu spoke evenly.

"I think they would make a fine match. What of her sister, the Princess Alicharia?" the Kor'nai probed.

"Alicharia is a mere whelpling! It will be many a moon before we address the question of her future?" Mes'khu ventured.

The Kor'nai eyed the younger man intently. "You have not, at any time, given private Counsel to the King in respect of the Princess Alicharia?"

"No, my Lord, I have not. The Princess Alicharia is a mere babe, of trivial significance to the future of the Duchy, despite her infectious charm."

"And the King has not sought your private Counsel in respect of the future of the Princess Miskal'ya?" the Kor'nai probed.

"No, my Lord, he has not." Mes'khu sighed irritably. "Nor has the King entreated me for opinion in respect of the Princess Kh'isa, or her sister, Haedi? Might I enquire as to your motive for this sudden interest in the King's granddaughters?"

"I feel certain Queen Lezika will raise the issue of the Prince Sea'gir?" the Kor'nai smiled thinly.

"Your spies have been thorough, haven't they?" Mes'khu drained his goblet and shrugged.

"The Persians are playing a dangerous game. I would be wary of their integrity in this matter?"

"For my sins, my Lord, I much prefer to keep those oily swindlers at arm's length" Mes'khu rose to leave. The meeting was over.

"They are our allies, are they not?" the Kor'nai smiled brightly.

"That is a matter of opinion, old friend. As well you know, opinion can be a highly dangerous commodity, especially in a climate of heightened suspicion, distrust, and even treachery."

The younger girl frowned at her reflection in the burnished bronze mirror. "I shall catch my death. I swear it so!"

"You swore a pledge to Mama to behave, as I recall?" the older girl chided.

"Are you touched, Mikhouri? My hair is as moist as a whore on Shabbat! I will surely freeze like a Shaman's tit!" the younger girl protested.

Mikhouri gaped in horror at her younger sister, aged only seven years. The young Handmaiden, Vy'lya, a year older than the nine-year-old Princess Mikhouri, giggled shrilly. "Hades aflame, Alicharia! Have you been sneaking into *The Spear and Sword* again? Such despicable language is not for the ears of little Princesses!" the older child remonstrated.

"The soldiers talk like that all the time, especially after a few rye beers" Alicharia protested.

"Which is why you are expressly forbidden from going there, are you not? You are a child, Alicharia! More to the point, you are a Royal Princess!"

"The soldiers like me. They give me beer" the younger girl sneered at her sister. Vy'lya turned away and grinned.

"You have been drinking beer again? What in Hades name will Mama say?" Mikhouri chided.

"She won't know, will she? As long as you don't tell?" the younger girl gazed pleadingly at her elder sister.

"I promise I won't tell. You need to promise that you will not go in there again? Mama will never believe me if I tell her that I didn't know."

"I promise, I swear it" Alicharia smiled sweetly.

The Handmaiden, Vy'lya, suddenly prodded the younger girl with her finger. Her eyes betrayed her terror. Mikhouri telegraphs a silent warning to her younger sister. Alas, both signals were regrettably lost in translation. "Stop prodding me, you thicket!" Alicharia spat.

"And what kind of language is that for a little Princess?" a voice clipped icily.

The Princess Alicharia turned and gaped dumbfounded at her mother, the Royal Princess Sychoria. "Hello, Mama!"

Mikhouri flushed hotly. "We are ready, Mama" she quipped.

"And don't you just look it?" the woman appraised them closely, smiling wryly. "I doubt there is a soul alive who would believe I have such a foul-tongued imp for a daughter!"

"I don't know what you are talking about, Mama?" Alicharia quipped.

"Perhaps you and I should talk, just the two of us, over a couple of jars of your favourite rye? You can regale me with the tales of soldiers you overheard at *The Spear and Sword*?" Sychoria said silkily.

"I should leave, Your Royal Highness?" Vy'lya blushed furiously.

"I should say so!" the Princess clipped icily.

The young Handmaiden scurried away. Mikhouri frowned and gazed at the floor. "I have tried my best, Mama."

"Your best is obviously nowhere near sufficient, my darling child!" Sychoria retorted. She turned and glowered at Alicharia. "As for you, young Lady, if you should cause a scene this day, I shall see you flayed a strip at a time!"

The Royal Party, including their esteemed guests, congregated in the late morning mist on the track by the ruins of Vol'yar, some ten miles northwest of Mamy'eva. The entire party, including Yari, were garbed in white. This seemed appropriate for the winter, yet white was the traditional colour for a Requiem, at any time of the year. Yari stood next to Ji'ri, rigidly still to the right of Queen Illir'ya, beside the Royal Princess Laeschalla. Yari wrinkled her nose in the chill of the day. She wore a white fur hat and thick fur cloak over heavyweight woollen kurta and britches. Soon thereafter, the Royal Party climb aboard their open carriages to begin the journey to Mamy'eva. Yari presumed that she and Ji'ri would ride with Queen Illir'ya, the Crown Prince Mais'ki, and the other Honourable members of the Royal Counsel in their two allotted carriages, but Laeschalla had different ideas, and requested that the two Handmaidens ride together with her mother, and the Dowager Countess Arialla. Queen Illir'ya consented with a smile, for it would at least spare the Sauromatae teenager from the steely glare of Commander Zar'cha, head of Her Majesty's Royal Guard.

The lead driver whipped his horses and the train headed east, moving slowly towards the Royal City. A little over an hour later, they were within a mile of the West Gate. Yari was greatly surprised by the size of the congregation of citizens who flanked either side of the Royal Avenue for much of the last mile of their approach. The soldiers who paraded on either side of the road, solemnly bowed their heads as the Royal Train passed by, but Yari had been equally astounded by the number of ordinary people who wept openly as the carriages passed by. Until then, she had little real idea just how much hope had been laid upon the shoulders of the young Crown Prince Ach'ti. Whilst the crowd stood in respectful silence, there were more than a few congregants who broke with tradition and loudly hailed their condolences to the Royal Princess Laeschalla, who was obviously held in deep affection by everyone.

The carriages passed beneath the formidable towers of the West Gate and entered the Royal City. Yari almost gasped at the mass of citizens who stood on either side of the Royal Avenue, heads bowed solemnly, as the Royal Train made its way slowly toward the junction with Wol'yi Way. To Yari's surprise, Laeschalla reached out to squeeze her hand affectionately, which made the Sauromatae teenager blush, for it was surely she who should be offering support to the elder girl. The carriages turned left at the junction and headed north for a short distance along Wol'yi Way, before turning right into Gor'khi Way to pass through the imposing marble edifice of the Gor'khi Gates. As they did, that Yari became keenly aware of the jeers hissed by many congregants on either side of the Wol'yi Way. These were aimed at the Ur'gai Queen and her party!

"There is much to lament, Your Royal Highness?" Queen Lezika remarked sombrely. "To see a life of promise, cruelly scythed before its ripeness, and in such tragic circumstances?"

"You have my sympathies and condolences, Your Majesty. Prince Ach'ti would have made a fine husband for your darling child, the Princess Cordicca" King Tagar sighed sadly.

The pair had met, alone, in the King's Private Chambers. Not even their respective Kor'nai's were permitted to hear what passed between them. The King drained his goblet and proffered his honoured guest a refill, which was graciously accepted. "Tell me, my Lady, do you believe the death of the Crown Prince was mere misadventure?" the King continued.

"I have heard whisper of the rumours, of course? Only a half-wit would credit them. Persia suspects the hand of Athens or Sparta, yet they would curse the Hellenics for the failing of the rains" Lezika scoffed.

"Our sources confirm a nest of dissident Armenians in the Crimea, yet they have neither the wit, nor the ambition, to accomplish such a feat" the King mused drily.

"Which leaves the Ur'gai?" the Queen smiled tightly.

"They have the resources, desire, and opportunity, yet a targeted killing of a Crown Prince seems a lofty adventure, even for a mind as unhinged as the 'mad maid'!" the King mused acidly.

"My previous Ambassador sung high praise of the young Princess Mikhouri. She will one day make a fine Queen?" Lezika sipped her wine and eyed the King closely.

"Not in this realm. I fear she is altogether too cultured, and far too delicate a soul to be gifted to that ill-bred wastrel in Mus'kyv!" Tagar snorted. He sipped his wine.

"Any such a union would surely raise the hackles of the Royal Army?" the Queen ventured.

"What of your own son and heir, my lady? Such a match would cement our two great houses in amity, now and forever?" the King smiled ruefully.

"It would not please the Orch'tai Royal Army? Nor would it be received favourably in Rost'eya or Mus'kyv?" Queen Lezika noted sourly.

"The Army will soon have enough to preoccupy itself. If a betrothal were announced timeously, how could they possibly oppose it?"

"Such a match meets with the approval of your Counsellors, my Lord?" Lezika pressed.

"The majority of my Counsel favour closer ties between our peoples. It is all too clear that Persia cannot to be trusted, we can surely agree on that?" the King spoke softly.

"We have furnished minimal assistance to the ongoing effort in the Ionian Sea, yet even now these fools fumble at the task of bringing Miletus to heel!" Lezika noted sourly. She sighed morosely. "It is the future, not the past, which vexes both mind and soul."

"My spies in Tyre assure me the new fleet will be ready to sail before the winter?" the King smiled tightly. It was a dangerous confession, on both counts.

"Our own agents report a catalogue of difficulties. They are constantly stung by pirates in the Dodecanese. And still the traitor Histiaeus remains at large" the Queen mused lightly.

"These are dangerous times, my Lady. We must exercise caution in our dealings with Persia. We have much to lose, do we not?"

"You have more to lose than I, Tagar? Your treasury has swollen by their need for timber. If reports from Attica are accurate, the Hellenics will never deal with you" Lezika stated baldly.

"I will deliver upon my promise, Lezika! The Ur'gai will be humbled. You have my solemn oath on that. You will have unquestioned authority in the Crimea" the King said earnestly.

"If that is so, we may yet find resolution to your dilemma. Unless one of your younger daughters sires a son, you must choose between them?" the Queen ventured searchingly.

"And how would your Counsel, wise and noble as it is, be of assistance in our grave matter of state?" the King quipped guardedly.

"I have a second son. You have a surplus of eligible granddaughters? Between the two of us, I feel certain a mutually beneficial compromise can be reached. One that will secure the succession and the future of your lineage for many a moon to come" the Queen smiled thinly.

"I must first think, and then discuss the matter with my Counsel. There is no denying the hand of fate rests heavily upon our souls?" the King sighed tiredly.

"I shall bid you farewell, Your Royal Highness, for the now, of course" the Queen rose to leave.

King Tagar watched her stroll across the room and exit. He reached for his goblet and drained it in a single gulp. "If only clarity of thought could grace a wine cup?" he pondered sourly.

Queen Lezika strolls along the pillared corridor, in whispered conference with her most trusted Counsel, the Honourable Counsellor Miris'kar. "Are you sure this course is wise, my Lady?" he ventured softly.

"The fool is rattled! Now is the time to topple him. Send word to my eldest daughter and her minions. Instruct them to proceed with her plan. Discreetly, I beseech you?"

As a King humours a Queen, so a Counsellor must indulge an ambassador, even one as scandalously indulged as the venerable Banassarias, plenipotentiary of His Royal Majesty, King Darius of Persia. "My agents have been quite thorough, I assure you?" Mes'khu's grey eyes twinkled wryly.

42

"As have mine, old friend. You require an honest broker in a Royal City plagued by pestilence and treachery?" Banassarias smiled thinly.

"You speak harshly, old friend, for Susa is no glory of Nineveh" Mes'khu smiled tightly.

"The King is weakened by this unforeseen tragedy. Perhaps we have been too generous in our appraisal of your virtue?" the Ambassador shrugged ruefully.

"Is that your own opinion, old friend? It was always my understanding that we have been at one on the burning issues of the day?" Mes'khu opined in a distressed tone.

"We are, old friend, and long may that continue. Nonetheless, with the capitulation of Miletus now a mere formality, who knows that the future may bring?"

Mes'khu eyed the Ambassador shrewdly. They had been close confidantes for the past seven years, ever since Banassarias' arrival in Mamy'eva, yet this Persian jackal rarely gave up his secrets readily. "It was my understanding that the traitor Histiaeus still eludes you? As long as he remains at large, the fires of rebellion will continue to burn brightly in Miletus."

Banassarias chuckled wryly. "Perhaps your agents in Ionia are not what they once were, old friend? Miletus is finished, and the war is over. You may rest assured of that."

"Has the city fallen? We have no news of this?" Mes'khu was astounded.

"The city capitulated several months ago. Naturally, we have been at some pains to delude the Hellenics and their allies in to believing otherwise" Banassarias shrugged apologetically.

"I was not aware that we were now considered allies of the Hellenics, old friend. Perhaps it is we who have misjudged your virtues?" Mes'khu spoke silkily.

Banassarias raised a hand to mollify the Counsellor. "The Royal City teems with Ur'gai spies. If your dignity is offended, I can assure you the Argata remain as much in the dark as you?"

"When do you plan to attack Athens?" Mes'khu spoke in barely a whisper.

"Athens can wait! The intolerable situation in the Crimea cannot!" Banassarias hissed. "King Tagar's position is plagued by a succession crisis. Naturally, there are concerns as to how that may adversely influence your commitment to our shared endeavours?"

"You may rest assured, dear friend, that we are at one on this matter, as we are many others" Mes'khu ventured emphatically.

"What are words, old friend? They are nothing but terms without substance? The Duchy needs an heir, one that binds the Royal Houses of the Orch'tai and Argata in perpetuity?"

"The King and Queen are at one on the matter of Prince Disch'al and the Princess Mikhouri" Mes'khu confided.

"That does not resolve the issue of the succession. A weakened King, bereft of a legitimate heir, is not a natural partner in our plans, old friend" Banassarias sighed regrettably.

"You speak for Susa?"

"Naturally, I do. A mind as keen as your own has surely grasped the solution to this riddle?"

"The Princess Alicharia would make a fine wife for the Crown Prince Sea'gir, would she not?" Mes'khu ventured airily.

"And a fine Queen, as long as she has the virtues of her mother?" Banassarias smiled thinly.

"It is settled, then?" Mes'khu ventured hesitantly.

"The Argata will drive a hard bargain in the matter of the dowry, for they are slaves to the altar of their traditions, as well you know?"

"I have your wholehearted support in my endeavours to resolve this matter to our mutual satisfaction. You will not abandon me in the breach?"

Banassarias adopted a pained expression, as if his honour were gravely wounded. "I promise to do all that is within my power to further these unions. You have my word, upon my honour."

A hasty conference was convened, later that evening, in a Private Room of *The Suckling Pig*, nestled in the far south of Mamy'eva, adjacent to the

South Gate. It was a notorious rough house, quite unfit for a Royal Princess, yet the Princess Perdicca had deliberately sought lodgings frequented by disreputable types, for here they would be assured anonymity. The Royal Princess, recently turned nineteen-years-old, strikingly tall, and stunningly pretty, with a flowing mane of luxurious red hair, was dressed in black from head to toe, including a dark hat, whose brim cast a shadow over her upper face. She had arrived in Mamy'eva two days earlier, accompanying a band of disreputable rogues, if appearances were anything to pass judgement upon. In truth, her eight companions were all battle-hardened warriors of Her Royal Majesty's elite, or *Khu'rok*, who had spent the past six years fighting a clandestine war against renegade Armenian bands in the foothills of the Caucasus. These men were adept killers, each one loyal to their beloved Queen. They were commanded by Captain Gy'dych.

"We are quite certain of our intelligence, my Lady?" Gy'dych probed.

"Indeed, we are, my good fellow. The covered carriage ferrying the Royal Princess Sychoria and Queen Illir'ya is destined to leave Mamy'eva for Or'vych in two days' time" Perdicca confirmed.

"They will be travelling with a detachment of Royal Guards?" Ka'vyn frowned in puzzlement.

"No more than twenty, I have assurances of that. These Guards will be Orch'tai, naturally, and will be commanded by a young and vainglorious fool" the teenager simpered.

"They are twenty men, my Lady? We are eight?" Gy'dych cautioned.

"Our objective is merely to sow consternation. We are not aiming to seize the Royal Party, are we?" Perdicca clipped coldly. "We will obviously kill a small number of Guards, which should be sufficient to give credence to the theory that a prescient threat to the life of the Royal Princess and her children exists, and that is all."

"We then make good our escape, heading due southwest for Kamy'ch, my Lady?" ventured Nas'ryn.

At the tender age of twenty, he was the youngest of the party by a good many years. In contrast with his fellows, Nas'ryn was softly spoken and serious, frequently embarrassed by the coarse language of his peers. He was also literate, a rarity among soldiers. The young Princess eyed him steadily, for he had unwittingly made a favourable impression upon her. "Our steeds should easily cover the distance in two hours, I would say?"

"If we take a scenic route, which would be well advised, my Lady, it should be more like four?" Nas'ryn blushed faintly at his temerity.

"In any event, we should be well away from the Kings hounds by nightfall" declared Gy'dych.

"We would surely be advised to conduct an initial scouting foray to appraise the lie of the land?" Dival'yn proposed. At over six-feet-three, he was one of the tallest men in the Argata Royal Army.

Perdicca smiled brightly at the man. "We shall conduct our reconnaissance tomorrow. Some of you will ride west, to assess the disposition of His Majesty's forces to the southwest of Or'vych, whilst a second party will head northwest and reconnoitre a decent ambush site."

"Two of us will remain here, to safeguard the Royal Princess. Is that understood?" Gy'dych said firmly.

"This should be a piece-of-piss, all things considered" Ka'vyn gushed.

"We are not expecting any serious opposition. The Royal Guards will likely believe we are mere brigands. Their first duty will be to protect the Royal Carriage" Perdicca mused.

"Some of them will die doing so!" growled Vor'dyl, a skulking brute of a soul, cursed with a face to terrify any child.

Rody'ska, March 493 BC

The visitors had been astonished by the thickness of the morning mist. It was almost impossible to discern your own breath, much less the ears of the steed that ferried you. Whilst the absence of snow was a blessing, the air was bitterly cold and seemed almost to cling to your body, permeating the thick woollen garments to chill the very bones. The three men cantered northwest through the valley, following the course of a barren riverbed, Gy'dych in the lead. All were armed with daggers, swords, and recurved bows. It was now several hours after first light, and the uplands of the broken escarpment to the immediate north were carpeted with a screen of snow. The entire landscape was barren, completely bare of trees, and offered little protection from the winter winds. This was shit country. The Orch'tai could keep it. Gy'dych reined his mare to a halt. Ka'vyn and Vor'dyl sidled close. "By the Gods, I don't wish to see the like of it ever again. This place is as bare as a baby's cunt!" Vor'dyl spat.

Gy'dych pointed northwest. "We should keep going that way. The terrain should become more bearable, according to the Princess."

"How the fuck does anyone live here?" Ka'vyn spoke in bewilderment.

"In case you hadn't noticed, they don't!" Gy'dych grinned. It should get easier from now on. There is a village about two miles ahead. We can stop for some tea and wodki."

"There aren't any bears, are there?" Ka'vyn hissed nervously.

"Why the fuck would any self-respecting bear take a shit in this place? There aren't even any woods to speak of" Vor'dyl mused gloomily.

"There are to the west. In case you didn't know, this *is* Bear country, at least according to the Princess" Gy'dych seemed to relish the prospect of encountering a bear.

"And they can bloody well keep it!" Vor'dyl cackled.

An hour or so later, when the mist was still thick, a covered wagon plodded west along a well-worn trackway, some two miles to the north of the escarpment on the plains of Rody'ska. The wagon was escorted by a detachment of twenty Orch'tai Royal Guardsmen, all hand-picked for this assignment. They were led by an experienced young Officer named Uh'gui, a veteran of the recent campaigns in the east, now aged in his middling twenties. Inside the covered wagon, a scowling Yari sipped a goblet of lukewarm tea from a flagon. "By the Gods, it's freezing! I don't think I have ever been this cold in all my life!" she lamented. The girl pulled her thick wool cap further down to cover her brow."

"Stop complaining, Yari! It will be nice in a few hours when the mists have cleared." Laeschalla smiled sweetly at the scowling girl.

"I am curious, obviously so? Why don't you live in Mamy'eva? It is the Royal City, and you are a Royal Princess, after all?"

"Mamy'eva is a filthy city. The air is foul, especially in the height of summer. There are far too many people now, it is not like it used to be" the older girl replied uncharitably.

"Rost'eya is much the same in the spring. That is why most of us head south with the Queen to the Saiga Plains" Yari sipped her tea.

"Where is Corelya? She is a little young to be sent away, is she not?" Laeschalla probed.

"The Queen sent her south to Tanais just after the solstice. I haven't seen her since."

Laeschalla gaped at the younger girl. "That was moons ago. She had still not returned before you left?"

"Corelya will turn up, sooner rather than later, likely with a glorious sun-tan" Yari mused.

"You aren't in the least concerned for her welfare?" Laeschalla stared wide-eyed at Yari.

"Corelya will be fine. To be perfectly honest, I don't really ask too many questions anymore…"

"What do you make of it, old friend?" Gy'dych turned in the saddle and addressed Vor'dyl.

"We *are* certain they will approach the crossroads from the west?" Vor'dyl seemed uncertain.

The trio of riders had reached the outskirts of the village of Ky'vych, three miles south of Or'vych and the Summer Palace. The men had spent a leisurely hour at a local tavern, sipping tea and drinking wodki. The mists had finally cleared, and the sky was an almost cloudless blue, yet it remained bitterly cold. The track leading to the junction was wide and firm, perfect for carriages, and even in the bleak of winter it was well maintained. "There is no other trackway on the approach to Or'vych which is suited to large wagons. They will turn right at the junction and continue north" Gy'dych seemed confident of his intelligence.

"And that is where we will hit them?" Ka'vyn grinned.

"I would say so" Gy'dych mused wryly. "They will almost certainly send outriders to screen the junction and the road ahead, in either direction."

"There is little in the way of cover on either side of the road north, my Lord?" Ka'vyn ventured hesitantly.

Gy'dych turns and points west to a small copse in the middle of the field. He turned and grinned wolfishly at his companions. "That will do splendidly, will it not?"

"It would give sufficient cover, and we can deploy and dismount in the field. The range would be perfect, I would venture?" Vor'dyl seemed enthusiastic about the potential of the site.

"Only if you can learn to shoot in the next few hours!" Ka'vyn sneered jocularly.

"I will shoot you in a moment, your jabber-mouthed cunt!" the brute sneered.

"Do you have anything of substance to add, Ka'vyn?" Gy'dych spoke mockingly.

Ka'vyn blushed hotly. "It will do perfectly, my Lord. If we wait for them to pass, and continue for a few hundred yards, we can hit them from the flank and rear?"

"It is settled, then? Now, if you promise to behave, I shall buy you a rye beer and a draught of wodki in the tavern before we leave?"

"My Lord...?" Ka'vyn hissed in a bewildered tone.

"Bear's tits...!" Vor'dyl gaped in astonishment.

A party of Royal Guardsmen morph on the horizon, half-a-mile or so to the west. They are accompanying a covered wagon, likely containing a person of importance. Ka'vyn gaped at his commander, his eyes betraying his incomprehension. "Is this the Queen and the Royal Princess?"

Gy'dych smiled wryly. "No, my old friend, it is not! I would have a little more faith in the young Princesses intelligence if I were you. This is almost certainly the Princess Laeschalla?"

The lead outriders of the Royal Train eyed the approaching strangers warily. One was a colossus, with an unruly beard and a face to frighten a tiger! Captain Uh'gui, spoke briefly with the driver, then spurred his mount towards the outriders and the oncoming strangers. "A fine morning for a hunt, is it not? The bears will not likely rouse for another moon at least" Uh'gui challenged the men pleasantly.

"We have ventured a mile or so further west, my Lord. An old sea-dog in *The Hemp Rope* told us the rabbits were numerous in these parts, even at this time of year" Gy'dych spoke evenly.

"You have ridden from Mamy'eva? You must have left early?" the captain probed.

"Indeed, we did, my Lord. Not that we have seen much in the way of rabbits" Gy'dych mused sourly.

"The ground is likely a little too frigid for them to leave their warrens. Give it a month or so and you may have a more profitable jaunt" Uh'gui ventured.

"We will warm our cockles with a couple of draughts of wodki at *The Bear and Honeycomb*, before we head back?" Gy'dych smiled brightly. He gazed past the young Captain at the wagon, now fast approaching the hostelry. "We did not expect to encounter Royalty on our little jaunt, my Lord?"

"The Royal Princess Laeschalla and a young companion are heading back to Or'vych. Have you heard of the place?" Uh'gui smiled tightly.

"Not at all, my Lord, for we are strangers in this land" Gy'dych shrugged apologetically.

"Then you might be best advised to continue back to Mamy'eva, dear fellow. The weather here can change at the drop of a hat, for you never know when a blizzard may strike" the captain suggested helpfully.

"Thank you for the advice, my Lord!" Gy'dych nodded his assent.

The riders kick their heels and trot west, past the entrance to the tavern and the Royal Wagon.

A brief while later, Yari and Laeschalla sat perched at a table in far corner of *The Bear and Honeycomb*, close to a roaring fire, cradling goblets of wodki and steaming mint tea. The tavern had not been busy, and the owner had been at pains to accommodate his Royal guest. "What in Hades name do you do out here in the middle of winter?" Yari chirped.

"You have missed the worst of it, for the thaw will soon be upon us. It is quite stunning during the summer. We have some of the best country in the Duchy for riding and hunting" the older girl gushed proudly.

"Do you ride often?" Yari sipped her tea.

"As often as I can, for it gets me away from the disapproving scowl of a repressive mother!" Laeschalla sighed morosely.

"She worries about you, Laeschalla, that is all. Did your brother like it here, or did he prefer to live in Mamy'eva?" Yari asked guardedly. This was obviously painful for the older girl.

"Ach'ti loved it here, especially when we were young. He spent a lot more time in Mamy'eva this past year, for obvious reasons, but still came home as often as he could" the blonde girl sighed sadly.

"When did you last see him? I do not mean to offend, or to intrude. It might be good for you to talk about him if you would like to?" Yari smiled encouragingly.

"It was just before the Solstice. Soon after the King had appointed him as Ambassador to the Royal Court in Archaeopolis" Laeschalla gazed down at her tea. "He spent a few weeks here, with me and mother, and then returned to Mamy'eva."

"I am terribly sorry, Laeschalla. I couldn't believe the news when I heard it" Yari smiled ruefully and sipped her tea.

"It was really nice to have him back, if only for a brief while. He does not disapprove of my new friends, not in the way that mother does" Laeschalla quipped.

Yari sensed there was more to this than met the eye. The older girl had much changed since the previous summer when they had met at Hopa for the signing of the *Accord Scythiac*, yet it was now clear what the true cause of this change was. "Your mother does not approve of you rolling in the clover with one of the local boys?" she asked in a hushed tone.

Laeschalla giggled. "She most assuredly does not? Her disapproval has been worse since Ach'ti died."

The younger girl leaned close and lowered her voice even further. "Are you in love?"

"I use him for sex, for he is very practical in such matters" the blond girl whispered.

"How would you know, unless you have been with others?" Yari gaped incredulously.

"His sister, who is the same age as me, certainly knows a trick or two. He is far more learned" Laeschalla blushed faintly.

Yari rolled her eyes in disbelief. "You have come out of your shell, haven't you?"

"I do hope your adventures were less memorable?" Perdicca quipped breezily.

"The journey should be less arduous later in the day, my Lady, provided we do not encounter a blizzard. The mist typically clears by mid-morning, at least according to the locals" Nas'ryn spoke evenly.

His party had departed Mamy'eva an hour or so after Gy'dych and his men, heading northwest towards the village of Tu'vyn, a few miles south of Rody'ska, before tacking west along the valley, in the shadow of the uplands of the escarpment to the immediate north. This landscape was as bleak and unforgiving as anywhere in the hinterlands of the Royal City in the winter months. Successive deforestation by a long line of Orch'tai Kings had left the soil with no protection against the permafrost and the deluge of the spring rains. No besieging army could prevision itself from the land around the city walls, and the absence of settlement offered little physical protection from the incessant cruelty of the winter winds. And yet, further west, the soils were rich and fertile, perfect for both arable and pastoral holdings, and dense forests carpeted much of the hinterlands of the great Don'yi. A few hours later, the party had reached the village of Oy'ska, where they stopped for an hour to warm their bones with a kettle of mint tea and a medicinal flagon of wodki.

They continued southwest, riding hard through mile after mile of snow-covered fields and meadows until they reached the village of Try'eva, a picturesque little spot, nestled on the shore of a small lagoon. They stopped for a brief respite and an obligatory flagon of wodki at *The Kings Pledge*, a small hostelry in the centre of the village, some twenty-five miles to the east of the port of Kamy'ch. The mercifully uneventful journey had taken a little over four hours, and, if the weather held, the trek southwest from Or'vych could easily be accomplished in just over two, riding at a gallop for most of the way. The return journey to Mamy'eva was surprisingly pleasant, given the time of year, and the three men had arrived back in the early afternoon. They were astonished to discover that the Princess had absconded with her bodyguards into the heart of the city itself. Upon her return, Perdicca had demanded a hot bath, for it would likely be her last for a week or so! Afterwards, the group had hastily convened in the Private Room of *The Suckling Pig*, prior to a light supper and an early night.

"You are confident no permanent garrisons exist in the hinterlands of Kamy'ch, Nas'ryn?" Perdicca enquired earnestly.

"We the exception of the Militia Guards, we have nothing to worry about, my Lady" Nas'ryn said confidently.

"We are obviously aware of the permanent divisions stationed at Loz'nye, twenty-five miles north of Or'vych, and at Mai'ske, sixty miles due southeast on the west bank of the Don'yi" Gy'dych interjected.

"Any immediate force despatched to apprehend us will undoubtedly come from Mamy'eva, my Lady" Nas'ryn spoke evenly. "They will surely expect us to head west for the Don'yi? Within a few hours, patrols will have visited every conurbation within a day's ride of Or'vych?"

"By which time, we will all be safely on the river heading south" Perdicca smiled sweetly.

"Once we reach the port of Ly'vyska, we can purchase horses and equipment for the journey south. I advise we split in to two parties, four men in each" Gy'dych proposed.

There were enthusiastic nods of approval. The ultimate decision would be made by the Princess Perdicca. "That seems a most appropriate course of action, Captain Gy'dych."

"We will leave Mamy'eva, shortly after first light, as two separate parties. Du'naik will join your band, Nas'ryn. You will leave first, following the same route as this morning. Once you clear the valley, you take the track north to Ky'vych" Gy'dych instructed them. He did not defer to the Princess Perdicca on this matter.

"We rendezvous when you clear the valley north of Rody'ska, my Lord?" said Nas'ryn.

"Then continue northwards as one party. Remember to wear an extra layer of woollen clothing. It will be bitterly cold in the copse. We could be there for several hours before the Royal Train arrives!" The men nodded vigorously.

"Let us toast our success, Gentleman!" Perdicca smiled sweetly at the assembled group.

To the glory of the Queen! To the glory of the Gods! Death shall be our testament!

Three

Or'vych, March 493 BC

A mysterious spectre, wrapped tightly in a heavy winter shawl to protect against the chill, hood drawn close, pads lithely along a dimly lit corridor. The ghoulish figure carries a small candle, fixed in a bronze holder in their right hand. They pause outside the door, glance furtively left and right, then reach for the handle and turn it gently, before slipping inside and closing the door silently. A sleeping girl lies on the bed, cocooned within several layers of blankets, blissfully ensconced in the land of dreams. She snores softly. The cloaked intruder stifles a giggle and pads stealthily to a small table next to the bed, where a fresh candle stands in a holder. The candle is lit by the flame of their candle, which is blown out and laid beside it. The intruder reaches out to the sleeping girl and strokes her hair. "Wake up, Yari-Bear!"

"What time is it? By the Gods, it is still dark outside, is it not?" Yari mumbles tiredly.

"There is someone I would dearly like you to meet. Come on. Get of bed and put your cloak on" Laeschalla chided.

"It's the middle of the bloody night, Laeschalla?" Yari mumbled grumpily.

"Mother is asleep. Come on. Get up."

Laeschalla leads Yari down a small flight of steps to the cellar. It was bitterly cold, and Yari shivers, despite her thick woollen cloak. Laeschalla opened the heavy oak door and ushered the younger girl through. The door is closed firmly. Yari blinks rapidly as her eyes adjust to the contrast, and, once they had, she gazes around in astonishment. The cellar is illuminated by the glare of at least a dozen candles. At the far end of the central aisle, a hearth burns brightly. "This is our special place. I hope you like it?" Laeschalla whispers proudly. "Come! I shall introduce you to everyone."

She led the astonished visitor down the aisle, flanked by trestle-tables on either side which are stacked with barrels of wine and wodki. At the far end of the aisle, a table is set to one side by the hearth, shielded from the entrance by rows of barrels. A group of teenagers sit at the table, three girls and two boys, whispering softly among themselves. Their chatter stills as Yari and Laeschalla morph at the end of the aisle. "Have you come to spoil our fun, Lally?" the nearest girl, garbed in a shawl of indeterminable age, eyes the newcomers mockingly. "Who is your new friend?"

"This is Yari. She is one of Queen Illir'ya's Handmaidens" Laeschalla smiled sweetly at the first girl. "You are to be nice to her, Yo'dyll, for she is lovely!"

"Hi" Yari smiled brightly.

"Is she Ur'gai? I hate the Ur'gai!" one of the boys scowled.

"Put a sock in it, Ga'vek! Does she look like an Ur'gai?" a second girl chided.

"You are quite right, Ny'vysa! Yari is Sauromatae!" Laeschalla quipped.

The teens are arraigned in an arc around an oblong table. Laeschalla beckons Yari to the table and makes the introductions. At the near end of the table, facing opposite end, sits Yo'dyll, razor-tongued with light brown hair. Ny'vysa, a raven-haired beauty with hazel eyes is to her left. Ga'vek is next in line, to the left of Ny'vysa. Vai'ska, a petite blonde girl with blue eyes, sits to Yo'dyll's right, next to Il'han, the oldest of the group by a mere few months. Last, but by no means least, is Ksen'ya, his younger sister, a twinkle-eyed brunette who sits directly facing Ny'vysa. There are two flagons of wodki on the table, both of which are now empty. "I don't suppose you bothered to save us a goblet?" Laeschalla raised an eyebrow mockingly.

"There is plenty to drink if you bothered to look. It is not like you are stealing, is it? Not when you own it all to begin with?"

"For your information, blockhead, this all belongs to the King. Our reserves are kept next door, safely away from your thieving hands" Laeschalla quipped snidely. "Sit down, Yari. I shall grab another couple of flagons" She turned and strolled away to the far side of the room, returning with two sealed flagons plucked from the shelves. "This is the cheap stuff we give to the locals! Nobody really notices if a few flagons disappear, from time to time' the blonde girl smiles sweetly at Yari, motioning her to sit in a vacant chair at the far end, facing Yo'dyll.

"I take it this is a regular gathering?" Yari accepts a goblet of wodki and sips gratefully.

"We normally meet at least once a month, always on a full moon" Yo'dyll grinned at Yari. "When we were young, we used to think Lally was a werewolf. We come to see if she will transform into one."

"That would be a sight to see!" Yari giggled.

"Not if I eat you, it won't" Laeschalla mused gleefully.

"We were thinking of going riding tomorrow, if you care to join us?" Vai'ska chirped.

"And where were you thinking of absconding with our horses?" Laeschalla raised an eyebrow mockingly.

"We are going to go to the woods and the lake at Gra'chi. Ny'vysa wants to check on the rabbit warren. She thinks it might have been disturbed" said Ga'vek.

"Why would anyone want to disturb a rabbit warren in the middle of winter?" Yari asked innocently.

"Poachers! They covet the meat and pelts at any time of the year" Ny'vysa scowled.

"Sounds like a decent adventure. You remember how to saddle a mare, don't you?" Laeschalla turned to Yari.

"Of course, I do. What do you take me for?" Yari replied.

"It is settled, then. We shall leave in the morning?" declared Il'han.

Rody'ska, March 493 BC

Nas'ryn frowned and raised a gloved left hand to his forehead, thumb outstretched, forefinger flat against the fur trim of his cap. He squints at the riders cantering west along the valley a few miles further north yet was unable to determine their precise strength. There were at least four riders, perhaps even five. "It must be them, surely?" Du'naik hissed.

"Don't be so presumptuous, friend?" Nas'ryn cautioned. He squints again at the riders as they continue west, certain that the lead rider was, in fact, two adventurers, riding side by side. His gaze suddenly switches to the plateau of the escarpment, high above the riders to the north.

"Shit! Who the fuck are those cunts?" Du'naik gasped.

A sizeable contingent of horsemen, some thirty in all, morph at the crest of the escarpment, heading west, almost as if they were shadowing the riders in the valley. Nas'ryn and his three companions watch in silence as the pursuers, who at this distance were discernible as a series of fast-moving silhouettes, snake west in staggered file. "They are Orch'tai cavalry! I am sure of it. They could well be a scouting party for the Royal Caravan" Nas'ryn said emphatically.

"What the fuck are we going to do now?" Du'naik mused gloomily.

"If it is Gy'dych and the Princess, it will be too risky to rendezvous with them at the junction of the track, not with those buggers on their tail" Nas'ryn spoke evenly. "If we kick our heels, we can reach Ky'vych in no time."

"You think the captain will simply head north?" Ha'jin ventured optimistically.

"If he isn't aware of those Orch'tai horsemen, he soon will be. I think we ought to work on the assumption he will head straight for Ky'vych. There is a hostelry there, is there not?"

"It is called *The Bear and the Honeycomb*, by all accounts?" Ha'jin confirmed.

"We can now presume that will be our rendezvous, are we clear?"

"Are you certain they are tailing us?" Perdicca whispered. The teenager shivered lightly, possibly with fear, rather than the cold.

"Quite certain, my Lady" Gy'dych smiled brightly. "I suspect they are outriders for the Royal Train. Considering what happened with the young Prince, they might consider it wise to prepare for every eventuality."

"If they follow us all the way to Ky'vych, we will have to reconsider the entire enterprise?" Perdicca mused gloomily.

"We will cross that bridge when we come to it, my Lady. By my reckoning, there are thirty to forty of them, trailing us across the escarpment. We can continue past the North Road and head for that forest in the distance" Gy'dych pointed due west. "If they elect to follow, we can easily shake them off in the woods and then double back to Ky'vych."

"Do you think they suspect anything?" Perdicca spoke urgently.

"No, my Lady, I do not. I think they are merely outriders. If I am right, they may not venture any further beyond the western fringe of the escarpment" Gy'dych replied confidently.

The Great Wol'yi March 493 BC

The Vanguard of the Royal Train reined in their steeds. It was now three hours after first light, and the air was bitterly cold. The Senior Officer, Captain Uh'gui, dismounts and strolls to the covered carriage, raising a hand to the driver, Var'ghyn. "This is a strange place to stop, if you don't mind me saying, Sir?" the scarred and grizzled veteran spat in disbelief.

"We shan't be here for long, I assure you" Uh'gui smiled brightly. He strolls to the rear doors of the carriage, nodding a silent greeting to Captain Ry'vach, the Commander of the Rearguard, and raps heavily on the rear doors. "We have arrived at Vol'yar, Your Royal Highness?"

"Then open the bloody door, you fool!" a petulant voice clipped from inside. The nearest soldiers grin inanely. Uh'gui glowers at them.

The two women alighted and followed the young Captain around to the left side. It was Her Royal Highness, the Princess Sychoria, who indicated a small escarpment, a little over two-and-a-half miles due northwest. It appeared to be roughly circular, bordered in the north by a small seasonal tributary of the great Wol'yi, enclosing a flat space of no more than a mile. "This is Vol'yar?" Illir'ya gaped at the site, barely able to contain her bewilderment.

"It isn't much to look at, is it? Yet, it was Queen Kh'our's first effort at a Royal City. Even when the site of the Royal Palace moved south, it remained pre-eminent until she died."

"The place is now completely abandoned?" the younger woman gasped.

"One of the line of fools she sired, I forget which one, took it upon themselves to deforest the surrounding valleys. After that, it became unbearable in the middle of winter" Sychoria mused cynically.

"The site remains revered, nonetheless?" Illir'ya spoke evenly.

"There are some among us, admittedly a rare few, who are not ashamed of our alleged barbarian roots" Sychoria grinned. "Kh'our remains an enduring source of inspiration to us."

"Matters of succession are rarely a bounty of blessings, my Lady" Illir'ya grinned.

"We should thank the Gods that your people did not see fit to crown your brother" Sychoria mocked lightly.

"In my experience, such blessings are a double-edged sword, Princess Sychoria. They impose a crushing debt of gratitude which stifles all hope of progress" Illir'ya mused cynically.

Yari and Laeschalla had risen shortly before first light and devoured a light breakfast of mint tea, freshly baked bread, and honey, before fetching and saddling the horses from the Royal Stables. Both girls carried military-grade recurved bows and a quiver of finely fletched arrows with razor-sharp iron points, capable of penetrating most armour. It was now an hour or so after first light, and the air is bitterly cold. Yari wrinkles her nose, adjusts the thick fur cap on her head, and turns to Laeschalla, or "Lally", as she much preferred. "Ready when you are?"

"Let us go, shall we?" Laeschalla grinned.

The pair trotted out of the stables and made their way to the Royal Aisle, which was apparently the correct name for the central avenue, heading west toward the main gates. "Will the others be waiting for us outside?" Yari asked.

"I would expect so. I doubt they would have gone ahead without us" Laeschalla replied.

"Is Il'han your boyfriend? He seems really nice?" Yari quipped innocently.

"You didn't think I was having it off with Ga'vek did you?" Laeschalla giggled shrilly.

"Your mother doesn't approve of him?" Yari blushed lightly.

"No, she does not! Cousin Sychoria seemed to be fine with it" Laeschalla confessed.

"You told your brother about him, did you not?" Yari asked.

"He guessed I had a boyfriend if that is what you mean? I didn't tell him who, obviously."

"Ach'ti wouldn't have approved?" Yari ventured hesitantly.

"As a mater of fact, I suspect he wouldn't have minded at all. Look! There are the others, just outside the gates" Laeschalla pointed ahead and waved energetically to the group.

"Do they get the horses from here?" Yari was astounded.

"Yes! They all hail from families that work the lands of the Royal Estate, so in many respects we are just like one big family. Given the reputation of some of my distant ancestors, we may be more closely related than anyone is comfortable admitting" Laeschalla smiled wryly.

The Royal Guards, some six in all, dutifully opened the ornate iron gates to allow the two girls to pass. With Laeschalla in the lead, and Yari to the rear, side by side with Vai'ska, the group trot west along the narrow, frozen trackway. Yari gazes at the surrounding landscape, which was bleak in winter, yet evidently majestic in the summer. She smiled inwardly. It was nice to be away from the Royal Palace of Rost'eya, even for a brief while!

When they reached the crossroads at the village of Ky'vych, Gy'dych spotted a clearly unimpressed Ha'jin, loitering at the entrance to *The Bear and Honeycomb*, stamping his feet on the icy ground to keep the blood flowing. He leaned in close and spoke briefly with Perdicca, before twisting in the saddle to scan the ground to the south. There was no sign of their pursuers. The party of five riders now head west in the direction of the copse. Ha'jin had disappeared, diving into the tavern to inform the others of the rendezvous. At this time of year, the landscape is barren and icy. There had been no snow for several weeks, and the open fields which stretched almost as far as the eye could see to the west and south were quagmires of ice. In the event of their escape, they would initially head west, keeping to the track, for only the Gods themselves knew what perils may await their horses in the fields.

The copse lay on a small rise, two miles west of the crossroads and a mile to the north. Whilst the trees were bare, they would furnish sufficient cover as they awaited the arrival of the Royal Train, which must surely now be on route from the Royal City. This was good country for hunting rabbits, and there was sound reason to check upon the health of the warrens prior to the coming thaw. The five riders, with Gy'dych in the lead, soon reach the entrance to a narrow bridle path on the right of the track. As they rode north towards the copse, Gy'dych glanced east and espied four riders trotting west along the trackway in the distance, a mile or so away. It was Nas'ryn and his merry band of adventurers!

Grak'ye, March 493 BC

The lake and forest of Grak'ye lay some four miles west of the Summer Palace and was accessible via a meandering bridle path, flanked to the north by dense clusters of bare trees. To the south, lay nothing but mile after mile of frozen earth which would, in the coming months, be utterly transformed into some of the richest arable land in the Duchy. Soon enough, the track veers south, away from the westerly course of the river Grak'ye, and is flanked by a gallery of mixed beech and maple on the left, surely a glorious sight from the spring through to autumn. "Do you ride often?" Yari asked Ksen'ya.

"As often as we can, which really depends on Lally, seeing as none of us could ever afford such horses" the girl smiled sweetly. "My parents have ponies, but they are used for ploughing and haulage. They are not for riding, certainly not now we are older."

"I wish I could get out on horseback more often. This is certainly a breath of fresh air from the Royal Palace of Rost'eya" Yari mused wistfully.

"You are one of Illir'ya's Handmaidens, are you not? She does not allow you to leave her sight, is that it?" Ksen'ya challenged mockingly.

"To be honest, I only seem to spend time in her company during the winter months, especially now I am older. The entire Household Division heads south to the Saiga Plains in the late thaw for the summer. I spend a lot of time riding there?" Yari confessed.

"And other things, I don't doubt?" Ksen'ya smiled wryly. "We have all heard tales of Ur'gai girls. You are most peculiar creatures."

"You mean 'the mysteries'?" Yari quipped.

"Despite what you might think, we are not quite the savages you paint us as. We know of the Priestesses of Lesbos, but nothing is formalised here. You also drill, do you not?"

"Not as much as people think we do?" Yari said guardedly. "I would not pay too much credence to wagging tongues."

Ksen'ya's eyes twinkle with delight. "You surely cannot be referring to Lally? Now there is a girl who definitely knows how to use her tongue!"

"Does she now?" Yari giggled. "She used to be such a sweet girl."

"She still is, trust me! She tastes as sweet as the first drizzle of summer honey."

The group soon reaches a beaten track to the right of the bridle path, which snakes north into the bare trees. Laeschalla clicked her mare and headed into the trees, as the rest of the group, with Yari at the rear, follow. Shortly thereafter, they reach the shore of the lake, skirted by a path along its perimeter. The group dismount and share a flagon of wodki. It was time to check on the rabbits!

The Royal Train made good ground during the next hour. They reached the hamlet of Gor'nii, nestled on an easterly inlet of Lake Varo'skye, some twenty-five miles to the west which was formed by a tributary of the great Don. They stopped for a quick restorative goblet of mint tea at a small hostelry, *The Royal Oak*, before continuing north. Soon enough, they reached the outskirts of Kra'nye, a small agricultural settlement, bordered to the west by a series of broken and barren plateaus and valleys. Uh'gui scans the horizon to the east with a wary eye, for he had been forewarned of a scouting foray from the garrison at Zar'khye, fifteen miles due northeast. He soon espies the wisps of smoke on the edge of a small escarpment, a sure a signal as any of their presence. Uh'gui grimaced at the tactical naivety of their commander and twists in his saddle to face his deputy, Navamir, a veteran of innumerable campaigns in the Western Plains of Kazakh'yi. "What do you make of them?"

Navamir spits on the ground in disgust. "The Sauromatae would eat the buggers for breakfast!"

"I would wager heavily on it, old friend" Uh'gui grinned. "At least we do not have to worry about that threat this far west. The fires will serve to advertise their presence to everyone in the area."

"Are we expecting trouble, Sir?" Navamir raised an eyebrow questioningly.

"There is talk of treachery. That Armenians, perhaps even Hellenics, may have been involved in the death of Prince Ach'ti. If you credit such nonsense, the apparent motive was to scupper the succession and destabilise the Duchy" Uh'gui confessed.

"Any such attack would be directed against the Royal Princess Sychoria and her children, is that it?"

"That is why our little jaunt was well advertised in advance, old friend" Uh'gui smiled slyly.

"Is this the real reason why the cubs are not travelling with their mother?" Navamir ventured.

"They will be leaving Mamy'eva in the next hour, without any formal escort, excepting those fools!" Uh'gui scowled at campfires on the horizon.

"I take it they have not been told in advance?" Navamir grinned.

"They shall be duly notified once we have safely reached Ky'vych."

"By which time they will have spent at least four hours in the cold, with the prospect of another three to come!"

"A soldier's life is no bed of roses, old friend. Didn't they tell you when you took the pledge?" Uh'gui quipped sardonically.

"I don't think anyone told those lazy twats, did they?" Navamir chuckled and cast a snook at the escarpment.

As luck would have it, the middle of the copse contained a large hollow, sufficiently wide, and long to conceal the horses and their riders. The floor of the hollow had been carpeted with autumn leaves, which offered protection for the underlying soil against the frost. All things being equal, this was not a bad little spot to hide for the next few hours, concealed by a screen of bare trees at the front and rear. Gy'dych and Perdicca elected to take first watch and scurry up the gentle incline of the east bank and then shuffle on their bellies across the frozen earth towards the edge of the treeline. There they lay motionless, longbows ready to hand, observing the main trackway heading north to the Summer Palace, a mile or so to the east. The field of observation was exemplary, and they would see the arrival of the Royal. Train from the south long before it reached the crossroads. Nas'ryn and his group had arrived and were now safely nestled in the hollow, concealed from prying eyes on all sides. All they could do now was wait, as patient as a viper poised to strike!

"It looks like the warren has been disturbed, just as I thought?" Ny'vysa eyed the deserted rabbit holes with an icy distaste.

"Ah, but not by locals, that much is certain?" Ga'vek ventured. Yo'dyll rolled her eyes. Ksen'ya giggled.

"Then by whom, smart arse?" Ny'vysa challenged.

"There is no evidence of butchery, is there? I would have expected the guts to be scavenged, but the heads…?" Il'han mused.

"Look at the earth around those holes? Does it look like the handiwork of poachers?" Ga'vek raised an eyebrow mockingly.

"Bears don't normally venture this far east in the winter, do they? Poachers may have brought dogs with them?" Vai'ska sighed irritably.

"It looks like it was done by a bear, and quite recently, if you ask me?" Il'han ventured.

"You didn't tell me we might meet a frigging bear!" Yari hissed at Laeschalla. The rest of the group giggled shrilly.

"You still know how to shoot an arrow, don't you?" Laeschalla grinned.

"I have never shot a bloody bear though, have I?" Yari retorted tartly.

"Are you a good shot?" Yo'dyll asked searchingly.

"I usually hit what I aim at" Yari blushed.

"She is exceptional! She hardly ever misses!" Laeschalla boasted.

"You always hit the spot, do you?" Ksen'ya mocked. The rest of group giggled hysterically.

"Hades aflame, Ksen'ya!" Ga'vek snorted. "You are like a bitch on permanent heat!"

Il'han turned to Laeschalla. "If a bear has been this way recently, we would be wise to inform the villagers?"

"If it was a bear, there must surely be tracks to the west?" Laeschalla mused.

"Let us get back in the saddle and trek further west. We never know what we might find?" Il'han proposed happily.

"A couple of handsome boys with massive cocks would be something to tickle a girl's fancy?" Yo'dyll quipped to Ny'vysa. Yari turned away and grinned.

"Perhaps what you seek has been hiding in plain sight all this time?" Ga'vek sneered.

"I think you have taken leave of your senses, needle-dick? I would much rather get frisky with Ksen'ya!" Yo'dyll retorted.

The group burst into hysterics, excepting Yari and Ksen'ya. The petite brunette did not even blush at the ribaldry. They climbed back on to their mounts and trot west along the shore of the lake.

"There! Do you see them?" Gy'dych extended his arm slowly and pointed southeast.

"I am tingling with the thought of killing them, Captain Gy'dych" Perdicca grinned slyly.

The vanguard of the Royal Train trot in staggered file toward the junction at Ky'vych, two miles to the south. Even at this distance, the sun reflected brightly off their helmets and armour. "We should get a clear idea of their strength as they approach the junction. We will know if the carriage is with them soon enough" Gy'dych mused.

"How many of the little darlings should we kill?" Perdicca mused gleefully.

"As many as we need to, my Lady. We should kill or wound enough to give credence to the seriousness of a threat, and to discourage any gainful pursuers."

"What of those riders this morning? Do you think it likely they are the rearguard?" Perdicca probed.

"I haven't given them much thought, my Lady. I doubt we shall have any trouble from them?" Gy'dych spoke confidently.

"Look! There is the carriage" Perdicca hissed. She pointed at the silhouette of a heavy covered wagon as it lumbers north in the distance. "They do not appear to have an excessive rear-guard, do they?"

"They do not expect to be attacked, my Lady. This is not Armenia?" the captain chided.

"Orch'tai fools! Now they will suffer their lack of judgement" Perdicca sighed happily.

"Indeed, they shall, my Lady. Indeed, they shall."

The thirty riders of the escort of the Royal Train were divided into three groups. Some fourteen men, including the Commander, were in the

Vanguard, and these had now secured the crossroads at Ky'vych. Six riders rode in the centre, on either side of the covered wagon, and the remaining ten are at the rear, also in staggered file. Of the mysterious riders from the escarpment north of Rody'ska, there was no obvious sign.

"I will warn the others to get ready" Perdicca spoke softly.

"Wow!" Laeschalla gasped in wonderment.

"I have seen paw-prints before, but never anything like this. How many bears do you think there were?" said Yo'dyll. She was kneeling by a smaller set of prints.

Il'han had also dismounted and was closely examining the larger prints. "I would say this one is female, at least judging by size. One female, recently pregnant I would wager, and two cubs?"

"They didn't come from the west, did they? These tracks head south?" Laeschalla pointed along the track.

The group had not ventured far from the shore of the lake. They rejoined the bridle path and headed west to a point where the track widened, at a junction with a small path leading south. To the immediate west, lay the small hamlet of Grak'ye. Yari politely refused an invitation to dismount and had her bow in hand with an arrow notched, her gaze focussed on the trees to the left. Ga'vek had trotted a few feet further along, and had his bow at the ready, his eyes fixed to the front. "This path leads to the grain silos, does it not?" quipped Ny'vysa.

"You think we have bears in the grain silos? Surely someone would have noticed?" Yo'dyll replied quickly.

"There is the fodder yard at the rear. No-one has likely been there in months?" Il'han ventured.

"That takes care of your hopes for a quickie, doesn't it? Not unless you had hopes of getting it on with a couple of bears?" Ga'vek mused snidely

"I don't howl loudly enough. He wants a real animal" Laeschalla retorted. The group giggled hysterically.

"The tracks head south, at least for a distance. Maybe we should trail them?" Ksen'ya suggested helpfully.

"Maybe *you* wish to be eaten by a bear? I bloody well don't!" Yari snorted.

"She will let anything eat her. She is quite the hussy" Ga'vek sneered.

"That is my sister you are talking about?" Il'han glowered at the younger boy.

"Ksen'ya is right" Ny'vysa beseeched. "If there is a den in the area, we have to inform everyone, surely?"

"They will kill them, Ny'vysa! You know what they are like?" Yo'dyll hissed softly. She stood up and gaped at Laeschalla, who had started along the track. "What the fuck are you doing, Lally?"

"Looking for bears, you thicket!" came the caustic reply.

"Maybe we should follow her?" Yari suggested helpfully.

Laeschalla did not get far before she stopped and immediately squatted on her haunches, examining the ground. She reached out and began tracing the paw-prints in the ground, frowning as she did so. Something was troubling her. "What is she doing?" Ny'vysa hissed.

"What is it, Lally?" Il'han hollered.

"You need to come and see this! All of you?" Laeschalla hollered back.

Yari reluctantly dismounts. Still armed with her longbow and quiver of arrows, she follows the rest of the group south along the track. As she did so, she made a mental note of the small copse sited atop a gentle verge, a mile or so away to the west.

"What the fuck was that?" Gy'dych hissed.

"It sounded like kids, Sir. There is a village a mile or so to the west. The ground here is slightly elevated, so any sounds, especially cries of children, would carry this far?" said Nas'ryn.

Perdicca noted the unease on Captain Gy'dych's face. The nine hunters were arrayed in a row, close to the edge of the undergrowth, watching the road to the west. The Royal Train had almost reached the crossroads at Ky'vych. *The last thing they had bargained for was a group of interfering children!* Gy'dych turns to Du'naik. "Go and check it out. Whatever you do, make sure they don't see you?"

Du'naik nodded silently and scurried away.

Du'naik was a fearless warrior. Battle-hardened and scarred on both arms, he was a veteran of the six-year-war against the Armenians and was not troubled by the prospect of a confrontation with a group of pesky children. He did, however, harbour a healthy respect for the local bears, if they existed. He scurried up the west bank of the hollow and slithered along the frozen ground toward the treeline, far enough to visualise the lie of the land. Du'naik smiled grimly at a group of eight teenagers, congregating at a track a few miles due southwest. One of them, a girl perhaps, judging by her long, blonde locks, stooped close to the ground, seemingly examining something. She stood and strolled east, her gaze fixed on the ground, for no more than six or seven yards. The girl stooped again, closely examining the earth, before she rose and let out a whoop of joy. To his horror, she turned and pointed to the copse, gesticulating wildly, as the others race to join her. "Shit!" Du'naik swore viciously. The last thing they had planned for was the undue interference of a group of witless locals, even if they were kids. *What in Hades name had gotten them so excited?* He glanced at the ground a short distance from his right hand and instantly felt a cold prickle of terror. "Holy shit!" he swore breathlessly.

These fucking kids might be the least of their worries!

"They head of in that direction, directly to the copse" Laeschalla grinned proudly.

"There are definitely four of them, aren't there?" Il'han whistled breathlessly.

"That is one seriously big fucking bear" Yo'dyll spoke nervously. "I didn't think they came this far to the east. The forests are miles away."

"It looks like the female was pregnant. They must have hibernated in the copse for the winter? It isn't unheard of, is it?" Ga'vek ventured.

"Maybe we should get back to the horses?" Yari whispered softly.

"They won't be awake at this hour, Yari?" Laeschalla chided. "But they have certainly ventured forth recently, perhaps in the past few days. Now that the thaw is coming, they will need food to bulk up the cubs."

"Which might be us, if we give them due cause?" Yari rolled her eyes.

"I think Yari is right? We should be getting back to the horses. We don't want to lose them, do we?" ventured Ksen'ya.

"We will need to inform the locals. I shall speak with the Guards when I return. We should be heading back, as Yari and I have plans for the day?" Laeschalla eyed the younger girl brightly.

Yari frowned in puzzlement. "We do?"

"Can't we watch?" Yo'dyll snickered. "Ksen'ya might even want to join in the fun?" Apart from Il'han, Yari, and Laeschalla, the group, giggled hysterically.

"What do you know that I don't?" Yari challenged Laeschalla.

"Mother told me that my cousin will be coming to stay for a couple of days. She is really sweet, I promise."

"I presume you mean the Royal Princess Sychoria? She was supposed to be coming with Queen Illir'ya, wasn't she?" Yari gazed at the elder girl accusingly.

"So, I was told" Laeschalla quipped.

"Hades aflame, Laeschalla! I am scarcely dressed to meet a Royal Princess, am I?" Yari scowled.

"And we are scarcely dressed to meet a Queen?" Laeschalla chided. "Anyway, it is time we left?"

"I would say so!" Yari mused sourly.

There was a sudden shrill of horns, far away to the west, to be quickly followed by another!

"Shit!" Yari swore. She turned on her heels and sprints across the field.

The rest of the group gape at the fleeing girl in bewilderment. Laeschalla started after her, the others close behind. By the time they had reached the horses, Yari was in the saddle, grim-faced and determined, an arrow notched and the ready. The shrill of the horns was now incessant.

"What is it, Yari?" Laeschalla gasped.

"It is the call to arms! There must be a fight in the offing, somewhere nearby!"

Du'naik slithered forward across the frozen ground towards Gy'dych. "It was just a group of local kids, my Lord. They are no threat to us. There is something that might interest you. I came across a set of bear tracks. They are undeniably recent, I would venture."

"I couldn't care less for the natural history of local bears, could I?" Gy'dych scowled.

Perdicca frowned. "I didn't think bears would venture this south and east? We are miles from the nearest forest, after all? Unless…Shit!"

"That was my thought exactly, my Lady" Du'naik mused gloomily.

"Would you care to enlighten me, perhaps?" Gy'dych eyed Du'naik sternly.

"A heavily pregnant female may have ventured this far east to give birth to her cubs, my Lord" Du'naik blushed hotly. "There is always plenty to eat in a place like this, especially if they have young mouths to feed. Contrary to popular opinion, bears are mainly omnivorous, and will scavenge anything that is edible. They do, occasionally, attack and eat people"

"You are quite the font of knowledge, Du'naik?" Perdicca teased. The scarred warrior blushed and even deeper shade of rouge. "There is something else, my Lord?"

"Please continue?"

"If it is a pregnant female and her cubs, there will likely be a male in tow, my Lord"

Gy'dych smiled thinly. "Well, it is a good job we will not be here for long, is it?"

Perdicca pointed east towards the main track, where the Vanguard trotted north, almost level with their line of sight. "I think our moment is now, Captain Gy'dych, you agree?"

"Pass the word along the line. Let's get back to the horses and get this over and done with."

The group made their way stealthily back to the hollow and untethered their mounts. The men glanced warily around the hollow, seeking any sign of the elusive bears. Some of the men muttered darkly, for few had any real experience of hungry bears! "Concentrate on the job in hand and forget about the fucking bears. I doubt they pose any real threat, for they have no arrows, nor any means to engage with ours" Gy'dych hissed menacingly.

"You heard the captain" Nas'ryn hissed. "Still your tongues and mount your steeds!"

Shortly thereafter, the riders trot south a short distance to a small clearing where they form up into two files, four riders in each, Gy'dych at the rear. Perdicca had elected, against the advice of the captain, to take the far right of the second file. "Let's get moving!"

Nas'ryn clicked his mare to a gentle trot and moved forward from the centre right of the first row. Vor'dyl, directly to his left, waited a few seconds to move. On the far right of the first row, Ka'vyn clicked his mare to a trot, and followed the brute, a few paces to his rear.

The rearguard of the Royal Escort was commanded by Captain Ry'vach, an energetic twenty-four-year-old veteran of the Western Plains of Kazakh'yi. The captain was stationed on the left side of the staggered file, almost in the centre, his eyes scanning west across the field as it rose gently toward a broken scar of copse, a mile or so away. He had seen nothing to concern him until, without warning, a rider looms from the bare treeline, slightly ahead of his position, and trotted gently down the shallow incline of the verge. They were followed by a second, and then a third, rider. "Shit!" Ry'vach swore. "I don't like the look of this at all!" he hissed.

"Riders to the left!" a voice bellowed from the front of the column. The Guards of the rear column twist in their saddles to appraise the unexpected threat.

The first mysterious rider kicked his heels to a gallop. The party behind him, for there were perhaps seven or eight now, follow suit, racing across the frozen earth, angling to attack the Royal Carriage in staggered formation.

"Sound the horns! Sound the horns!" Ry'vach roared. "Left Wheel! Left Wheel! You insolent curs!

The Orch'tai cavalry wheel their mounts to face the unexpected threat from their left flank.

Nas'ryn was not a man given to excitability, especially in a fight! The incessant blasts of the horns did not faze him in the least. He was both an expert horseman and a seasoned and competent commander. The effective range of their recurved bows was just under half a mile, but it would pay dividends to be certain. The Royal Guards to the fore-and-rear of the Royal Carriage were busily shuffling themselves into staggered ranks, to face the threat from the west, whereas the men in the centre had dismounted and were, even now, unslinging their bows and notching their arrows. They would be the first to die, Nas'ryn decided. He leaned forward in the saddle to chide his mare to a canter, as his right hand plucks an arrow from the quiver at his right shoulder. "Halt!" he bellowed. "Right face!" He glanced quickly at Vor'dyl, who reined in beside him and nodded silently. Ka'vyn grimaces as he notches his arrow. They had now been joined by Du'naik, who eyed the preparations of the bowmen at the front of the Royal Carriage and spat on the ground. "Draw!" Nas'ryn bellowed. "Loose!"

The arrows flew true, and four of the six archers were downed, writhing briefly, before stilling forever. Arrows were immediately notched. "Draw!" Nas'ryn commanded. "Loose!"

An arrow flew past his head as his own struck a surviving Guardsman in the chest. To their right, the Princess Perdicca had, with breathless insouciance, downed two of the rearguard before she had even taken her place at the far right of the arc. "Draw!" Gy'dych bellowed, as he reined in beside the Princess. "Loose!"

A crescendo of horn-blasts was met with a withering hail of arrows. Death had come to Or'vych!

Captain Ry'vach hissed with pain and glowered malevolently at the arrow shaft which protruded through the outer flesh of his upper left leg. He had a small cut on the right side of his head, sustained when his horse had fallen to an arrow strike. Mercifully, he had been pitched forward to topple from his mount as it had slumped, avoiding the certainty of a broken leg had he remained in the saddle. Two of his men had been less fortunate and would likely never ride again. Three were dead. His survivors had now dismounted to engage their attackers, and yet, whoever these bastards were, they were clearly no strangers to a fight! They extended their line, increasing the distance between themselves, constantly manoeuvring, whilst effectively engaging with their bows. Whilst their effectiveness was now hindered, it would be sheer suicide for the survivors of his detachment to charge them. They must protect the Royal Carriage, at all costs! "Move forward and protect the Royal Carriage, you hear me!" Ry'vach bellowed.

Where in Hades name were the support units from the Royal Palace?

When the attack had commenced, Captain Uh'gui had cursed with petulant fury. He twisted in his saddle and roared at the lead rider, Hy'dryg, entreating him to make for the Summer Palace and inform the Commandant of this disturbing development. Hy'dryg was seasoned and dependable, yet the young Captain shivered briefly as he watched the man gallop north. *What if there were more of the bastards in the area?* Such a brazen attack by some nine riders, against a party of thirty elite Royal Guards, was an act of breath-taking lunacy, yet they had slaughtered all the men by the carriage and inflicted serious damage of Ry'vach's detachment. "Left Wheel, you bastards!" he roared at his men. "Keep your dressing! Advance at the trot. Ten yards, no more, arrows at the ready. I want those bastards dead!" Uh'gui seethed.

The men shuffle to face the west, keeping their formation, and adjusting their dressing. They wait for the command, to trot forwards into the frozen waste, grim-faced and determined, hell-bent on exacting revenge upon these infernal violators of the King's Household.

Yari turns her mare east and kicks her heels, urging it to a gallop. She leant forward in the saddle, right hand clutching the reins, her left clasping the recurved bow, an arrow clenched between her teeth. The girl did not glance behind, for she knew the others, all seasoned riders, would surely follow. The party raced along the track in single file, Laeschalla a short distance behind the lead. Yari felt a tingle of exhilaration, which dampened all fear, as she thundered along the track. Even as the blood pounded in her ears, she became aware that the horns had silenced. There were no screams, or peals of clashing swords, instead there was an ominous, and even eery, silence. Her eyes scan the horizon to the east, where the fields rose gently to meet the copse on the verge. As her mare raced towards a sharp bend in the track, Yari made her fateful decision. She would leave the track and make for a narrow break in the copse, almost at the centre of the verge, a mile or so away. Here the ground seemed shallow. She twisted in the saddle and pointed toward the break in the distance, before spurring to the right, away from the course of the track.

The girl did not even glance behind her, for the others must surely follow.

Perdicca scowled as an arrow flashed past, perilously close, fired by a survivor of the rear-guard who had raced forward to secure the carriage. "Insolent cur!" the woman hissed.

"We should be going, my Lady!" Gy'dych yelled, from a few feet away. "There must surely be reinforcements on the way from the Royal Palace?"

"Not yet, Captain Gy'dych, for we still have further damage to inflict upon these vainglorious fools!"

Gy'dych gaped at Perdicca in astonishment, for it was clear that she had lost all control in the heat of the melee. Far to their left, Nas'ryn, Vor'dyl, and Ka'vyn were busily engaging the Vanguard with devastating accuracy. At least four men were now down, with not a single loss of their own. It was almost as if the Gods themselves were smiling upon them! Suddenly, there was a scream to his left. Ar'duc topples from his saddle, blood venting from his mouth in torrents, an arrow protruding from his throat. As he clicked his mare to face northeast, an arrow flashed past, fired by one of the surviving Vanguard. Thus far, they had seized the initiative and inflicted a devastating reversal upon their historic enemies, yet everything could change for the worse in a heartbeat. They must disengage and make good their escape.

"We must go, my Lady! It is time!" Gy'dych hissed.

The deathly silence was shattered by a shrill of horns!

Yari raced up the verge and clicked her mare to a canter. The shrill of the horn-blasts startled her, but this must surely be reinforcements from the Palace. The girl followed the well-worn path through the small gallery of bare woodland and soon reached its edge, halting in the shadows. She could scarcely credit the spectacle unfolding in the field below. Yari notched an arrow and scowled. Laeschalla reined in beside her, her cheeks flushed pink from exertion. "I doubt you spared a moment's thought for the poor bears?" she noted acidly.

"Shit! I had completely forgotten about them! What do you make of this?"

"That is the Royal Train! I have no idea as to the identities of our mysterious assailants" the older girl smiled wryly.

Yo'dyll suddenly morphed beside them on foot, with Il'han and Ksen'ya in tow. "What's going on?"

"You can see for yourself?" Laeschalla quipped mockingly. "They appear to be having the best of it thus far, but they won't when the reinforcements arrive."

Yari pointed to the distant rider on the right wing, far to the south, who was hastily turning their mare west, readying their escape. "They are making good their escape. They will head back to the copse and use the broken ground to cover their escape. If we head back, we might be able to cut them off?"

"You aren't seriously thinking of fighting them?" Ksen'ya gaped in horror.

Laeschalla giggled at the younger girl. "Of course, she is! Yari is Sauromatae. If we make haste, we can engage them in extended line as they break cover?"

"It is a tempting proposition, to be sure? They surely won't be expecting us, will they?" Il'han grinned.

"Let us get going? We have no time to waste!" Laeschalla clipped.

The surviving renegades, the Princess Perdicca in the lead, Gy'dych close behind, race across the field to the safety of the copse. Gy'dych glanced to his rear. Sixty reinforcements had arrived from the Summer Palace to secure the carriage and the survivors of the Vanguard were in hot pursuit, a half mile or so behind. Nas'ryn twisted in his saddle, took steady aim, and fired at their pursuers, striking the lead rider in the chevron. The man toppled from his saddle as his comrades on either side gallop past. Ka'vyn and Vor'dyl follow suit, the latter missing his target by a mere whisker, whilst the former hit his man in the throat, in an edifying explosion of crimson! "Keep going!" Gy'dych bellowed. "We should yet outrun them!"

The riders thundered up the verge to vanish into the trees, as their pursuers warily slowed their pace!

The reinforcements from the Summer Palace were commanded by a seasoned officer named Bar'zakh, aged in his middling thirties, a veteran of the wars against the Argata in 'the lands between the seas'. He twists in his saddle and scowls in fury at the fleeing assailants, who even now inflicted further insults upon the survivors of the Vanguard. "I want those bastards hunted down and killed! All of them! Do you buggers' hear me?" he seethed.

"I hear well enough, Commandant Bar'zakh" a youthful, mocking voice chirps from close by.

The officer turned in his saddle and gaped at Queen Illir'ya, who is busily buckling a sword belt across her light green winter cloak. "Your Majesty! I humbly apologise for any offence I may have unwittingly given!"

"Do you intend to pursue?" the Queen clipped.

"We can at least give them chase, my Lady!" the Commander mused grimly.

"Shall we go?" the young Queen suggested helpfully. Before the Commander could respond, the woman turned and hollered to a young cavalryman some twenty yards away who was steadying a fretting mare. "Bring her to me, young man!"

"Captain Dro'khu! Your detachment will escort the carriage and wounded to the Royal Palace. Captain Vis'ghal, you are with me. Head straight for the far edge of the copse and secure the road, you understand?"

"Yes, my Lord" Vis'ghal replied.

Commandant Bar'zakh turned to the young Queen, now in the saddle, a recurved bow in her left hand and quiver of arrows at her right shoulder. "Shall we go, Your Royal Highness?"

"Lead on, my good fellow" Illir'ya grinned slyly.

"Right, you lazy bastards, follow me!" The Commandant kicked his heels and thundered west across the field, following the course of the fleeing assailants.

The tables had turned, and the hunters were now the hunted!

Gy'dych reins in and turns quickly in his saddle. The Princess Perdicca kept her gaze firmly west. Ha'jin and Dival'yn soon arrive and, shortly thereafter, are joined by the last of the four survivors, a grinning Nas'ryn at the rear. "A grave pity about Ar'duc?" Gy'dych lamented. "He was a fine soldier, as good as any I have ever commanded."

"Are we going to split into two groups of four, my Lord?" Nas'ryn turned and glanced quickly to his rear. The thunder of pursuing hoof-beats drums ever closer to the copse.

"I will take the Princess due south to Roi'skya, with Ka'vyn and your own good self. Ha'jin will command the second party, taking Dival'yn, Vor'dyl, and Du'naik dues west to Vaia'chi. That should split our pursuers into two groups, which should give them cause for concern."

"We rendezvous at *The King's Pledge* in Try'eva, is that it?" Ha'jin smiled wryly.

"As good a place as any, wouldn't you say?" Gy'dych mused wistfully. He twists in his saddle and grimaces at the thunder of the approaching riders. "Let's get going!"

Ha'jin clicks his mare west and kicks his heels. At the rear of his party, a grim-faced Du'naik watches as Ka'vyn disappears into the woodland screen to the south.

Yari afforded herself a brief smirk of triumph as she trotted west to take her position at the far right of the hastily formed defensive arc. To the far left, Yo'dyll gritted her teeth and steadied herself in the saddle. She turned to Ga'vek and hissed urgently. "They are coming! I can hear them!"

The warning was passed along the line. Yari notched an arrow, drew her bowstring taut, and sucked her teeth. An unsuspecting Ha'jin bursts from the treeline, ten yards to their front, and gaped in dumbstruck horror at the unexpected threat. Yet, before he could holler a warning, Yari roared her command.

"Right wing, hold your fire! Left wing, fire at will!"

It was Vai'ska, the petite blonde, barely a moon beyond her thirteenth birthday, who killed Ha'jin with an expertly aimed strike through the right cheek. His head snapped violently back, a font of blood exploding from his mouth, as a second arrow, fired by Ny'vysa, punches through his throat. Yo'dyll took Dival'yn clean from his steed with a strike to the ribs, and, before he even hit the earth, Ga'vek fired a well-aimed strike to his stomach.

"Right wing, fire at will!"

Laeschalla and Il'han took careful aim at the bewildered Vor'dyl, as the brute reached forlornly for an arrow from his quiver and dropped him instantly. At the edge of the woodland, Du'naik clicked his mount to a halt and tried in vain to turn east and race into the cover of the copse, when he was struck twice in the left flank by arrows fired in quick succession by Ksen'ya and Yari. Suddenly, two riders break cover from the treeline, sixty yards to the south, angling southeast towards the road from Ky'vych. "Shit!" Yari swore. "They are getting away! Let's get after them!"

The girl reached for an arrow and notched it expertly, just as a second pair of riders broke cover, following hard on the heels of the first. Yari steadied herself in the saddle, took careful aim at the second rider, and fired. Her shot narrowly missed its target, much to the eternal relief of a cursing Princess Perdicca!

Commandant Bar'zakh dipped low in his saddle and gritted his teeth, a reflex action to reduce his visibility, as he thundered up the verge towards the treeline, the young Queen close behind him. He clicked his mare to a canter as they followed the course of the well-worn path, soon reaching the clearing. "That way!" he gesticulated eagerly toward the winding path which first veered north, then west. He would leave it to Captain Dro'khu's own good sense to take the trackway heading south from the clearing. If he failed to do so, he would be summarily strung up from the nearest suitable branch by his balls!

The grim-faced Commander kicked his heels as the screen of woodland before him began to thin and his eyes scanned warily ahead for any sign of their quarry. To his eternal astonishment, as they cleared the treeline and raced down the west verge, there was none!

Not of the living, at least! Yet, this day's surprises were not yet done!

Yari gaped in astonishment as the lead riders of the Royal Guard, including a well-dressed person of considerable social status, who was clearly no soldier, burst from the treeline to race down the verge, some thirty yards ahead. "They are ours! They are ours! Nobody is to fire!" Laeschalla hollered. She trots forwards, turns in the saddle, and grins at Yari. "Is that who I think it is?"

"You know who it is?" Yari grinned sheepishly. She raised a hand in greeting.

Commandant Bar'zakh and his Royal Guard were now keenly aware of the group of teenagers, including the Princess Laeschalla, huddled a short distance away to the north. The scowling Commander had espied the four assailants fleeing south and roared at his main force to give chase. The lead party, comprising some ten riders, including Bar'zakh and Queen Illir'ya, slow their horses to trot and wheel north, as the party of triumphant, blushing teens trot down from the verge to greet them, the Princess Laeschalla in the lead. "Your Royal Highness!" the Commandant smiled warmly at the girl he knew well. "You have met Her Royal Majesty, Queen Illir'ya of the Ur'gai, I am sure?"

"Indeed, I have, Commander Bar'zakh!" the girl grinned. She turned and nodded at Yari. "May I have the pleasure of introducing Her Royal Majesty's Handmaiden, Yari, for it was she who planned the slaughter of these four assailants?"

"Are they yours as well?" the Commandant growled, pointing east. Laeschalla gasped at such unblushing rudeness. Yari flushed hotly looked quickly down at the ground.

Illir'ya stifled a giggle. She raises her right arm and points east. "I think he means our furry friends?" The teenagers twist in their saddles and gaze towards the woodland's edge.

A family of brown bears, rudely awoken from their precious slumber, had encountered an unexpected bounty that would see them through the current moon! The four cubs, barely a moon old, are a glorious sight to behold!

Four

The four fugitives gallop south, Gy'dych in the lead, following the winding course of the Roi'skya as it circuited the gentle uplands of the escarpment. They are now some eight-and-a-half miles south of Ky'vych and the copse. Gy'dych reins in and trots a short distance to the stream to allow his stallion to drink, gazing warily at the plains to the east of Stapy'nye. There is seemingly no sign of their pursuers. "It looks like we have lost them, my Lord?" Ka'vyn grinned.

"I would not be so certain, old friend?" Nas'ryn ventured curtly.

"Is there something troubling you? Perhaps you would care to share it?" Perdicca spoke evenly.

"What of the enclosed perimeter to the southwest of Stapy'nye, my Lady? I suspect it is nothing more than a granary. And yet, its size is considerable, is it not?"

"You think it might be a Royal Granary?" Perdicca quipped.

"If it is, my Lady, it might be best to presume that a detachment may be stationed nearby to protect it?" Nas'ryn ventured.

"I doubt the King, or his grain reserves, have anything to fear from the local peasantry?" Gy'dych said dismissively.

"What of the riders we saw on the escarpment northeast of Rody'ska earlier this morning? They were no peasants, surely?" Ka'vyn spoke gloomily.

"I suspect they have already returned to their garrison" Gy'dych clipped curtly. "There is nothing in our available intelligence to support any sizeable

84

garrisons in the immediate area. I maintain they were a scouting party sent from Mamy'eva to confirm the track was in good order for the carriage, what with the uncertainty of the weather this time of year?"

"Perhaps we should get moving, my Lord? I doubt we have lost our pursuers so easily" Nas'ryn spoke evenly.

Gy'dych glowers at the man, a gesture not lost on the Princess. "I make it just over an hour's ride to *The King's Pledge* in Try'eva. With any luck, we will have shaken our pursuers by then."

Gy'dych turned his horse southeast, kicks his heels, and spurs away.

Hy'dryg kicked his heels and spurred his mount ever faster along the icy track. He had been informed that a detachment of thirty riders from Zar'kye were camped on the plateau, a mere six miles from the crossroads at Ky'vych. He was heading due east, with the escarpment directly ahead, and could now discern wisps of smoke from a string of small campfires dotted along its southern ridge, affording a clear view of the valley below and the road south. As far as he knew, Captain Dro'khu and his men were heading south to Stapy'nye, where a small garrison was stationed at the Royal Granary. No matter how unseasoned in combat, these men would be vital in the hunt for the surviving fugitives. Once he had raised the alarm, he would ride east, to the garrison at Zar'kye. A survivor of the Rearguard, Din'van, was heading north to inform the Commandant at Loz'nye of the day's events. Hy'dryg grinned wryly, for he was positively giddy at the prospect of instructing the Commander of the detachment that one of his precious little darlings was to undertake the arduous journey southwest to impart the news of the attack on the Royal Train to the Commandant at Mai'ske, a journey of nearly sixty miles!

Hy'dryg soon reaches the junction with the south road to Mamy'eva, which veers to the right. He turned his stallion northeast, left the track, and kicked his heels to race across the frozen ground and up the gentle incline at the foot of the escarpment. A veteran of countless operations against the hated Argata in 'the lands between the seas', he could barely keep his composure as his sudden appearance caused mass panic among the idling soldiers, who race to their mounts, abandoning kettles of steaming mint tea and half-empty flagons of wodki. "Halt!" a petulant and imperious voice challenged from a nearby campfire. "Halt, I say, damn you!"

Hy'dryg twists in the saddle and glowers at a young officer, aged in his early twenties, who stands apart from the congregants, his sword drawn. "Who the fuck might you be?" Hy'dryg spat contemptuously.

"I beg your pardon?" the officer gaped in disbelief.

"You can beg all you want to, dickhead! It is time you did some proper soldiering!"

The officer blinked. "I am Captain Lyn'ska of His Majesty's Royal Army, you insolent swine! And who might you be?"

"My name is Hy'dryg. I have ridden from Ky'vych. There has been an attack on the Royal Train. As I have already stated, it is time for you, and this shower of prinked-up wannabes, to do some proper soldiering!"

"An attack?" young Lyn'ska was ashen.

"You heard me, Captain Lyn'ska. I need one of your men, your best man, to ride for Mai'ske and inform the Commandant. We have four fugitives heading for the Don'yi" Hy'dryg spoke evenly.

"Have you informed His Royal Majesty of this day's treason?" Lyn'ska quipped. Hy'dryg smiled inwardly. *This whelpling might just be up to the job, after all!*

"Good thinking, Captain Lyn'ska! Send another of your men to Mamy'eva. I am to ride to your Commandant at Zar'kye."

"What of the rest of us?" Lyn'ska raised an eyebrow challengingly.

"You will ride for Stapy'nye and rendezvous with Captain Dro'khu at the Royal Granary. He is heading there to pick up reinforcements. Your arrival will be expected" Hy'dryg smiled brightly.

"You think the fugitives are destined for Try'eva?"

"That would be the safest course, you would agree. It would be a suitable place to hide for the night and procure fresh horses and a change of clothes" Hy'dryg mused drily.

"Is there anything else?" Lyn'ska smiled tightly. He sheathed his sword. "Pass me one of those flagons! I could do with a fucking drink!"

Or'vych, March 493 BC

Queen Illir'ya, the Royal Princess Sychoria, and the Dowager Countess Arialla sat on exquisitely carved cushioned chairs in the palatial Sitting Room of the Morning Lodge sipping scalding goblets of freshly brewed mint tea. The Ur'gai Queen, barely a woman, appeared to be unfazed by the morning's horror, whereas the Royal Princess was pale and withdrawn. As for the Dowager Countess Arialla, she was dismissive of the affair, almost to the point of contempt. "I doubt you will find the fugitives alive. Any soul with the wits of a hen will be eager to silence them!"

"I had no idea things had deteriorated so badly in the Duchy. Perhaps the attack was directed against me, after all?" Illir'ya ventured smoothly.

"Do not flatter yourself unnecessarily, Your Royal Highness!" Arialla quipped rudely.

Illir'ya smiled tightly. Sychoria glanced quickly at the rug. "If I do so I apologise. There are those within my own lands who will see things differently, of course" Illir'ya mused.

Arialla snorted. "That half-wit must bear responsibility for his own actions! If you care for my opinion, no good could ever have come from fawning over that detestable harpy."

"Is there any news of my children?" Sychoria asked eagerly.

"I am sure they are safe and well, my Lady" Illir'ya smiled reassuringly. "No harm will come to them. You must banish such bleak thoughts from your mind."

"And where is my own reckless girl? Has she gone a-sallying to sully her repute further with another spate of slaughter?" Arialla noted acidly.

"The Princess Laeschalla acquitted herself with commendable resolve, Dowager Countess!" Illir'ya bristled. "We should be thankful we have only four fugitives, not twice that number, to contend with."

"Your own Handmaiden played a significant part in their adventures, did she not? I see you have not yet managed to tame the brute?" Arialla retorted tartly.

"Yari may be Sauromatae, Dowager Countess, yet she is no brute!" Illir'ya bridled. "I trust her with my life, and she repaid that trust this day with no thought for her own safety!"

"Nor anyone else's, I might add!" Arialla quipped tartly.

"Your daughter was never in any danger, my Lady, even from herself. You ought to be proud of the fine young woman she is fast becoming" Illir'ya soothed.

"She could have been killed! I have heard word of a family of bears now residing in the area!"

"Whom your Guard would have slaughtered as a matter of course, had they not been placed under your daughter's protection, my Lady" Illir'ya countered.

"She is a silly girl! Even as a child she was a slave to her own sweet nature, as now she is prisoner to her lust" the Dowager Countess noted acidly. Her two guests shared a bemused glance. "You take me for a simpleton? I know full well the identity of the peasant boy who roots my child!"

"And you shall do nothing detrimental to the matter, dear Aunt!" Sychoria quipped icily.

"Perhaps it runs in the family, you would agree? Our noble King is bewitched and besotted by a feral slattern from the wrong side of the mountains. He conducts the affairs of state with the piteous guile of a lustful teen."

"You think the attack on the Royal Train was prompted by the King's courtship of the Argata Queen, my Lady?" Illir'ya mused.

"If you consider yourself the target of this day's misadventure, Your Royal Highness, I fear you have lost your wits entirely" Arialla challenged. "I am rather more versed with the Kings designs than he would credit. So too are the Hellenics, I don't doubt?"

"Such talk is treacherous and distressing. I will not tolerate it in the presence of my children" Sychoria hissed.

"Even if it directly concerns them, my Lady" Arialla smiled sadly.

"I have no earthly conception of the matters to which you refer. My strongest advice, my Lady, is to desist with any interference in the grave matter of the succession" Sychoria bridled.

"This grave matter of the succession cost my own dear son his life" the Dowager Countess hissed. "And may nearly have cost you your own this day?"

"I have nothing more to say on the matter, my Lady. Now, if it may be too much to ask, I would like to take a bath" Sychoria drained her goblet and twirled away without another word.

"That was unduly harsh, my Lady" Illir'ya spoke evenly. "Sychoria and her family must surely bear no responsibility for the tragedy of your beloved son."

"My tragedy is something I shall bear for the rest of my days, your Grace. Nonetheless, there are those to whom Ach'ti's demise was a blessing in disguise, you agree?" the woman glowered at the young Queen.

"Everyone's death is a blessing to someone, dear Lady, even yours?" Illir'ya noted silkily. She drained her goblet and left the room.

The Dowager Countess watched her leave in silence. She reached for a flagon and poured a large measure of wodki, sipping tentatively. She smiled wryly. The parting shot of the young Queen had confirmed one thing, at least.

Your enemies have misjudged your ruthlessness for far too long, little rose!

The fugitives gallop across the plain, heading for a dense patch of woodland four miles to the south. This would provide good cover against their pursuers, who would be keenly aware of the prospect of an ambush. Whilst their pursuers would have the benefit of the high ground, the broken topography of the landscape to the immediate south was consistent with a shallow valley and a small stream, which stretches far to the west. Gy'dych surveyed the treeline with a professional eye, seeking the safest point of entry. He reined and turned in the saddle to face the Princess Perdicca. At the rear, Nas'ryn and Ka'vyn instinctively turn their mounts to face the rear. He pointed to a thin break in the treeline, where a narrow track threaded its course. "We would be strongly advised to keep to the beaten track, my Lady."

"I would agree. She glanced quickly behind her. There was no sign of their pursuers, but surely, they could not have given up the chase so easily.

"Shit!" Nas'ryn cursed feelingly.

"By the Gods!" Ka'vyn gaped in horror. Gy'dych and Perdicca twist in their saddles and blanch.

On the northeast horizon, some three miles away, a posse of sixty Royal Guards thunder across the frozen plain in hot pursuit. Further east, a stream of riders raced southwest to join them. A grim-faced Gy'dych turns to the Princess Perdicca. No words were required.

All prior exuberance had been misplaced. They would need a miracle to escape this!

Captain Lyn'ska kicks his heels and spurs his mare faster still. He grinned for sheer joy as the icy breeze whipped his face. *This was soldiering!* He could see the four fugitives, a little over three miles away, galloping for the safety of the copse. In addition to his twenty-eight men, there were at least sixty other hunters, all garbed in the uniform of His Majesty's Royal Guard.

These beleaguered fugitives would pay dearly for this insult to the Royal Household!

Quite regardless of their perilous predicament, the fugitives slow their pace to a canter as they approach the narrow track which led in to the copse. They soon reach a small clearing, where Gy'dych reined in. "I think it might be wise if we split into pairs?" he glanced quickly at the Princess Perdicca, who silently nodded her ascent. "Once we clear the valley, it should be clear plains for the next few miles, with little in the way of cover."

Ka'vyn glanced nervously to his rear. "They would surely not expect us to head due east, would they?"

"I suggest both parties find a suitable place to hide for the rest of the day and then move again in the late afternoon. We rendezvous at *The King's Pledge* in Try'eva at sunset. Hopefully, we will have shaken them by then."

"We need to get moving, my Lord?" Nas'ryn suggested urgently.

"And so, you shall, soldier!" Gy'dych clipped curtly. "You will head east with the Princess. You are to guard her life at all costs, do you understand?"

"I understand, my Lord" Nas'ryn replied.

"Get going, then! Ka'vyn and I will head west, threading through the forest, following the lower slope of the ridge" he and Ka'vyn watched as Nas'ryn, and the Princess turned their steeds east and disappeared into the trees. "What do you say, old friend? Shall we give these useless twats a gallop for their gold?" Gy'dych smiled wryly. Ka'vyn grinned.

They two warriors kick their heels to canter east, weaving through the trees, as the hoofbeats of their pursuers thundered ever closer. They soon reach a small stream and cross to the opposite bank, continuing eastwards, whilst paying little heed to the trail of their pursuers.

It was implicitly understood that neither man could afford to be taken alive!

It was a visibly shaken King Tagar who received a suitably diplomatic Queen Lezika shortly before midday. His Royal Majesty had recently left a hastily convened assembly of his Royal Counsel and was ensconced in his Private Chamber, together with his smouldering Kor'nai. The King looked pale and withdrawn, almost as if he might crumble under the weight of this recent strain. "This is a brazen outrage, Your Majesty. I could scarcely credit the news when it reached my ears. If there is anything I can do, anything at all, you may only ask? An attack on an ally is an affront to us all, is it not?" Lezika mused silkily.

"You refer to your two-hundred Royal Guards to the southwest of the city, Your Majesty? Are you offering assistance in the apprehension of the fugitives?" the Kor'nai quipped icily.

The Queen smiled sweetly. "My dear fellow, whatever your personal opinion of my people, you may rest assured we are in no way involved in this ghastly affair."

"We have no reason to suspect your involvement, Your Majesty" the King said quickly. "I have it on authority that four attackers were slain whilst attempting their escape. I have ordered their bodies to be brought to Mamy'eva with haste."

Queen Lezika smiled thinly. "You intend to publicly display their heads in the hope they will be recognised?"

"These vermin may be known to certain elements in the city, Your Majesty. We have our own ways of loosening tongues, just as you do?" the Kor'nai mused breezily.

"I am sure that you do, Honourable Kor'nai" the Queen smiled brightly. "Can we be certain that this attack was not directed at Queen Illir'ya? The declaration of a Protectorate over the cities of the Crimea is a source of festering resentment among the political and merchant classes?"

"We fear the attack may have been directed against the Royal Princess Sychoria" the Kor'nai replied evenly.

Queen Lezika was aghast. "What of her children? Are they safe?"

"The Royal Princesses travelled separately from their mother. They departed Mamy'eva several hours afterwards in a covered wagon with the minimum of fuss" the Kor'nai confided.

"They are safe and well, Lezika. Their carriage was secured, and they are now re-united with their mother and Queen Illir'ya in the Summer Palace" the King confirmed.

"It is the opinion of the Royal Counsel that this day's outrage was orchestrated by a shadowy clique of dissidents opposed to the marriage of the Royal Princess Mikhouri and your own darling son, the Crown Prince Disch'al" the Kor'nai smiled tightly. "This was treason! You may rest assured, dear Lady, that the perpetrators and their ilk will be hounded to justice!"

"I cannot countenance such egregious malice, directed at a mother and her sweet babes" Lezika gaped in bewilderment.

"This does not alter your own position, my Lady?" the King spoke softly.

"You may rest assured that this day's outrage will not weaken my resolve. I remain committed to the matrimony of my own sweet child to the young Princess. I am incandescent by the thought that such calculated wickedness could have been contrived to weaken my heart."

"The two girls are badly shaken, as I am sure you understand?" Tagar sighed sadly.

"The Royal Princess and her delightful husband are most welcome to visit Archaeopolis in the summer. We have much to discuss, do we not?"

"Indeed, we do, Your Majesty. You may rest assured that my own resolve will not waver" the King spoke fervently.

"My sons will be heartbroken when they hear news of this atrocity. They ask constantly ask of the good health and virtues of your darling granddaughters" Lezika sighed morosely.

The Kor'nai and the King exchanged knowing glances. "The grave matter of the succession will be resolved, Your Majesty, you have my word on it. By the end of the summer, I will announce my chosen heir and successor" the King confided.

"My husband and I are at one on this matter. We feel the Princess Alicharia will make a fine wife for our youngest son, the Crown Prince Sea'gir, if it pleases your Grace?" Lezika spoke softly.

"I am honoured, Your Royal Highness, truly honoured" the King smiled brightly.

"These marriages would join our two Royal Houses in perpetuity, my Lady. Our two great nations will be at peace, now and forever" said the Kor'nai.

"Once the Ur'gai and Nur'gat are tamed, my dear fellow. Only then shall we have lasting peace."

"We are ready to do our part, as you must do yours?" said the King.

"It is done, then? We shall speak no more of it" the Queen quipped curtly.

Gy'dych and Ka'vyn venture west along a narrow track, skirting the lower fringe of the escarpment. They listen intently as the incessant thunder of hoofbeats, which pound the frozen earth in a drumbeat of death, gradually fade into the distance. Both were seasoned campaigners and had been separated from their fellows on several occasions in the wilds of Armenia. Neither man feared death. After a time, as the height of the escarpment began to gradually fall, Gy'dych reins in and instinctively turns to face west, listening intently for any sounds of their pursuers. "You think we have lost them?" Ka'vyn whispered softly.

"I am not sure, old friend. Now is the dangerous time, for the treeline ahead is thinning. We have no idea what dangers lie ahead" Gy'dych smiled grimly.

"They will hound us to the ends of the earth, will they not?"

"That they will, old friend. Yet, for the now, you may smile. There is no-one following our trail. We should get moving!"

"Yes, my Lord!" Ka'vyn nodded obediently.

The pair continued west until they reached a small clearing, almost at the far edge of the copse. Here were remains of a small settlement, once the abode of a humble family, long since abandoned. Apart from a small hut at the far south of the clearing, the rest of the buildings had been severely pillaged. Gy'dych drew an arrow from his quiver, slipped from his saddle, and strolled towards the hut, arrow notched, and bowstring taut. Ka'vyn drew an arrow and notched it expertly. Gy'dych rapped softly on the door, and, when no answer came, he pulled it ajar. The hut was empty. He smiled tightly. It was as good a place as any to hideout for the rest of the day and he felt sure he could reach Try'eva in just over an hour, provided he did not encounter any hostile parties on route. *All that now remained was the inevitable!*

Gy'dych lowered his bow and removed the arrow. He turns and smiles at Ka'vyn, raising his hand to signal of their good fortune. Ka'vyn slipped his arrow back into his quiver. He slid down from the saddle and strolled across to Gy'dych. "Take a look inside, Ka'vyn. I think it should suit us fine?"

As Ka'vyn stepped past to appraise the suitability of the hut, Gy'dych dropped the arrow and moved his hand quickly to the sword at his left hip. He drew the blade, only a little at first, enough to ensure it was free, and then, with an insouciance that was truly chilling, the blade hisses from its scabbard to plunge deep in to Ka'vyn's lower back. Gy'dych reached around with his left hand to clamp the man's mouth, as the point was driven clean through the front of his belly in a sickening vent of blood. Ka'vyn's legs buckled. The blade was drawn free, and his body slumped to the earth. Gy'dych grimaced as he cleaned his blade on the dead man's cloak. This was no time for sentimentality.

Ka'vyn was a good man. He had died an ignoble, yet necessary death. Now, what to do with his body?

Nas'ryn and Perdicca ventured east for several miles until they reached the edge of the copse. Nas'ryn reined in and turned his stallion west, listening intently. He was certain they were not being followed. "I think we have lost them, my Lady" he whispered softly.

Perdicca eyed him coldly. "If we both wish to survive this day, it might be wiser if you stopped addressing me as 'my Lady'. You may call me Perdicca, Nas'ryn."

"As you please, Perdicca" the young soldier blushed faintly.

Perdicca was bemused by his evident shyness. "Do you know what would please me right now?"

"I think I can imagine, Perdicca?" Nas'ryn smiled slyly.

"Can you imagine fucking me, Nas'ryn? Can you imagine how moist I must be right now, sat on this horse, yearning to be fucked like a savage?"

"I think we ought to leave, Perdicca" Nas'ryn blushed hotly.

"You are no man's fool, nor are you a shrinking violet. My lust can wait, at least for now. It was extremely foolish of you to think you could escape me forever?" the girl smiled sultrily.

The pair broke cover to canter east along the plain for a few miles, where they reached an ancient trackway that headed southeast. They had not encountered a single soul, which was surprising, given that scouting parties must surely have been sent out from the Royal City, some twenty miles due southwest. The two riders slow their pace to a gentle trot and tack south along the trackway, which skirted a small patch of bare woodland, offering little prospect of cover. This was the dangerous time, for the landscape was an unending expanse of frozen earth, devoid of cover, apart from a thin screen of bare woodland flanking the north bank of a large stream, two miles due south. The pair kick their heels and gallop southwest across the plain, heading for the north bank of the river and the settlement of Ry'gykh. It would be as good a place as any to rest, if only for a few hours. Perdicca led the way, with Nas'ryn a yard behind. Within an hour, they had reached the gates of Ry'gykh and ambled slowly along the central street towards the welcoming embrace of *The Old Barleymill*, the only hostelry in the settlement. They were assured by a friendly farmer on the outskirts of the village, who appeared unperturbed by the sight of two armed travellers, that they could obtain food, drink, and a room. As they reached the stable-yard, Perdicca smiled brightly.

A hot bath and a good fuck would be just what the Surgeon ordered!

Captain Dro'khu reins in and swore furiously. The fugitives were nowhere in sight. His sixty riders, fortified by Lyn'ska's twenty-eight cavalrymen, had reached the east bank of a large stream, six miles east of Try'eva. He glanced to his rear, blinking in the glare of the midday sun, and scanned the landscape. If the fugitives had gone to ground, it would be nigh on impossible to locate them, even at this time of year. Surely, they would not be stupid enough to light a fire, for the smoke would signal their location many miles away. Lyn'ska trotted forward and reined in beside him. "Have we lost them, my Lord?"

"Do I look like a fucking Lord to you, matey?" Dro'khu growled.

"If they have gone to ground, they could be anywhere, could they not?" Lyn'ska ventured.

"That's rather stating the bloody obvious, is it not?" the older man clipped curtly. "What would you do, if you were in their shoes, Captain Lyn'ska?"

"I would look for a good place to hide, at least for the rest of the day" Lyn'ska smiled thinly. "They would be taking an awful risk if they remain as a party of four?" Dro'khu ventured.

"We would now be seeking two parties of two riders. Even in this shithole, we will be searching for the proverbial needle in a haystack!" Dro'khu sighed despondently.

"They will surely make for Kamy'ch? If that is true, it would be too risky to rendezvous there. By now, everyone will be looking for them?"

"If they have gone to ground, they will likely rendezvous at Try'eva. It is sufficiently remote and lies only a few hours ride to the east."

"I will order my men to establish piquet's on all of the approaching roads, north and south. We can rotate our rosters, three hours on, two hours off?" Lyn'ska spoke evenly.

"We will take the first shift. Take your men to Try'eva and get yourself warm. This promises to be a long day indeed" Dro'khu mused grimly.

Gy'dych adds fuel to a small fire and dropped mint leaves into his kettle, stirring them vigorously. He glanced at the sky. It was now mid-afternoon, and the sun was far to the west of its zenith, promising several more hours of light before sunset. He felt certain his pursuers were now far away and could only hope that Nas'ryn and the Princess had fared equally well on their travels. Gy'dych stands and pads across to his steed to retrieve a flagon of wodki. He removed the wooden stopper and took several grateful slugs. He replaced the stopper and slid the flagon back into his knapsack. The tea was bubbling nicely, and the smoke from the small fire would not reveal his location. Within a few hours, he would be ready to leave for Try'eva.

Two riders trotted amiably toward the checkpoint at the crossroads, a mile or so north of the hamlet of Ka'poi, nestled on the banks of the small river from which it derived its name. Perdicca raised a hand in greeting to the Guards and reined in, a few yards from the group. "Let me do the talking, you understand?" she hissed.

"I understand" Nas'ryn replied simply.

"It is a strange hour for a lovers jaunt, is it not?" clipped Zai'gyhn, a youthful cavalry officer. He had approached the two travellers in the company of two other guards.

"We are brother and sister, my Lord" the girl quipped shyly. "We have come from Pai'shyn on an urgent errand for our father."

"Where are you going at such an hour?" Zai'ghyn pressed.

"We are going to visit our uncle in Kamy'ch. We are on an urgent errand for our dear father, as I have said" the girl replied softly.

"Have you heard the news from Ky'vych?" the soldier challenged.

The girl looked bewildered. She turned and glanced quickly at her brother. The gesture was not lost on the officer, whose right hand moved swiftly to the sword at his left hip. The girl blanched with terror. "We don't know anything, I swear it!"

"I don't believe you!" Zai'ghyn clipped icily. There is a hiss of metal as the two men beside him drew their swords.

"No! I beg of you!" Nas'ryn pleaded.

"We know nothing! I swear it by all the Gods!" Perdicca sobbed.

"We are seeking four fugitives who attacked the Royal Train to the south of the Royal Palace of Or'vych early this morning" Zai'ghyn spoke menacingly. "These vermin are both desperate and dangerous, yet I suspect that you already know this, don't you?"

"They swore they would kill us if we told anyone where they were. They have taken hostages at a small farmstead just outside Ry'ghyk."

"You have seen them? When was this?" Zai'ghyn probed.

"It was a few hours ago, my Lord. We have known the family for many years and stopped to pass on our father's blessing. We had no idea they were there" Perdicca sobbed bitterly.

"There were four of them? What can you tell us of them?"

"Their leader is called Gy'dych. They were speaking Armenian" the girl confessed. "This scum threatened the entire family with death. They forced us to head to Ry'ghyk and get supplies for them. They swore they would kill us if we ever breathed a word."

"They were still there when you left? That must be little under an hour ago?" Zai'ghyn gaped at the girl.

"Gy'dych had left for Try'eva when we returned. We overheard them talking about it" Perdicca sighed morosely.

The young officer and the two guards exchanged excited glances. Their delight was not lost on either Perdicca or Nas'ryn. "You are quite sure of this?"

"Gy'dych had ridden ahead to *The King's Pledge* in Try'eva. I swear it by all the Gods!" the girl beseeched.

"If you are lying, we know where to find you?" Zai'ghyn glanced contemptuously at Nas'ryn. "Not even your brother will save you from the King's wrath. Now, begone with you!"

"Of course, my Lord, for we are loyal subjects of our noble King Tagar" the girl mumbled in a chastened tone. She appeared to be visibly shaken by the ordeal, almost on the verge of tears.

The two riders trot through the checkpoint and turn left, heading south toward the hamlet of Ka'poi. Perdicca turns in the saddle and espied two riders galloping northwest across the frozen plain towards the southern crossing at Try'eva. She turns back to Nas'ryn and raised an eyebrow mockingly. "What did you make of my performance, my darling?"

"You are an accomplished actress, Perdicca. I have yet to witness finer" Nas'ryn smiled slyly.

"And you have a wayward tongue, handsome. You can use it on me anytime you choose!"

Gy'dych turned right at the main square, heading toward the welcoming embrace of *The King's Pledge*. He duly arrived at the stable-yard and glanced warily around for any sign of Nas'ryn or Perdicca's steeds. There was none. The stable yard was deserted. He dismounted and lashed his stallion next to the watering trough, then turned towards the rear entrance. To his astonishment, a group of six Royal Guards stood menacingly in the near corner of the yard, just inside the gates. All were armed with military-grade recurved bows, arrows notched and ready. An officer stands framed in the rear doorway of the tavern. "You have nowhere to run, you heathen Armenian shit-bucket!" Dro'khu snarled.

"I think you have me confused with someone else, friend?" Gy'dych smiled thinly.

"You are Gy'dych, are you not?" Dro'khu smiled tightly. "Your comrades will see you in hell!"

Gy'dych reached for his sword, yet, before he could draw his blade, a salvo of arrows thump into hist chest. More were fired into his prone form with murderous intent. Dro'khu smiled grimly. "Get this slag on to the wagon and get him on the road to Mamy'eva!"

Nas'ryn smiled brightly at the agent and handed over two silver pieces. "That is sufficient, my good man? I require an early morning charter south for two passengers and their steeds?"

"Then you shall have it, my Lord" the agent grinned. "I suspect that you and the Lady would require accommodation for the night?"

"Do you have any suggestions?" Nas'ryn smiled slyly.

"You might try *The Hearth and Kettle*. It is the best hostelry in Kamy'ch. They are famed for their excellent food and comfortable beds!"

"Thank you, my good man!"

Nas'ryn strolled back to Perdicca, who waited patiently at the side of the wharf. He smiled ruefully. "We will have to spend the night in Kamy'ch, my Lady?"

Perdicca raised an eyebrow mockingly "Have you tired of me already, my sweet?"

"I intend to tame the savage in you this night, my Lady!"

"You talk too much, my handsome. You should find another use for that wagging tongue" the girl's eyes flashed sultrily.

Mamy'eva, April 493 BC

The apartment was on the second floor of an old residential block in the moderately affluent northern suburbs, favoured by the wealthy merchant class, a great many of foreign extraction. As a precaution, the visitor alighted his carriage a few streets away to slip into the night without remark, for his driver and footman knew exactly where to be stationed for his return. A frigid wind chilled the air, perhaps a herald of further snow, unusual for the time of year. The lone figure was wrapped in a heavy wool cloak, its hood drawn close, and strolled unchallenged through the warren of backstreets, glancing occasionally to his rear to check for pursuers. In the current political climate, treachery was everywhere, and his master had been most insistent in this most delicate of matters. Not even His Majesty's Chief Counsellor must know of this meeting, much less of what might pass between confidants. The man stepped into the shadows at the side gate and paused, glancing quickly around for any signs of life. Once he was sure he was alone, he continued along the narrow alley to slip into the shadows of a flight of steps to an underground cellar, where he rapped a brief tattoo on its heavy oak door. The door opened immediately, to usher the visitor inside, and was then closed and bolted. "I am Arzal, my Lord. My master is expecting you. Please, follow me!"

The visitor was led along the central aisle of a cellar, almost to its middle, where they turn left and make their way along a narrow aisle between trestles of wine barrels on the right, and poppy oil on the left, until they eventually reach a flight of steps that leads upstairs to the residence on the second floor. When they reach the landing, Arzal fishes out a key, and, to the visitor's surprise, unlocked the door on the right side, which could never have led to the main residence. "My master awaits you, my Lord. Please, go inside." The visitor nodded silently. He opened the door, stepped inside, and closed it firmly behind him.

The visitor found himself inside a small closet, no more than two feet wide and a foot-and-a-half deep, lit by tallow candles. The brick walls had been plastered and panelled with oak. On the far right, clearly illuminated by a candlestick on the opposite side of the wall, was a secret doorway. The visitor stepped to the side and pushed the door open. He stepped into the room next door. "I trust you were not followed, Honourable Counsellor? It would not enhance either of our reputations if tongues were to wag, you agree?" Faizil smiles wryly at his visitor.

"I have been careful, my friend, as always. Not even the King knows of your existence, much less where your true allegiance lies" the Honourable Counsellor Mes'khu spoke softly.

"I would be surprised if he did, for I am a humble merchant? Have some wine, old friend! It is Gaullish and is far superior to anything the Hellenics produce."

The Honourable Counsellor accepted a goblet and sipped it appreciatively, for it was every bit as fine as promised. "We must act with haste. His Majesty is determined to resolve the thorny issue of the succession, once and for all."

"My mistress desired a husband for her beloved daughter. Now he is dead. There is no other heir to the Orch'tai crown who would willingly take the hand of the Princess Cordicca" Faizil said silkily.

"Alas, there is not" Mes'khu shrugged apologetically. "The King remains committed to the ideal of a historic union of our noble houses. We may yet contrive a solution that resolves the matter of the succession and serves our noble purpose in equal measure."

"You presumably speak of the young Crown Princes? How could their marriages to two minor Princesses influence the succession? The claim in right of the Princess Sychoria is a distant third to her elder sisters" Faizal mused wryly.

"I had been led to believe that Queen Lezika had warmed to the marriage of the Crown Prince Disch'al and the Princess Mikhouri? Am I mistaken?" Mes'khu gazed shrewdly at the man sat opposite.

"A marriage of Prince Disch'al and Princess Mikhouri is no solution to the issue of the Orch'tai succession. Mikhouri will be the consort of the heir to the Argata Crown, not the Orch'tai."

"Such a union would strengthen the claim of the Princess Sychoria. Few in Mamy'eva, or elsewhere in the Duchy, welcome the coronation of the Princess Naemoria" Mes'khu smiled ruefully. "The Princess Miskal'ya is much regaled for her devotion to the poor, yet does not have her younger sister's natural gifts for statecraft, you would agree?"

"Do you honestly believe the Royal Army would warm to the idea of a line of succession which places the Princess Alicharia and her Argata consort in direct line to the Throne?"

"The Royal Army will have more than enough to preoccupy them in the forthcoming years. We cannot discount the possibility of war with the Nur'gat?" Mes'khu ventured.

"The Princess Sychoria is in her prime. She could rule for decades before the Crown passes to her whelpling?" Faizal smiled tightly. "There is the potential of a future son and heir to consider, one with far greater natural rights than his elder sister?"

"There is much in the future that is unknown, old friend. And yet, there is little in the future that is impossible, even implausible, as recent tragic events have shown?" Mes'khu sipped his wine.

Faizal smiled thinly and reclined in his chair. "Do you have any evidence at all to implicate the Ur'gai, or the Hellenics, in the death of Prince Ach'ti? There are rumours, of course, but there are always rumours?"

"That would be a matter for the King and his Counsel, surely? We have the grave matter of this recent outrage against the Royal Household to contend with."

"It is my understanding that three of the fugitives remain at large. You rightly fear the prospect of a further outrage?" Faizal spoke evenly.

"Your spies have been thorough, haven't they? We shall deal with those responsible in due course. You have my assurances on that" the Honourable Counsellor spoke with a chilling certainty. "The furtherance of the marriages of the Crown Princes to the Royal Princesses must be the focus of our efforts from this day forth. That is the surest means to ensure longevity of the current peace, is it not?"

"Their mother is receptive to the unions?" Faizal asked.

"The Argata Princes are fine children and a credit to their parents. I see no reason why the Royal Princess and Crown Prince will oppose the betrothals if the incentives are agreeable" Mes'khu stroked his chin and sipped his wine.

"The Orch'tai Crown, perhaps?" Faizal smiled wryly. "What makes you think Queen Lezika, as wise as she is virtuous, would welcome her children being used so bluntly in the resolution of a political dilemma in a foreign state? That would be especially true in the case of a neighbour with whom we have been recently engaged in hostilities?"

"We are now allies, old friend? The Argata would lose nothing, and gain everything, by the success of this initiative?"

"Not if the Princess Sychoria were to sire a legitimate heir, old friend?"

"The Orch'tai Royal House is plagued by tragedy, is it not? I see no reason why such misfortune might not continue for many moons to come" Mes'khu smiled tightly.

"The King's health is a constant concern to you, is it not?" Faizal smiled thinly.

"That is why time is of the essence in such a grave matter of state as this! I need an answer within the moon, and no more than that, for there is considerable work to be done!" Mes'khu drains his wine and declines the courteous offer of a refill.

"You have hopes to be anointed Kor'nai before the winter Solstice, old friend?"

"As I have said, tragedy stalks this Royal House! I will be Kor'nai, I assure you. As for the grave matter of the King's health, who can truly predict the future?" Mes'khu said airily.

"We have an understanding, old friend. I am certain I can impress upon my mistress the virtue and urgency of your proposal" Faizal spoke softly. "Once you have cemented your power in the Royal Court, you can guarantee that things will proceed smoothly?"

"I can do so, old friend. The Princess Sychoria may be Queen within the year, for the King's health is precarious. Once she is, she will be guided by her Chief Counsel, and by none other!"

"As will her daughter, I presume?"

"It is the way of things, is it not? And you and I shall speak no more of it, not until our fruit is ripe, of course."

Or'vych, April 493 BC

The Dowager Countess Arialla was greatly surprised when a General of His Majesty's Royal Guard was ushered into the Sitting Room one afternoon toward the twilight of the thaw. "What in Hades name are you doing here, General Nal'gi? Has that insufferable fool demoted you to a mere errand boy?"

"I serve His Majesty, my Lady, as I always shall. Once upon a time, I served your husband with equal devotion, if you care to remember?" said General Nal'gi.

"You used to call me Arialla back then, not my Lady, if my memory serves" the woman smiled sweetly at the man she had not seen for the better part of a decade.

"Indeed, I did, Arialla. I am deeply sorry for your loss and my infidelity" the General smiled sadly. "I would have come here sooner, but I have been away in the north liaising with the Lords about the arrangements for the harvest.

"At least you came, which is more than I can say for certain others I could mention. For that, I am in your debt. Please, sit down and take a draught of wodki." It was an entreaty spoken with the authority of one born to command.

"How is the little Princess?" Nal'gi asked earnestly.

"Laeschalla has not been a little Princess for quite some time" Arialla clipped. The General saw a flicker of sadness twinkle in her brown eyes. "She is quite beside herself, the poor lamb. She and Ach'ti were devoted to each other. You knew that, of course?"

"I did, Arialla, as did your husband. He often spoke of them when we were away at the front. He was justifiably proud of them both."

"Has the King anointed a suitable successor to the Crown?" Arialla asked bluntly.

"I am a humble soldier, my Lady, and have no knowledge of the decisions of Counsel?"

"What do you make of them? You may speak candidly, old friend" Arialla's eyes twinkle with mischief.

"It is not my place, my Lady, as well you know. I have the highest regard for the Kor'nai, of course, and Counsellor Har'juk is wise and just, despite his youth" the General sipped his wodki.

"What do you make of the Honourable Counsellor Mes'khu?" Arialla raised an eyebrow.

"He is an extremely talented man, my Lady. You know far more about his virtues and vices than I? Nal'gi smiled tightly.

"A Kor'nai in the making, is he not?" Arialla pressed.

"So, it is rumoured, my Lady. I know he has the ear of the King, within and without, the Royal Counsel."

"How are my darling nieces bearing the strain of this recent tragedy?" Arialla smiled grimly.

"The Princess Sychoria is plagued by melancholy since the death of Ach'ti and that unspeakable outrage in Ky'vych" said the General.

"Sychoria is a sweet child, Nal'gi, she always was. I suspect she is not in the least impressed with the insidious scheming of certain less than honourable fellows of the Royal Counsel?" Arialla smiled mischievously.

General Nal'gi was startled. "I am not certain I follow you, my Lady?"

"Surely, old friend, you have heard word of the impeding betrothal of her two little doves to the Argata Royal Princes?" Arialla smiled wryly.

"I have heard whisper of it, my Lady. The consensus is that the Princess Mikhouri would make a fine consort for the future Argata King?" Nal'gi spoke softly.

"What of the whelpling? The incorrigible Alicharia! Do you think she will make a fine bride for an Argata Prince?"

"Alicharia is adored by the soldiers in the Palace. She is blessed with mother's mind and cursed with her grandfather's tempestuous streak!" the General grinned.

"Perhaps she has the makings future Queen?" Arialla sips her wodki and let the statement hang in the air.

The General eyed the woman steadily. She was nobody's fool, and it was clear that the Dowager Princess had learned something he himself was not aware of. "Has the King confided with you in this grave matter of State?"

"No, he has not! Nor, for that matter, would he ever deign to do so. It may strike you as unkind, but I doubt the King is in command of either his senses, or his Counsel, much less the pressing matter of the succession" Arialla smiled tightly.

"Are you alluding to a dangerous vacuum within the Royal Counsel? Where individual ambition, not to mention personal vanity, might take precedence above the security and prosperity of the realm?" Nal'gi eyed the Dowager Princess sternly.

"I have said no such thing, young man! You would do well to take care in what you may divulge, unwittingly or otherwise!" Arialla clipped.

"My Lady, you malign me? I would never betray a confidence. You know that, surely?" Nal'gi beseeched.

"Would it be true in a matter as grave as the security and prosperity of the realm, with the entire future of the Duchy imperilled? I never thought you a fool, General Nal'gi? Perhaps I have been mistaken all these years?"

The General smiled tightly. He was a professional soldier, never a politician. "Are you aware of something I am not, my Lady?"

"All I shall say is this, General Nal'gi. The Honourable Counsellor Mes'khu is vain, ambitious, and decidedly unconventional, to put it mildly. Moreover, he has been a rather busy little bee!"

Mamy'eva, May 493 BC

General Nal'gi arrived at the villa shortly after nightfall, having ridden hard from the Royal Palace at sunset. He dismounted his steed, opened the gate, closed it firmly behind, and leapt agilely back into the saddle. Horses were in his blood, for he was a cavalryman, and the gentle trot up the path to the villa was as much a courtesy to his host as it was an insult to his stallion. As he neared the main residence and outbuildings, Nal'gi was met by the formidable figure of Ny'azmi, the retired General's loyal retainer and battle-scarred veteran of innumerable campaigns, most recently against the Argata in 'the lands between the seas'. Despite his rank, General Nal'gi was wary, for Ny'azmi was as dutiful as he was fearless, regaled as having slain more men in hand-to-hand combat than any soldier in the annals of the Royal Army! "It is good to see you again, General. My master has been expecting you" Ny'azmi smiled grimly.

"It is good to see you again, old friend. You weather the sands of time with the same contempt you showed those bastard Argata bowmen!"

"They were always lethal with a bow, to be sure, my Lord, but useless with a sword at close quarters. That is why they lost!" the grizzled old soldier spat on the ground with contempt.

"Indeed, it is, old friend. And how is the old bugger?" Nal'gi smiled wryly.

"A soldier without war is like a courser without a hare, is he not?" Ny'azmi mused.

"Or a loose woman denied a train of disreputable suitors!" Nal'gi grinned.

"I can only hope your visit improves his mood, my Lord. He is even more irascible than ever."

Nal'gi felt a prickle of foreboding. General Az'nai was likely better briefed that anyone in the Duchy! "The tidings I have brought may be as favourable as a winter storm."

General Nal'gi found the scarred and weather-beaten General Az'nai sat alone in his study, frowning over a communique scribbled on a scrap of parchment. On the desk to his right sat a goblet of his favourite plum wodki. "It is good to see you again, General. It has been some time, has it not?" Az'nai did not glance up from his parchment.

"I have been engaged on urgent business for the Crown, my Lord. It has taken me far and wide across the Duchy" Nal'gi replied.

"This new army is a source of considerable scribble, young Nal'gi. I receive an almost constant flow of correspondence, most of it sour!"

"It is not popular with the Counts. They are resentful of the levies, as they always have been."

"The recent years have been good to them. They rightly fear a significant shortfall in the harvest in this, and many more years to come. Tell me, young Nal'gi, do you think the King is misguided in this venture?" the older General eyed the younger man intently.

"If recent news from the east is even half true, then we have much to fear. These pesky siblings are a cause considerable consternation among our southern allies. They seek a stern remedy" Nal'gi mused bleakly. He remained standing.

"Sit yourself down, man! This is not a Commandant's Office. You too, Ny'azmi, for I value your opinion. Help yourselves to a drink, for you know where everything is?" Az'nai rapped.

The three men were soon sat around the General's desk, their goblets filled with plum wodki. "I see you are keeping busy, General Az'nai? You know there was a wager as to whether or not you would be spending more time in the garden?" Nal'gi smiled wryly.

"How is the Dowager Countess Arialla holding up to the recent tragedy? The unforeseen death of the Prince Ach'ti is a devastating loss to us all" Az'nai sipped his drink.

"As well as can be expected, Sir. Nevertheless, when I met with her, the Dowager Countess left me with the distinct impression that she does not believe it was an accident."

"Do you give any credence to the rumours that an assassin, engaged by the Ur'gai or their allies, may have targeted the young Prince for death?" Az'nai smiled tightly.

"Our sources confirm that the Ur'gai have strengthened their existing intelligence networks in Chersonesus and Nymphaion these past summers, my Lord. It is rumoured that Queen Illir'ya has appointed a new retainer, though I would give little credence to it" Nal'gi confessed.

"A whelpling assassin? Perish the thought!" Ny'azmi noted sourly.

"Such a spectre would not be beyond the realms of possibility? There have been dark whispers for centuries of a shadowy group of female subversives who effectively regulate order in their society. If my memory still serves, they were implicated in that dark business in Olbia several years ago?" General Az'nai noted in a bemused tone.

"This would be these so-called '*Sisters of the Rose*'? Can we be sure they even exist?" Nal'gi was equally bemused by the legends.

"It seems likely, does it not? The Ur'gai have always had strange tastes where their daughters are concerned." Az'nai noted with a grin.

"And so, it is entirely possible that a female, even an older child, might be engaged in sanctioned killings at the behest of the Queen and her Hellenic allies?" Nal'gi proposed.

"You suspect that this girl, if she exists, despatched Ach'ti on route to Archaeopolis?" Az'nai smiled thinly. "Given the terms of the *Accord Scythiac*, it is provocation to war! For myself, I think it most unlikely the Ur'gai would engage in such an egregious outrage. I would not be surprised in the least if the Armenians were somehow involved?"

"They are sworn enemies of the Argata, my Lord, and with good reason" Nal'gi conceded. "And yet, they assisted us in the recent war by harrying overland convoys on route to Bu'khu, did they not?"

"And we repaid their amity by turning a blind eye to a slaughter of innocents during the recent Argata campaigns" the General mused wryly.

"You think that the Armenians may have retaliated by targeting Prince Ach'ti?" Nal'gi ventured.

"What is your opinion, old friend?" General Az'nai turned to Ny'azmi.

"The Armenians are a ruthless people, but I cannot envision any gain from killing the heir to the Crown, beyond simple revenge" Ny'azmi sighed.

"People have always killed to avenge themselves, in the name of honour, family, even justice! An eye for an eye, a tongue for a tongue, and a soul for a soul" mused Nal'gi.

"I still cannot envision any gain from such an overtly hostile act" Ny'azmi continued. "Unless it was motivated by the impending betrothal of Prince Ach'ti to the Princess Cordicca, for she is the younger sister of the whore-bitch Perdicca, the most hated woman in Armenia?"

"It is an interesting hypothesis, old friend, and not without merit. If there was foul play in the death of the prince, and I remain unconvinced this was anything other than a tragic accident at sea, it must have come from outside the region" Az'nai said emphatically.

"There is rumour that the Princess Cordicca may have left Archaeopolis before the death of the prince. She has not been seen in public since the Solstice. It may be entirely unconnected, but it is more than a little strange, don't you think?" Nal'gi mused. He sipped his drink.

"I doubt that there is anything sinister in the reclusiveness of the young Princess, nor in any sudden departure from Archaeopolis" Az'nai drained his goblet and replenished it. "What is surely of greater concern, are the rumours concerning the impending betrothal of the King's granddaughters to the Argata Royal Princes?"

"The Princesses are not in the line of succession? The Princess Sychoria is third in line, is she not?" Ny'azmi quipped.

"In case you hadn't noticed, there are few contenders remaining, now the presumptive male heir has vanished without trace!" General Az'nai replied brutally.

"A King and his indomitable den of vixens?" Nal'gi noted cynically. "There are concerns for the King's health, that much is true, for he cannot survive forever?"

"None of us can, old friend" Az'nai sipped his drink. "What is now of the utmost concern is this hitherto inconceivable pivot towards a formal entente with the Argata. I am not alone in expressing my reservation, even my distaste, for there are a great many whom are aghast at the prospect!"

"The army is opposed to the *Accord*. Is that what you are saying?" Nal'gi spoke softly.

"I appreciate the political benefits to marrying the eldest girl to the Argata heir, yet I cannot see any grace in wedding the whelpling to the younger boy, not unless she is unspeakably ugly!" Az'nai mused glibly.

"The Princess Alicharia is reputed to be a pretty girl, is she not?" noted Ny'azmi.

"She is an extremely pretty girl, with her mother's mind and grandfather's fire. When I spoke with the Dowager Countess, she hinted that there may be more to this than meets the eye. She was concerned the King may not be driving the carriage, so to speak" the younger General confessed.

"I would presume that the King would be guided in this matter by his Kor'nai?" Az'nai frowned. He drained his goblet and reached for the flagon.

"The Dowager Countess is alarmed by the rising influence of Counsellor Mes'khu" Nal'gi confided.

"As well she should! I have it on some authority that it was Counsellor Mes'khu, and not the Kor'nai, who took the lion's share of the credit in the negotiations which led to the *Accord*. His views on a deeper alliance with the Argata are well known" Az'nai spoke acidly.

"A union between the two Royal Houses, cemented by multiple bonds of marriage, would be unshakable! Even more so if the parties ascend to their respective thrones" Ny'azmi mused.

"You surely cannot be serious?" Nal'gi was incredulous. "In the event the marriages succeed, the King would anoint his youngest daughter, the Princess Sychoria, as his chosen heir?"

"I think we may be closing fast upon the Honourable Counsellors train of logic?" Az'nai smiled tightly.

"The army would be rightly outraged by the prospect of an Argata Prince as consort to their lawful Queen? Especially one sired by the womb of that treacherous whore! She murdered her own brother, the rightful King, to seize the Crown for herself!" Ny'azmi seemed genuinely outraged by the Argata Queen's shameful betrayal.

"Her brother was a born fool! His recklessness imperilled the entire Kingdom. Had the Princess Lezika not contrived his end, others would have surely done so. She had the lives of her young children to consider" General Az'nai ventured soothingly.

"As does the Princess Sychoria, my Lord? In a matter as grave as the succession, treachery is everywhere, especially within the confines of the Royal Palace" Ny'azmi noted gloomily.

General Nal'gi was astounded. "You are not seriously accusing Princess Sychoria of contriving the murder of Prince Ach'ti to secure her own succession?"

Az'nai waved a hand to silence the bewildered Ny'azmi. "No, he does not! We can dismiss that theory as entirely baseless" Az'nai smiled at the horrified officer. "Nevertheless, my old warrior-brother may have resolved the riddle of the Honourable Counsellor's machinations?"

"The Princess Sychoria would become Queen upon the King's death, with the Crown passing to her youngest child, the bride of the Argata whelpling!" Nal'gi nodded respectfully at Ny'azmi, who smiled tightly back at him.

"Who would be her consort, and her de-facto successor, in the event of her untimely demise" the General mused, his voice rich with cynicism.

"The army would never tolerate such a grave insult!" Ny'azmi spoke feelingly.

"And risk a prolonged and bloody war with our partners in peace? The Nur'gat and Ur'gai may be inclined to support the Argata?" General Az'nai smiled ruefully. "I think it would be wise to keep a close eye on the Honourable Counsellor Mes'khu, you would agree?"

"I am confident that such a thing could be arranged, my Lord?" Nal'gi replied emphatically.

"As could more robust initiatives, should this prove necessary" the General intoned silkily, a twinkle of malice in his eyes.

"I think you have all you require at your disposal, my Lord" Nal'gi turns and grins at Ny'azmi.

The grizzled veteran was quite perplexed. "I do not understand, my Lords."

"How would you feel about murdering the King's closest confidante, in the event of necessity, of course?" General Nal'gi smiled thinly at the astounded warrior.

"There may be far graver necessities than that, my friend, if these unions are blessed" General Az'nai spoke chillingly.

Five

Mamy'eva, June 493 BC

The Royal Princess Sychoria, aged in her late twenties, slim and attractive, eyed the two men sat perched on elegant, cushioned, chairs a mere few feet away with an icy politeness. She remained standing, as was expected of her in the presence of the King. "I was led to believe we would be alone, father?" Sychoria glanced witheringly at the man to the right of the King.

"Were you now, sweet child?" the King gazed searchingly at his youngest daughter. "You have reservations discussing such a delicate matter in front of the Honourable Counsellor? And yet, I see you have brought your husband?"

"The matter in question directly concerns my husband. After all, Mikhouri and Alicharia are his daughters as much as they are mine!" Sychoria quipped. "Where is your Kor'nai?"

It was the Honourable Counsellor Mes'khu, who answered. "The Kor'nai is feeling a little under the weather at the moment." He raised a hand to soothe the startled visitors, "It is nothing serious, and we expect him to devote his energy and talent to the matter at hand in due course. For myself, Princess Sychoria, I offer my sincere apologies if you were not advised of my attendance beforehand. I assure you that I only have the best interests of the Royal Princesses at heart, as you do?"

"I presume that satisfies your curiosity?" the King eyed his daughter closely. "Now, you may sit, for we have much to discuss."

"I shall take a cup of wine, if it pleases Your Royal Highness?" said Counsellor Mes'khu.

"Of course, my old friend, and for our guests, for there is much to celebrate."

"You have made your decision, father?" the woman asked hopefully.

"Perhaps I have, sweet child. Yet, I cannot speak for the Argata, of course?" the King replied.

The Honourable Counsellor filled four silver goblets, intricately embossed, with fine Hellenic red and passed one to the King, then to both guests. "I am curious, darling child, for your contentment is surely a priority in this matter. Are you and your husband happy with the proposed union of your daughters to the Crown Princes?"

"We are in agreement, are we not, darling husband?" Sychoria smiled lovingly at Prince Voskar. "We have met the Crown Princes, and their parents, and feel they would be impeccable suitors for our beloved girls. They are noble, virtuous, and of pure-blood descent."

"Your eldest daughter Mikhouri would be Queen one day? You could not have hoped for a more fruitful and prosperous union, my Lady?" said Mes'khu.

"We are honoured that Her Royal Majesty, Queen Lezika, and her husband, the Crown Prince Mor'kur, consider our children to be worthy of their heirs and successors" the Prince Voskar spoke for the first time.

The King eyed his son-in-law sternly. "Did it never occur to you that it is we who are furnishing the greater blessing? No, I doubt for a moment that it did. The Ur'gai have a coterie of suitable daughters of marriageable age, yet none are as pure as your own little doves."

"I am only concerned with my children's future happiness, Your Majesty. Nothing more, and nothing less!" said Voskar.

"You are a bigger fool than I would have credited, Prince Voskar!" the King hissed. "The little Princesses are more valuable than you think. They are now even more so, in light of our recent tragedy."

"My husband is nobody's fool! Not even yours!" Sychoria bridled. "Our beloved girls will never be pawns in anyone's game. Do I make myself clear on this?"

"The thorny issue of the succession cannot be ignored any longer, my Lady" Counsellor Mes'khu soothed. "You must surely have considered the matter?"

"I?" the Princess Sychoria shot the Honourable Counsellor a withering askance. "The question of the succession is not one to which we have devoted much consideration, unlike others I may care to mention."

"We have no suitable male heir, my Lady. Such a situation is unprecedented in the annals of history" Mes'khu quipped curtly.

"My beloved cousin, so tragically drowned at sea, may well have been your preferred choice in secret. Yet, you made no public announcement to that effect?" Sychoria addressed the King, not his most cherished advisor.

"You would see your sister, the Princess Naemoria, sat upon my throne?" King Tagar gazed searchingly at his youngest child, who was also his favourite. "Perhaps you prefer Miskal'ya to wear my crown, once I am gone?"

"It is the way of things? I have no opinion on the matter. I never have?" Sychoria replied evenly.

"Perhaps I misjudged you, darling child, just as I misjudged your husband? I thought you wise, yet now I see you are as guileless as a puppy" Tagar sighed heavily. "Surely you must see that your sisters can never be Queen?"

"I know my own place in the line of succession, and that of my children. I would be correct in my presumption that my elder sisters are quite unaware of your concerns as to their suitability?" Sychoria smiled brightly.

"The prospective union of the Royal Princesses with the Argata Royal House presents a glorious opportunity to settle this thorny issue, once and for all" Counsellor Mes'khu confided.

Voskar and Sychoria exchange startled glances. "I am not sure I follow your reasoning, father? If Mikhouri were to wed Prince Disch'al, she would one day be his Queen? Perhaps I am as dim as my sisters? I cannot see how the security of the Argata line of succession could have any bearing upon our own?"

117

"If the Princess Alicharia were to wed Prince Sea'gir, a match to which you freely consent, it would cement her rightful claim in the line of succession, would it not?" said Mes'khu silkily.

"I see" the Princess Sychoria sighed. "You would be prepared to publicly declare me as your legitimate successor, in right?"

"If you can persuade that insufferable bitch in Archaeopolis to acquiesce to the union of her sons to your own little doves then you, and you alone, are my preferred heir" the King spoke softly.

"I am to say nothing of this to my sisters?" Sychoria smiled thinly.

"You are to say nothing to anyone! Am I quite clear on this?" the King hissed dangerously. "There are a great many who will not be best pleased with the course upon which I am now resolved. Do we understand one another, darling child?"

Sychoria glanced quickly at her husband, who nodded his ascent. "We do, father, indeed we do" the Princess replied softly.

The Royal Princess Sychoria studies her reflection in a polished bronze mirror with a sense of supreme satisfaction. She had lost several pounds since the thaw, her skin had lost its winter pallor, and her long limbs had been toned by a morning exercise regime which included a six-mile run, followed by a half-mile swim. Her young Handmaiden, the thirteen-year-old Sierna, turns and apprises her mistress with equal delight, for she too has been a willing beneficiary of the Royal Princesses' exacting dietary and fitness regimen. "Do you wish me to pack your winter cloak and fur-lined cap, my Lady?" the girl asked.

"Why would I require a winter cloak and cap in the height of summer?" The Princess Sychoria stifled a giggle and appraised the girl mockingly.

"It must be terribly cold, my Lady? So close to the mountains?" the girl insisted.

"Not at this time of year, sweet child. There is surprisingly little in respect of the climate in the Argata homelands that need concern you. The lions and jackals, on the other hand…"

"They have lions in Archaeopolis!" Sierna was now terrified at the prospect of their planned sojourn in the Royal City of Archaeopolis.

"But of course, sweet child. The lion is the true King of the plain, not the pretender in his Royal Palace in Susa" Sychoria eyed the girl in mock severity.

"Begging your grace, my Lady, but I know nothing of such things. I have never been anywhere."

"Archaeopolis is a beautiful city, Sirena. It is far prettier and grandiose than Mamy'eva. I am sure you will be suitably impressed" declared Sychoria.

"I have never even been on a boat, my Lady?" confessed Sierna.

"We will be travelling by ship, sweet child, not by barge. It is a ship so large that it will speed us across the Kas'pa in a day. Are you afraid of the water?" Sychoria watched the reaction of the girl with some curiosity.

"I am afraid of drowning, my Lady, ever since I was a child. One summer, when I was young, a boy I knew drowned in the Wol'yi. We were all afraid of the water afterwards" Sierna replied softly.

"The Kas'pa is perfectly pleasant, sweet child, and you will be in no danger of drowning. Have the new chitons arrived?"

"They will be arriving later today, my Lady. The Mistress Mischal'ya received a note from the merchant confirming that the consignment will be delivered today."

"I think you will be suitably impressed by the new garments I have selected for you" Sychoria smiled sweetly at the teenager. "We must endeavour to make a good first impression upon our hosts. The success of our entire enterprise depends upon it."

"I don't know how to thank you, my Lady. My parents could never afford such things for me or my sisters" Sierna sighed wistfully.

"We cannot have you twirling around the Royal Palace in Archaeopolis dressed in the garb of a common beggar? You must dress as a Princess. Now, my young Handmaiden, have you packed my jewellery safely?"

"I have, my Lady, it is secured within your trinket case. Should I entrust that to the Guards for safe keeping?" the girl asked earnestly.

"Only when we are ready to depart, and not before, is that understood?" the girl nodded her acquiescence. "We have yet to receive confirmation of our departure date. The Royal Guard are liaising directly with the captain, but I would not concern myself with such trivialities, sweet child. We will be leaving within the week, as planned. Now, would you be so kind as to inform the Mistress Asel'ya that I desire time alone with my eldest child?"

"Of course, my Lady, I shall go at once" the girl curtseyed and left, closing the door behind her. Shortly thereafter, a pretty girl, garbed in a simple white chiton with emerald-green trim, knocked respectfully and awaited her mother's command to enter. Her younger sister, in stark contradistinction, would have sauntered into the room leaving the door ajar! "Hello, my petal, how are you feeling today?"

"I feel a lot better Mama, thank you for asking. My throat isn't all that sore anymore and my tummy is a lot more settled" the girl replied softly.

"You still look a little pale, darling child, and you are thinner than ever. Your little sister could eat you for breakfast?"

"Alicharia has been banished to her room again" the child sighed.

"Your sister has a habit of not doing what she is told! I promise I shall look in on her later."

"Will you be away for the whole summer?" the girl looked anxious.

"That is why I sent for you, Mikhouri. I think it is time that you and I had a talk, for you are not a baby anymore, are you?"

"I shall be ten before the Solstice, shall I not?" Mikhouri beamed proudly.

"You are fast growing into a remarkably poised young Lady. Your father and I are immensely proud of you. You know that don't you?"

"You will be spending the summer with Queen Lezika and her family?"

"We shall, my love, and I shall miss you terribly, both you and Alicharia. You know why we must head south this summer?"

"Am I to be betrothed to the Royal Prince Disch'al?" the girl smiled shyly.

"Has your father spoken with you?" her mother eyed her searchingly.

"I spoke with him just the other night" Mikhouri confessed. "Father told me I was fast becoming a perfect little Princess and that he loved me more than words could ever convey. He also told me I would make some lucky boy a fine Queen one day" the girl gushed.

"Has your father spoken to Alicharia?" Sychoria spoke tonelessly, yet her eyes telegraphed her alarm.

"I know he spoke with her in her bedchamber the other night, shortly after he spoke with me. I do not know the matter on which they spoke."

"I see" Princess Sychoria smiled affectionately at her eldest child. "There is something I need you to do for me, my sweet child. You cannot tell your sister what we have spoken of, do you understand? When we have finished talking, you will understand why."

Mikhouri looked bewildered at the thought of deceiving her sister. "Yes, Mama, I understand" she nodded.

"You are a little girl no more, Mikhouri. You have now reached an age where there are expectations of your future, and it is of those which we must now talk." Sychoria indicated a cushioned bench near the window, with a majestic view of the River Wol'yi and its meadows. "Please, my sweet, let us sit. What do you know of the Royal Prince Disch'al?"

"I hear that he is very handsome and is destined to be tall. He can read, and he has a great love for ballads, music and the theatre, or so I am told" Mikhouri smiled sweetly.

"Then you know far more than most girls in this world, little rose. He sounds like a fine young man, does he not?"

"That he does, Mama. I also hear he is fast becoming a fine horseman and has learned to shoot an arrow" the girl quipped blushingly.

"Is that so important to you, my love?" her mother smiled warmly at the girl.

"I think it is important for him, is it not? For he will be a King one day, will he not?" Mikhouri ventured.

"Important to men, perhaps, yet less so to his future Queen, you would agree?"

"And why would the Prince Disch'al care for my lowly opinion of his virtue as a husband, much less a King?" Mikhouri seemed genuinely surprised.

"Would it surprise you to learn that Prince Disch'al would be greatly interested in your opinion on such things, for he has made regular inquiries of your opinion on many things?"

"I cannot believe that is true. Surely, you mock me, mother?" the child smiled shyly.

"No, darling rose, I do not. By all accounts, the Royal Prince is quite taken with you and would dearly love to meet you."

"There must surely be other girls? There must be thousands of girls who are far prettier than I, or will ever hope to be?" Mikhouri blushed.

"No, Mikhouri, there are not. At least not according to the Royal Prince?" Sychoria smiled brightly at the girl.

"But we have not even met? How could he know what I look like?"

"Do you remember the Royal Banquet in honour of the Argata Ambassador last year? You wore that beautiful gold dress and had your hair in ringlets, rather than pleats?"

Mikhouri blushed. "I remember it well, mother, for I have not had chance to wear that beautiful dress since. Everyone complimented me and told me how beautiful I looked."

"Including the Ambassador himself?" Sychoria chided.

"The Ambassador is a diplomat? Alicharia doubted he could tell a truth from a goat!" Mikhouri snickered.

Sychoria giggled. "Your sister spends too much time listening to the crude chatter of soldiers! The Ambassador was telling the truth. By all accounts, the dashing young Prince is now besotted by your reputed charms."

"You surely tease me, mother?" the girl implored.

"I do not, my love. Prince Disch'al has requested a lock of your hair, if you would be gracious as to offer him such a keepsake?"

Mikhouri was astounded. "But we are not yet betrothed? What would my future husband think of me if he learned I had given freely of such a treasure to another?"

"I think your future husband would be grateful for such a keepsake, for he has asked repeatedly for it?"

"Now you do tease me! It is not proper!" Mikhouri bridled. "The Royal Prince wishes for my hand in marriage?" Mikhouri's cheeks flush brightly.

"Would you give it, if he asked?" Sychoria asked earnestly.

"Of course, I would. For I would be his wife and his future Queen" Mikhouri cooed.

"And so, you shall, my darling rose, for that is what you were born to be" Sychoria smiled sweetly at the blushing girl.

"I cannot tell Alicharia? It would pain me to keep such a secret from her?" Mikhouri seemed disconsolate at the prospect.

"You may tell her, my little dove, of course you may. Your sister has too inquisitive a mind and is not easily fooled. What you cannot tell her is that she too made a favourable impression upon the Ambassador."

Mikhouri giggled shrilly. "The Ambassador wishes to wed my little sister when she is older?"

Sychoria chuckled. "No, my little dove, your darling sister has made a favourable impression upon the young Prince Sea'gir, and his parents, for that matter."

"They obviously haven't met her!" Mikhouri giggled breathlessly. She frowned and eyed her mother steadily. "Is that why you and Papa will be spending the entire summer in Archaeopolis? To betroth us to the Royal Princes, when we are of suitable age, of course?"

"That is exactly why your father and I must go to Archaeopolis. It is time for you to become a true Princess. And one day, in the not-too-distant future, you shall become the most beautiful Queen that has ever lived?"

"Even more beautiful than Helen of Troy? Was not she the most beautiful girl in the world?" Mikhouri cooed softly.

"You will be more beautiful, more gracious, and more faithful a Queen than Helen of Troy ever was. You are a true-blooded Scythian Princess, and never a half-breed Dorian! One day, my little pearl, the poets will write legends of your virtues."

"I shall tell my sister only what she needs to know and nothing more, I swear it!" Mikhouri pledged solemnly.

Archaeopolis, June 493 BC

Almost a world away, in the Royal City of Archaeopolis, the Crown Prince Disch'al was being led by the hand by his Governess, the Princess Sorkh'ya, first cousin to his mother, Queen Lezika, through the busy throng of shoppers in the Jewellers District. The young Prince, who would be ten in the early autumn, was in jovial spirits this day. He had been instructed by his mother to select a trinket, no matter its price, to be a gift for the most beautiful girl in the world. Such an errand would normally have struck the prince as unnecessary, for surely such trivialities could be left to one of Her Majesty's retainers. In this case, the young damsel was to be his betrothed, his loving and faithful bride and, at a suitable time in the future, his loyal and obedient Queen! "What is the name of this fellow, again, Mistress Sorkh'ya?" the boy quipped.

"His name is Mesticrates. He is the finest jeweller in Archaeopolis, as I have informed you a thousand times this morning" Princess Sorkh'ya sighed exasperatedly.

"I like to be certain of these things, darling Sorkh'ya. Is certainty not a virtue of Kings?"

"Perhaps it is, young man, but you are not yet a King" Sorkh'ya teased.

They arrived presently at the jewellers' premises and entered. A chaperone of six Guards, including the gruff and chiselled Dru'khim, all garbed in civilian attire, loiter in the street immediately outside the door. "It is an honour, my young Prince, truly an honour" the jeweller greeted the Prince and his Mistress with a flourish. "If it may please the Royal Prince and, acting upon Her Majesty's instruction, I have taken the liberty of selecting my finest pieces for your appraisal, for I am certain you will appreciate the craftsmanship."

"Let me see them, dear fellow" the young Prince quipped.

"Child!" the jeweller commanded, momentarily startling the prince and his ward. A bright-eyed girl aged several years younger than the prince, looms in the doorway at the far end of the room. "Would you be so kind as to fetch the trays from the desk in my office?"

"Of course, master", the girl replied meekly, then vanished as quickly as she had materialised. She returned, a few moments later, pushing a trolley upon which rested several trays of exquisite trinkets.

"Thank you, child, you may leave us!" Mesticrates spoke icily, as if her very presence was an embarrassment to such a regal personhood as the young Prince.

"Yes, master!" the girl spoke softly, and turned to leave.

"Stay, my Lady!" Prince Disch'al spoke sharply, startling the child, her master, and his mistress.

"Master?" the girl looked nervously at the jeweller.

"Forgive me, my Prince, for it would please me to make the introductions" Mesticrates spoke silkily. *Perhaps the little bitch might be worth more than he had paid for her at the Slave Market, for she had certainly made an impression on the Royal whelpling.* "This is Avielle. She is a native of Gaul. She is a Celt, would you believe?"

"You are a long way from home, my Lady?" the young Prince smiled warmly at the girl.

"Yes, my Lord" the girl replied simply, her cheeks blushing lightly.

"Now, my young Prince, I have heard much of your passion for all things beautiful. We have many a wonder guaranteed to play upon the strings of a Lady's heart?" the jeweller smiled at the Princess Sorkh'ya, who he sincerely hoped would chivvy the prince in the direction of the two most expensive pieces. The young Prince stepped towards the trolley and appraised the pieces, each laid carefully upon its own polished wooden tray. "You are allowed to choose any piece you wish, my young Prince, for the honour is mine."

The young Prince made his selection in surety that it would annoy this oily swindler. "They are exceedingly fine, my dear fellow. Yet, I feel unable to choose between two of the pieces."

Mesticrates flashed his teeth, for this was music to his ears. Of course, the young Prince could not distinguish between the two most expensive pieces, just as he had hoped. He might yet be persuaded of the merits of buying both. "Perhaps a Lady may assist you in your endeavour?" he smiled brightly at the Princess Sorkh'ya.

Prince Disch'al struggled not to laugh out loud. "I agree, my dear fellow, perhaps she might. Which would you choose, Lady Avielle?"

The jeweller was astonished. "Forgive me, my Lord. This is no Lady. She is a mere brute."

The prince glowered at the jeweller and smiled shyly at the girl, who blushed hotly. Her eyes, of the purest emerald green, briefly flash with anger at the jewellers' casual insult to her honour. *She was nothing but a slave to him, yet to the prince she was the most dazzling creature he had ever seen.* "It would please me, Avielle, if you would select a piece for me?" the prince spoke softly, and with obvious reverence.

The girl smiled slyly and made her choice. "I would choose this one, my Lord."

It was not a piece her master would have chosen, yet it was the one the prince himself had deemed the most beautiful, excepting that most exquisite of jewels, young Avielle herself!

As was her custom, Avielle rose early and, after a light meal of unleavened bread and a small portion of fruit, washed down with a goblet of watered wine, she commenced her duties cleaning the floor and tables prior to the arrival of her master. Despite her status, Avielle liked her life in Archaeopolis, for it was a far less hostile than her previous two years in Tyre. She had been employed by a famed distributor of opia who had treated her harshly, ever since her arrival from Gaul, shortly after her sixth birthday. Now, aged eight-and-a-half, she had at least found some semblance of peace with Mesticrates, who seemed to like and value her, provided she was dutiful and considerate in her labours, which she invariably was. He trusted her with polishing the jewellery, and this was important, as it steadily facilitated ever-greater freedoms than she could never have imagined in Tyre.

After seven months in Archaeopolis, Avielle's daily duties included running errands for her master, mostly mundane chores like fetching fresh fruit and wine from the Bazaar for the customers, yet this afforded the liberty of strolling about the city with money, mainly copper coins, but sometimes silver, held in a small leather purse around her neck. This morning, she was tasked to deliver an urgent request to a notorious money lender with whom Mesticrates had an account. And so, shortly after her master had arrived to supervise the arranging of the displays, followed by a cup of freshly brewed mint tea and a ration of apricot wodki, which she secretly adored, Avielle left the Jeweller's District and sallied fearlessly through the throng of shoppers and merchants in the Bazaar. Her destination was *The Pilgrim's Rest*, where a money lender of dubious repute, Mustafir, domiciled his lucrative business. If one needed money in Archaeopolis, no matter the sum, you were strongly advised to approach Mustafir, or else suffer the consequences of your lack of foresight!

The girl strolled through the entrance to *The Pilgrim's Rest*, blithely ignoring the lurid advances of several drunks perched on the steps, and made her way to the private bar, ignoring everyone. She nodded a polite "Hello" to two burly retainers stationed in the corridor and they acknowledged her with a warm smile. Mustafir was in conference with a customer when she appeared in the doorway, but instead of waving her away, the man smiled and nodded in the direction of a vacant seat. Avielle sat down and watched the unfolding drama with interest. "I can't go any higher than two Persian pieces, not without security, you know how this works?" Mustafir spoke softly to the customer, a man named Sestarches.

Sestarches was not to be dissuaded. "I need four. I told you that when I came in, didn't I?"

"Your credit isn't good enough for four pieces, is it? Perhaps three at the most, but even that is pushing it."

"With interest you charge?" the man said sullenly.

"That is exactly the point, isn't it? You cannot cover the interest payments on three pieces, let alone four. Do you take me for the village fool, Sestarches?" Mustafir challenged sourly.

"I need at least three, and you'll get your money, I promise. I have a nice little score coming in, and that is all I can tell you. You will thank me for it, I guarantee it."

"Three it is! And don't think I won't forget this, Sestarches! I am putting my neck out for you here, you understand. If you fail to pay on time, as per our arrangement, it will be on your own head!"

"This is a guaranteed score! You will have the first instalment in three days and the remainder by the next Shabbat" Sestarches said softly.

"Then you can go and see our mutual friend and tell him you have cleared this with me. There is my chit. He will honour it, upon my word."

As the man got up to leave, Mustafir eyed the pretty child with a toothy grin. "Now, my little honeycomb, what service can I do for your master this day?" He reached for a flagon on the table and poured two generous measures of apricot wodki, beckoning the girl to join him. "That is on the house, my little peach. I know it is your favourite, so drink up." Avielle sat down across from him and sipped her drink. It tasted heavenly. "Is that miserly old prick still treating you well? I will lower his credit line if he isn't?" he grinned conspiratorially at the child.

Avielle grinned back. "My master requested a meeting with you later, if that would be possible?"

"I don't see why not? The usual arrangement, is it? I shall arrive just before closing time."

"My master would be indebted to you, as always."

"He always is, isn't he?" the man grinned.

"You have always been good to me" the child sighed. "I just wanted to say thank you."

Mustafir eyed the girl steadily. "He hasn't been mistreating you, has he?"

Avielle blinked. "No, my Lord, he has not. Mesticrates always treats me with courtesy. It is just that, for the past few days, I have a feeling I am being watched, even followed about the city. I don't know anyone here, apart from the few people I meet on my errands, so I don't know why anyone would be so interested in me."

"Why don't you finish your drink, and then you can be on your way. I will have a word with a few people I know, and they will follow you and make sure you get back safely."

"I am sure I will be fine, my Lord. Perhaps it is nothing" Avielle looked wary.

"It is always better to be safe than sorry, my petal. Now, be on your way, like a good girl, and I will ask some of my lads to keep an eye out for you?"

Mustafir climbed out of the chair and left the room. When he returned a brief time later, the girl had left the tavern to venture back to her master.

King Tagar turned to his Steward, Hai'jil, nodded at the small table in front of him and clicked his fingers. The Steward strolled across the palatial private study to a dresser table, where a silver tray, flagon, and goblets stood. Hai'jil, a favourite of the King for nearly two decades, places the tray down on the table. "Would you like me to pour, Your Majesty?" "That will be all, my old friend, you are dismissed. You may inform the Guards outside the door that I am not to be disturbed, you understand?" the King smiled thinly.

"I am at your service, as always, Your Majesty!" Hai'jil turned and made his way towards the door, closing it firmly behind him.

Tagar eyed his unexpected visitor coolly, despite their affection. "I see you came alone this time, darling child?"

"My husband has business in the city, as I had here. I thought it would be courteous to pay you a visit, father?" Princess Sychoria replied.

The King smiled slyly at his favourite child. "You were always a thoughtful child, Sychoria. I take it you have no concern as to the presence of the Honourable Counsellor on this occasion?"

"I expected you to be here, Counsellor Mes'khu? Is the Kor'nai still feeling under the weather?" Sychoria challenged in a mocking tone.

Tagar chuckled lightly. "What do you want of me, Sychoria?"

"I have a request for you, darling father. I have heard from the Captain of the Royal Guard that you intend to send an increased contingent north with my children?"

It was the Honourable Counsellor who answered. "We thought it the wisest course, in light of recent events?"

"Perhaps you might consider keeping them in the Sar'kta Plains for a week, instead of returning to Mamy'eva immediately. We do not wish to alarm the children, do we?"

"What would a detachment of my own Royal Guard do during their extended sojourn?" the King enquired coolly.

"They could assist the Crown Prince with the supervision of the harvest. It would be a gesture of reassurance, for the sake of the children, if you will?" Sychoria quipped.

"Very well, I will inform the Captain of the Guard to make the necessary arrangements. Is that all you wished to speak with me about?" Tagar stroked his chin.

"I have arranged to meet with my sisters this evening. I merely thought it courteous to inform you in advance?"

"You intend to keep your silence, darling child?" the King appraised the Princess warily.

"Of course, father? What else would you have me do?" Sychoria replied evenly.

Tagar smiled tightly. "These matters could easily have been dealt with through normal channels, could they not? What did you really want to speak about?"

"The Argata will enquire about our preparations for the forthcoming campaign?" Sychoria smiled ruefully.

Once again, it was the Honourable Counsellor, rather than the King, who answered the Princess. "You may inform Queen Lezika and her Royal Counsel that matters are in hand. We stand ready to fulfil our obligations in the enterprise, as they must surely fulfil their own."

"Do you think the Argata Queen will be placated by such dismissive twaddle?" the Princess seemed bemused by her temerity. Mes'khu blushed hotly.

"You will be in Archaeopolis to further your daughters' betrothals to the two Princes, will you not?" Tagar clipped testily. "You have no martial experience, and neither does your husband. You cannot be expected to have a firm grasp of the finer details of the forthcoming campaign."

"I simply wished for your counsel, nothing more. On the matter of my daughters, I take it you consent wholeheartedly to the marriages?"

"Of course, I do, for the reasons we have already discussed. I intend to keep my side of the bargain, darling child, you may rest assured of that. Now it is up to you to deliver upon your own terms of the bargain" the King confirmed.

Avielle strolled through the crowds congregating at the fruit-sellers, stopping briefly to purchase oranges, grapes, and plums from Dischaeus, the preferred merchant to her master. She knew instinctively that she was being followed, yet this intrigued, rather than frightened her. She smiled at the kindly old man and nodded a silent "Hello" to his daughter, Chirelle. Glancing to her left, she noted a boy of perhaps nine or ten years, who blushed hotly and averted his gaze. *Why are you so interested in me?* The child mused silently. Avielle reached into the purse that hung around her neck to pluck a single copper disk to pay the fruit seller when, to her astonishment, a cultured voice, soft, yet resonant, spoke up from her right shoulder. "A fine morning, is it not, Dischaeus? I shall pay for the young Lady's goods." A startled Avielle turns and gazes into the eyes of a boy who is no stranger.

"It is you?" she gasped.

"Might I escort you back to your master, Avielle?" Prince Disch'al smiled at the girl.

Avielle smiled shyly at the boy. "Seeing as you are already here, you might as well."

131

The pair left the fruit seller and strolled through the crowds. "Have you been watching me these past few days?" Avielle spoke softly.

"Yes, and I am sorry, I never meant to cause any offence, my Lady."

Avielle snorted. "Stop calling me that! My name is Avielle, and that is what you may call me. Did you not hear my master? I am certainly no Lady."

"Would you expect me to care in the slightest what your master thinks?" Disch'al grinned.

"Do you truly care for anything, or anyone? I doubt that you are in the least bit sorry for having me followed these few days past. You are a Prince, and may do as you please, may you not?" Avielle quipped.

"That is true, Avielle, but even a Prince can be human. Perhaps we are not as different as you think?"

"I am a slave, my Lord! I cannot change my destiny. I belong to my master, as I did the master before him. Mesticrates is good to me. He treats me far better than my last master in Tyre, of that you may be thankful."

"You may call me Disch'al, not my Lord, Avielle. I am a Prince, by the way?"

"Do you take me for a simpleton? I know who your mother is? Am I to be your new plaything, Prince Disch'al?" the girls emerald pools twinkled mischievously.

"I simply wanted to talk to you, Avielle, and that is all."

The girl smiled shyly, her cheeks flushing lightly. "Then you may talk with me."

As the pair cleared the Market, Disch'al nodded to a marble bench nestled in the shade of a Sycamore tree. "Would you like to rest for a while? It is as perfect a place as any in our fair city, wouldn't you say?"

The girl smiled mockingly. "I am not tired, Disch'al, and I have a full day's work ahead of me. But it would please me, to sit and talk, at least for a little while."

As they sat down, another boy approached the prince and passed him a flagon. "Thank you, Milaeus! You are a true friend. Now, bugger off!"

Avielle giggled. "You certainly have a way with people, don't you?" the girl's eyes twinkled once more. "What is in the flagon?"

"It is apricot wodki, sourced from the finest merchant in all Archaeopolis. I was led to believe it is your favourite?" the prince smiled slyly at the girl.

"Is there anything you have not discovered about me?" Avielle smiled shyly.

"Everything" the prince passed the girl the flagon.

Avielle took a gulp of the liquor. "You must meet lots of other girls, surely? Sweet and virtuous girls, from wealthy and noble families?"

"Not like you, Avielle" Disch'al blushed.

"You don't know anything about me? You don't know who I really am, how I came to be here, or what has happened in my past?" she remonstrated.

"And you don't know anything about me, do you?" the prince countered.

Avielle smiled shyly. "Then we have rather a lot to talk about, don't we?"

The girl, recently turned seven years old a moon after the thaw, stood defiantly in the centre of the room, watching as the woman filled a chest with light-weight summer garments dyed in a variety of shades. Most of the garments were new, fashioned from fine materials with intricate embroidery. "I do not wish to go! I don't see why we have to!" the child protested.

Asel'ya eyed the child steadily. "Every summer it is the same with you, Alicharia? You know the answer to your question and yet, ever since you were able to talk, we must endure your annual tantrum. It is fast becoming a little trying if you care for my opinion?" she sighed exasperatedly.

"I am old enough to understand. You do realise that don't you?" Alicharia eyed the woman sternly. "Father and Mother are leaving for Astrach'yi early tomorrow and will be away for the next two moons. Why must we go north? We could stay here, with you?"

"Your Grandparents are expecting you, young lady? Do you wish to disappoint them?"

The child grinned slyly. "They could come to Mamy'eva, could they not? There is no reason why they could not do so?"

"And who will supervise the harvest in Sar'kuc? I doubt you have given any consideration to that small matter, have you?" Asel'ya chided.

The child grinned. "Grandfather has retainers who can undertake the responsibility. I do not see why he could not simply instruct someone to supervise the harvest. What is the point in having a title if you cannot exercise power?"

"Spoken like a true Princess! Do you believe the key to real power lies in imposing your will upon others?" the woman sighed. "Those who truly exercise power in this world have responsibilities unto others. Your Grandfather cannot abdicate supervision of the harvest to his Retainers. He must undertake that responsibility himself."

"And so, we must go north?" the girl sighed despondently.

"And so, we must go north! And you, young lady, will exercise some decorum in the matter. Why can't you be more like your sister? She does not feel the same as you?"

"Mikhouri is an idiot! She is simple in the head! Everybody agrees on this, didn't you know?"

"And you, young lady, are simple in the heart!" Asel'ya replied tartly. "This world of ours does not revolve around you, didn't you know?"

"Well, maybe it should. One day, and that day will come soon enough, for I shan't be a child forever, I shall order the world be exactly as it ought to."

Asel'ya eyed the girl with genuine affection. "And who said you would be Queen? Your sister precedes you in the line of succession, for she is older. You surely understand that Alicharia?"

"An idiot, a simpleton, will reign over the kingdom? Whatever will you think of next?" Alicharia sneered.

"If your sister heard you speak like this, she would surely box your ears!" the woman teased.

"That is only because she is bigger than me, and that is because she is older than me. That also means that she will continue to grow older than me, until she dies, and that will be long before me!"

"You are a child, Alicharia! You should not speak of such things. It is dangerous talk!" Asel'ya hissed.

"Is somebody throwing a 'hissy fit'?" a polite voice, a girl's, interjected.

The startled Handmaiden turns away from the younger girl to appraise her elder sister, who stands in the doorway smiling brightly at the pair. "Your baby sister is entreating me to her annual melodrama. You are just in time for the finale!" Mikhouri grinned at her sister, who stuck her tongue out.

"I was simply enquiring why Grandfather and Grandmother could not come to Mamy'eva for the summer. And do not mention the harvest, for I refuse to accept that the responsibility could not be derogated."

"I think you mean 'delegated', darling sister?" Mikhouri teased.

"I think you will find you are wrong, darling sister. All I was asking for is a temporary departure from the accepted norm. Isn't that so, Asel'ya?"

"You think it wise to depart from the rules, simply because you can?" Mikhouri frowned.

"We are Princesses, are we not? Grandpapa is a Crown Prince, is he not?" Alicharia quipped.

"The title is honorary, as well you know. It was conferred upon him by the King" Mikhouri replied evenly.

Alicharia grinned at her elder sister. "Nice isn't it, to confer titles on people simply because they allow their son to marry your daughter? I think I would like to be Queen. I think it would suit my temperament" she declared.

"Your temperament would be better suited if it were tempered more frequently, young Lady" Asel'ya chided.

"Perhaps I could speak with my sister alone?" Mikhouri asked politely.

"As is your wish, my Lady. I shall continue supervising the packing."

"You do have a way with people, little sister?" Mikhouri smiled sweetly at the younger girl when the Handmaiden had left the room.

"I don't want to go! I don't see why we have to?" Alicharia protested.

"We are children, Alicharia. We must do as we are told. It is expected of us." Mikhouri chided.

"Nobody asked for my opinion on the matter, did they?" Alicharia mused sadly.

"It will be different this time, I promise you. You are old enough to learn to ride?"

"Grandmama won't allow it, will she?" the younger girl sighed despondently.

"Grandpapa might, if you promise to be good?" Mikhouri posited.

"What has that got to do with anything?" Alicharia rounded tartly. "Grandpapa will do as Grandmama tells him! No more, no less, for she is a woman, and he a man! They *are* beneath us; don't you know that? We *are* Scythians, are we not?"

"Do you think you will ever get married?" Mikhouri grinned.

"No, I do not! I can't ever imagine being married, not ever!" Alicharia spat indignantly.

"Then what will you do with the rest of your life? When you are older, that is?"

"I would like to fight! I was born to conquer, just like that idiot in Susa! When I am older, I will beat him. King Darius if he still lives. If not, then his idiot son. They are both born simpletons and will be no match for me" Alicharia sneered.

"I do worry about you, little sister? I truly do?" Mikhouri smiled wryly the girl.

"Well, you shouldn't worry, for I shall be fine. It is this world that ought to worry!" Alicharia declared confidently.

"Mother and Father have asked to see us. You will promise to be good, won't you? You know how upset mother can get at this time of year?" implored Mikhouri.

"I will, I promise."

"Then you can go back to your dreams of conquering this world of ours?" Mikhouri mocked.

"I will conquer the world, darling sister, just you see! You can help me if you want to?"

The boy climbs agilely over the back wall and merges into the shadows. What few candles burn from within the building, or from the adjacent properties on either side of the lane, could never reveal his presence to any watchful eye in the upper storeys of the business premises or tenements.

The boy smiles mischievously and drew his dagger, the blade held at an angle so as not to catch the gleam of the moon, and silently pads to the window. He glances warily around, though he is sure he has not been followed, and strokes the tip of the blade thrice upon the corner stone. The boy waits patiently, and repeats the strokes, only three, and no more, when a candle flame appears on the opposite side of the hollow. The candle is withdrawn, and the boy felt his pulse quicken with a joy he had never felt before. He retrieved the flower, a single bud of a glorious pink rose, cut from the flower garden of the Royal Palace earlier that afternoon, and slips it through the hollow. "I knew you would come. A Prince must keep his promises" a sweet voice whispered from within.

"And a Lady must honour her own, sweet Avielle" whispered Disch'al. "I will unlock the door for you."

Avielle unlocked the door and ushered the prince inside. Her quarters, situated at the rear of the Jeweller's shop, were small, yet even in the meagre glare of a few candles the prince could see the girl was far better treated than most slaves could ever hope to be. "I have brought a present for you" the prince handed over a small flagon.

"Is it apricot wodki? You truly are sweet!" Avielle smiled shyly at the prince.
"And you are the fairest of maidens, sweet Avielle" the prince replied.
"I think you say that to every girl, don't you?"
"I have never uttered those words to anyone before, sweet Avielle."

Avielle poured two generous measures into two battered wooden goblets and the pair sat down on the edge of the bed. "Does anyone know you are here?" Avielle whispered.

"No" the boy grinned conspiratorially. "I accomplished my escape without alerting any Guards. They think I am asleep in my bed."
"Did you have to scale the perimeter wall?" the girl frowned.

"There is a secret entrance to the Royal Palace near the old stables by the north wall" Disch'al confessed. "Only a few people know that it even exists. The Palace Guards patrol the area at night, but not so regularly that I couldn't slip past them. I found out about it a few years ago, but I have never used it to abscond to the city."

"Until now?" said Avielle.

"Until now" replied Disch'al. "What would you like to talk about?"

"Why don't you tell me about yourself? I don't really know anything about you, do I?"

And so, the children talked, as children do, and it mattered not than one was a Prince and the other a pauper, for nothing could sour the simple joy of their companionship. An hour or so later, Prince Disch'al bade his fair maiden good night, with a promise to return early the following morning. For a Prince should keep his promises, should he not?

He had no intention of disappointing a girl who had, in the space of a single hour, stolen his heart forever.

Prince Disch'al kept his promise. He woke earlier than ever and tip-toed through the Palace and the Ornate Garden, successfully navigating the routine patrols of the Guards, before slipping through the gap in the perimeter wall near the crumbling ruins of the old stables. The streets of the city were largely deserted at this hour, and the young Prince felt confident that no-one would recognise him, garbed as he was in a thick winter cloak with its hood drawn tightly to cloak his face. Disch'al was not afraid, for he was a Royal Prince, the heir to the Argata crown, and this was *his* city. He carried his dagger at his left hip, attached to a leather belt around his silk chiton.

He arrived in the Jewellers Quarter and slipped down the backstreets to the rear of Mesticrates premises. Disch'al checked left, then right, and then stealthily scaled the wall. He approached the window and drew his dagger, scraping the tip three times on the edge, as he had done so the previous night. "Do you have a present for me, sweet Prince?" Avielle whispered shyly from within the room.

"I have only myself to offer, sweet Avielle. Will that suffice?"

"Yes" the girl whispered softly and drew back the bolt on the door. "I have made some mint tea, if you would like some?"

"That would be lovely. I could not get any wodki this morning. I am sorry."

"I have some of my masters. I will pour us a goblet to share if you would like?"

"That would be lovely, sweet Avielle" the boy smiled shyly.

The prince and the girl shared their tea and wodki, and then commenced their chores, sweeping the floor, dusting, and polishing the tables, before arranging the display trays for the arrival of her Master for the day's trade. Two pairs of eager hands made light of the work and the pair brewed another cup of mint tea and sat and talked, as they had the previous night. "I wish you didn't have to go" Avielle whispered sadly.

"I shall return this evening, if you would like me to?" Disch'al smiled shyly.

"You know I would. More than anything, even my freedom" the girl sighed happily.

The prince smiled sweetly at the girl and kissed her lightly on the cheek. "I will come after the rising of the moon, I promise, sweet Avielle."

The girl closed the door and bolted it, sighing happily. Disch'al quickly scaled the wall and strolled through the backstreets towards the Bazaar. At this hour, the streets were no longer deserted, and a steady stream of traders, assistants, and early morning shoppers had begun to flock to the Bazaar for the start the day's trade. As the young Prince threaded through the lanes and alleys of the Bazaar, it never occurred to him that he might be recognised. The Queen had a legion of spies in the city, and little passed without notice, especially a well-dressed boy with his hood drawn close to avoid recognition, who strode innocently towards the Royal Palace.

Astrach'yi, June 493 BC

It is now a few hours after first light. The sun has risen on the horizon in the east, the sky is cloudless, and the air is unusually cool for the time of year, fast approaching the height of summer. A covered carriage canters northwest along the avenue towards the Docklands and the Wharf. The port city of Astrach'yi has been awake for several hours, yet the arrival of the Royal Train and its entourage of heavily armed Royal Guards was a rare spectacle. As the Royal Train arrived at the South Wharf, a tall and elegantly dressed seafarer, aged in his early thirties, paced energetically to meet it. "It is as glorious a morning as any to raise a sail, Your Royal Highness" Captain Zakhari declared Sychoria as she alighted from her carriage.

"I am glad you think so, Captain Zakhari" the Princess shivers lightly in the early morning chill.

"I have supervised the loading of your luggage personally, my Lady. It is safely stored in your cabin. Let me show you the way. The weather is fair and there should be no unexpected delays in reaching Bu'khu by early tomorrow morning."

The passenger vessel, *The Flower of Astrach'yi*, departed soon afterwards on her journey south to the port of Bu'khu, sited on a promontory on the western shore of the Kas'pa, south of the Caucasus Mountains. The port was nominally controlled by the Argata, ever since their cruel oppression of the Armenians several years ago and was the largest port in the sea. In addition to the captain, a native of Sar'kta, the vessel boasted eight seamen and a detachment of elite Royal Guards who would accompany the Prince and Princess throughout their stay in Archaeopolis. The Princess was accompanied by her two Handmaidens, Sierna and Gh'aena, and the prince retained his Private Secretary, U'vohn. They planned to be away from

Mamy'eva for six weeks, sufficient time to negotiate the terms of the dowry for their cherished daughters.

The weather was fair and the sea calm, almost perfect conditions for sailing. *The Flower of Astrach'yi* was a fast vessel, sleekly built and well-maintained by her Captain and crew. None carried personal weapons, for there was no plague of piracy in the Kas'pa to contend with, quite unlike the Ionian and Aegean seas. The Royal Princess occupied her time aboard sewing with her Handmaidens, whilst the Crown Prince and U'vohn busied themselves with the prospective figures of the dowries of the Royal Princesses. A light meal would be served in the Captain's Galley soon after midday, with a lavish supper planned for the evening. The promise was for a most enjoyable and uneventful passage.

Bu'khu, June 493 BC

A detachment of thirty veterans of the Argata Royal Guard, commanded by Captain Nakh'ga, arrived at Bu'khu later the same morning, stabling their mounts at *The Gypsy Rose*, a famed tavern on the outskirts of the settlement. They had ridden hard from Archaeopolis for three days, escorting a carriage and covered wagon across the unforgiving terrain east of the Colchian plains, a landscape perennially plagued by marauding bands of Armenian renegades. The detachment had not encountered any hostile elements on the outward journey, but it was well-known that Armenian spies in Bu'khu often tipped off their compatriots about tempting consignments heading east. If the identity of the passengers became known, the return journey might prove to be anything but uneventful! With that prospect in mind, an entire cavalry troop was scheduled to arrive from the garrison at Neh'ma, eight hours ride to the east, early the next morning.

The soldiers slaked their thirsts with tankards of rye beer and wodki chasers, warily eyeing the customers for anyone who might have taken too keen an interest in their arrival. In the far corner, two old men sit engrossed in a table game, presumably regulars who posed no obvious threat. A group of stevedores slaking their thirsts at the bar in the middle of their shift were a different matter entirely. Captain Nakh'ga eyed them shrewdly, hoping to determine their ethnicity and gauge whether they had been piqued by their unexpected arrival. Nothing seemed out of place at *The Gypsy Rose*, and the soldiers paid little heed to the old man as he passed their table on route to the stable yard. In retrospect, they should have paid the man notice, for he was Isair, the Commander of a notorious and ruthless band of renegades, *The Sons of Sevan*, and their sworn enemy.

Isair spoke briefly to the stable boy, who turned on his heels, sprinted from the yard and headed along the street to the stall of a fishmonger named Luska, who could be entrusted to relay the news of the soldier's arrival to the rest of the band, camped in a valley several miles to the south. The information was explicit, for these were not ordinary soldiers, but members of Her Royal Majesty's Guard, no less! They had obviously ridden from Archaeopolis on some secretive assignment and would be staying overnight in Bu'khu. They would make a fine series of scalps for *The Sons of Sevan*! Shortly thereafter, the fishmonger's apprentice, a ruddy-faced youth named Sal'ka, gallops southwest toward the rugged hills and valleys, clothed with dense woodland, where the renegades had waited patiently for the past few moons.

PART TWO

Six

Archaeopolis, June 493 BC

Queen Lezika was a habitual early riser, a legacy of a misspent youth in the hedonistic backstreets of Corinth, when her Tutors thought her safely asleep in her chalet. She invariably slept alone, except on rare occasions, and during the summer months she could be found at a desk in her private study attending to her correspondence a few hours after first light, fortified with a kettle of scalding mint tea. Her Royal Majesty had spent the virginal hours poring over recent intelligence reports from Armenia, prior to her morning bath, followed by a repast of bread, honey, and an obligatory goblet of spiced Hellenic wine. Her Kor'nai found her in fine spirits an hour or so later, yet her morning glow did not survive intimation of a most disturbing revelation. "Are you quite certain of this information, Honourable Kor'nai?" the Queen spoke coldly.

"The man in question ranks among my most reliable and trusted sources, Your Majesty. He would never knowingly lie to me" Miris'kar confided.

"And this source claims to have encountered my eldest boy sallying through the Bazaar in the early hours of the day, when everyone thought him sound asleep in his bed?" Queen Lezika was astounded by the revelation.

"A loyal retainer followed the young Prince on his return journey and observed him entering the grounds of the Palace via a secret passage in the perimeter wall, adjacent to the old stables."

"Did the man have any idea where my son had been? And to whom he had paid his clandestine early morning visit?" the Queen spoke evenly.

"We cannot be certain of his destination, Your Majesty, for the man encountered the Prince in the Bazaar. He appears to have journeyed from the direction of the Jewellers Quarter."

"Did he now? Perhaps my son should answer these allegations for himself?" the Queen sighed irritably.

"The prince is not accused of any prescribed offence, Your Majesty. It is possible he was merely engaged on an errand?" the Kor'nai replied soothingly.

"My son, the heir to the Argata Crown, has willingly assumed the duties of a lowly errand boy!" the Queen bridled. "I am naturally curious to learn who he visited at such an ungodly hour. His behaviour has been strange these few days past, you would agree?"

"From what I know, he has taken to spending a lot of time alone in his quarters. In of itself, that is no evidence of anything untoward?" the Kor'nai ventured.

"A visit to the Jewellery Quarter in the early hours hardly constitutes typical behaviour for a Crown Prince, Honourable Kor'nai? You would correct me if I were mistaken, my old friend?" the Queen said icily.

"My source merely inferred it was likely the prince had arrived in the Bazaar from there, Your Majesty?"

"I wish my son's activities to be closely monitored. Considering this disturbing revelation, I now harbour grave concerns as to his conduct and desires. Perhaps the foolish whelp has gotten into a spot of trouble?"

"Surely, he would have intimated something, Your Majesty?"

"Discreetly, Honourable Kor'nai, if you please? I wish to know where it was my son went, and to whom he paid a visit. Do we understand one another?"

"I will see to it personally, my Lady!"

"See that you do, old friend?" the Queen sighed irritably.

Bu'khu, June 493 BC

A cavalry detachment of fifty warriors from Neh'ma arrive on the outskirts of Bu'khu shortly after first light the following morning. As the men lit fires for a hasty brew, a scout from the Royal Guard arrived and chatted briefly with the Commander, Captain Ais'gar, over a quick goblet of wodki and scalding mint tea, before returning to the Wharf and his comrades. By the time he returned, *The Flower of Astrach'yi* had berthed and was busily discharging its luggage and passengers. The passengers bade their farewell to Captain Zakhari, who had proved a congenial host, whilst their luggage was loaded aboard the covered wagon. They boarded the carriage and, headed east along the main road with an armed escort towards the waiting cavalry, who were by now ready to move. The promise was for yet another glorious summer's day, with a clear blue sky and the breath-taking panorama of the snow-peaked mountains on the north horizon. *It was a beautiful day to be alive, and a glorious day to die!*

As the retinue reach the reinforcements on the plain, their arrival was watched with considerable interest by a group of men on the high ground concealed at the fringes of a screen of dense woodland, several miles to the south. "Dandy looking bastards, aren't they?" growled Tis'cu, the grizzled and weather-beaten commander of the renegades, who looked older than his thirty-five years.

"We have more than enough archers, my Lord, provided we engage them from the high ground. They won't have a fucking clue what has hit them when it starts" Zargu grinned wolfishly.

"Their mobility will be encumbered by the carriage and the baggage cart" Tis'cu mused happily. "Whoever is in that carriage, I want them alive. Do we understand one another? They might be valuable hostages, given the size of their escort?"

"Are you thinking what I am thinking?" Zargu smiled mischievously.

"It is perfect, is it not?" Tis'cu grey eyes gleam with mischief.

"We can use the valleys as cover as we head west. As long as we don't encounter any routine patrols from Neh'ma we should be well ahead of them in a few hours?" Zargu mused.

"We will make a defensive position on the knoll, with archers concealed in the treeline, and our cavalry poised to attack to the left and right. With the grace of the fate, when the attack commences, they will corral in defence of the carriage. Then we can encircle them?" Tis'cu grins wolfishly.

"I humbly request the honour of leading the right flank, my Lord?" Zargu asked hopefully.

"You can take the left, old friend, and have the honour of leading the attack from the front. I will engage from the rear and destroy them. Victory will be yours this day, I promise you!"

"I will inform the men and get them ready to move" Zargu nodded solemnly.

"With this action, we could turn the tide of the war! The Gilded Whore of Archaeopolis will weep bitter tears and poets will sing sonnets of *The Sons of Savan*!" declared Tis'cu.

The Sons of Savan, one hundred and seventy seasoned veterans, had good reason to be supremely confident of victory. Within a mere few hours, they would be positioned to launch a devastating attack against their hated enemy. The Argata would pay a heavy price for this day's foolishness.

What could possibly go wrong?

Prince Disch'al was blissfully unaware that he had been followed, ever since he had left the grounds of the Royal Palace. He had visited Avielle the previous night, but had, unbeknown to him, lost his tail in the warren of alleys of the residential quarter north of the Bazaar. His watchers were fearful for their lives, having received a stern rebuke from their controller, yet these men were now certain that whatever the Crown Prince's ultimate destination was, this was no random expedition. Prince Disch'al was secretly visiting someone twice a day, at first and last light. *They must determine who this was, and, what hold they exercised over the heir to the Argata Crown!*

Sweet little Avielle was besotted with her charming Prince and was blissfully unaware of the gravity of their togetherness. She had begun to cherish his clandestine visits, and even pined for him once he had left. The prince felt the same, which is why he kept his promise. This morning he carried a small flagon of apricot wodki and a knife, which he used to cut a pink rose from a flower garden by the fountain in the Central Square. His stalkers were bemused by such innocent courtesy, for only a girl could kindle such chivalry! *The young Prince was in love, was he not? But for whom did his heart pine with such ardour?*

They watched with interest as he made his way through the Bazaar, eerily empty at this hour, for it would be another hour before the fruit sellers arrived and set-up their stalls. Once the wayward Prince reached the Jeweller's Quarter, he dived into the anonymity of the covert of backstreets. Disch'al was nobody's fool and, fearing he may have attracted the attention of a gang of thieves, he elected to take a circuitous route, weaving back upon himself, loitering at the corner of passages, concealed in the shadows, until he finally arrived at the rear of Mesticrates premises. He checked left and right, and scaled the wall with ease. He did not see his pursuer skulking in the shadows at the corner of an alley a short distance away, nor did he hear his muffled cackle. This man knew the identity of the Jeweller, and of the little dove who had, astonishingly, stolen the heart of the heir to the Argata Crown. *Her name was Avielle!*

When Disch'al left, some two hours later, his heart was bursting with a joy that he had never felt before! *Would his friends even believe him?* He had kissed his first girl, fully on the lips, and savoured her sweetness! Sweet little Avielle, now alone in the shop awaiting her master's arrival, sighed blissfully.

She was truly no longer a slave!

Eastern Plains, June 493 BC

"This place is worse than Hades! How could anyone live here?" the Royal Princess Sychoria gazed distastefully at the unforgiving landscape, rocky and threadbare of greenery.

"They don't, my love, for there is no major river and the soil is unsuited to cereals or grazing, even to the hardiest of goats" replied the Crown Prince. "From what I have heard, this is worst of it. We should be free of it within a few hours at the most. Thereafter, the landscape is far prettier."

"I still cannot fathom why anyone would put a major port in a place like this. It is brutish, is it not?" Sychoria mused grimly.

"It is rich in mineral ores, including gold. That, in addition to the strategic significance of the promontory, is why the Argata sought to take it from the Armenians in the first place" Voskar mused airily.

The hinterlands of the promontory were an alien landscape to an Orch'tai native sired in the lush pastures of the floodplains of the Wol'yi or the Uras'ka, barren of both greenery and settlement. Nevertheless, the landscape, as bleak and as unforgiving as it was, inspired awe in all those who gazed upon it, and might even be described as majestic, in a raw and rugged way. The soldiers were understandably wary, for treachery could lurk, concealed and ready to pounce, at every step along the meandering track as they headed east. The Argata scouts were in the lead, the main contingent of their comrades some distance to the rear, within sight of the Orch'tai Royal Guard who shadowed the carriage, whilst the remainder of the Argata Royal Guardsmen formed the rear-guard. Despite the raw desolation of the place, there was comfort in knowing that only a reckless and desperate foe would dare to mount an attack on such a large contingent of professional soldiers, given such scant cover, and security of escape.

A few hours later, the caravan duly halted some distance from a forbidding pass at the foot of a canyon. The entire left flank was shadowed by an imposing massif, perfect for enemy archers, with cavalry in reserve. The soldiers were understandably coy and had judged the pass to be a perfect 'killing ground' for an ambush. The rearguard, comprising thirty veterans of the recent Armenian campaign, instinctively turned their horses to face any threat from the rear.

"Why have we stopped?" the Royal Princess sighed irritably.

"I will endeavour to find out, my rose. Do not trouble yourself, I beseech you" the Crown Prince smiled thinly.

Voskar was desperate to allay his wife's fear, for he well understood the danger of their passage through this hostile terrain. He opened the door and stepped out into the blinking sun, closing the door firmly. Instinctively, his right hand touched the pommel of his sword, and he smiled grimly as he stepped away and sought out the Argata Commander, nodding respectfully before he spoke. "Is there a problem, Captain Nakh'ga?" the prince asked softly, indicating by his pitch that it was wise not to upset the ladies.

Captain Nakh'ga smiled respectfully. "As you can see, My Lord, this next phase in our journey presents obvious difficulties?" the young Captains eyes sparkled briefly with mischief, almost as if he relished the prospect of action.

"We have archers, do we not?" the Crown Prince nodded at Kai'vygh, Commander of the elite detachment of the Orch'tai Royal Guard.

"We do, my Lord! We were simply appraising the lie of the land" the Argata Captain smiled thinly.

"I fear that time is of the essence, if we are to reach our preferred camp before nightfall?"

"I assure you, my Lord, that it has not escaped our notice. Now, if you care to avail yourself of the security of the carriage, then we can be on our way. The scouts have signalled that it is safe to move" the young Captain, aged perhaps in his middling twenties, spoke respectfully.

"As you are, Captain Nakh'ga" the Crown Prince grinned, and paced back towards the carriage.

The retinue canters at a steady pace along the rocky path and soon enters the pass, the gateway to a narrow canyon bordered by rugged and breath-taking uplands. The soldiers had every right to be wary for, if they were engaged by archers from the high ground on either flank, this would prove a perfectionist's death trap! The Orch'tai Royal Guard shadows the carriage on either side, longbows at the ready, as they eye the massif grimly. Whilst they had never faced Armenian renegades, they had been briefed on their tactics and capabilities prior to departing Mamy'eva. Bitter personal experience in the hinterlands of the Uruk Mountains had taught that a landscape such as this presented enticing opportunities for ruthless and determined assailants. *Local bands of renegades would surely never look such a gift-horse in the mouth?*

To their relief, the convoy cleared the canyon without incident and entered a wide expanse of grassy plain, dominated in its centre by the course of the River Naya, and bordered on its northern and southern flanks by high ground. It would take a little under three hours to reach the stronghold of Neh'ma, burdened by the carriage and baggage wagon, whereas cavalry could have covered the distance in less than two! Whilst the next phase of the journey was not without foreboding, there was some comfort in the knowledge that any attack must now be spearheaded by cavalry, pitting bloodthirsty and ill-disciplined cut-throats against the finest horsemen in the world, on a battleground offering them supreme advantage of training and experience. It would be nothing short of massacre? *In such a landscape, fortune favours the skilled and disciplined, rather than the desperate, no matter how motivated or brave!*

On the high ground to the south, concealed by an outcrop of rocky massif, Tis'cu, Zargu, and a small retinue of senior comrades, watched the Royal caravan trailing west towards the Naya. "What do you make of them thus far?" Tis'cu enquired of the assembly.

"They are impressive, my Lord, of that there can be no doubt. They will be expecting a quiet ride for the next few hours, won't they?" Zargu replied.

"That is what we shall grant them" Tis'cu grinned wolfishly at his second-in-command and closest confidante. "We shall grant them safe passage for a pleasant morning, followed by a leisurely evening's respite within the walls of Neh'ma."

"Am I to take it such courtesy will not be extended on the morrow, my Lord?" Zargu grinned.

"But of course, my dear fellow? After all, we are not savages?" Tis'cu grinned. "We shall afford them the courtesy of a safe departure and onward journey, for the morning, at least. I take it we are all in agreement on this matter?"

"We shall extend them all due courtesy in the morning, before granting the grace of slaughter in the afternoon" Zargu hawked and spat on the ground.

"Not the passengers, for they may prove their weight in gold" Tis'cu said sternly, stressing his prior edict.

"With a bit of luck, they will be numbed with the fog of a pleasant evening's drinking" Zargu raised the prospect of an easy day's hunting.

"The Orch'tai contingent may be, but I would not expect anything so rash from those Argata slime. They will keep clear and focussed heads upon their shoulders, until we take them with our swords."

"We are ready, my Lord, and we will not fail" Zargu said emphatically.

"See that you are, my friend? This could prove the most decisive blow we have struck against the Argata for many a moon. Depending on the identity of the guests in that carriage, it may even turn the tide of the war in our favour" Tis'cu mused solemnly.

"Then we shall relish killing them all the more, my Lord."

River Wol'yi, June 493 BC

Her Royal Highness, the Princess Alicharia, stands on the prow of the Royal Barge, surrounded by heavily armed soldiers, surveying the great Wol'yi and its hinterlands on the west and east banks. As far as the eye can see, the plains of the east bank are green and lush, with none of the broken and majestic ruggedness of the western plains. Whilst there was little secret that the young Princess was exceptionally fond of soldiers, she was intrigued and suspicious of the size of the detachment accompanying them north to the Sar'kta Plains. The child turns to the nearest officer, an infantryman, standing a few paces away, and challenged him curtly. "Are you expecting to be attacked?" Alicharia asked searchingly. There was a twinkle of mischief in the child's pale blue eyes.

"Would you expect to be, Your Royal Highness, the Princess Alicharia?" the soldier grinned at the little girl.

"We have enemies, do we not? There are also quite a lot of you aboard this time. More than in any previous year, I would wager?"

"Is there anything else you might have noticed?" the soldier asked inquisitively.

"There are four barges this time, not the usual three. We only require the one, do not? Why are we travelling with an extra guard detail?" Alicharia's eyes sparkled with suspicion.

"And how would the horses travel, Your Royal Highness, the Princess Alicharia?" the soldier raised an eyebrow.

"You mock me, truly you do?" the child grins at the man. "They would travel with their riders, for there is little wisdom in segregating cavalrymen from their steeds! Even an infantryman would be expected understand that" she remonstrated.

"The King's orders were quite specific. We are to keep you safe, at all costs. How did you know I was an infantryman?"

"You have neither bow, nor quiver, but instead have a spear and shield. Your armour is the bare minimum. Cavalry are issued with far better protection, are they not?"

"Do you believe the life of an infantryman is worth less than a cavalryman?" the soldier smiled ruefully.

"I do not! Yet horses win wars, do they not? They are virtually impossible to defeat unless you have archers?" replied Alicharia.

"Who require elevated ground to be truly effective?" the soldier ventured.

"That is true. So, you pick a battleground with a view to defeating cavalry?" the child probed.

"Yet those archers would require protection, would they not? Our enemies are all equipped with recurved bows, every inch as lethal as our own. Yet, clusters of archers sited on elevated ground provide a tempting target, you would agree?"

"And so, we have infantry to protect them?" the child grinned.

"And so, we do, sweet child. Yet, an infantryman must also be able to fight an enemy at close quarters. The armour issued to cavalrymen is unsuited to the vigour of close-quarter combat. It is too heavy, too cumbersome, and not entirely practical" the soldier smiled wryly.

"I follow your logic, I truly do. Yet I do not see how that would work on a barge such as this?" Alicharia chirped.

"We are a floating target, with everything packed tight. In the event of attack, archers would engage first, probably from both the front and at least one bank, and we would assemble to meet that threat" the soldier confided. "That would be a compact mass of suitable targets, you would concur. Our own cavalry would have to moor and disembark to engage the threat."

"And that is why most of the cavalry are in the two barges behind us? We have twice the normal protection, do we not?"

The infantry Commander smiled ruefully, for this was no ordinary Royal whelpling. "The King's orders are quite specific, as I have said. You should not worry about such things, for we have all sworn a solemn oath to protect you."

"I was simply curious, that is all. If it were up to me, I would not even be here. It is a stupid and dangerous way to travel, especially if one is expecting to be attacked!"

The soldier grinned at the child. "As an infantryman, I heartily agree, Your Royal Highness, the Princess Alicharia. Nevertheless, it remains the quickest way to reach your destination."

"If we agree, Sir, you may refrain from using the honorific. You may call me Alicharia" the girl smiled sweetly.

"As you wish, Alicharia!" the soldier grinned.

"As I command, dear fellow" the child grinned back.

At the rear of the barge, Mikhouri and Asel'ya sat on cushioned chairs under a canopy, sheltering from the intense glare of the midday sun. Mikhouri carefully threads a needle to start embroidering a pair of gloves she had made as a gift for her grandfather for the winter months that would soon be upon them. "Where is your sister?" Asel'ya asked sternly, already suspecting the truth of the matter.

"I presume she is busy annoying the soldiers at the front of the barge. She seems to think that we might be attacked?" Mikhouri confessed.

"Why ever would she presume such a thing? We are quite safe, I assure you" Asel'ya quipped.

"You cannot fool her, Asel'ya, you surely know that by now?" Mikhouri chided.

"I didn't wish to give cause for alarm, my Lady" Asel'ya whispered softly.

"We are travelling north with almost twice the number of men as in previous years. That was always going to arouse her suspicion" the girl smiled wryly. "Alicharia is obsessed with soldiers, as well you know. She talks to the Guards at the Palace at every opportunity. She wants to be one when she is older."

"Now, there is a fine vocation for a Royal Princess! Though not one that is naturally suited to motherhood."

"I cannot imagine Alicharia as a mother, can you?" Mikhouri giggled hysterically. "She would dress her daughter's in uniform. Their toys would be instruments of war; bows, spears, swords, and shields."

"Your sister will soon learn acceptance of her feminine fate. She cannot escape it. It is not in our nature to be instruments of violence" Asel'ya mused airily.

"We are Scythians, are we not? We are not as war-like as the Sauromatae and their *Amazons*, but Scythian women wage war, do they not?" Mikhouri countered.

"The Sauromatae are a brutish people, young Lady, and are quite unsuited to a civilised supper table. They are not role models I would commend to a Royal Princess!" Asel'ya sneered.

"Alicharia is enchanted by them. She wants to be just like them when she is older."

"Does she also hope to grow horns, a tail, and cloven hooves?" Asel'ya mocked.

Mikhouri giggled. "You cannot frighten her with such nonsense, Asel'ya, surely you know that? Alicharia is far too intelligent to fall for it anymore."

"Your sister is far too clever by half! Your father, for all his virtues, has indulged her once too often. It is high time her baser nature was bridled, if your mother hopes for a suitable husband."

"Best wishes in your endeavour, fair Asel'ya, but I would expect to be beat" Mikhouri snickered.

"Whipped, you say, by a mere whelpling? Perish the thought?" Asel'ya sneered.

"This is no ordinary whelpling" Mikhouri grinned. "Alicharia hopes to conquer the world when she is old enough. She wishes to wage war with Persia, the Hellenics, and then tame the threat from the east forever."

"Your darling sister must learn her place in the world. The sooner her true education starts, the better for us all."

Northern Plains of Armenia, June 493 BC

Thirty Argata scouts cross the bridge across the Naya and dismount, stretching their legs as their horses graze in the plain and drink greedily from the river. The pasture was lush, among the richest in the historic homeland of the Armenians, and the men settle down around hastily lit fires for a brew of mint tea and shared flagons of wodki. The sun was hot, a few hours shy of its zenith, with barely a cloud above, yet the peaks of the mountains on the north horizon are clothed a virginal white. These men were seasoned cavalrymen, veterans of a long war with the indigenous Armenians, and they knew this landscape almost as well as the hills and plains of their birth. They had ridden hard since their last rendezvous with the Royal train, several hours earlier. Here they would remain, for the next few hours, securing the

all-important river crossing until the Royal Train arrived. The bridge across
the River Naya had been built a few years earlier and was a glorious feat of
engineering. It was sufficiently wide and sturdy to ferry a convoy from the
west bank of the Naya to the east, including cavalry, baggage trains, and
siege equipment.

Some two hours ride to the east, the Royal Train, its escort, snakes
unwittingly across the grassy plain into a carefully laid trap set by their sworn
enemies. Their effective strength is bolstered by fifty additional horsemen
from Neh'ma. The lead scouts are some distance ahead of the main body
and carriage, yet the plain was narrowing with every rhythmic hoofbeat.
The gentle slopes of the escarpment on either side of the wide expanse of
plain below was carpeted with dense woodland, perfect concealment for a
determined enemy hell-bent on their ruin. Surely, they would never dare
attack such a sizeable contingent. Armenian renegades typically operated in
insignificantly small bands, numbering no more than fifty-to-seventy men.
With the sun now fast approaching its zenith in a clear blue sky, the Royal
Train and its entourage would face the threat of a hundred and seventy
assailants, including mounted warriors and archers!

General Tis'cu had selected a perfect site for a massacre. He had watched
the passage of the Argata lead scouts and tracked their journey far to the west
to the bridge over the Naya. The plain was bordered on either side by rugged
escarpment, broken in several places on its northern and southern flanks, yet
the incline of the southern escarpment was gentler and more suited to a fast
attack by mounted warriors armed with spears and recurved bows. To the
far west, a large re-entrant cleaves the uplands from their highest point, a
dome-shaped pinnacle with gently curving slopes. This was graced by a thin
screen of trees on its brow, which offered concealment for his archers. These
would be the first to engage the enemy from the front. The massif was an
imposing feature and dominated the narrowest point of the plain. Fifty of his
best warriors, all superb horsemen, commanded by the loyal and dependable
Zargu, were corralled in the re-entrant; poised and ready to strike!

In the centre, a quarter of a mile east of the re-entrant, the sixty men who would lead the main attack were in position. These would be led by the General's younger brother, Tirka, in whom he had complete faith. They were tasked with killing the guards and securing the carriage and its occupants. A quarter of a mile further east, far from the edge of the escarpment, some forty veterans of the recent campaigns against the Argata stand poised to engage the rear-guard. Tis'cu had every faith in their fighting abilities, for these were his chosen elite, to be commanded personally. Whilst all his men were superb archers, for the bow was as much a part of their souls as the horses they rode, a detachment of twenty archers, commanded by his brother-in-law, Nescu, lay flat on the grass at the edge of the central escarpment, stalking their quarry. These were not the mindless brutes proclaimed by the Argata to the world, for they were a proud *family*, bound forever by blood, honour, and a litany of past injustices. All were motivated by a keen desire to avenge the insults inflicted by the hand of this most recent violator of their lands, their kin, and their birthright.

General Tis'cu smiled thinly as the vanguard of the Royal caravan cantered ever closer to his position, as he lay flat on the grass in the centre next to Nescu and his archers. He turned to Nescu and whispered in his ear. "Are you ready, brother?"

"We are ready, my Lord. We will hit them as soon as the baggage wagon reaches us, just as you instructed" Nescu grinned conspiratorially.

"Do you have any thoughts on the plan of attack? I would appreciate your honesty, my brother, as I always have."

"I am confident of both the range and our marksmanship" Nescu grinned. "We will aim to kill as many of those flash Orch'tai bastards as we can before Tirka, and his men make their charge. That will be their best hope of survival in the early phases of the attack. Once they are on their way, we will continue firing right up until they close. If the passengers remain within the carriage, they will be in no danger from us."

159

"Good man!" Tis'cu said emphatically. "This day we will have revenge upon this infernal plague that has violated our lands, our families, and our birth right, for far too long."

"I look forward to killing this filth! I wish only to repay the insults they have wrought upon us as much as any man under your command!" Nescu replied.

"Happy hunting, fair brother, for the hour of deliverance is nigh!"

Tis'cu scurried away on hands and knees a safe distance to the rear of the escarpment, where Tirka and his men readied to mount their steeds and lead the main charge. Confident in the assurance that he could never have been seen by the Argata vanguard on the plains below, he stood and strolled casually across to his younger brother. Everything was ready, nothing had been left to chance, and there was no prospect of failure on this most glorious day. Death would come to this most hated invader and victory would be theirs.

It had been ordained by will of the Gods themselves!

Queen Lezika received her Kor'nai in her Private Chamber later that afternoon. "Our Guests should have arrived in Bu'khu early yesterday morning, should they not? With any luck, there might even be rain in the next two days?" the Queen smiled thinly.

"Have you made your decision concerning the Royal Prince Sea'gir and the Princess Alicharia?" the Kor'nai enquired.

"I think the Princess Alicharia would make a fine match for my youngest son. Though she is distant in the line of succession that could easily change, should she bear a son?" the Queen mused breezily.

"I would concur with that assessment, Your Majesty" the Kor'nai replied.

"I also hear that she takes after her mother and is quite the cutie, if not a little badly behaved on occasion."

"She is a mere whelpling, Your Majesty, yet she will flower over the next few years" the Kor'nai replied.

"Speaking of whelplings, have your agents brought further tidings of my wayward boy?" the Queen eyed her most trusted Counsel closely.

The Kor'nai sighed sadly and shrugged his shoulder apologetically. "They do, Your Majesty! I fear this may be graver than I initially thought."

The Queen blinked. "How so, my most trusted Counsel? Is my child in peril?" she eyed the old man sternly.

"I fear he is sickened in both heart and mind?"

"You surely cannot be serious? *He is a mere boy!*" Lezika remonstrated hotly.

"And she is a mere *girl*, Your Majesty?"

"Who is this infernal little minx?" the Queen demanded.

"My agents have established that the young Prince has been regularly visiting a certain premises in the Jeweller's Quarters, belonging to Mesticrates. The man has a girl, a slave from Gaul named Avielle. She is a year or so younger than Prince Disch'al. I regret to inform you that the prince has been taking her tokens of affection, roses and such like."

"A slave girl, you say! And this brute has bewitched my darling child?" the Queen was incensed.

"She is a pretty girl, by all accounts, my Lady, and we know nothing of her heritage, do we?" the Kor'nai cautioned.

"What would you suggest we do?"

"Given their age, Your Highness, this may be nothing more than mere friendship. The prince is well known for his kind heart and sweet disposition. Perhaps he has merely found an intriguing new playmate?"

"And if this were more serious than that?" Lezika pressed.

"I cannot begin to fathom how the prince could expect a friendship with a slave girl, however affectionate, to have any meaningful future?" the Kor'nai ventured.

"It is decided, my Honourable Counsel, let my son continue with his clandestine visits to this girl, at least until our Royal visitors arrive. In the meantime, I will have a little chat with him about his obligations and his future" the Queen sighed.

"I think that the wisest course of action, for the present, Your Majesty" concurred the Kor'nai.

"For the present, that is my command" the Queen said coldly.

Nescu waited patiently at the edge of the escarpment as the carriage cantered steadily towards them in the centre of the plain below. The vanguard of thirty Argata cavalry had halted some distance from the re-entrant and massif at the far end of the valley to allow the carriage and its bodyguard to draw close. Once the distance had closed, the vanguard would advance at the gallop to clear the valley and secure the plains, which furnished excellent vantage on all sides. The river and bridge lay several hours ride further west. The carriage was now almost level, and Nescu licked his lips in anticipation of the slaughter that now lay within his grasp. The carriage, which was driven by two of the most stunning horses he had ever seen, passes by and the lumbering baggage wagon and its stout ponies drew ever closer. Nescu's hand tightened around the grip in the centre of his recurved bow. "Let's make sure we miss the horses, eh?" he hissed softly to his men. "On your feet, you glorious bastards! Let us give this heathen filth a death they so richly deserve!" The men on either side were on their feet in an instant. Arrows were notched and bowstrings drawn taut, as the men elevated their aim to an angle of some forty-five degrees, awaiting the command. "Loose!" Nescu roared. The bowstring slapped hard against the leather gauntlet encasing his left wrist.

Miraculously, the horses were spared, but six of the Orch'tai Royal Guards were down, felled in an instant, likely dead before their bodies hit the dirt. The surviving Guardsmen on the nearest side of the carriage unfroze and dismounted, scattering like rabbits to form a defensive screen, several yards to the front of the carriage. The driver yelled a warning to its occupants, before vaulting agilely from the cabin and racing to his comrades, his own recurved bow in hand. "On my marker!" Nescu yelled, aiming his weapon at a slightly higher angle so that his arrow would fall short and target the ever-increasing screen of bowmen, fortified by Guards from the opposite side of the carriage, who raced to bolster their thin defensive line. Nescu loosed. He and his comrades now waited with bated breath for the arrow to strike. "Draw!" he bellowed, following with a brief pause. "Loose!" he roared, smirking in triumph as his arrow took an Argata bowman in the chest. The man had only just reached the line and now fell dead. The men release their volley and cheer, before notching another arrow and taking aim. "Draw!" The command came, followed by the pause. "Loose!"

"On! You bastards! On!" Tirka roared, as he kicks heels in the flanks of his steed and gallops towards the brow of the escarpment. His men, loyal and true, follow swiftly behind and the stream of riders roar their battle-cry as they clear the brow and thunder down the incline towards the thin line of horrified Guardsmen. The rear-guard were galloping frantically west to engage them, yet Tirka kept his focus on the defensive screen to the front of the carriage and baggage wagon. "Draw!" Nescu commanded, glancing quickly at the plain below. The vanguard shuffle quickly into staggered files, two ranks deep, facing the threat of Zargu's contingent as it bears down from the west, readying a charge at their hated enemy! "Now, you glorious bastards, make this count!" Nescu roars at his men. This would likely be their last salvo, and it was surely the most important, for it could thin the line of bowmen who now stood defiantly, aiming their bows at Tirka's warriors, as they bore down upon them with a terrifying certainty of victory. Then, within an instant, everything changed!

Death had come to the field, and its spectre wore a grisly guise.

Sar'kta Plains, June 493 BC

The yearling filly was a stunning creature, one of the Crown Prince's finest, sired from a noble thoroughbred line. She was a little above the average withers for her age, with a pelt of the most luxuriant chestnut. She had a white stripe from her forehead to her muzzle, a vestige of her esteemed pedigree. The Crown Prince led the eager child across to meet her. "What do you think of her, sweet child?" asked the old man.

"She is truly beautiful, Grandpapa, but will she carry my weight?" cooed Alicharia.

"You are still young enough to ride on my shoulders, are you not? She may look a little skinny, especially compared with her peers, but she is only a yearling. She has good stamina and I think she would suit you perfectly."

"Grandmama surely won't let me ride her, will she?" Alicharia sighed sadly.

"She allowed your sister to ride at your age. Horses are in our blood, are they not? Without them, we would not even exist?" the old man opined.

"Is that really true?" Alicharia quipped.

"Of course, it is true, little rose. We are descended from ancestors who first domesticated these fine beasts from their wild progenitors. We owe everything we are to them."

"Can I ride her? Please?" Alicharia beseeched.

"Not today, for you require a saddle. I think there may be one that would fit her, and you, but it might have to be modified" the old man smiled as the child gaped in bewilderment. "I will ask Yur'ki the saddler for advice. You will be able to ride her in a few days, I promise."

"Mikhouri rides well, does she not?" the younger girl nodded to her elder sister, riding in the meadow to the east.

"Your sister seems comfortable in the saddle. It suits her." The old man waved at the older girl, who now obediently trotted toward the pair. "How are you finding him?" the old man asked as his Granddaughter slid cautiously from the saddle.

"I love him! He is so easy to ride" Mikhouri gushed happily. "I had forgotten how peaceful it is here?"

"You haven't even pressed him. He can certainly gallop and has excellent stamina. Perhaps he would make a good stud, even at his age?"

"Mother and father don't often let me ride at home. They say it is far too dangerous, what with the traffic in the streets and such" Alicharia mused glumly.

"The joys of city living, how well I remember them? You couldn't drag me to that flea-pit, not unless I was already dead, of course?" the old man mocked.

"Not even to the Royal Palace?" Alicharia teased.

"Still a hotbed of intrigue, is it? I shouldn't wonder with the way things are right now?"

"Why would you say that?" Alicharia glanced quickly at her grandfather, then at her sister. Neither the old man, nor the elder girl, cared to enlighten her on the malaise which plagued both King and Duchy.

"Are you hungry? I am sure you must be? Let us go back to the farmhouse. I am sure that your grandmother has prepared a midday meal for us. The sun will be too hot soon enough."

"No-one ever tells me anything!" Alicharia sighed morosely as the pair trooped along the dusty track towards the farmhouse, a short distance behind the old man.

"You promised to be good, remember?" Mikhouri cautioned. "We are children, Alicharia, and there are things that we are simply not permitted to hear."

"Is the Duchy in trouble?" Alicharia asked searchingly. Her blue eyes twinkle with mischief.

"Let it go, Alicharia! These are things that do not concern us" Mikhouri implored.

The arrival of Tis'cu's mounted warriors, their valiant commander in the lead, was heralded by cheers as they thunder down the incline to close with the massed rear-guard. The Argata Commander forms his men into staggered files to face the threat from the south. The archers of the Royal bodyguard, Argata and Orch'tai, loosed a murderous volley at the closing wedge of Tirka's horsemen, and Nescu saw his brother-in-law fall from the saddle, almost certainly dead, alongside at least eight of his comrades. To the far west, an almost two-to-one superiority of Zargu's warriors ensured the melee was currently going their way, despite heavy losses sustained by a murderous volley of spears from the Argata horsemen, who charged to close with a ferocity that was blood curdling. Suddenly, the screams of the dying and the peals of clashing swords were drowned by a herald of trumpets. From his vantage point high on the escarpment, Nescu stares aghast as three columns of Argata cavalry, some two-hundred-and-forty men, morphed from woodland on the horizon of the northern escarpment to stream across the plain towards the melee below.

"Where the fuck did these twats come from?" Nescu bawls petulantly, all certainty of victory eclipsed by an equally chilling certainty of doom, when the man standing next to him grunted and dropped, an arrow-point protruding through his chest, unleashed by an unseen enemy that had fastened without warning. Nescu turned to face the threat from the rear and died instantly, and arrow punching through his heart, as his men fell all around him. A force of sixty Argata warriors had infiltrated the southern escarpment, tethering their horses in a patch of woodland a mile to the south and advanced to contact on foot, armed with spear, sword, and lethally accurate recurved bows, taking advantage of the low ground where they would not be seen by their prey. Nescu's men were slaughtered in a mere matter of seconds, and their hated enemy race forward to form two staggered ranks, turning sharply at an angle with parade-ground precision, notching arrows, before taking careful aim at Tis'cu's horsemen as they close with the rear-guard. "Loose!" the Commander roared. A hail of arrows hissed in the air, looping high, to dive murderously upon their hated foe!

The three streams of Argata cavalry thunder down the rocky slopes of the northern escarpment to engage the remaining Armenian horsemen in the west, centre, and east of the valley. To the east, Tis'cu parries a slash from an attacker with expert skill and skewers the man in the throat. "Filthy scum! Argata pig-shit!" he screamed his challenge to the next man when, suddenly, an arrow took him in the side and topples him heavily to the dirt. He was quickly finished by a thrust of a spear-point to the throat. *Death had come, and victory was assured.*

The Armenians, who had never massed in such strength, were soon slaughtered to a man by a merciless and vengeful foe. It was sheer serendipity that had led to the discovery of a camp on the southern plains of Bu'khu by a routine patrol from Neh'ma, two nights earlier. The warriors had returned to the garrison to inform the Commandant of an enemy presence on a hitherto unprecedented scale. The Commandant, the scarred and prickly General Tuly'si, had quickly determined that such a concentration of the enemy boded certain disaster for the Royal caravan travelling west.

The Old Count sat alone in his study, a medicinal goblet of wodki on the table to his right, reading an old fairy-tale, composed almost an eon ago, then faithfully recorded for future generations, when he was pricked by a sense he was no longer in solace. He glanced up to see Alicharia, standing in the open doorway, gazing at him silently. "What are you doing up and about at such a late hour, my petal?" said the old man.

Alicharia yawned tiredly. "I couldn't sleep, Grandpapa."

"Come and sit down, child. I will fix you some warm milk and honey. Would you like that?"

"Yes please!" Alicharia sighed happily.

A little while later, Alicharia was snugly curled in her grandfather's lap, sipping a cup of warm milk, generously laced with honey from the hives of his estate. "Is something troubling you, little rose? Perhaps you miss your mother?"

"I do, obviously I do, but it is lovely to be here" Alicharia spoke softly.

"Your sister intimated the contrary, sweet child? Perhaps you are not as honest as she?" the old man teased lightly.

"Mikhouri talks too much. Everyone say's so, didn't you know? She is quite the jabberer!"

"You would have much preferred it if Grandmama and I visited Mamy'eva, would you not?"

"Asel'ya also talks too much" the little girl sighed. "Why have the soldiers stayed here? It is not what they usually do, is it? Has there been trouble here lately?"

"No, darling child, there has not. I would scarcely have acquiesced to your visit if there had been so, would I?" he ruffled his Granddaughter's hair affectionately. "The King is rightly concerned for your safety, and that is all. The soldiers will remain here for a week or so and then return to Mamy'eva."

"So, the Duchy *is* in trouble?" Alicharia sighed despondently.

"There is little which escapes your notice, is there, Alicharia? The mysterious death of the King's nephew, young Ach'ti, your mother's first cousin, is a cruel blow to all our hopes" the old Count smiled sadly.

"I never really knew him, though I did like him. Mikhouri was terribly upset when we were told. She cried all afternoon in her room" Alicharia confessed. "I cannot see how his death is a cruel blow to our hopes, simply because he was a man? That does not make any sense. Why do you consider a King to be more righteous a successor than a Queen?" she protested.

"The question of the succession is one that has plagued the Duchy for a generation and more, my love. Yet, it is not a concern that you should trouble your sweet little head about."

"And why should I not? Is it because I am a little girl? Yet, I will not be a little girl forever, will I? One day, soon enough, I shall be a woman, and this woman will take no such Counsel from a *mere* man!" Alicharia spat indignantly.

The old man chuckled. "You have the fire of your ancestors, sweet child. And yet, if we are to prosper, the Duchy requires peace and stability, not treachery and usurpation."

"You think I am a treacherous usurper?" Alicharia quipped mischievously.

The old man grinned. "No, Alicharia, I do not. I think you are fast growing into a highly intelligent and naturally inquisitive girl who devotes more time than she perhaps should to matters that may only spell trouble for her" he rebuked the child lightly. "The question of the succession will be decided peacefully, as it always has been, of that I am certain. As I have said, it is not something you should trouble your sweet head over. It would upset your sister, would it not?"

"Mikhouri and I have nothing to fear?" Alicharia beseeched.

"You have nothing to fear, little rose. Not whilst you are here under my protection. Yet, I would have something to fear from your Grandmama if she knew we were up talking the whole night, wouldn't I? It is time for you to go back to bed, my petal" the old man chided.

"I can't wait to start learning to ride! I will be the best rider the world has ever known!" the girl gushed proudly.

The old man smiled affectionately at the girl, as he led her, hand-in-hand, towards the door and, beyond it, the stairs to her bedchamber in the upper tier. "Do not worry about the soldiers, for they will be gone within the week. I assure you."

Queen Lezika and Counsel received their esteemed visitors, the Princess Sychoria and Prince Voskar, in the Throne Room a few hours after their arrival in Archaeopolis. It was early afternoon, four days after the fateful engagement in the valley, far to the east of the Colchian Plains. The Orch'tai delegation, including the survivors of the Royal Guard, was greatly relieved to be safely billeted within the walls of the Royal Palace. "I deeply regret that you experienced such an arduous and dispiriting journey from Bu'khu, Your Royal Highness. I assure you, my Generals are sitting as we speak, formulating our response to this outrage" the Queen clipped.

"The perpetrators were slaughtered by your gallant warriors, Your Majesty. Surely there is no necessity for any further bloodshed" the Royal Princess Sychoria replied evenly.

"*Really?*" Queen Lezika spat indignantly. She eyed the younger woman with thinly veiled disdain. "We have suffered serious losses, Princess Sychoria. These must be avenged, must they not?"

"Eight of our own Royal Guards perished in the attack, Your Majesty. My husband and I do not wish to hold innocents accountable for an outrage perpetrated in their name by others" Sychoria replied coolly.

"In their name, you say, Your Royal Highness. I think that is precisely the point!" the Queen clipped tersely.

"It is the allies of the perpetrators who must surely pay for the actions of their kin?" Sychoria insisted. "To do otherwise would pour hot oil on smouldering coals?"

"You have a mind for strategy, Princess Sychoria?" the Queen smiled tightly. "I agree with your assessment of the crime, and its remedy. The collaborators and any of their known sympathisers involved in this outrage will be hunted down and brought to justice." The Queen smiled sweetly at the couple. "Given your recent travails, perhaps you might wish to spend time alone in your chambers before this evening's Banquet. I will entreat my Steward to send food, wine, and anything else you may desire?"

"That would be most gracious of you, Your Majesty. We are both tired from our travels and would very much enjoy whatever hospitality you may extend to us" Sychoria smiled sweetly.

"It is settled, Your Royal Highness. I look forward to getting to know you both over the next few weeks. We have much to celebrate, do we not?"

"We do, Your Majesty, and the pleasure will be ours, of course."

Soon after the guests had left for their private quarters in the East Wing, the Queen and her Kor'nai sat alone in Her Royal Majesty's Audience Chamber. The Queen accepted a goblet of watered wine and sipped it gratefully. "Give my Generals full permission to extract whatever penalties they may insist upon."

"These penalties are to be extracted upon the known allies of the perpetrators, Your Majesty, rather than the local populace?"

"I will leave the precise details to my Generals, don't you think?" the Queen smiled slyly.

"I would agree entirely, Your Majesty. This outrage must be redressed as a matter of urgency!"

"What do you make of her?" the Queen asked pointedly.

"You refer to the Royal Princess Sychoria, Your Majesty?" the Kor'nai raised an eyebrow.

"She is a pretty thing, isn't she, if not a little delicate, and more than a little naïve? I have heard her daughters are comely and that the eldest takes after her mother, at least in her appearance. The whelpling may be as ugly as a dyspeptic piglet, for it matters not, as long as she is fertile" Queen Lezika mused caustically.

"I have heard it said the Princess Alicharia is a pretty child. She is a strawberry blonde, or so it is rumoured."

"My elder son might be envious, when the whelpling duly flowers and grows pretty coloured hairs around her treasure. He may feel he married the wrong daughter?" the Queen mocked.

The Kor'nai smiled thinly. "You have heard my opinion on the matter, Your Majesty. So often, that I fear I may be in grave danger of boring you. The young Princesses would make entirely suitable brides for the young Princes."

"Provided my son and heir forgoes his silly obsession with this doe-eyed slave girl!" the Queen's lips tightened with distaste.

"The Crown Prince continues to pay the girl regular visits, in the morning and evening, Your Majesty" the Kor'nai sighed despondently.

"After tonight, he will learn the truth of the matter" the Queen eyed her Kor'nai steadily.

"Of that I am certain. The prince will realise his destiny and renounce his childish infatuation with this little shrew" the Kor'nai smiled tightly.

"I hope you are right, my trusted Counsellor, I truly do" the Queen sighed irascibly.

"The Crown Prince is a good child, Your Majesty, and a noble one. It is time for him to cast his childhood asunder and grow into Kingship. His betrothal is the first of a great many steps to his becoming."

"You are quite right, of course, Honourable Kor'nai. This slave girl is nobody, after all? We have absolutely nothing to fear from her, you would agree?" the Queen eyed her Kor'nai evenly.

"She is a *mere* child, Your Majesty, who poses no threat to the realm. I assure you of that."

"See to it that she remains so, Honourable Kor'nai, I beseech you?" the Queen said curtly.

His Royal Majesty, The Crown Prince Mor'kur, loyal consort of Queen Lezika of the Royal House of the Argata, doting father to his beloved sons, The Royal Princes Disch'al and Sea'gir, knocked lightly on the door to his eldest son's chamber. "Come" a voice commanded from within. Mor'kur opened the door and appraised his eldest boy with affection. "We may yet make a Royal Prince of you, my son?" he smiled wryly.

The Royal Prince appraised himself in the polished bronze mirror. "I am not sure it suits me, father? I would not have chosen such a colour for myself."

"Your mother thought it would suit you splendidly, my son. For myself, I will freely admit I may have had some reservations, though not anymore" said the Crown Prince.

The Royal Prince was dressed in an elegant two-piece tunic and britches, fashioned from the finest oriental silk, dyed a vivid shade of pale green, edged with gold trim at the collar, cuffs, and trims of the trouser legs. "I would have much preferred my brother's outfit, for his is blue, is it not? This is a girl's colour!"

"It is a shade fit for a Royal Prince, my child, and none other. I do feel it lacks something, don't you?" the Crown Prince smiled wryly.

"A sword!" the Crown Prince grinned.

"Something a little more subtle, don't you think, darling child? Especially so, given the travails that befell our guests this past week, you would agree? I had this made especially for you, and for no other." As if by magic, Mor'kur conjured a small wooden box from within the folds of his robe.

"What is it?" Disch'al asked eagerly, unable to cloak his expectation.

It was a gold brooch. It was heavy in the palm, as fine a thousand as ever was crafted, fashioned in the form of a Celtic torc, traditional symbol of prestige and birthright of the Celtic Princes of the Atlantic Coast and, so it was rumoured, even the "Cursed Isles" themselves. "It is beautiful, father, it truly is. It is Celtic, is it not? Yet, we are not, are we?" the boy smiled slyly.

The Crown Prince Mor'kur smiled wryly at his younger son. "As well you know, my child, the Princely Houses of the Argata, including the Royal House itself, have retained Celtic mercenaries for the much of the past Century. Perhaps it is not only your mother who became infatuated with their virtues, for they have many, do they not?"

The Royal Prince blushed and glanced quickly at the floor. "They do, father! More than they will ever be credited with."

The Crown Prince Mor'kur sat down on a chair and indicated that his son should be seated. "My Great-Grandmother certainly thought so" the prince grinned conspiratorially. "She caused great scandal when, as a teenager, she fell in love with, and then married, the eldest son of a notorious Celtic mercenary in the employ of our House. His name was Dubolen. He was a great warrior who served us with loyalty and honour, eventually rising to the rank of Captain of the Household Guard."

"Your Great-Grandfather was a Celt?" Disch'al was astounded by the revelation.

"The Celts are not quite the untamed brutes some would have us believe. They are a proud people, with a love of music and poetry as dear to them as it is the Hellenics."

"So Sea'gir and I have Celtic blood, is that true?" Disch'al grinned slyly.

"That is true, my son, and I see no earthly reason why we should be ashamed of it. The Celts will forever be remarkable and alluring souls, especially their daughters, you would agree?"

Prince Disch'al blushed hotly. "How did you know?"

"Come, Disch'al! You are surely not so naive? Your mother has agents throughout the city. You were recognised, and your movements have been closely monitored ever since."

Disch'al's eyes flashed with anger, and then sadness. "Her name is Avielle. She belongs to her master, Mesticrates the Jeweller. She arrived in Archaeopolis just before the winter solstice" the boy spoke softly.

"Is she beautiful? Is she sweet? Is she virtuous?" his father asked.

"Avielle is all of those things, father, and so much more" the young Prince smiled shyly.

"Are you in love, my son?" the Crown Prince eyed his son closely.

"I love being in her company, listening to the sweetness of her voice, hearing her stories. Is that love?" the prince asked softly.

"And yet, you are to be promised to another. You must surely understand this?"

"I have not even met the Princess Mikhouri, have I?" the boy remonstrated. "I hear tales of her, of her beauty and her virtue, yet I cannot breathe her."

"As you have breathed this lowly Celtic child?" his father asked, almost dreading the answer.

"Avielle is not lowly! She is a prisoner of a world we have created" Disch'al bridled. "It is not a world of which we should be proud, father?"

"I am sorry, my son, I truly am. You cannot see her again, not after tonight. You must surely understand this?" Mor'kur spoke softly, yet firmly.

"I cannot even say farewell to her. Is this Honour, Father?" the boy chided.

"Your honour is now keepsake for another, my son. Yet, you are right, of course. You must tell Avielle the truth, no matter how it pains her. It is the only honourable course."

"I will see her tomorrow morning. She knows I cannot come tonight" Disch'al confessed.

"And that must be the last time you ever meet. Not as you have been meeting, you acquiesce?"

"I do, father. Upon my honour I do" Disch'al sighed sadly.

Seven

The Princess Alicharia, her cheeks flushed a radiant pink, sits unsteadily in the saddle on to the back of her mare as her doting Grandfather checks to confirm the harness, bit, and reins, are secure. They are at the near edge of the paddock in the far north-east of the village of Sar'kuc, on the west bank of the Illov'ya and the water meadow. In the far corner of the water meadow, a dozen yards from the riverbank, Mikhouri canters gaily on her mare, her equestrian skills improving with each passing day. Alicharia leans forward in the saddle, her knees clenched tightly, to ruffle her mare's mane. She glances down at the Count, who catches her eye and grins. "Does the saddle seem comfortable enough?" asked the old man.

"It seems strange. Are you quite sure I am safe?"

The old man chuckled. "You are high off the ground, little rose. *You* are no longer in control of your destiny, *she* is" he indicated the yearling.

Alicharia looked startled. "I thought *she* was supposed to obey *my* commands?"

The old man laughed heartily. "She is your guide, no more, no less! As you, sweet child, are her conscience."

"This doesn't sound much fun at all!" Alicharia scowled.

"Your sister seems to be thoroughly enjoying herself, doesn't she?" the old man teased.

"Mikhouri is a strange bird, didn't you know? She is soft in the head!"

The Old Count chuckled. "Your elder sister is no longer frightened by the thought of supplicating her destiny to another. You are terrified of the prospect. It is perfectly natural, the first time you are in the saddle, and will remain so for quite some time. After that, you will learn to breathe as one. Your heart, and her heart, will beat as one."

"I don't understand. I am the rider?" Alicharia blinked.

"And she is your spirt, little bird? The more you learn of her, and as she learns to trust you implicitly, the closer you become to being one. After that, she will spirit you anywhere you wish her to" the old man soothed. "She will carry you faster than the wind. For the present, you must become accustomed to one another. If she does not take to you, you were never destined for one another. It is that simple."

"She will never obey my commands?" Alicharia furrows her brow in puzzlement.

"She is not your Handmaiden, sweet child, and will never be your slave!" her grandfather admonished the child lightly. "You can never truly *own* her, but you can *possess* her. You can be as one with her as with no other. She is a free spirit, my sweet. Now, enough of this nonsense, for it is time to ride."

"I don't even know how to get her to move. She seems perfectly happy standing still and eating grass!" Alicharia mused cynically.

"You need to take tight hold of the reins. Are you ready?" counselled the old man.

"Yes" the child grinned.

"Now, make sure your knees are tight together, as tight as they can be. You won't hurt her; I assure you of that? Are you ready?"

"Yes" Alicharia grinned.

"Keeping tight hold of the reins, and your knees together, now lean forward in the saddle and whisper in her ear" the old man smiled mischievously at the little girl.

"What am I supposed to say to her?" the child was quite bewildered.

"*Yoi'ka!*" the old man said softly.

"What?" Alicharia frowned in puzzlement.

"*Yoi'ka!*" the old man bellowed.

To Alicharia's horror, the yearling startled to a brisk canter and headed off towards the far corner of the paddock where her elder sister had dismounted to allow her steed to drink from the Illov'ya. "Waaah!" the child screamed. Her face twisted with rage as she desperately tried to gain some degree of control over her destiny. As the horse and rider sped away at a steady pace, she could hear her grandfather chortling loudly. Within an instant, her whole world changed forever, and she became immersed in a crystal pool of pure exhilaration. As the wind whipped through her hair and her cheeks flushed rouge, she felt her soul soar as never before. Alicharia felt truly liberated, for the first time in her life, supplicating her destiny to another being, an *animal* at that! This was her birthright, for the horse was an extension of her soul. She had heard the lore often enough, that horses were in their blood and that their ancestors owed their very existence to these creatures. "You are nothing without me, and I am nothing without you!" she whispered softly, as her steed slowed its pace to a gentle trot as they approached her sister and her mare. Mikhouri stood grinning at the younger girl as the yearling headed towards the bank of the stream.

As the pair reached them, Mikhouri steps forward to soothe the yearling to a halt. "Whoa girl, easy girl" she spoke softly. "How did you find it?"

"It was exhilarating! There is no other way to describe it" Alicharia gushed.

"Were you scared? It is not unusual, the first time you are in the saddle."

"I was not!" Alicharia protested. "Well, maybe a little, but only a little" she gushed.

"Everyone is scared, at least a little, their first time. It will get easier, as you get used to one another."

"Can I take her home with me? *Please?*" the child implored.

"We have horses back home, don't we?" said Mikhouri. "I am sure Mama and Papa would get you a fine yearling from the Royal Stud, provided you promise you will ride her and take care of her. They are a lot of work,

Alicharia, for they need to be fed, watered, and cleaned up after, especially when stabled."

"Don't we have servants for that?" Alicharia quipped.

"No, we do not!" her sister remonstrated hotly. "You must take care of her, or him, for they will be your responsibility, now and forever."

"I will take good care of *her*, I promise" beseeched the child.

"I will speak to Mama and Papa, when we return to Mamy'eva, I promise you. I am sure that they will get you a fine horse."

"She is the finest I have ever seen. I don't want another horse, I want *her*."

Mikhouri smiled at her sister affectionately. "You have not even named her?"

"Yes, I have" Alicharia grinned. "She is called *Silka*. We shall conquer the world as one!"

Archaeopolis, July 493 BC

Queen Lezika was as angry as her Kor'nai had ever seen her in all his years of faithful service. She paced the polished floor of the Throne Room like a soul possessed. And yet, it was not the sanctity of her own soul that she now felt was imperilled. "What manner of dark magic has this Celtic slave bitch conjured to bewitch my son and heir?" she hissed dangerously.

"From what I have learned of the child, Your Majesty, I have no suspicions of any vile mystery in their liaisons. The Royal Prince is simply fond of the girl, exceptionally so, it would appear."

"My son, the *idiot*, my first-born and heir apparent, has entreated this lowly slave bitch with a token gifted to him by his own father?" the Queen demanded hotly.

"So, it is rumoured, Your Majesty" the Kor'nai sighed. "The child was seen wearing the trinket the morning following the young Prince's final visit to her, and again the following day. She has not been seen wearing it since."

"You think she may have sold it?" the Queen bridled.

"I have my doubts of that, Your Majesty. It is more likely she has realised its true value and no longer wishes to attract any undue attention."

"The trinket in question is the brooch given to my son by his father on the eve of his betrothal to the Royal Princess Mikhouri, is it not?" the Queen probed.

"Indeed, it is, Your Majesty. It was a gold torc, I seem to remember."

"Of considerable sentimental value, you would concur. Notwithstanding the cost of materials and craftsmanship?"

"Perhaps the Royal Prince was merely bestowing upon the girl a token of his esteemed remembrance, now their lives must diverge along their separate paths. For the Royal Prince, it would be a point of honour, would it not? I doubt Prince Disch'al intended any offence to his father" the Kor'nai soothed.

"*Really?*" the Queen enquired icily.

"My agents inform me Disch'al has refrained from visiting the girl since the morning following his betrothal" the Kor'nai seemed perplexed by Queen Lezika's smouldering rage.

"And your agents have witnessed nothing unusual in the daily habits of Mesticrates the Jeweller, my most trusted Counsel?" the Queen's eyes twinkled with mischief.

"I assure you, Your Majesty, they have not witnessed anything untoward. Neither in the early morning, before the start of trade, or in the evening, in the hours after her master has left."

"And have they kept their vigil on the crumbling wall near the abandoned stables?" the Queen raised an eyebrow.

"They have, Your Majesty! I have their assurances on the matter" clipped the Kor'nai.

The Queen smiled thinly. "Perhaps your agents are not as diligent as they claim, my faithful Counsel! If they were so, they would surely have noted a most unusual development in the Jeweller's Quarter these few days past."

"They have reported nothing to me, Your Majesty. I would have informed you of such, you may rest assured of it" the Kor'nai frowned in puzzlement.

"Our mutual friend, Mesticrates the Jeweller, has developed a newfound fondness for rye beer in the course of this past week?"

"Not to my knowledge he has, Your Majesty. And yet, even if it were true, I cannot see how such a thing would be of any concern."

"My own agents have divulged something that presents a most intriguing riddle?" the Queen smiled slyly at her Kor'nai. "Our little Gaulish dove has been observed frequenting a shop adjacent to Kalich's Brewery, leaving the Jeweller's Quarter an hour after her master has left, to return a few hours thereafter. My agents inform me our little dove is in the habit of accepting a lift to the brewery, and back to the Jeweller's Quarter, on a wagon driven by Old Caester's Grandson!"

The Kor'nai glanced at the floor and grinned slyly. *The little Prince had tried to play them all for fools!* "Perhaps it was naïve of me to think the matter would be settled so easily?" Miris'kar apologised unreservedly.

"So, it would appear!" Queen Lezika said hotly. "My son, the heir to the Crown, is now in the habit of smuggling himself out of the Royal Palace on the back of Old Caester's wagon. Safely corralled inside an empty beer barrel! Only Hades would dare countenance such conduct!"

"Have you spoken to the Royal Prince about his scandalous behaviour, Your Majesty? Given the delicacy of the current arrangements, with our esteemed guests, you would prefer it that I should speak with Prince Disch'al."

"The matter is in hand, Honourable Kor'nai, you may rest assured of it!" the Queen hissed with a chilling certainty.

"With all due respect, Your Majesty, is this a wise and just course. The girl is a child, is she not?"

"A child who has bewitched my son!" the Queen bridled. "My son made his father a promise, upon his honour. And my son is betrothed to another, upon my own honour? I have allowed this indulgence of his upon my conscience for long enough! It is time to remedy the matter, once and for all!"

"I see, Your Majesty" the Kor'nai sighed sadly. He glanced quickly down at the polished floor.

For he did see, all too clearly, and Avielle would pay dearly for the young boy's foolishness!

"They certainly seem to be getting the hang of it, my Lord," said the soldier.

The two Princesses had crossed the Illov'ya and were riding in the meadow beyond, with its lush pasture and vivid kaleidoscope of wildflowers, including roses and poppies. Their Grandfather stood in the near corner of the paddock, watching their endeavours in the company of a young Officer of His Majesty's Royal Guard. "They certainly do. I remember full well the joys of learning to ride at their tender age, don't you?"

"I am a simple farmer's boy, my Lord. The only horses we had in the village were to plough the rye and barley we grew" Commander Zu'ki smiled wryly.

"You are an infantryman, are you not? Am I to take it that you hold such majestic creatures, not to mention their riders, in distain?" the old man chuckled.

"It is a beautiful part of the world, my Lord. I could imagine being happy here?" the soldier said woodenly.

"Not for you the intrigues of Court, young man?" the old man smiled slyly.

"Intrigues, my Lord? I am not quite sure what you mean?" Zu'ki's eyes twinkled with mischief. "The Royal Palace has always been fertile soil for rumour, but it is no different from any large garrison. Rumours are to soldiers like the pox is to a whore!"

The old man laughed. "Is there any truth to the rumours of a nascent Sauromatae Confederacy in the east?"

"There is talk of such, but it has been so ever since I was their age" Zu'ki nodded to the two Princesses, who were now giving chase to one another in the meadow at a brisk canter.

"So, there is nothing to it?" the old man persisted.

"We have a strong military presence east of the Wol'yi, my Lord, perhaps the largest in recent memory, both cavalry and infantry. According to the rumours I have heard, these units are currently engaged in aggressive patrols against the Shal'kha, south of the Uras'ka, and in the Western Plains of Kazakh'yi" Zu'ki confessed.

The old man whistled. "So, there is an increased threat to the Duchy, after all?"

"It would seem odd to have such a large contingent of men stationed in the region if there were nothing to fear, would it not?" Zu'ki ventured. "I know a few older Guards who are mercenaries now, providing security for the caravans travelling west. This year, there has been little for them to do."

"Trade along the Upper Darya has been disrupted?" the old man was incredulous.

The soldier sighed. "There is certainly a lot less traffic this summer, my Lord. Then again, it is still early days, for there is at least another month of summer."

"A caravan takes at least three weeks to make the journey from the eastern fringes of the Kas'pa Sea to the port of Olbia" the Count replied sternly. "It is for that reason the traffic is always at its briskest in the early summer months."

"As I said earlier, my Lord, I am just a simple famer's son who grew up and joined His Majesty's Army. I am no expert on such matters, and nor do I pretend to be!" said Zu'ki.

"When did you last hear whisper of these rumours?" the old man pressed.

"It was at least a moon ago, certainly before the last new moon? I wouldn't put much credence in the gossip of soldiers, my Lord, far too much of it is nothing but idle chatter!"

"You are likely right in that regard?" the old man sighed tiredly. "If there was any truth to the rumours, the King himself would have seen fit to intercede in such a delicate matter. We would have heard something, even this far north?"

"Delicate, my Lord, I am not sure that I follow?" the soldier asked.

"Even a simple farmer's boy, and an Infantry Officer no less, would comprehend how crucial security of the east-to-west trade flow is to the *Accord Scythiac*? If it were ever seriously disrupted, it could destabilise peace with the Nur'gat and Ur'gai" the old man sighed tiredly.

"Do you think there might be some mischief afoot, my Lord?" Zu'ki raised an eyebrow.

"Perhaps it is nothing, merely the lamentations of a weary old man. When are you leaving?"

"We are due to leave the day after tomorrow, my Lord."

"Then I shall arrange a feast in your honour? We will dine on roasted hogs and a bull."

"Such generosity would be an unforgivable indulgence, my Lord? We are only doing our duty, after all?" Zu'ki protested.

"My youngest granddaughter, the Princess Alicharia, has grown fond of you this past week" the old man smiled.

"She is a talker, to be sure? And such questions? The like of which I have never heard from the mouth of a young girl. She seems to be obsessed with soldering and war!"

"A true Scythian Princess, wouldn't you say?" the old man chuckled.

"Perhaps we cannot tame the *Amazon* in her, my Lord?" Zu'ki grinned.

The old man eyed the man coldly. "I would be strongly advised to forget any such nonsense if I were you! Do we understand one another?"

Zu'ki was acutely embarrassed. "Forgive me, my Lord, I have misspoken. I beseech you!"

"You have said nothing wrong, young man, and there is nothing to forgive? It might be best to forget such nonsense, for that was a long time ago. We have nothing in common with the vast swathes of uncivilised folk east of the Uras'ka"

"You are quite right, my Lord. We are a civilised people. The Sauromatae are nothing but wild animals. They shall never be tamed."

"They are not, and will never be, wild animals!" the old Count said testily. "And yet, through circumstances entirely of their own making, they are the gravest threat to all we have accomplished in the last Century. You would be strongly advised to remember that!"

Mesticrates the Jeweller was a man of habit and a stickler for punctuality. He rose early in the morning, with the first spears of light, regardless of the season. After a light morning meal of bread, honey, and a goblet of watered wine, he left his apartment in the northeast of the city and made his way on foot to his premises in the Jeweller's Quarter. Now fast approaching the twilight of his fourth decade, Mesticrates had always preferred young slave girls in his employ, certainly not for any improper and disreputable motives, simply because they had always proven more diligent and trustworthy. Young Avielle, whom he had purchased from a reputable trader some eight months earlier, was fast becoming his best employee yet, for the girl was apparently blessed not only with a sweet and charming disposition, a fastidious ethic, but also intelligence. Given her looks, for she was assuredly a pretty child, it would only be a few years before some oaf approached him with an offer for her services, and Mesticrates had long ago learned that it simply did not pay to delve too deeply in to motives of his fellow men! Sweet little Avielle may yet have a bright future ahead of her in Archaeopolis, even as the dutiful wife of a fellow trader, for he would certainly recommend her virtues. Of her vices, none seemingly existed.

Upon arriving at the shop, Mesticrates was astonished to discover that the drapes were drawn, for the girl always opened them first to allow natural light to assist her with the cleaning of the floor and tables prior to his arrival. Mesticrates was perplexed, rather than alarmed, for Avielle was almost as fastidious in her habits as he himself. It was even more of a surprise when, upon entering the front of the shop, he noted that, whilst the place was spotless, the girl had made no preparations for the day's trade! The tables had not been polished since the previous day, nor were the jewellery trays set upon them. *Something was clearly wrong!* Perhaps the child had taken ill in the night? He opened the door at the far end and strolled down the narrow passage, past his office on the left and storeroom on the right and reached the door to the small room at the back of the property, where the child had her personal quarters.

Mesticrates knocked lightly upon the door, yet no answer came. He knocked again, this time with more vigour, yet was rewarded with silence. He tried the door. It was locked from the inside. By now, any irritation he felt at the child's neglect of her duties had given way to a prickle of foreboding, for it was most unusual for the child to have overslept and, even if she had, she must surely have heard him knocking? He strolled down the corridor to the office and quickly retrieved his spare key. He inserted this into the lock and pushed open the door. *Nothing could have prepared him for the sight that awaited him upon entering the room!*

Avielle dangled lifelessly from the rafters, a length of hemp cord fashioned in a noose around her neck, as naked as the day she had been born. Upon her left breast had been pinned a solid gold brooch, fashioned in the form of a Celtic torc, the pin driven through the nipple itself! As the surgeon would later attest, the child had been obviously dead when the grisly deed had been performed by her murderer, for, there was little question that she had been strangled prior to being hoisted from the ceiling! There was equally little doubt that, in the hour or so prior to her death, the sweet child had been brutally raped, perhaps by more than one assailant! *What mind could have contrived such wickedness upon such a sweet and innocent soul?*

News of the murder spread like wildfire among the shocked populace, for such grisly deeds were almost unknown in Archaeopolis. Despite the revulsion and outrage, few would shed tears over the death of a mere slave girl! Upon hearing the news, Prince Disch'al had wept inconsolably. *He knew only too well the unbridled ruthlessness of the woman who had nursed him at her own nipple, a mere decade earlier!*

The Royal Princess Sychoria frowned at her reflection in the bronze mirror. She reached for the small ceramic pot of *blush*, made from ground red Rose petals and white wine vinegar, and dabbed a little on each cheek, etching the colour into her skin with deft circular strokes of her index finger. She re-appraised her reflection and scowled. Her husband poured two goblets of fine Hellenic red and strolled across the room, preferring a cup, which was graciously accepted. "You are troubled, my love?" the Crown Prince Voskar caressed his wife's lower jaw affectionately with his index and middle finger.

"Should I not be so, darling husband? You have surely heard the rumour circulating in the city?" The Princess Sychoria was quite bewildered. Tears film in her eyes.

"It is the nature of commoners to gossip, for they are no different from us in that regard. In my experience they are rarely happier than when they revel in the scandal of their masters" Voskar soothed.

"Do you believe there is truth to the rumour? Do you think it possible the Crown Prince was enchanted by a mere slave girl? And that this girl was the poor child so cruelly slain in the Jeweller's Quarter?"

"I would venture that as children our sensibilities are quite different from those as adults, my love. I find it not in the least scandalous that the Crown Prince was enchanted by a mere slave girl. He too is a child, is he not?"

"How did they even meet?" Sychoria whispered. "Not to mention the high talk that the Crown Prince was gaily smuggling himself from the Royal Palace in an empty beer barrel in order to meet with the poor wretch, quite against his mother's express command."

"And such conduct, even if it were true, is the reason for your melancholy these past few days?" Voskar gazed searchingly at his wife.

"Perhaps such conduct is excusable for a man?" Sychoria replied hotly. "Would you grant the Crown Prince such grace in the matter of his wild oats?"

The Crown Prince smiled wryly. Sychoria was all the more lovely in his eyes when roused to passion. "I must protest, my love. There is no evidence at all that the Crown Prince Disch'al behaved dishonourably. I would venture that his conduct was quite the contrary."

"You accept that Prince Disch'al entreated this girl with a trinket of esteem? And not just any trinket, I might add, but a gift from his father on the night of his betrothal to our eldest child?" Sychoria gaped in astonishment.

"I think the Crown Prince gifted the girl a token of his esteem for her, and nothing more. The little Prince chanced upon a new playmate, a girl-child who both enchanted and intrigued him. Is that so difficult for you to understand?" Prince Voskar smiled sadly.

"That is entirely the point, darling husband!" Sychoria bridled.

The Crown Prince eyed her steadily. "I have heard the rumour, my love. I am not sure I would credit it."

Sychoria turned away to gaze through the window in the Palace yard. "I think we have made a terrible mistake. Mikhouri is such a sweet and loving girl. It would surely break her heart if she were to hear word of such malice" she bows her head in despair.

"These are rumours, my love, nothing more. Do you really believe the Queen would order the brutal murder of an innocent? An act of unfettered wickedness, contrived to remind a wayward boy of his duty?" Voskar whispered softly.

Sychoria turned to face him, as tears streamed down her cheeks. "I don't know what to believe any more, truly I don't? What if the rumours are true? What if Lezika did order the slaying of the girl?"

"Crown Prince Disch'al is not his mother, my love. Surely you realise this?" Voskar whispered soothingly.

"We can only pray, my love, can we not? If he was to grow to be so, it would surely poison our daughter against us" Sychoria sighed disconsolately.

"That would never happen, my love. We shall speak no more of this, for no good will come of it."

Sychoria frowned as the soldier opened the door, without her acquiescence, to usher the Queen's young Handmaiden, Myletia, into the room. At least the soldier had knocked first, yet this breach of courtesy seemed contrived to insult and infuriate her. "How may I help you, young Lady?" Sychoria spoke evenly.

"Begging your pardon, Your Royal Highness, but Her Majesty wishes you to join her for a light repast in the Ornate Garden?" said Myletia.

"That would be quite delightful, young Lady? Will my husband and the Crown Prince Mor'kur be joining us?"

Myletia blushed lightly. "The Crown Prince Mor'kur and your husband have not returned from the city, my Lady." Sychoria noted the calculated disavowal of her husband's honorific with an icy distaste.

"You may lead on, young Lady" Sychoria smiled sweetly.

Sychoria and Myletia left the Master Bedchamber, at the far south of the Residence Suite of the East Wing of the Palace. This was situated on the upper tier and was nominally reserved for esteemed guests. They headed the short distance along the corridor, turning left into the Portico, with its elegant marble pillars, and strolled towards the steps at the north end. These led to the ground floor of the East Wing, which housed the offices of State, including the Kor'nai's private residence. Two soldiers garbed in ceremonial dress courteously open the door and the pair step blinking into the glare of the afternoon sun. The Royal Garden is spectacular, surpassing anything of its kind in Mamy'eva. The layout of the garden is perfectly symmetrical, with two ornate flower gardens facing the entrance to the East and West Wing. The West Wing houses the Great Hall and the Royal Residence, also on the Upper Tier, home to Queen Lezika and her family. The centrepiece of the Royal Garden is a spectacular fountain, directly facing the Throne Room on the Lower Tier of the Central Wing, flanked on either side by an ornate semi-circular sitting area. Here Queen Lezika sat, sipping wine from a silver goblet. On the table next to Her Majesty, sits a silver tray with two flagons, one filled with wine, and the other with water infused with citrus. A second conveys a selection of sweet and savoury pastries. Queen Lezika gazed up and raised her right hand in greeting. Myletia escorted the Royal

Princess to the table and then graciously bade her leave. "I am so pleased that you could join me, Princess Sychoria! We have barely had chance to talk alone since your arrival, have we?"

"No, Your Royal Highness, we have not. I am honoured to be invited to join you here. You have an incredibly beautiful garden."

"I am blessed with a beautiful gardener, Lady Sychoria, though admittedly he is not as fine as those of certain Honourable Counsellor's" Queen Lezika smiled mischievously.

"My husband is quite taken with your blessed city, Your Majesty. It is certainly far sweeter than Mamy'eva" Sychoria confessed.

"Please, you must call me Lezika, for we should be at ease with one another, don't you think? I am pleased you like it here, for you will be a welcome and frequent visitor in the future?" Queen Lezika smiled warmly.

"I would hope so, Your Majesty. I would most certainly not wish to disavow myself of the joys of my future Grandchildren, Lezika" Sychoria smiled sweetly.

"I have heard nothing but good things about your daughters, Lady Sychoria. They do you credit, especially the Royal Princess Mikhouri, who I am led to believe is fast becoming a prefect little Princess?"

Sychoria smiled tightly at the barbed compliment, whose praise did not flatter the Royal Princess Alicharia. "Both of my daughters are a credit to my husband and I, Lezika, as your sons are to you. Strange, is it not, that I have not yet been introduced to the Princess Cordicca? She is surely too young to be married?" Sychoria's eyes twinkled mischievously.

"Cordicca is well, my Lady, and is currently residing in Corinth, where I hear nothing but praise for her accomplishments" Lezika smiled tightly.

"Is she enjoying the delights of Corinth?" Sychoria asked politely.

"She is literate, artistic, and has a taste for all things musical, at least in the opinion of her tutors. You were schooled in Corinth, were you not?" Sychoria nodded. "So too was I, yet in my case I fear my tutors despaired of my endeavours!"

"You are a highly accomplished personhood, Your Royal Highness, and are much loved by your subjects, rich and poor, or so it is said. I would not pay too much heed to the opinions of your learned tutors, dear Lady" Sychoria sipped her wine.

"Do you have plans to educate your children in Corinth, Lady Sychoria? It is an expectation of us nowadays, at least with respect to daughters. In my case, I do feel the fees were an expense well justified, as I am sure you shall in the case of your eldest girl."

"I have high hopes for both of my daughters, Lezika. Alicharia is not, and will never be, a pale reflection of her elder sister" Sychoria replied firmly.

Queen Lezika's eyes flashed briefly, for it was clear that she had found a weakness that might be readily exploited, if not simply for pleasure. "I honestly did not mean to give offence, my Lady. I know only too well the bane of being the runt of my particular litter?"

Sychoria eyes blaze with anger at the insult. "I do not value my children differently, Lady Lezika, for it is not the way of my people. I cannot speak for the culture or practices of the Argata, of course?" she replied icily.

The Queen smiled thinly. "You are quite right, Lady Sychoria. My father always did harbour a strange attitude to women. Our womanly sensitivities are not best suited to martial endeavours, is that not so? And yet, I hear rumour that the Princess Alicharia is quite the little *Amazon*, in her own inimitable way?"

"As is your eldest child, Lady Lezika, or so it is regaled" Sychoria replied with icy politeness.

"The Princess Perdicca is her father's daughter, Lady Sychoria. That much is certainly true. We are a nation surrounded by enemies, on all sides, at least until recently."

"And yet we are friends, Lady Lezika, are we not? For, my husband and I would not be here otherwise" Sychoria smiled sweetly.

"I am curious, Lady Sychoria, for there must surely have been *other* suitable matches for your darling girls? The Nur'gat King Ni'ghul has fine sons, does he not?" the Queen sipped her wine.

Sychoria bristled at the suggestion. The youngest scion of King Ni'ghul, the Crown Prince Mor'gai, was a decade older than Mikhouri and a notorious drunkard and wastrel. "That is true, my Lady, yet neither my father, nor my people, would have consented to such a match. There is something of a history between our peoples, is there not? As there is between you and the Persians, I might add?"

"And yet, my elder daughter, the Princess Perdicca, is happily married to a fine Persian man, as you are aware, my Lady. You attended her wedding, did you not?"

"Have the God's blessed their happy union with a child, my Lady? Have they graced the happy couple with a healthy son, or else a sweet and virtuous daughter?" Sychoria's eyes twinkled mischievously.

"Alas, my Lady, they have not, as yet, seen fit to bestow such blessings" Queen Lezika smiled tightly, yet her eyes flash dangerously. "My daughter is still young, of course. I do hope you enjoy your refreshments, Lady Sychoria, as I have enjoyed your company. I am afraid that I must bid you my leave, for I have a pressing matter of State to attend to?"

"Of course, Your Royal Highness, for grave matters of State must take precedence over all else? That is a lesson my beloved daughter, Mikhouri, will undoubtedly learn in due course." Sychoria flashed her teeth.

"As I am sure you are aware, Lady Sychoria, such an education is a costly investment? I can only hope, as you can, that it will be money well spent."

Queen Lezika rose from her seat and strolled towards the entrance to the Palace.

Mamy'eva, July 493 BC

General Nal'gi reached for a flagon of wodki and fills two goblets. He handed one to his visitor, then sat down, directly facing the youthful Commander, recently returned from his jaunt in the north. "Did you enjoy your recent assignment, Commander Zu'ki? A welcome little furlough from the humdrum of Palace life, I would venture?" General Nal'gi asked interestedly.

"I have never been that far north along the Wol'yi, my Lord. It is a beautiful part of the Duchy" replied Commander Zu'ki.

"I was born there, young man, in case you didn't know? I know of Crown Prince Sor'chir, of course, for my family lands lie to the west. He was merely a Lord back then, obviously, before his eldest son married the Royal Princess Sychoria. Do you have anything of interest to report?"

"As per your instructions, I kept the men occupied throughout our stay in Sar'kuc. There was more than enough work, what with the harvest and other routine administrative tasks. We were little more than glorified labourers, yet it seemed more than appropriate, given the congeniality of our host." Commander Zu'ki confirmed.

"I am sure your efforts were appreciated by the Crown Prince. So, we have nothing to fear in the northeast?" General Nal'gi asked searchingly.

The young infantry Commander was puzzled. "I was not made aware of any explicit concerns before my departure, my Lord. Nor did we learn anything consistent with any increased threat to the northeast sector."

"You are obviously aware of the rumours circulating from the east?" the General probed.

"There have been rumours of a Sauromatae Confederacy ever since I was a child, my Lord! The Sauromatae are too loosely organised, too widely dispersed, and too fractious, to pose any grave threat?" Commander Zu'ki exclaimed.

"I would be inclined to agree with you, Commander. Nevertheless, there is a sizeable contingent of our own people who seem ready to believe such nonsense. And therein, Commander, lies the seeds of treachery, you would agree?" the General mused.

"With all due respect, my Lord, I am not entirely certain what it is you allude to?" the young Commander confessed. "I was not informed beforehand of any ulterior purpose to our mission, and nor would I have expected to be. The young Princess, on the other hand, would have little difficulty deducing your train of thought?"

"*Really?*" exclaimed General Nal'gi. "I presume you refer to the Princess Alicharia?"

"She asks the most searching questions for one so young, especially of military matters! There is little that escapes her notice, I assure you?"

The General chuckled. "I have heard rumour of her interest in the soldiers of the Palace Guard, yet I was not aware this extended beyond mere familiarity. You had never met the Princesses before, had you?"

"No, my Lord, I had not. I was closely questioned by the Princess Alicharia for much of our journey north along the river" Commander Zu'ki confessed.

"In what regard, Commander?" probed the General.

"The young Princess' suspicions were aroused by the presence of infantry and by the additional cavalry. She appeared bemused by my preparations for an attack, however unlikely. I fear the sweet child may be pre-occupied with concerns that the Duchy is plagued by enemies, external and internal."

"Perhaps the young Princess is wise beyond her years? Or else she was simply besotted with you. A young girl, naturally inquisitive in nature, thrown together on a barge with such a dashing young Commander?" the General smiled mischievously.

"Perhaps that is all it was, my Lord. She is an engaging child and made a real impression on the men" Zu'ki replied, blushing hotly.

"Thank you, Commander, you are dismissed."

"Of course, my Lord, and a good evening to you" the Commander stood to attention, saluted crisply, and left the room.

After Commander Zu'ki had closed the door, the General poured himself a generous refill of apricot wodki, a personal favourite that was richer than the plum varieties. The General sipped his drink and smiled thinly. *The rumours were true, after all?* The little Princess did possess a natural inclination to martial ambition. Or, at the least, a sage appreciation of martial affairs! *Such spirit would be a rare blessing in a potential heir to the Orch'tai Crown.*

Especially so, in a scion of this unfortunate dynasty!

Sar'kta Plains, July 493 BC

"I would gladly trade a honeycomb for your thoughts?" Mikhouri chided.

"I was thinking about the soldiers. It was nice having them around, at least for a short while. I miss them." Alicharia sighed.

"I thought you had changed your mind about being here. Are you homesick?"

"I miss Mama and Papa, of course. It is lovely here though, isn't it?" Alicharia sighed happily.

The girls sit on the west bank of the Illov'ya, in the heat of a glorious sun, as their horses graze nearby on the lush grass. "I think we are blessed to be able to escape Mamy'eva and stay here for the whole summer" Mikhouri cooed.

"It is far too quiet now, ever since the soldiers left. Nothing exciting ever happens in Sar'kuc, does it?" Alicharia sighed.

"You might marry a soldier one day, darling sister? If you do so, he will be the one to wear the trousers, not you" Mikhouri teased.

"If I did marry a soldier, he would have to ride better than I, and shoot an arrow better than I!" Alicharia scoffed.

Mikhouri giggled. "You can't even shoot an arrow?"

"Nor could I ride a horse until a week or so, but just see how I have taken to it? I will be a fine archer, and an even better swordsman!" Alicharia declared. "And who will you marry, darling sister? Don't tell me you still pine for that dog-eared little puppy from Archaeopolis?"

"His Royal Highness, the Prince Disch'al, is no dog-eared little puppy! He is a Crown Prince and is the heir to the Argata Throne!" Mikhouri retorted.

"Is that supposed to impress me? I can assure you, it does not!"

"Prince Disch'al is blessed with virtues of which you have no comprehension, darling sister. Sadly, he is cursed with a stern and unforgiving mother" Mikhouri reproved.

"According to the soldiers of the Palace, his mother is cursed by Hades and has horns and a tail. Do you think it is true?" Alicharia giggled.

"She is a Queen, Alicharia? You must never speak so disrespectfully of her. Such crudity is the curse of the commoner, and we are not of them!" Mikhouri reprimanded sternly.

"I was only echoing what I heard from the soldiers. I like listening to the talk of commoners. They can be very forthright, and they make me laugh."

"The talk of commoners is not for the ears of Princesses" the older girl chirped sternly. We are born to rule. We are not, and will never be, the same as commoners. It is the way of the Gods" she protested.

Alicharia stuck her tongue out. "I shall not marry his younger brother. You may rest assured of that" she said firmly.

"You will marry whoever you are betrothed to. We are daughters, Alicharia, and we are supposed to be dutiful" she sighed. "The Crown Prince Sea'gir will grow to be a fine man, perhaps even a fine husband. It is a privilege to be considered a suitable bride for such a fine boy, though you must endeavour to change your ways!"

"What in Hades name do you mean by that? I am only seven years old" Alicharia bridled. "Why should I care about such things? It is all such a long way off."

Mikhouri turns quickly away and espies their grandfather strolling across the meadow towards them. She glanced up at the sky, noting the locus of the sun, which was a little further to the right of the tallest mountain in the distance than it had been some earlier. "You are quite right. We should not talk of such things" she soothed her sister. "It must be time to eat. Come now, let us go." The girls lead their horses towards their grandfather.

"How old will I be when Papa betroths me?" Alicharia asked suddenly, when they were a short distance away from where their grandfather stood waiting for them.

"Hush! We will not talk of such things right now."

Alicharia suddenly stops and turns to glare icily at her sister, her fists balled with rage. "Why have Mama and Papa gone to Archaeopolis this summer? What do you know that I don't?"

"Nothing, darling sister, I swear it! They always go away for the summer, don't they?"

"Why are you lying to me, Mikhouri?" Alicharia spat indignantly.

"What in Hades name is going on?" their grandfather gasped.

Alicharia ignored him and eyed her sister witheringly. "I hate you!" she screamed. "I shan't marry him! I swear it by all the Gods! You can't make me!"

She burst into tears and raced past her dumbstruck Grandfather towards the farmstead.

The Princess Sychoria had elected to take a leisurely mid-afternoon stroll around the Royal Garden at the rear of the Palace. It was another glorious summer's day, blessed with a sky of the purest blue and the barest whisper of a wind. If an enmity existed between Lezika and she in the tender matter of their offspring, it had not soured the blossoming friendship between her husband and Crown Prince Mor'kur. Sychoria welcomed this blooming amity, for it was entirely conducive to the success of their endeavour, yet she could not dispel a gnawing conviction that the guiding hand of the Queen was secretly shepherding this to pastures of her own choosing. She nodded courteously to the Guards, stepped through the doors into the light, and stopped dead in her tracks. Her heart skips a beat. In the far corner of the West Garden, close to the Guard Tower, young Prince Disch'al sits alone with his thoughts. Sychoria strolls across the Pavilion towards the West Garden, hoping to snatch a few words with the young prince, who had been plagued by a strange melancholy ever since their arrival in the Royal City.

"It is a fine day, fair Prince, is it not?" Sychoria hailed the boy from the opposite corner of the garden.

Disch'al turned, blinking in the light, to face the woman. He smiled warmly. "Lady Sychoria! I was not aware that you were fond of strolling in the garden?"

"It is a fine garden you have, young Prince. Finer than anything we have in Mamy'eva!" Sychoria came to stand beside the boy, gazing up at the imposing edifice of the West Tower. "It is a day blessed by the Gods, is it not?"

"I have never been to Mamy'eva, Lady Sychoria. I must defer to her Ladyship's grace" the boy said awkwardly.

Sychoria stifled an urge to giggle and smiled sweetly at the boy. "Come now, Prince Disch'al! I surely do not frighten you, do I?"

"Of course not, my Lady, it was a simple statement of truth."

Sychoria giggled, startling the young Prince, who frowned at her. "You remind me of Mikhouri, for she would have said much the same thing."

"You must miss her? In ways I cannot imagine" the prince smiled warmly.

Sychoria sat down next to him on the lawn. "I miss them as you would miss the sight of the mountains were you parted from them, no matter the season. My children are the most precious thing in the world to me, as you and your darling brother are to your mother."

"I have heard tale the Princess Mikhouri is a sweet and generous soul, every inch a Royal Princess? Is it true that she has a kindling fondness for the Greek ballads?" Disch'al asked.

"She is a little young for Homer, yet she is smitten with the fables of Aesop, and more rustic ballads, those which our ancestors bequeathed to us" Sychoria confessed. "It has said you are a devotee of the Greek ballads, fair Prince?"

"That is true, my Lady" the boy blushed shyly. "My mother insisted upon my private tuition here in Archaeopolis" the boy smiled shyly.

"Would you not wish to attend school in Corinth or Athens, as your sisters were?" Sychoria asked earnestly.

197

"I would, my Lady, yet it is not something to which my mother would willingly acquiesce. At least not until the signing of the *Accord*" the boy sighed sadly.

"And yet the *Accord* is now a year old? The cords of peace hold fast" Sychoria replied.

"They do, my Lady, yet there is the delicate matter of the Persians to consider, is there not?" the boy looked sheepish.

Sychoria smiled sympathetically at the boy. "The Orch'tai and Corinthians are scarcely on speaking terms, yet I never once feared for my safety in all the years I spent there. It was one of the happiest times of my life, far away from the restrictions of Palace life"

Disch'al grinned. "You are not fond of Mamy'eva, my Lady, is that so?"

"I much prefer my husband's estate in Sar'kta, young Prince. For there, even the lowliest beggar is of sweeter soul than the loftiest Courtesan" Sychoria smiled slyly at the prince, who grinned back at her.

"You have not seen much of our Royal City since you arrived, Lady Sychoria? You must at least see it, before you leave" the boy implored.

"A city is a much as any other, is it not?" the woman replied guilelessly.

The boy smiled shyly. "We have a fine Bazaar, my Lady. Several of them, to be exact, and our craftsmen are regaled as the finest in the world, except for the Royal City of Susa."

"I think that you would make a fine guide, fair Prince. My husband spends more time in your father's company than in my own?"

"The Crown Prince is a fine man, my Lady, my father has remarked so. It is little wonder that the God's have blessed you with two obedient and dutiful daughters" Disch'al mused.

"You have yet to meet the Princess Alicharia, sweet Prince" Sychoria giggled softly. "She is not without virtue, to be sure, yet obedience is sadly not among them!"

Disch'al grinned at the woman. "I have heard it spoken of the little Princesses fondness for soldiers, yet I freely admit I found it difficult to accept, for she is a pretty girl, is she not?"

"When she refrains from scowling, it is true!"

"I am sure that you will find many wonderful gifts in our markets, my Lady. We have some of the finest toy-makers and dress-makers in the region."

"I have heard tale of it, young Prince. Perhaps you might accompany into the city one day, for I would be grateful for your company and your keen eye. Was it not you whom chose the gift for my daughter, Mikhouri?" Sychoria enquired.

The pain was raw in the boy's eyes. "I did not, my Lady, a girl who worked in the shop assisted me. It was her choice?" the boy whispered.

"I meant no offence, Prince Disch'al, upon my soul I did not" Sychoria smiled sadly at the boy. "You can talk to me, about her, if you would like to?"

The tears sprang freely in the boy's eyes. Then, without deference to either protocol or courtesy, he stood and strolled away without a further word, heading towards the doors to the West Wing. Sychoria frowned as she watched, for it was clear the boy had been exceptionally fond of the murdered child, regardless of their difference in status. She was not the only witness to the prince's shameless disavowal of decorum, for the Kor'nai had been watching the pair for some time, cloaked in the shadows of the upstairs balcony!

The Mistress Asel'ya eyed the sullen child sternly. Alicharia sat on her bed, maintaining a brooding silence she had affected for several hours. A plate of bread, cheese, and fruit sat on a small table to the side of the bed. "You must eat, Alicharia! You will wither to nothing if you do not" Asel'ya beseeched.

"I am not hungry! I just want to be left alone!" Alicharia spat indignantly. "Why can't anyone understand that?"

"You haven't eaten a thing since breakfast? That is not like you at all, is it?" the Handmaiden sighed.

"You think me porky? Perhaps it will do me good to miss a few suppers!" Alicharia spat.

"I do not think you porky, young Lady, and you shall refrain from putting words into other people's mouths" Asel'ya rebuked mildly. "You must keep your strength up, young lady, if you are to survive the coming winter. What will your parents think of me if you return from here as slender as a hairpin?"

"I don't care what they think! I don't care what anyone thinks of me!" the child spat feelingly.

"Your sister is downstairs talking to your Grandparents. We shall uncover the mystery of what has upset you so?" the woman smiled slyly.

"Mikhouri is a liar! She lies all the time!" Alicharia hissed.

"You have never intimated such things before, so why should I believe you now? Lies are not true to your sister's nature. She is a good girl, as you are, when your hunger is satiated!"

"I don't want to eat! I do not care whether I survive the winter! I care for nothing anymore and I simply wish to be left alone!" the child mused bitterly.

"Do not speak of such things, young Lady! Your parents would be heartbroken if you did not live to see the spring, surely you know that? Whatever it is that has upset you so, then a good meal, and an early night, would do wonders for your troubled soul."

"Why would they be heartbroken? They don't care about me at all. All they care about is selling me off like a slave!" Alicharia remonstrated.

"You are Royal Princess, Alicharia! No-one will sell you like a slave!" Asel'ya chided.

"Yes, they will. And my sister knows all about it?" the girl blazed indignantly. "It may amuse you to learn that my parents plan to sell me to that dreary whelp and his horn-tailed mother. That is my future, is it not?" the child wrinkled her nose with distaste.

"So that is what has gotten you so upset?" Asel'ya ruffled the girl's hair affectionately. "Now we know the source of your bitterness, we might discuss the matter, if you would pacify your woe? Perhaps you would prefer to talk about this with your Grandparents?"

"I don't want to talk about it with anyone! Not now, not ever! I shall not marry him! You can't make me!" Alicharia was on the verge of tears once more.

"Hush, sweet child!" Asel'ya soothed. "You should not distress yourself over matters so distant in your future? Now, young Lady, you will dry your eyes and put on that nice frock I spent so much time pressing and present yourself at supper as a Royal Princess should."

"All so I can marry that dreary little whelp?" Alicharia mused bitterly.

A knock came at the door, followed by a brief pause, then the Crown Prince entered the chamber with a flourish. He bowed respectfully to Asel'ya. "Might I have a moment alone with the young Princess, my Lady?" he asked courteously.

"Of course, my Lord, I will dress for supper" Asel'ya stroked the little girls head affectionately and quickly left the room.

The old man closed the door firmly. "Your sister is very upset, Alicharia?"

"She deserves to be, after the way she has lied to me!" Alicharia mumbled softly.

"No, my child, she does not!" the old man reproved her softly. "Your parents are only looking out for your best interests, and that is all. You will thank them for it one day, I assure you of that."

"Why do I have to marry him? I don't even like him!" Alicharia spat.

"You don't even know him, do you?" the old man said soothingly.

"Do you like him?" Alicharia probed.

"I do not know him, my love. Your parents have never met him, not least until now, yet I assure you they have considerable effort to learn as much of him as they could. They would never broach such an important matter as your future had they not done so, you have my word on that" the old man sighed.

"Mikhouri wants to marry his older brother, doesn't she?" Alicharia eyed the old man steadily.

"She has intimated as much. I think he would make a fine husband, and she a fine Queen."

"I don't get to be Queen, do I?" the child replied sadly.

"You do know your parents love you, don't you? Your future happiness is all that they care for" the old man smiled at the girl reassuringly.

"And I love them! And Mikhouri too! Why did they not speak with me before we came?"

"It is not yet certain that Queen Lezika and Prince Mor'kur will acquiesce to your betrothal to Prince Sea'gir" the old man smiled reassuringly at the girl. "I cannot lie to you, my petal, but your sister will likely be betrothed to Prince Disch'al before the end of the summer."

"Why should they not acquiesce to my betrothal? I am not too ugly, am I?" the girl spat tartly.

The old man chuckled. "You are beautiful, little rose, perhaps even more so than your sister, yet there is the delicate matter of Queen Illir'ya of the Ur'gai."

"Queen Illir'ya doesn't even have kids, does she?" Alicharia quipped.

"Yet, if she were to bear a daughter in the next few years then everything would change. You and Sea'gir are both young. There is much that could change in the next few years."

"Mikhouri will turn ten before this winter's Solstice, is that what you mean?"

"That is precisely what I mean. You should not trouble yourself too deeply over your future, sweet child. It is far too distant to be a cause of such distress" the old man sighed.

"Then we should pray that Queen Illir'ya is with child before the end of the summer" Alicharia grinned.

The old man laughed heartily. "Your sister has intimated that you would like to learn to shoot a bow?"

"I would!" Alicharia said eagerly.

"Then dress for supper, my little rose, and we will talk further about this on the morrow."

Eight

Mamy'eva, July 493 BC

The rider trots along the gravelled path, admiring the majestic grace of the plum trees which adorn the lawn on either side. It had been many years since his last visit to the Summer Palace of Or'vych, yet the place had little changed in the interval. Soon enough, he reached the end of the track and turned north, heading for the Morning Lodge. The rider, aged and weather-beaten, was one of the most celebrated soldiers in the Orch'tai Royal Army. He was greeted by the Chief Steward Guy'nim, who smiled warmly in greeting. "It has been a long time, my Lord?"

"Indeed, it has, old friend!" the General smiled warmly. "I trust the stables are still well staffed?"

"That they are, my Lord. There are still those among us who cherish our traditions. You may follow me, my Lord, for Her Ladyship is waiting? My men will take care of your stallion."

"See that they do, old friend" The General agilely leapt from the saddle and followed the Chief Steward up the steps to the front door.

The Dowager Countess Arialla was seated in the Sitting Room, sipping a goblet of fine Hellenic red when her visitor was ushered through. She rose and padded across to embrace the man she had not seen in more than six years. "It is good to see you again, my Lady. The God's in their wisdom be praised for this blessing. You are holding up, I trust?" said the General.

"I am well, all things considered. The past few months have been the darkest in many a moon" the woman sighed sadly. "It was good of you to come, General Til'koi?"

"I came at my Lady's request, as I always shall. You have my word on that, now and forever" the General said dutifully. "The loss of a son, especially one upon whose shoulders we all placed such high hopes, is the cruellest of blows" the General bowed his head reverentially.

"Thank you, my loyal and trusted friend. You cannot know how such words sustain me at this most difficult time" the Dowager Countess Arialla smiled sweetly at her visitor. She motioned the General to a vacant chair and poured him a goblet of wine.

"How is young Laeschalla holding up to such a crushing loss?" Til'koi smiled sadly.

"As well as can be expected, given the circumstances. Her brother doted on her, as you know?"

"His affection for his sister was always deeply touching" the General sighed.

"The poor girl has been deeply affected by the recent news from Mamy'eva" Arialla adopted a pained expression.

Til'koi smiled tightly. "The grave news from Bu'khu has affected us all, my Lady. Mercifully, the Princess Sychoria and her husband were unharmed in the attack."

"Anyone would think the poor woman cursed. She has suffered two attempts on her life in twice as many moons?" Arialla mused glibly. "I should be grateful the King did not consider my sweet child a rightful contender for the Crown."

"I have heard whisper of the rumour circulating the Palace. There is more than a grain of truth in it, my Lady?" the General sipped his wine.

"The King has either lost his wits, or his Counsel. Even Laeschalla harbours grave fears for the future of our Duchy, as should we all?" the Dowager Countess said despairingly.

"The King and Counsel have consented to these rumoured unions?" Til'koi asked searchingly.

"The King summoned his elder daughters to a meeting three nights ago. They were aware of the betrothal of young Mikhouri to the Crown Prince Disch'al, for that has been the worst kept secret in the Duchy. I fear news of the King's plan for a union between the Princess Alicharia and the Crown Prince Sea'gir came as rather a shock to them" the Dowager Countess mused drily.

"It is settled, then? Queen Lezika and her Counsel have consented to the marriage of Princess Alicharia and the Crown Prince Sea'gir?" Til'koi grimaced at the prospect. He sipped his wine.

"That gilded tramp will undoubtedly press for a dowry which redresses any perceived historic insult against her people, no more, no less!" Arialla smiled brightly.

"I cannot countenance the King's motives, not in respect of the Princess Alicharia. There are many fine sons among our own noble families?"

"I would venture that nothing is settled, old friend. I would never underestimate the resolve and cunning of my dear niece, certainly not least in the matter of her cubs. There will be no public announcement of the betrothals, not until the issue of the dowry has been settled and Sychoria and her husband have returned" Arialla mused bitterly.

"When do you expect them to return?" the General spoke evenly.

"Not for another moon, at the least. There are innumerable obstacles to be overcome, for the Argata have their traditions, do they not? One can only hope that my niece is not totally out of her depth?" Arialla sipped her wine.

"You do not approve of the union of the Princess Alicharia and the Crown Prince Sea'gir? This would surely advance the claim in right of the Princess Sychoria as her father's chosen heir?" Til'koi spoke softly, for this was dangerous and treacherous ground.

"Much as I love and respect my niece, this egregious breach of all we hold dear must be stopped at all costs! Surely you, of all people, must see the danger?" Arialla hissed.

"I am a soldier, my Lady, and I follow the King's orders" Til'koi spoke warily. "I shall speak candidly, my Lady. There is great disaffection in the

Army with this perceived shift in our allegiance. We are not natural allies, the Argata and ourselves, are we?"

"My sentiments exactly!" the woman concurred. "These unions will neither bear the glory, nor ensure the stability, that His Majesty craves. We have an understanding, do we not?"

"As always, my Lady, we do?" the General spoke softly.

"There are others, a great many perhaps, who share in our despair?" Arialla ventured.

"Indeed, there are, my Lady. You may rest assured of it" Til'koi replied emphatically.

"Perhaps the King might be dissuaded from his current course? If not by reason, then perhaps by love itself?"

"Then we shall secure the future of the Duchy, and of our people, by love itself!"

Archaeopolis, July 493 BC

"I trust you enjoyed your day's ride, darling husband?" Sychoria smiled sweetly as she proffered the Crown Prince Voskar a goblet of wine. He removed his riding boots, laid them on the floor next to the bed, and reached for the goblet.

He sipped it gratefully. "I did, my sweet. This is fine country for riding and hunting. Perhaps you might care to join us tomorrow?"

"I think I might, provided our hosts have a suitable mount for me?" Sychoria mused airily.

"I am sure one can be arranged, my love. I shall speak with Prince Mor'kur later, if it pleases you?" the Crown Prince sipped his wine. "This really is exceptional wine, is it not?"

"You are due to meet with the Crown Prince again this afternoon? I presume this is in relation to the dowry?" Sychoria smiled sweetly.

"It is my love" he sighed lengthily. "I am making progress on the most delicate matters, I assure you?"

Sychoria frowned. "You make it sound like pulling teeth? Is there anything I ought to be aware of? My father is most insistent that we succeed in our efforts."

"Forgive me, my darling, for I did not wish to trouble you unnecessarily" the Crown Prince blushed lightly. "There is a specific matter which remains a subject of vigorous discourse. We are making headway toward a common understanding, I promise."

"What additional demands has that haughty bitch made?" Sychoria bridled.

"Darling, please?" the Crown Prince hushed her to silence. "Remember who you are, and where we are? It might be wiser if we talked about this after supper, don't you think? I will have a far clearer idea of the lie of the land by then."

"What are they demanding? One hundred pieces of gold for our eldest, is that it? And what of Alicharia, may I ask? What price has our gracious host placed upon our darling runt?" Sychoria hissed.

"This isn't simply about money, Sychoria? The Argata have their traditions, and they are quite different from ours. That is the impasse we have reached." the Crown Prince blushed furiously.

"*Pri'ciz fornicuja*? Is that the matter to which you refer? Or is it our daughter's honour? What additional demands has this infernal woman tabled to further her son's right to our daughter's honeypot?" Sychoria spat malevolently.

Crown Prince Voskar was astounded. "I was not aware that you knew of the custom, my love. It has not been practiced in our Duchy for more than a Century?" Voskar muttered bleakly.

"I should bloody well hope not! Nor shall it ever be again, I should pray? It is the purview of the heathen Sauromatae" Sychoria spat tartly. "They trade a daughter's virtue for a blood-debt and a train of ponies! They want land, as well as gold.

Voskar nodded. "That is the impasse we have reached, my love."

"And what land, I may ask? The richest pastures in the Duchy, is that it?" Sychoria seethed. "Perhaps they covet the port of Astrach'yi, or of Tanais, or possibly both! There are always the grounds of the Royal Palace of Mamy'eva, for I am certain that would satiate Her Majesty's desire?"

"The Crown Prince is not his wife, my love, and this is a matter between men" Voskar drained his goblet and poured himself a generous refill. "You mentioned this morning you might take a stroll around the city, did you not?" The Crown Prince deftly changed the subject.

"I did, my love, for you have sung its praises often enough" Sychoria smiled sweetly.

"It is a fine city, my love, far sweeter than Mamy'eva, with many fine markets and craftsmen" the Crown Prince smiled encouragingly at his wife.

"I shall look forward to my adventure. Why should you men have all the fun?" Sychoria teased.

"Perhaps we may yet enjoy it together, my love, at least for a week or so? I am confident that my discussions with the Crown Prince Mor'kur will bear fruit soon enough."

Her Royal Majesty, Queen Lezika, graciously accepted a silver goblet of wine from the Honourable Counsellor Miris'kar. She was still visibly reeling from the revelation so recently imparted to her. She sipped her wine and eyed her Kor'nai steadily. "Are you quite sure of this?"

"I observed Prince Disch'al and the Princess Sychoria together in the garden yesterday for a matter of minutes, Your Royal Highness. I am quite certain of what I saw" replied Miris'kar.

"My son was left distressed by whatever passed between them?" the Queen demanded hotly.

"Indeed, he was, Your Majesty. Whatever did pass between the Crown Prince and the Princess, it appears to have touched a raw nerve with the young man" the Kor'nai ventured.

"Do you think this matter is something we ought to be concerned about?" the Queen scowled.

"It could be anything, Your Majesty. The young Prince has not been himself this past week, has he? I do not believe the Princess Sychoria set out to wilfully injure the young pup?" the Kor'nai smiled sadly.

"If you believe that, then I fear you have taken leave of your senses? You will soon be preaching the woman has not a vindictive bone in her body?" the Queen hissed.

"Is there anything I need to be kept abreast of Your Majesty?" the Kor'nai beseeched. "I was obviously aware that you and the Princess Sychoria spent time together the other day? Did things not quite go as well as planned?"

"She rose to the bait, just as you predicted. The Ice Maiden is quite the lioness in the matter of her cubs, especially the younger girl" the Queen smiled thinly.

"That is only to be expected, for she loves her children dearly" the Kor'nai replied evenly.

"I could not care less if she detests them. It is quite clear that my eldest son is not entirely enthusiastic at the prospect of his union with that drab little girl."

"Has he intimated anything to that effect, Your Majesty? I thought that you were pleased at the union with the Royal Princess Mikhouri?" the Kor'nai raised an eyebrow.

"As long as she is dutiful, and fertile, I have no opinion on the matter. It is the issue of the runt, the whelpling Alicharia, which now intrigues me. You have read the recent communiqué from our agents in Mamy'eva?"

"I have, Your Majesty, and think it entirely credible. The union of the two Royal Houses would strengthen the Princess Alicharia's future claim to the Crown?"

"Perhaps we might exercise greater resolve in the matter of her dowry, regardless of the pleasure I derive from needling her mother" Queen Lezika smiled mischievously. "It is clear that she adores the girl, no less than her sister, but if the younger bitch is more valuable to us, there are new accommodations that must be met in her dowry?"

"I take it that you are satisfied in respect of the eldest girl, Your Majesty?" the Kor'nai smiled thinly.

"My husband assures me that they are slowly, yet surely, navigating the impasse of our design" the Queen's eyes sparkle with satisfaction.

"If that is so, then all of our efforts should be directed to a finalisation of the betrothal. As for the whelpling, perhaps the cold winds of reality will soon chill their resolve? After all, they are our guests, and we have more than sufficient time in our favour?" the Kor'nai mused.

"Those are my own feelings, Honourable Kor'nai. Let our guests trouble their own consciences with the matter, at least for a week or so, you would agree?" the Queen mused.

The aged General, long since retired from a lifetime of duty east of the Wol'yi, passed a large goblet of fine Gaulish red to his visitor. They were old friends, almost as close as kin, and the older man, fast approaching the mid-point of his seventh decade, had known the younger General since he was a spotty and eager youth. General Az'nai eyed his visitor with genuine warmth and affection. It had been a long time since they had last talked. "So, young man, how goes the season's hunting in the Western Plains?"

"They are giving us quite the run-around, as usual! They are a hard enemy to break, my Lord, as they always were" General Til'koi smiled tightly.

"Is there any truth to these recent rumours? Not that even a silly old goat such as I would give them credence!"

"Perish the thought, General Az'nai?" General Til'koi protested. Both men roared with laughter and sipped their wine. "You honour me, my old friend, truly you do. This is a rare treat from the swill I have become fond of imbibing!"

"You never give a damn thing away, do you?" General Az'nai teased.

"Such conduct would be tantamount to dereliction in the plains, especially against a foe as cruel and merciless as we have faced?" the younger General placed his drink down on the table. "I suspect you would appreciate honesty, even if it will make for uneasy table-talk at the Royal Palace?"

"Let me do you both a favour and a service, my old friend" General Az'nai sipped his wine and glowered at his visitor with barely suppressed rage. "Sauromatae patrols have increased in strength, tenacity, and in their capacity to penetrate our forward screens. Our supply lines are stretched, nothing unusual in that..." the General raised a hand to silence the younger man, "yet they are more vulnerable than ever to concerted enemy attack. We have sustained deplorable losses to combat and fever, and our supplies are desperately low. You have made enemies in every village in the Western Plains, and in the far reaches of the Upper Darya, and will pay for it. The Sauromatae never let a blood-debt go unpaid! It is a point of honour!"

"We have to feed an army of a size never before deployed east of the Wol'yi. Our orders were to severely restrict the overland traffic from the east. What would you have done differently, Sir?" the younger man smiled thinly. He had not been stung by the older General's words, his tone, or his barely suppressed disgust.

"If you do not know the answer, you are clearly unfit to command!" General Az'nai said icily. "You must withdraw as a matter of urgency. If you do not, then you are finished!"

"The King will not hear of it" General Til'koi sighed.

"The King must hear of it! His reckless adventure against the Ur'gai has made the Duchy more vulnerable than ever. Even the Nur'gat may be inclined to waive their neutrality?"

"What of the Argata?" General Til'koi raised an eyebrow.

"Bugger the Argata! Have you considered the possibility that they might be playing us for fools? In the event this misadventure falls, they are far removed from its consequences!" General Az'nai sighed irascibly. He sipped his drink.

"The King is blindly committed to deepening our alliance with the Argata and with Persia" General Til'koi ventured.

"The Persians want revenge for the calamity at Urzbin? There is not a single community in the Upper Darya, or the Western Plains of Kazakh'yi, who have not heard tale of General Dra'ghiz' exploits" the older General remarked bleakly.

General Til'koi grimaced. "Our agents in the Upper Darya report little else. They have elevated this feral she-bitch, Dali'yah, to an almost god-like status!"

"She brought them victory! There is the not insignificant matter of the young Queen in Khoda to consider, for it is plainly clear that she is no friend to Persia?" Az'nai smiled tightly.

"You think Queen Tae'gryn may have fanned the flames of discontent in the western reaches of the Upper Darya?" Til'koi smiled grimly. He sipped his wine.

"We have stirred the hornet's nest and may yet be badly stung for it!" the older man remarked glibly. "It is my understanding that you met with a Lady, or so I have heard whisper? Perhaps you have grown foolhardy with the advancing years?"

Til'koi was visibly astonished. "I thought you lived by the maxim that soldiers should disavow politics. It is a dirty, dangerous, and thoroughly disreputable business?"

"That is so, old friend, yet times change. Is there any truth to the rumour now circulating in the capital?" General Az'nai probed.

"It is the worst kept secret in the Duchy, is it not? The King is set to announce the betrothal of the Royal Princess Mikhouri to the Royal Prince Disch'al. That at least has been agreed among both parties. I cannot speak for the Royal Princess Alicharia...?"

"The intention is to marry her to the whelpling, the Crown Prince Sea'gir?" Az'nai pressed.

"Given the current malaise in the Royal House, and the poor health of the King, there is merit in the unions? Our alliance with the Argata will be bound by blood" General Til'koi mused.

"Not everyone is so sanguine, old friend!" General Az'nai quipped testily. "A great many rightly fear the consequences of any such union?"

"Whilst that may be true, they cannot thwart the King's desire?" Til'koi sighed.

General Az'nai smiled slyly. "Every problem has a solution, as well you know. Our problem may require robust initiatives which may transpire to be as unpalatable as they are unspeakable?"

General Til'koi gaped at the older man. "You surely can't be serious?"

"But I am, old friend, you may rest assured of it! The guiding ministrations of Athena must be thwarted by all necessary means, do we understand one another?" the aged General growled.

Sar'kta Plains, July 493 BC

A doleful Princess Mikhouri fishes another handful of rye from the pail and threw it in the direction of the chickens, grimacing as the birds peck furiously at the grains in the dirt. She reached inside the pail and drew another handful, throwing this carelessly toward the flock. Her mind and heart were clearly elsewhere. The countess looms unseen in the doorway, watching the girl in silence. She strolls across and ruffles her hair affectionately. "We missed you at breakfast, sweet child! Are you feeling under the weather?" asked the old Lady.

"She hates me, doesn't she?" Mikhouri sighed despairingly.

"And who is 'she', my little dove? Is it your sister to whom you refer?"

"I thought that she would be happy. It was supposed to be a surprise" Mikhouri mused sadly.

"Are you happy with the arrangement, sweet child?" the old Lady smiled sweetly.

"I don't really get to choose who I marry, do I? I am old enough to understand that. Alicharia is still young" Mikhouri sighed.

"Your sister is a mere whelpling, petal. She has an awful lot to learn about the world" the old Lady soothed.

Mikhouri grinned. "I wouldn't let Alicharia hear you saying that!"

"You still haven't answered my question, little dove?" Her Grandmother pressed.

"Mama has spoken to me about Prince Disch'al, obviously she has. He is rumoured to be exceedingly kind and virtuous, blessed with sweetness as pure as honey. In that respect he is quite unlike his mother or elder sister. He is a fine horseman, though not as accomplished as some boys his age, and he adores animals, music, and poetry. It is also rumoured he is an avid reader" Mikhouri gushed.

The old woman smiled sweetly at the child. "He sounds like a fine boy, does he not? He also sounds like even finer husband material, if you care for my opinion on the matter."

"I am not stupid, Grandmama, despite what Alicharia thinks? I have heard stories of his mother, everyone has. Is she really as cruel and as unforgiving as everyone says?"

"Queen Lezika is a ruthless woman, sweet child, and don't you ever believe differently. Yet, she came to power at a difficult time, when the future of her line, and of her Kingdom, was imperilled. She has shown an enviable resolve in securing her realm especially during the turmoil of the past decade. It is not a peaceful region, little dove. It has always been so?"

Mikhouri gazed deeply into the old woman's eyes. "Is it true she murdered her own brother, the rightful King, to seize the Crown for herself?"

"And what do you know of such things, little dove?" the old woman clipped coldly.

"I have heard the rumour, everyone has. Did she also order the death of her first husband, the father of her daughters?"

"So it is said, sweet child. You would not be marrying Queen Lezika, would you? You are to be betrothed to her son, and he is not his mother" the old Lady sighed.

"But what if things change? What if he grows into a man like his mother?" Mikhouri protested.

"As his Queen, you will have more influence on his mind than any Counsellor. Prince Disch'al will not grow to be like his mother, not with you as his conscience. I am quite certain of that?"

"I would dearly like to meet him, Grandmama, and settle the truth of the matter for myself" Mikhouri declared.

"Then you must speak with your parents when they return. Such a departure from the accepted norm is not as uncommon as you may think. If you wish for my advice, sweet child, the more you learn beforehand, the happier, and more prosperous, your future together will be!" the old Lady reassured the child.

"What of Alicharia? What am I going to do about her?" Mikhouri sighed despondently

"You just leave Alicharia to the tender bosom of her Grandpapa. It is time your darling sister learned the truth of this world" the countess sighed.

The Royal Bazaar, situated in the north of the Royal City of Archaeopolis, thronged with shoppers enjoying another glorious summer afternoon. The Royal Princess Sychoria had ventured from the Palace in the company of her teenage Handmaidens, Sierna and Gh'aena, and a retinue of Her Majesty's Royal Guards, all bristling with weaponry, who loitered a respectful distance away. The throng of shoppers appeared unperturbed by their presence, yet nonetheless gave the men a respectful berth. Sychoria eyed a stunning creation, which hung from a rack at one of the more bespoke garment merchants. "What do you think of this?" Sychoria pointed to a beautiful saffron chiton, edged with gold trim, sized for a child of eight to ten years,

"It is beautiful, my Lady. I am certain the Princess Mikhouri will adore it so" replied Sierna dutifully.

"I asked what *you* thought of it, young Handmaiden" Sychoria raised an eyebrow in mock severity.

"I think it would suit me perfectly, my Lady. It would be more than a match for my hair and eyes, as it would the Princess Mikhouri" Sierna smiled sweetly.

"You do not think it would suit Alicharia?" Sychoria raised an eyebrow challengingly.

"Alicharia has rose-blonde hair, my Lady? I do not think the colour would complement her. And besides, why not try blue, red, or purple? Those are the colours of soldiers."

Sychoria giggled. "I do like the little Princess in purple! What do you think of that one?"

It was a stunning creation, dyed a luxuriant deep purple with elegant silver trim around the hemline, neck-line and on either sleeve. Sychoria presumed it was Persian, for surely only they could craft something of such quality. "Is this Persian, my good fellow?"

"No, my Lady, it is not. It is made by the Saka who live west of the Hindi Kish. They are, I believe, of Sauromatae extraction" the merchant replied.

Sierna giggled. Sychoria was astounded. "This is Sauromatae?"

"Of course, my Lady, and there a few who could imitate it? Sauromatae garment makers rank among the finest in the world!" the merchant smiled brightly.

"Is this silk?" Sychoria pressed.

"Indeed, it is, my Lady! It is from the Orient" the merchant eyed the woman steadily, for he was now certain that he would make his sale.

"I am sure that the Princess Alicharia would be smitten with it" Sierna added helpfully.

"I am equally sure she would" Sychoria frowned.

And yet, the merchant was determined not to be thwarted. "Now, my Lady, perhaps your beautiful young companion would consider this offering, for I would dearly love to hear her opinion?" The merchant reached for a pile of garments that were laid on a table behind him, and removed an elegant *gown*, for that was surely what it was. The length was longer than a kurta or chiton, and the cut of its silk was crafted to closely film the natural contours of its wearer. Neither Sychoria, nor Sierna, had ever seen such a colour, for it was a most radiant and delicate hue of rose, like the cheeks of a pale child in the hot sun after a chase with her playmates. "What do you make of it, Gh'aena?"

"I think is very beautiful, my Lady" said Gh'aena.

"What colour is this, my dear fellow?" Sychoria quipped.

"I believe the Sauromatae call it *blush*, my Lady. I have never seen the like in all my life!" the merchant smiled ruefully.

"This is Sauromatae?" Sychoria gasped.

"It is from the Saka people, who live west of the Hindi Kish, as I have already said."

"I'll take it!" Sychoria said instantly. She turned and flashed a smile at Sierna. "It is a gift for my young companion. I think it would complement her most commendably?"

"Now, my Lady, I would appreciate your opinion on this particular item. In deference to your dark hair, pale eyes, and light complexion, I think it would suit you perfectly?" the merchant smiled thinly.

"What shade is this? It is the palest green I have yet laid eyes on" Sychoria cooed with delight.

"The Sauromatae call it *winter mint*, my Lady?" said the Merchant.

"What do you make of it, Sierna?" Sychoria asked earnestly.

"I think it is truly stunning, my Lady, as are you" the young Handmaiden replied sweetly.

"I think it could have been crafted for you, and you, alone" Sychoria beamed at Gh'aena.

The Merchant could scarcely credit his fortune. There were days, as rare as a summer frost, when the Gods truly graced you with their blessing. "It would be a travesty, my Lady, if we could not accommodate your own desires?" The man smiled brightly and, turning to his right, plucks a garment from the rear of a rack suspended from the canopy. Both Sierna and Gh'aena gasped with joy. Sychoria gazed at the garment in silent disbelief. It was a most vivid shade of blue yet seemed to dazzle in the rays of the sun. "You are a Lady of exquisite taste! One who genuinely appreciates the glory of exemplary craftsmanship?" the merchant beamed.

"What colour is this?" Sychoria chirped.

"The Sauromatae refer to it as *lazuli*, my Lady."

"It is truly beautiful, my Lady" Gh'aena chimed blissfully.

"I'll take all five of them, my good man" Sychoria smiled sweetly at the merchant, who nodded gnomishly. The garments were expensive, yet he could always add a little extra to the total, for this was clearly a woman of considerable wealth.

A gruff looking and heavily armed soldier, plainly identifiable as a member of Her Majesty's Royal Guard, an officer no less, morphed beside the trio. "A quiet word, if I may, Sir?"

The merchant was not to be deterred from closing the sale. "Of course, dear fellow, for I am ever at Her Majesty's service. If I may be permitted the small courtesy of finishing my service to these three Ladies, I shall attend to you presently. An Officer of Her Majesty's Royal Guard needs no lesson from a humble merchant in the value of a courtesy, is that not so?" the merchant replied silkily.

"I will cut your fucking balls off, pal! Courteously, of course" the soldier hissed.

The merchant blanched. "How may I be of service, Sir!" he spoke softly, and with due respect.

"This is the Princess Sychoria, of the Orch'tai Royal House, is that understood? I will broker none of your fucking 'Gypo tricks, like beefing up the price, just because you can, is that understood?" the soldier whispered malevolently. "This is your lucky day? You wouldn't want to spoil things, would you?"

"This is a rare pleasure, Your Royal Highness! I am at your humble service and in your grace" the merchant beamed at Sychoria, who nodded appreciatively, her eyes twinkling with delight.

"Thank you, my good man! I appreciate your courtesy and consideration, Captain Galligalcix."

"In was merely doing my duty, Your Highness, nothing more than that" the man smiled tightly at the Princess, then gazed warningly back at the merchant.

"My Lady, this is my pleasure, to be sure, and I will charge only twenty-three silver drachms for the lot, for I shall make no commission for myself" the merchant smiled ruefully.

"I think you mean twenty, don't you, Sir?" the soldier's eyes twinkled with malice.

"I must protest, Sir, for these are most expensive items" the merchant spoke softly.

"I heard you the first time, Sir, but I doubt you can even count to twenty-three? I will be paying twenty, isn't that so?"

"I think we can reach an accommodation, my Lord" the merchant smiled tightly, for he now had the measure of his man. The brute would hand over twenty-one pieces, in front of the three females, and a single silver drachm would be slipped back to an underling, likely the last man in the detail. The soldiers would get their cut, and he would still make a tidy profit, so everyone was happy.

"Our friend will take twenty-one pieces of silver, my Lady, for it is fine attire, is it not?" the captain smiled thinly at the Princess and her Handmaiden.

"I am in your debt, Captain Galligalcix" Sychoria simpered.

The captain fished out a purse and handed twenty-one silver pieces to the merchant, who duly handed over the garments, carefully wrapped and fastened with bright coloured twine, to Negorias, a fellow Celt. As the group turned to leave, a silver coin was passed to the last of the soldiers in the guard detail, a lithe and dangerous-looking teen name Astoriax, the younger brother of Negorias. And, just as the merchant hoped, all was well in the world.

The Princess Sychoria and her teenage Handmaidens, accompanied by their retinue of Guards, stroll leisurely towards the Jewellers District. The party strolled south along Nineveh Way, delighting in the Royal Gardens, a spacious area of public greenery with flowerbeds, well-manicured lawns, a lake and fountain, and its small theatre. The visitors marvelled at the lake, fountain, and flower beds to the north of Garden Avenue, which had no comparator in the Royal City of their birth. On such a beautiful day, the Royal Gardens were especially busy, and crowds continue to flock to the theatre, where a performance was underway. "Would you mind if we stayed, if only for a while? I am curious about the performance" Sychoria smiled sweetly at Captain Galligalcix, who nodded through gritted teeth. Such a large gathering of people in such proximity was an obvious security risk to the Royal Party, and one he was ill-prepared for.

The group make their way to the edge of the arena and seating platform and sat down. It was obvious that the performance had been underway for some time, yet the crowd seemed enchanted, particularly with the actors, which included a dwarf, who was unusually cast in a serious role. This greatly surprised Captain Galligalcix, for dwarves were typically figures of fun. Then again, by his own admission, Galligalcix was neither a scholar, nor devotee of the arts, yet it became clear that the Princess was, despite her criticism of the cultural trappings of Mamy'eva. This was not altogether surprising, given her education in Corinth. The scene, being enacted before them, went as follows:

King Priam: Whose fates are heaviest in the scales of Jove, tomorrow's light (O haste the glorious morn!). Shall see his bloody spoils in triumph borne, with this keen javelin shall his breast be gored. And prostate heroes bleed around their lord.

Helen: Oh worthy better fate! Oh early slain! Thy country's friend, and virtuous, though in vain, no more the youth shall join his consort's side? At once a virgin, and at once a bride! No more with presents her embraces meet or lay the spoils of conquest at her feet. On whom his passion, lavish of his store, bestowed so much, and promised so much more!

A group of nearby women, perched a few yards to their left on a lower tier, turn to glance quickly at Sychoria, then giggled shrilly among themselves. A scowling Captain Galligalcix drily noted they were not the only offenders. Sychoria had also noted the reaction of the crowd, yet seemed surprisingly nonplussed, and kept her gaze fixed on the stage. "Do you know what this is, Captain?"

"I freely admit that I do not, my Lady" the captain spoke evenly.

"It is from the Iliad by Homer. It is an epic poem of the war between the Greeks and Trojans?"

"Can't say I have ever heard of it, my Lady" the captain spoke brusquely, his irritation at his lack of learning as clear as the bright blue sky above.

King Priam: Thus, rank on rank, the thick battalions throng. Chief urged on chief, and man drove man along. Far o'er the plains, in dreadful order bright, the brazen arms reflect a beamy light. Full in the blazing van great Hector shined, like mars commission to confound mankind. Before him flaming his enormous shield, like the broad sun, illuminated all the field!

Kassandra: Thou art up shit-creek now, oh silly boy! Our father is now cursed with asinine nobility! Do you think ye truly sired of the gods? Thou art but man-like gristle, void of celestial wisdom, which lives, breathes, bleeds, and dies. No grace from spear or arrows deliverance, in thy duplicity!

Helen: Great Jove has placed, sad spectacle of pain! The bitter dregs of fortune's cup to drain, to fill with scenes of death his closing eyes, and number all his days by miseries! My heroes slain, my bridal bed overturned, my daughters ravished, and my city burned! My bleeding infants dashed against the floor, these I have yet to see, perhaps yet more!

King Priam: My Lady, sweet child, your hands doth tremble! Dwell no more upon such distressing fates, instead of victory, the glorious triumph of our race, awaits!

Kassandra: And now we see there is a first for everything, for it is usually her knees which tremble!

Helen: Shall, ignominious, we with shame retire, no deed performed, to our Olympic sire? Come, prove thy arm! For the first war to wage, suits not my greatness, or superior age. Rash as thou art to prop the Trojan throne, forgetful of my wrongs, and of thy own. And guard the race of proud Laeomedon!

Paris: Nor must thy course lie honoured in the bier, nor spouse, nor mother, graced thee with a tear! Far from our pious rites those dear remains, must feast the vultures on the naked plains.

Helen: Ah suffer that my bones may rest with thine! Together we have lived, together bred. One house received us, and one table fed, that golden urn, thy goddess mother gave, may mix our ashes in one common grave.

Paris: But since the god his hand has pleased to turn and fill thy measure from his bitter urn. What sees the sun, but hapless heroes' falls? War, and the blood of men, surrounds thy walls. What must be, must be! Bear thy lot, nor shed, these unavailing sorrows o'er the dead! Thou canst not call him from the Stygian shore, but thou, alas, may'st live to suffer more?

King Priam: 'Blest is the man who pays the gods above, the constant tribute of respect and love! Those who inhabit the Olympian bower, my son, forget not, in exalted power. And heaven, that every virtue bears in mind, even to the ashes of the just is kind.

Kassandra: O sire! Can no resentment touch thy soul? Can mars rebel, and does no thunder roll? What lawless rage on yon forbidden plain, what rash destruction! And what heroes slain! Venus, and Phoebus, with the dreadful bow, smile on the slaughter, and enjoy my woe! Mad, furious power! Whose unrelenting mind, no god can govern, and no justice bind!

The bawdier quotations, clearly not from the pen of Homer himself, caused raucous laughter among the enraptured spectators. And yet, it was the smug, all-knowing glances that were continuously shot at the Princess Sychoria, accompanied by gleeful smirks, that failed to pass without notice, even the uncomprehending Captain Galligalcix. "Perhaps we might leave, my Lady, for the sun is getting hot in the sky?" said the Captain of Her Majesty's Guard.

"Of course, honourable Captain, and I rather fear that we have missed the best of it!" Sychoria smiled sweetly.

"If that is your jar of rye, my Lady" the captain mused through gritted teeth. He was irritated at being singled out as an additional source of merriment by the crowd.

And yet, there had been a coded message in the quotations, and the shared and almost intimate comprehension of the adoring crowd. The Royal Princess, schooled by the finest tutors in Corinth, as Queen Lezika had once been, correctly deciphered it and was, at one, bemused and pricked. "I would like to see the play in full, Captain Galligalcix, privately, of course? Do you think that might be possible? Perhaps you may speak with your Lady?"

Captain Galligalcix bristled at the deliberate discourtesy. "I will speak with Her Majesty, on your behalf of course, my Lady" he replied evenly.

"Excellent! Now, lead on, Captain Galligalcix?" Sychoria smiled sweetly. The briefest twinkle of satisfaction flashed in her pale blue eyes.

Chief Counsellor Kol'cha, *Kor'nai* to His Royal Highness King Tagar of the Orch'tai Royal House, greeted the General formally in the antechamber to the Great Hall of the Royal Palace of Mamy'eva. The old Kor'nai limped tiredly towards the younger man, each footfall betraying his advancing age and declining vigour. Kor'nai Kol'cha was approaching his eighth decade, an exceedingly rare feat, and had loyally served King Tagar and his father, the "Warrior King" Mag'kar, before him. Despite his advancing years and unsteadiness of feet, the old man remained blessed with a razor-sharp mind. He was at one and the same, a kind and loyal friend, and a dangerous and merciless enemy. Many a traitor had died at the hands of his loyal coterie of retainers, all in preservation of the security of the realm. "General Til'koi, it is a pleasure to see you again. We have said regular prayers for the safe return of you and your men against this most pernicious of enemies."

"Thank you, Honourable Kor'nai, the pleasure is mine, as always. It is good to see you in good spirits" the General smiled warmly.

"Perhaps my spirit is as fickle as the autumnal winds, pending the gravity of your report." The Kor'nai leaned close to the General and spoke in barely a whisper. "Much as the King's mood, I might add, and His Royal Majesty's health."

"How is the King's health?" the General enquired respectfully.

"His Majesty has been plagued with melancholy ever since the unfortunate tragedy which befell his beloved nephew. His passing was a great loss."

"I met with the Dowager Countess Arialla a few days ago" the General confided. "She is heartbroken by her loss. I fear that only her devotion to Laeschalla keeps her from winnowing to nothing" There was little point in denying he had met with the countess, certainly not to this wily old fox.

"She was a delightful child, was she not? Arialla was always deeply fond of you, General Til'koi. Indeed, she remains so" the Kor'nai sighed.

"And I of her, Honourable Kor'nai, for we have known each other for many moons. Such a terrible plague of sadness, in one so youthful, it truly breaks the heart."

"Her husband's untimely death was a bitter blow to the King and the realm" the Kor'nai sighed despondently.

"He was a fine man and an exemplary Commander. It was an honour and a privilege to serve under his Command" the General concurred.

"And now, you have risen to the rank of General? Newly appointed Supreme Commander of His Royal Majesty's Army east of the Wol'yi, no less?"

"It is an honour to serve the King and the realm, Honourable Kor'nai. It is a solemn and sacred duty, to protect our borders from the infernal perils of the east."

"How fare your endeavours?" the Kor'nai's eyes twinkled with suspicion.

"Perhaps we might respectfully speak of these matters before the King?" the General smiled tightly.

"Of course we shall, my dear fellow? You may rest assured the Royal Counsel will appreciate honesty in such matters. To do otherwise, would be a grave dereliction, would it not?" the Kor'nai spoke softly.

"I must advise you, Honourable Kor'nai, that there is much in my report to unsettle a queasy conscience" General Til'koi cautioned.

The King's health was a subject of constant rumour, both in Mamy'eva, and in the garrison outposts of the Signet. His Majesty certainly appeared jaded since the last time that General Til'koi had seen him. Then again, perhaps they all did. King Tagar was perched on the High Throne, flanked by his Kor'nai and Honourable Counsellors, as the General stood before him. His Majesty cleared his throat, smiled thinly, and addressed the most senior serving soldier in the Orch'tai Royal Army. "It has been far too long, General Til'koi. We are honoured by your presence before this Counsel" said King Tagar.

"The honour is mine, Your Royal Highness, for I faithfully serve His Majesty and Counsel" the General bowed with a flourish.

"How long is it since you were last in Mamy'eva, General?" the King asked interestedly.

"It has been some three winters, Your Majesty?"

"Three long, cruel winters were they not?" the King smiled warmly.

"The menace of the Sauromatae requires constant vigilance, Your Majesty. I swore a solemn oath to defend the realm. I fear I cannot do that oath justice, guarding a Royal Princess' privy!" General Til'koi replied, to raucous mirth from King and Counsel.

"How are the new recruits faring? I trust they conduct themselves with honour and vigilance?" the King eyed the General closely, searching his reaction for anything amiss.

"Regrettably, Your Majesty, they do not" the General's words cut through the chamber like a Siberian wind in mid-winter.

"They do not fight, as Orch'tai should fight?" the Kor'nai demanded evenly.

"They are ill-trained and ill-prepared for the rigours of combat operations beyond the Signet, my Lord. A vast majority are mere boys, with little experience of the hardships of the plains, or of the cunning and ruthlessness of our enemies."

The Signet was the defensive ring of fortresses, one hundred and twenty miles to the east of the River Uras'ka, spanning the entire breadth of the plain from the Uruk Mountains in the north to the Kas'pa in the south. It had been established four decades earlier, under the auspices of the 'Warrior King' Mag'kar to stem a renewed tide of Sauromatae aggression across the Western Plains in the years following the rise of Persia under Cyrus the Great. The Signet were permanent garrisons for Cavalry and Infantry, who aggressively patrolled the vast expanse of the Western Plains of Kazakh'yi and the far westerly reaches of the Upper Darya, in search of enemy marauders.

"We have received word of increased Sauromatae aggression, of course?" the King sighed. "And yet, these are dismissed as mere fancy by a great many, for such is the legacy, and the lunacy, of a Sauromatae Confederacy!" The Royal Counsellors chuckled contemptuously.

"Would it surprise Your Royal Highness and Counsel to learn there may be more than a sliver of truth in these latest rumours?" the General said icily.

"You surely can't be serious?" gasped Counsellor Mes'khu.

"I could not be more so, Honourable Counsellor" the General said coldly. "We are all aware of the calamity at Urzbin in the summer of 495 BC? Our intelligence sources report a new cordiality between the fiefdoms of the Upper Darya and their kin in the Plain of Tu'mysch, and beyond."

"This is the girl Queen, Dali'yah? Strange, that the Sauromatae would rally to the standard of a child?" mused Counsellor Har'juk, widely acknowledged as a rising star of the Royal Counsel, despite his comparative youth, at twenty-seven years of age.

"She is no ordinary child, Honourable Counsellor. Dali'yah has the support of her kin further east, and perhaps even an earthlier benefactor?" Til'koi mused sourly.

"The whore Queen in Khoda? Is Tae'gryn even pure blood Sauromatae?" the Kor'nai scowled.

"She is. I believe, of Saka extraction. She is the richest woman in the world!" Til'koi smiled thinly. "According to our reports, hostility between the fiefdoms of the Tu'mysch and Zy'ghuk continues to smoulder and may yet erupt in open war. Nevertheless, it cannot be denied that vast swathes of the Sauromatae dominions are now loosely confederated."

"Then we must act, with vigour!" the King bristled. "I would have expected a new seasonal campaign against the recalcitrant communities of the Western Plain and the Upper Darya?"

"The new Divisions are simply not up to the job, my liege. They cannot withstand the rigours of incessant patrolling in the plains" the General eyed the King closely.

"If what you say is true, General Til'koi, such a deplorable situation reflects badly on their Supreme Commander? The Honourable Counsellor Mes'khu shot the General a glance of withering disdain. "The training and preparation of these Divisions is your responsibility? Do you deny it?" he challenged.

The King studied the General's reaction. "These so-called warriors were mere farmhands at the last harvest" Til'koi spoke icily.

"This Counsel saw fit to appoint you their Supreme Commander, General Til'koi? Perhaps our faith has been misplaced?" Mes'khu simpered.

The General gritted his teeth. "They are poorly equipped, my Lord? The weapons that we were promised have not materialised in sufficient quantities. Sadly, this may be the least of our concerns?"

"Would you care to clarify that statement, General Til'koi" the Kor'nai said evenly.

"With your grace, Honourable Kor'nai, I shall. The calibre of our newly appointed officers, many of whom were, until recently, idle sons of the favourably born, is deplorable. They are not suited to martial endeavour, and this has had a degrading influence on the men they purport to lead. In the worst instances, they exercise little, if any, authority over an ill-trained and ill-disciplined rabble. There are reports of atrocities, savagery even, against innocent communities of the Western Plains."

"You are their Commander, are you not, General Til'koi" the King bridled.

"I have that Honour, Your Majesty" the General bowed respectfully.

"For the moment you do so, General Til'koi. Considering these wholly unsubstantiated rumours of atrocities against the communities of the Western Plains, I take it they are Sauromatae?"

"They are, Your Majesty" the General said tonelessly.

"These feral brutes are our sworn enemies!" the King challenged his Counsellors, all of whom nodded like obedient donkeys, except for the Kor'nai, who eyed the General warily. "We facilitate their existence, by allowing their stinking caravans to journey unmolested through our realm. The lands of *our* ancestors! And how do they repay such generosity and amity? With wickedness and disobedience, for that is their nature! These new Divisions were raised and deployed to tame their threat forever. They will never darken the borders of our realm! Never!" the King roared hoarsely.

"Begging your grace, Your Majesty, but the severe restrictions imposed upon the passage of caravans across the Wol'yi, coupled with a logistical dilemma of securing sufficient food for such a large contingent of men, has exacerbated a growing discontent that has festered for a decade" the General ventured.

"Are you seriously petitioning this Counsel to consider the suffering of these infernal wretches?" Mes'khu ridiculed.

"The harvests have been woefully poor for several years, my Lord" Til'koi confessed. "That is the root of the present malaise. If the communities of the plains refuse to sell us their surplus emmer and barley, or if the seasons cannot furnish this surplus, we simply cannot feed an army of this size?"

"They have no right to deny us their annual tribute!" the King seethed. "Therein is the key to their very survival. If they continue to abstain from their obligations, we are within our rights to exact punitive measures!"

"Hence the increased incivility towards the local communities, Your Majesty, at the hands of ill-trained, ill-equipped, and ill-disciplined troops!" the General said coldly.

"If what you say is true, General Til'koi, we must conceive an urgent remedy to this malaise?" interjected Honourable Counsellor Har'juk.

"A remedy shall be prescribed! This plague of disobedience cannot be permitted to flourish!" barked Counsellor Mes'khu.

"Perhaps we might consider lifting our restrictions on the passage of caravans, Your Majesty?" General Til'koi suggested helpfully.

"And what good would that do, so late in the season?" sighed the Kor'nai lamentably.

"Securing a food supply for these new Divisions, even in the short term, must be our overriding imperative!" growled King Tagar. "I will not broach any relaxation in the flow of traffic across the Wol'yi! Do we understand one another, General Til'koi?"

The General looked steadily at the old King, his expression betraying nothing of the swirling undercurrent of his emotions. "I understand, Your Majesty."

"We will take only what we need from them, no more, no less! That is my command?"

"I understand, Your Majesty, but if the communities of the plains resist such demands?"

"You will quell their petulance at once, with fire and fury, as necessity demands! Our indulgence of these untamed beasts has brought nought but trouble! If they will not yield, they will be wiped from the plains! Is that understood, General Til'koi?" the King hissed.

The General smiled congenially at the mad old bastard! "And if the Sauromatae take up arms against us? All of them?"

"If you are no longer capable of carrying out your solemn duty, General Til'koi, then I will find a suitable replacement who is!" the King hissed menacingly.

A rigid Captain Galligalcix stood before his Queen and Kor'nai. Quite regardless of the cool of the stone room, a bead of sweat trickled down the grim-faced Officer's cheek. The Queen eyed the brute with interest. "I hope that the Royal Princess Sychoria enjoyed her little sojourn to the Bazaar this afternoon, Captain Galligalcix?" Queen Lezika enquired.

"That she did, Your Majesty. I think the Royal Princess was more than a little surprised by the variety and the superior quality of the wares on offer in Archaeopolis, compared with those of the markets of Mamy'eva" the captain reported dutifully.

"Have you ever been to Mamy'eva, Captain Galligalcix?"

"I have not, Your Majesty" the captain replied curtly.

Queen Lezika grimaced. "It is a dreadful city, Captain Galligalcix, and you may take my word as authority on the matter! And yet, the Royal Palace is spacious and splendorous. So, the Royal Princess could not find fault with our little spot of the world, could she?"

"Quite the contrary, Your Majesty, for she repeatedly sang its praises. I got the impression that she and her husband prefer to spend time at their country estate, whenever possible."

"That would not surplice me in the slightest, for the hunting grounds of the Orch'tai King are quite remarkable. Is there anything else, Captain Galligalcix?"

"If it may please Your Majesty, there is?" the captain spoke evenly. "As we passed the Royal Gardens, we came across a performance by a travelling troupe of actors at the Theatre. The Princess Sychoria requested that we stay a while. It was a play, based on the Iliad, or so the Princess intimated, and it drew a large crowd of spectators, who were most enthralled by it."

"And the Royal Princess has expressed an interest in inviting this travelling troupe to the Royal Palace for a private performance?" the Queen smiled thinly.

"She did, Your Majesty, very much so" Galligalcix replied.

"I see, Captain Galligalcix. Are you a devotee of the theatre?"

"I am a simple man, Your Majesty. I could follow much of what was being said, and it appeared to be somewhat humorous, bawdy even, for there was much mirth among the spectators, from time to time, of course" the captain confessed.

"The Iliad is a tragedy, Captain Galligalcix, if you were not aware?" the Queen quipped sternly.

"That is what the Princess intimated, yet this is an adaptation, and is rather humorous in places. The Princess Sychoria confessed she thought it 'delightfully witty', Your Majesty."

"Did she indeed? Do you happen to know where this travelling troupe is staying in the city?"

"I have subsequently learned from some of the lads that they are staying at *The Horn and Crown*. They are to be found there almost every night, at least for the past week. I have no idea when they plan to leave Archaeopolis?" said the captain.

"If the Princess Sychoria wishes for a private performance of this 'delightfully witty' rendition, perhaps you might pay the *Horn and Crown* a visit this night and inform these actors I would be honoured if they would extend me the courtesy of a private performance at the Royal Palace?" the Queen smiled tightly.

"It will be done, Your Majesty. When do you request the performance to take place, Your Majesty?" the captain enquired.

"Tomorrow evening would suit perfectly. They would be afforded the courtesy of an invitation to dine with us at a lavish supper in their honour. Do you think they may be amenable, Captain Galligalcix?"

"How could they refuse tan invitation from Her Royal Majesty? Delivered in person, by a loyal Captain of Her Majesty's Royal Guard, no less?" Galligalcix said woodenly.

"I fear our beloved city is becoming quite unruly of late, especially during the evening hours" the Queen smiled ruefully. "You will take all necessary precautions for your own personal safety, will you not?"

"I will indeed, Your Majesty, as will the rest of my detachment!"

"You have my confidence in this matter, Captain Galligalcix. Tell this travelling troupe that I look forward to the performance and the pleasure of their company at supper."

Nine

Archaeopolis, July 493 BC

The Horn and Crown is a spacious hostelry with ample stabling at the rear. It stands at the far end of Brewery Street, a short distance from the Jewellers Quarter, and was run by a cheery soul named Cenarius and his flock of nubile daughters. Cenarius was a proud Celt and retired mercenary, formerly in the employ of Queen Lezika's Royal Guard, who married a local girl and purchased the inn upon his retirement. He was a loyal and faithful servant of Her Royal Majesty, and, whilst he had been horrified by the rumours circulating the city in the aftermath of the murder of Avielle, he had discouraged public discussion of the incident within his walls. He knew only too well the whims of this Queen! He was a first cousin to Vetinaeus, Queen Lezika's first husband and father of the Royal Princesses, Perdicca and Cordicca, his beloved nieces. The bar was unusually busy this night, as it had been for the past week, ever since the arrival of the merry band of performers whose antics, both on and off the stage, provided a welcome tonic to the clouds of gloom which had shrouded the Royal City ever since the Avielle's brutal slaying.

The troupe had spent the past eight days in Archaeopolis. Whilst the city was no Susa or Babylon, its understated opulence and manicured public gardens had surprised and impressed the senior members, a husband and wife named Daladaeus and Bellatae. These were otherwise known to those who had seen their performance of *The Sceptre and the Serpent: a tragedy of Helen and Paris*, as King Priam and Queen Helen. The reception had been warm, generous even, and the troupe had rarely dipped their hands in their

233

purses for a drink in the bar of the 'Horny Jewel', as it was affectionately known to its regulars. Such generosity may have had more to do with the youngest member of the troupe, a green-eyed and pretty Sauromatae girl named Cerrae, who joined as a child some six years before. Cerrae had been virtually adopted by the people of Archaeopolis, especially its teenage sons, regardless of the insignificance of her role. Bellatae, or 'Bella', smiled sweetly as the teenage barmaid, Atlantes, approached with a fresh tray of drinks. "These are on the house, my lovelies! My father told me to tell you that you can stay as long as you please, for you have certainly brightened our little abode!"

"Thank you, my petal! Have you ever thought of a career as an actor? You could have a bright future, anywhere you wished?" Bella flashed her teeth at the girl.

"And where are our two little love-birds tonight?"

"Fucking!" Bella grinned.

Atlantes giggled. "I think I might like the life of a professional actor; drinking, fucking, and basking in public adoration!"

"Spoken like a true Celt, my petal!" Bella smiled sardonically.

"Don't worry about the drinks, my love, for our love birds have gorged their hunger" Atlantes declared, nodding towards the far end of the bar. Framed in the entrance of a corridor leading to the stairway and the upstairs accommodation wing, stood Novaetis the dwarf and the quiet young teenager, Charaen, her pale cheeks flushed by her recent adventures between the sheets. A group of rowdy young teens cheered their arrival. Novaetis, with typical sangfroid, waved airily in acknowledgement. The cheer was taken up by the rest of the regulars, not in deference to their recent ardour, but because the troupe, especially the loquacious and ribald Novaetis, had been a welcome gust of perfumed air.

Novaetis beamed at Atlantes as he approached the table. The girl blushed faintly. "I do declare, 'twas not the beer which brought me low, but as fair a maid in all the world, who graced a smile to thaw the deepest snow!"

"You are a deplorable scoundrel, I do confess, and yet I meet thy lance! Thy sheets to grace, with sweet embrace, my heart doth twirl in trance!" the girl snickered.

"Spoken like a true Thespian, my child, and now I rest my case! Thy father, reverence held, in chained devotion fast, must surely see light at last! Thy future glory dances on a different plane, for the stage betokens, upon which, thy virtues, surely grace!" said Daladaeus.

"I would not trust him, my Lady, for he promised me the self-same future" Novaetis winked at Atlantes, then plucked a goblet of Gaullish red, and passed it to his young lover.

"Is he an honourable man, my Lord?" Atlantes smiled sweetly.

"He is a disreputable rogue, blessed with silver tongue and cursed with copper purse" Novaetis turned and winked at Daladaeus. "He promised me a life of unbridled variety. Do you know how many stables I have rested my weary head?"

"You may tell your father we have travelled far and wide, and a better welcome we have never known!" Daladaeus smiled brightly at the child.

Atlantes blushed and twirled away to the bar. "You never fail to impress, do you?" Bella giggled.

"I like this little town, don't you? Not Babylon, to be sure, but certainly fairer than Medes" Novaetis gulped his wine and reached for a jar of beer.

"Nothing to do with that unfortunate incident in the market, was it?" Bella's eyes twinkled mischievously.

"I was not myself. I was ill, you remember?" Novaetis scowled.

"You can't fucking ride, is all!" Bella snickered.

"He rides like a thoroughbred! You can rest assured of that!" Charaen quipped.

The table dissolved into laughter, for there was much to be pleased about. The play, composed within a day of their arrival, had been a resounding success with record crowds, rich and poor alike. The laughter suddenly died, as sure as a candle's light in an unwelcome gale, as a detachment of armed soldiers' troop through the door, to be greeted by hushed silence. "Breach that fucking gate!" a resonant voice boomed from the bar.

"You think that an acceptable way to address a Captain of Her Majesty's Royal Guard, you miserable old bastard!" Captain Galligalcix grinned.

"Is this a social visit, 'Galli? You are certainly dressed for the occasion?" Cenarius mocked.

"I have it on good authority you have a troupe of actors staying here?"

"And if we do, Captain? What concern would that be of yours? I never had you pegged as an aficionado of the theatre, 'Galli?" Cenarius raised an eyebrow mockingly. The men behind the captain grinned.

"Her Majesty would like to request a performance at the Royal Palace, nothing more than that?" Galligalcix smiled tightly.

"Why don't you ask them? They are over there, at that table?" Cenarius jerked his thumb at the gaggle of thespians. "Ask for Daladaeus."

Captain Galligalcix led his group over to the table, where the actors sat in stunned silence. "Is one of you named Daladaeus?"

"I am Daladaeus. How may I be of service, Captain?" the man said tonelessly.

"I have it on some authority, my own, I might add, for I witnessed the act myself, that you are giving a rendition of the fabled Iliad in the Royal Gardens?"

"That is correct, Captain! Did you enjoy the performance?" Daladaeus smiled thinly.

"The Princess Sychoria was very taken with it. So much so, she asked me to speak with Her Royal Majesty, Queen Lezika, who commanded me to pass invitation to perform at the Palace tomorrow evening. There is also an invitation to a supper afterwards, to be held in your honour?" Galligalcix smiled tightly.

"How could we possibly refuse Her Majesty's grace and favour?" Daladaeus smiled brightly.

"I can inform Her Royal Majesty that you accept?"

"You may indeed, Captain!" Daladaeus smiled brightly.

And with that, Captain Galligalcix followed his men out into the night, without giving anyone, including Cenarius, a second glance. After he had left, Novaetis turned to Daladaeus and whispered softly across the table. "We are up shit-creek in a leaky barge, old friend!"

Sar'kta Plains, July 493 BC

"Can you forgive me, Alicharia? I cannot bear the thought of us never speaking again" Mikhouri sighed sadly.

"We are speaking now, aren't we?" Alicharia quipped. "From what Grandpapa told me, I may not have to marry that horrid little toad after all? His mother may choose someone else, for we are both children."

Mikhouri smiled wryly at the girl, whom she adored. The pair sat on Alicharia's bed in her dorm room, in the upper quarters of the farmstead. She snakes her arm around the younger Alicharia's neck and ruffles her hair. Mikhouri sighed. "I am sorry I deceived you, little sister, more than you could ever know. Mama made me promise not to tell you, not until they return. Nothing has been decided until they receive formal assent from Queen Lezika, for both of us, at least that's what I was told" she confessed dolefully.

"Do you truly wish to marry Prince Disch'al?" Alicharia gazed searchingly at her elder sister. "That would mean having his babies, would it not?"

"I suppose it would, but it isn't anything that women ought to be afraid of. It is why the God's made us. Our children would be Princes and Princesses and will be heirs to the Argata Royal Crown" Mikhouri smiled at the younger child.

"What if they have horns and tails, just like their grandmother?" Alicharia sneered.

"Queen Lezika has neither horns, nor a tail, Alicharia! You are surely too old to believe in such nonsense?" Mikhouri chided.

"Nobody seems to like her very much, do they? I doubt many people will like you anymore, not if you marry into that family" the younger girl snorted.

"Queen Lezika is a stern woman, Alicharia, but she is also a just woman. Everybody says so."

"I have heard it said that she kills people. That she kills them in horrible ways. What if her son grows up to be just like her?" Alicharia implored.

"He will not grow up to be anything like her, I promise. As his Queen, I will be his most trusted and faithful Counsellor, don't you see?"

"You are not very bright though, are you?" Alicharia snickered.

"You have an awful lot to learn about the world, darling sister? I can read and write, and that is something you struggle with. So too can Prince Disch'al, by all accounts?"

"He can read his mother's spells?" Alicharia grinned.

"Queen Lezika is not a witch, or a *shamani*, Alicharia! Nor is she in league with Hades" Mikhouri chided.

"Why doesn't anyone like her? Everyone likes Mama and Papa? Is it because she kills people? I have heard whisper that she is unspeakably cruel."

"All Kings and Queen's must be cruel, Alicharia, at least from time to time. How else do you hope to conquer the world? You must be cold and cruel, rather than meek and mild!" Mikhouri teased.

"I will only be cruel to my enemies, never to my friends!" Alicharia affirmed.

"You won't have any friends at all, not if you plan to conquer them all?" Mikhouri giggled. "A Queen must be just and fair, Alicharia. You cannot have your own way all the time, simply because you are the Queen. Being a Queen carries the burden of responsibility for others, just like Grandpapa" the older girl cautioned.

"What is the point of being Queen in the first place?" Alicharia protested. "A Queen must tell people what to do, and then expect it to be done. If people do not obey your commands, you throw them in a dungeon."

Mikhouri giggled. "I think there is more to being a Queen than throwing people in dungeons?"

"I could have people put to death, could I not? Just as Queen Lezika does with her enemies" the younger girl grinned. "Come to think of it, when I grow up and raise my army, I can conquer the Argata lands and have you and that little cloth-head put to death!"

"Don't say such things, Alicharia! It is dangerous talk. What if Mama and Papa heard you talking so? We could all get in to trouble!" Mikhouri castigated her sister.

"Would they kill us?" Alicharia seemed suddenly troubled.

"Why would anyone want to kill us? We are children?" Mikhouri smiled wanly.

"We won't be little forever, will we? There could be many reasons to have us killed?"

"Do not think of such things, little sister. No-one will ever want to kill us. Mama and Papa love us dearly, as we love them. For as long as they are alive, we are safe. We are a good people, Alicharia, and we hail from a proud and noble people. For now, we have peace. Nobody would ever want to hurt us, I promise you."

Mamy'eva, July 493 BC

"I am pleased you could spare me a brief moment of your time, General Til'koi" the Kor'nai ushered the General into his private study. "Please be seated, you are my guest. Would you care for a small wodki, perhaps?"

"Thank you, Honourable Kor'nai. I take it I am not yet under formal arrest?" the General smiled grimly.

The Kor'nai was astonished. "Why would you think such a thing, dear fellow? We are two Counsellors to his Royal Majesty, having an informal and friendly discussion. There is no treason, despite what that slippery fool Mes'khu may venture!" he mused acidly.

Til'koi smiled wryly. "I did try to warn you that my report might cause consternation among His Majesty's Counsellors, Honourable Kor'nai" he sipped his wodki.

"You might at least have signified the gravity of the matter beforehand, preferably in private? I could have spoken with His Majesty before Counsel was convened" the Kor'nai sighed tiredly.

"Forgive me, my Lord. The King is angry with me?" the General enquired tonelessly.

"The King, for all his virtue, is not blessed with his father's grasp of military affairs, particularly those pertaining to the security of the plains" the Kor'nai sighed lengthily. "As you know, I have watched your career with interest, ever since you were a young Officer serving under Kour'zan Az'nai. It was I who persuaded the King to appoint you Supreme Commander, because in my opinion you are the most experienced field officer in the Royal Army."

"I am honoured by the compliment, Honourable Kor'nai, yet I am certain General Zu'ghir would disagree?"

"You have different strengths, different qualities of leadership, and different methods. Zu'ghir is universally admired, that much is true, but lacks your experience in commanding such large detachments. I would be inclined to give regard to any recommendations you have in respect of the logistical issues raised by our current dispositions?" the Kor'nai smiled warmly.

"There is little further to add to what I presented to His Majesty, Honourable Kor'nai" replied the General. "But, given my respect for you, both as a man and a mind, I will re-state my position, and to Hades and be damned with any snivelling sycophant on His Majesty's Counsel. These new divisions are not suited to the rigours of duties in the plains. They have been hastily raised, poorly trained, and lazily provisioned, in respect of equipment and in their officers. They are simply not up to it. I am sure you have spoken with General Az'nai?"

"Does the General share your pessimistic assessment of the present situation east of the Wol'yi, and of the dire performance of the new Divisions?" the Kor'nai raised an eyebrow expectantly.

"Begging your pardon, Honourable Kor'nai, but the General practically tore me a new arsehole when I met him the other night. He was exceptionally well-briefed on the current situation and of the precariousness of our position."

The Kor'nai smiled mockingly. "Perhaps the General would be perspicacious enough to share his insights with His Majesty and the Royal Counsel?"

"I would not advise such a course of action, Honourable Kor'nai, for the General is not a man inclined to mellowing with age" Til'koi chuckled wryly.

"I appreciate your honesty, General Til'koi, and your integrity, which is beyond reproach. It is all too clear that something must be done to urgently redress this depressing situation" the Kor'nai mused softly.

"I am a simple soldier, my Lord, never a politician. If you appreciate honesty, then you shall have it" the General eyed the Kor'nai steadily. "The misadventure upon which we are now resolved could bring the entire Duchy to its knees. The Sauromatae are stirring, old friend, and I fear we have not the capacity to face down the threat. Instead, we are now committed to a war with those who might aid us in our hour of need."

"The King must be made to see reason in this matter, it goes without saying?" the Kor'nai spoke softly, yet firmly.

"I will say no more, Honourable Kor'nai, and I bid you good-night" the General swallowed his remaining wodki in a single gulp and left the Royal Palace immediately.

Archaeopolis, July 493 BC

The following morning, Crown Prince Voskar and Princess Sychoria were sat in the flower garden, sipping wine from silver goblets, when Queen Lezika's Handmaiden, Myletia, coughed lightly from a respectful distance. "Hello Myletia, would you like to join us?" Sychoria smiled sweetly at the girl.

Myletia blushed lightly. "Begging your grace, my Lady, but Her Majesty told me to inform you that we have something special planned for this evening. A troupe of actors will be staging a performance in the Great Hall, prior to a commemorative public Banquet, to be held in your honour. Her Majesty would be honoured if you would attend, despite the short notice."

"You may tell Her Royal Majesty we would be delighted to attend, and we are honoured by Her Majesty's most generous hospitality" Prince Voskar smiled warmly at the girl.

"Thank you, my Lord. I shall inform Her Majesty at once. Once again, my sincere apologies for the intrusion into your privacy and humbly beg forgiveness" Myletia curtseyed respectfully.

"There is nothing to forgive, my Lady, I assure you of that," said the Count.

"Are you sure you would not care to join us for a small cup of wine?" Sychoria pressed.

"Alas, I have other duties to attend to, My Lady, but thank-you for your generosity" the girl curtseyed again, and twirled on her heels, heading back to the Royal Palace.

"A generous gesture on Her Royal Majesty's part, to be sure it is? Perhaps we are making better progress than I thought?" Voskar smiled reassuringly at his wife.

"I would have thought it the least she could do, after she was so horrid to Alicharia!" Sychoria seethed.

"Her Majesty simply wished to goad, my love? You should not let it unsettle you so" Voskar soothed his plainly irritated wife. "I have a mind as to why the Queen saw fit to place a lesser status on our youngest daughter, and I will play my hand with the Crown Prince Mor'kur most deftly. You have my word on that, now and forever."

"You have my complete confidence, my love, as you have the King's. My father is not the easiest of souls to reason with. You knew that before you married me!" Sychoria teased.

"I did not propose to your father, did I? I was vying for the hand of the most beautiful girl in the whole Duchy, without realising that she could only ever be eclipsed by her own girls!"

"I miss them! I can't wait to see them again!"

"Nor I, my love, and when we return, perhaps it would be nice to spend a few weeks in Sar'kta, if you would like?" the Count spoke softly.

"I would love nothing more, my love, except, perhaps...?"

"You yearn for another child, is that it?" the Count smiled ruefully. "I suspect another addition to the family would be welcomed by your father, though only Hades knows what our youngest child would make of it?"

Sychoria smiled mischievously. "It might be best to start thinking about how we intend to break the news to them, you would agree?"

"My love, I...? Are you saying what I think you are saying?" the Crown Prince stared at his wife in wonder and adoration.

"I have missed my monthly bleed, my love. For quite a time, I should add" Sychoria confessed.

"You have not been beset by the morning trials, have you?" the prince seemed worried.

"I have a terrible feeling that is due to commence in the next two weeks, my sweet. I do hope this will not discolour your rosy appraisal of this fine city" Sychoria teased.

"No, my Lady, it will not. If you are convinced that you are now with child, perhaps we might edge the scales in our favour?"

Sychoria smiled at her husband, her eyes twinkling with delight. "I am feeling rather frisky, my love! Would you like to hear me howl the walls down?"

The *caravan*, if you could call it such, trundled into the village of Sar'kuc in the mid-morning, an hour or so before the sun reached its zenith. It comprised three covered wagons, and its occupants were Sauromatae traders, an extended family group comprising some fourteen individuals, including a baby boy born only a week earlier. The travellers hail from a community to the immediate east of the Uruk Mountains. They had hoped to be welcomed by the villagers and make a tidy profit on a sale of their wares. They were sorely disappointed, on both counts. Mikhouri and Alicharia were excited by their arrival, the younger girl especially so, yet both had noted the troubled expression upon their grandfather's face as the caravan rolled in and camped on a vacant plot in the far northwest of the village. "How long do you think they intend to stay here?" he whispered to his Chief Steward, Ais'ka.

"We will have them out before the night, if that suits you, my Lord?" Ais'ka spat indignantly.

"There are presumably small children aboard? Leave them be, at least for a while. They will need to replenish their supplies, I don't doubt?"

"There might be trouble, my Lord, if they hang around for too long. What with things the way they are right now."

"Make sure that they have protection, those are my instructions. Do you understand?"

"As you wish, my Lord, yet some of the lads may not be happy. They have sons serving in the east" Ais'ka noted pointedly.

"Do these people look like mortal enemies to you?" the kindly Crown Prince sighed sadly.

It would have been astonishing if they had been so, for many of the occupants of the wagons were children, eight in all, ranging in age from eleven years to a mere week, six of them girls! Mikhouri and Alicharia were bewitched by the attire of the children, who sported kurtas and britches in a rainbow of colours, exquisitely embroidered around the neckline, hem-lines, sleeves, and trouser-ends. In contrast to her sister, Alicharia was rudely disappointed to discover not a single child was endowed with either horn or a tail! "They are impostors, for sure. I doubt they are even Sauromatae" she noted coldly. Mikhouri giggled.

The first signs of trouble became apparent an hour later at the communal well, not far from the vacant lot where the travellers had camped. At this hour of the day, the well thronged with a steady stream of visitors, typically small groups of women and young girls. On this day, there is an unusually large number of men, all muttering darkly about the new arrivals. Three traveller girls, aged between seven and nine years, trooped across to the well with sturdy wooden pails and respectfully took their place at the back of the queue, away from the rest of the throng. They were soon joined by a young girl, who raced gaily across to join them. The child, who had celebrated her fourth birthday a week earlier and answered to Nir'ah, wore a vivid red kurta, which reached almost to her knees, embroidered with saffron-coloured thread of the purest silk. She was a pretty child, blessed with eyes of the palest blue and blonde hair fashioned in pleats at the sides.

The Sauromatae children were chatting quietly amongst themselves when a group of five local boys, well known in the village, strolled across to sit on the grass, a few yards away. None had a bucket or pail. The older traveller girls were keenly aware of their hostility, as the boys made lewd comments about their clothing and appearances, oblivious to the fact that they were readily understood. Nor, for that matter, were they aware of the arrival of two other girls, also visitors, who now stood silently to their rear, pails in hand. Mikhouri grimaced with distaste at the bawdier comments of the boys, secretly hoping her younger sister was still too young to understand such things. She was quite wrong, obviously, for Alicharia spent far too much time in the company of soldiers and was inwardly seething at the base insults hissed at the children. *Except for the youngest child, the older girls surely understood what was being said about them?*

The atmosphere inevitably turned uglier as the queue gradually thinned and the girls moved closer to the well to draw water. "Hey! We were here before you? Get to the back of the queue!" one of the boys, Tiz'ga, challenged angrily. The older traveller girls were startled by the outburst, whilst Nir'ah chewed her lip and reached for an older girl's hand. The boys remained seated and had only now become aware of the two Princesses waiting patiently with their pails at the rear. Mikhouri had been equally startled by the outburst, whereas Alicharia glanced quickly at her sister, her blue eyes flashing angrily. "Where are your pails?" Mikhouri challenged pointedly.

"We were going to use theirs, weren't we?" Tiz'ga smiled mischievously. He was a confident little scamp and, despite his tender years, already had a reputation as a trouble-causer. The traveller girls could neither hide their surprise or embarrassment at the admission.

"Have you asked their permission? No, I doubt the thought even occurred to you? Perhaps you should head home and fetch your pails? Then you can take your rightful place in the queue?"

"In front of them?" Tiz'ka asked unsurely.

"Behind us, obviously, for you cannot secure a place without a pail, can you?" Mikhouri smiled sweetly.

"You are siding with them?" a second boy, Amas'ki, spat indignantly.

"We are not siding with anyone, for there is no dispute, is there? Without a pail, you never had a place, did you?" Mikhouri mocked.

"That isn't fair!" Amas'ki whined.

"Are you thick?" Alicharia challenged, drawing gasps of astonishment from everyone. The elder Sauromatae children giggled shrilly.

Amas'ki turned swiftly and glowered at the travellers, who were immediately cowed. "You don't belong here, remember that!" he growled.

"Neither do you, at least not without a bucket or a pail!" Mikhouri smiled brightly.

The boys were beaten, and they knew it. They shrugged their shoulders and filed past the two Princesses in sullen silence, their heads bowed. Only Amas'ki had the temerity to meet their gaze and glowered malevolently at Alicharia as he stomped past. Alicharia stuck out her tongue and grinned slyly at the scowling boy, drawing snickers of glee form the traveller girls. "You may collect you water now" Mikhouri implored, once the boys had retreated.

"Please, you must go first. We are visitors here, are we not?" the eldest girl blushed.

"You are our guests? If that is so, it would be quite wrong of us not to extend you such basic courtesy, you would agree?"

The girl smiled brightly. "I am called Azal'ya. This is my sister, Xelia, and my cousins, Xalya, and Nir'ah" she introduced her companions.

"I am Mikhouri. This is my sister, Alicharia."

"Thank you for your assistance. We are in your debt. If we can ever repay you with a service, you need only ask?" Azal'ya ventured.

"Where did you get your kurta? It is quite beautiful?" Alicharia asked Nir'ah, without any trace of embarrassment.

"I can't believe you sometimes, Alicharia?" Mikhouri hissed as the four traveller girls strolled away, their buckets filled. "Would you have the poor child stroll around naked?"

"I was only being friendly" Alicharia sighed exasperatedly.

General Az'nai's aged Retainer, *Sar'ku* Ny'azmi, escorted the visitor to the garden at the rear, where his master sat enjoying the late afternoon's sun in conference with three guests. The General's visitors were current or retired Senior Staff Officers of the Ur'gai Royal Army, grizzled veterans of the campaigns against the Sauromatae in the east, the Argata in 'the lands between the seas' and, in the case of General's Az'nai and Zu'ghir, the last campaign against the Nur'gat, some twenty-five years earlier. As Ny'azmi and Til'koi loomed in to view, Az'nai raised a hand to silence the buzz of conversation and rose to greet his visitor. "It was good of you to come, my old friend. Would you care for a goblet of wine?"

"After the week I have had, I could drain a flagon or two?" Til'koi grinned. The other Generals laughed heartily.

"Make sure we are well supplied, old friend" the General smiled at Ny'azmi warmly.

"I certainly will, Sir!" Ny'azmi nodded and promptly disappeared.

"Sit down, Til'koi, for you know everyone here, I presume."

"Indeed, I do, General Az'nai."

Til'koi knew the men sat at the General's table. General Az'nai poured his guest a goblet of Hellenic red and resumed his seat at the head of the oblong table. General Til'koi took his, directly facing General Nal'gi, Commander of His Royal Majesty's Guard and, to his right, the retired, battle-scarred, and pugnacious General Zu'ghir, victor of the Battle of Gor'khi, some twenty-five years earlier. Immediately to his left, sat the irascible General Bash'tu, feted as the most brilliant cavalry Commander in the Army, a view Til'koi's shared. Bash'tu had been a scourge of the Argata in 'the lands between the Seas' and, more recently, of the Sauromatae to the east of the Uruk Mountains. As Til'koi sat down, it was Bash'tu, rather than their venerable host, who spoke first. "At least now we can stop chirping about Grandchildren and get down to some proper business!" The men laughed raucously.

"How did your meeting go with His Majesty, old friend?" General Az'nai enquired once the laughter had died.

General Til'koi sipped his wine and smiled tightly "I doubt there is a man among us who doesn't know the answer, General Az'nai." There was no laughter, merely an ominous, brooding silence.

"The King is enthralled by his Counsel?" Az'nai smiled wryly.

"Not his Kor'nai!" General Nal'gi spat gloomily.

Til'koi sipped his drink reflectively. It was Generally Az'nai who eventually broke the uncomfortable silence. "Which brings us readily to the point, Gentleman? The King has been ill-advised on this entire adventure, we agree? Our army in the east is now swelled by ill-trained, ill-equipped, and poorly led troops who are little more disciplined than the savages they face in the plains. Our forces in the Caucasus have been deprived of the vital supplies they so urgently need to protect our southern frontier and, most worryingly, there is barely a hem-line of protection in the northeast sector of the Ka'myka Plains!"

"A pair of 'knick-boos' would do nicely!" General Bash'tu remarked acidly. Nobody laughed this time.

"I do not trust the Argata! I never have!" General Zu'ghir spat.

"The *Accord Scythiac* was a sham, right from the very outset!' General Bash'tu growled. "There is logic in sympathising with the Persian effort in Ionia, but where is the grace in seeking ever deeper ties with them? It only weakens our hand, at least to my mind?"

"The King and his Counsel have placed the entire Duchy in an impossible predicament! We have elected to choose a side, have we not?" said General Az'nai.

"Then let at least us speak the truth of it, and to Hades and be damned! We have elected to side with those heathen bastards south of the Caucasus!" sighed General Nal'gi.

General Az'nai looked pointedly at General Til'koi. "Your silence on this matter is instructive, my old friend?"

"Not so, my old friend, I am simply listening. I agree with everything said thus far. We must accommodate Persia, to be sure, but surely nothing more than that? Despite their amity with the Argata, they are scarcely equipped to attack us? The Ur'gai pose no grave threat to us, not since the Battle of Za'kuva, and we have always had a mutual interdependency in respect of our enemies in the east, do we not?"

"With all due respect, my Lord, and there is none I would trust more with my life, we are in agreement on the state of this rabble the King's Counsel has bestowed upon us?" General Bash'tu turned to his right and studied the younger General closely.

"They are beyond description! I have to feed and water these worthless twats!" Til'koi spat.

"They are our brothers, surely?" General Az'nai smiled politely.

"They are not fit for purpose! And since when were you a fucking virgin?" Bash'tu glowered at the older General. For the first time in what seemed like an eternity, the table convulsed into raucous laughter.

"We have an intolerable situation in the east, which has, and I have never been a disciple of old wives' tales, unified the Sauromatae in their enmity with fervour unknown since the early years of Cyrus?" Zu'ghir stated baldly.

"I think that we can all agree on that, my Lord" Til'koi confessed.

"We have weakened our forces in 'the lands between the seas' to such an extent that the Argata, now bolstered by hired Mercenaries, seek greater leverage in the region?" ventured Bash'tu.

"Under the terms of the *Accord*, we have effectively derogated power in the entire region, my Lord" replied Nal'gi gloomily. "Is it little wonder the Argata now covet the Crimea so openly?"

"There is the obvious question of the Ur'gai? Would you be so courteous as to enlighten us, General Nal'gi?" said General Az'nai.

"As you wish, my Lord, for there is much that is troubling in the recent reports from Qu'ehra and the Southern Plains. The Ur'gai succeeded in infiltrating an agent into the region and, whilst I confess there is much about the affair that is wild rumour, this alleged agent may have learned much of our strategic dispositions."

"This is the Sauromatae girl that some have named the 'gold witch'?" Bash'tu bristled.

"When does the King intend to launch his attack against the Ur'gai?" asked Til'koi.

"*His* attack, General Til'koi? You surprise me, for such talk may constitute treason?" Az'nai smiled wryly.

"Do not toy with me, my Lord? This entire meeting may be construed as treason!" Til'koi spoke pointedly.

"Within the moon, my Lord, according to our latest intelligence?" replied Nal'gi.

"Perhaps it would be wise if you continued, General Nal'gi?" General Az'nai said silkily.

"With respect, my Lord's, I shall. According to our sources, the security situation in Nymphaion deteriorates by the hour. This is certainly an unstated aim of Persia, and even the hand of King Darius himself may be at work in these matters. We continue to receive worrying reports of collusion between our brethren in the Civis Militia and known Persian agents in the polis. Even the criminal fraternity may have been seduced into their schemes."

"And these initiatives have received the King's blessing?" Zu'ghir hissed.

"The Argata convinced him of the wisdom of such endeavours?" replied Nal'gi tonelessly.

"As they did the involvement of this Celtic rabble, is that not so?" Zu'ghir growled.

"This is an intolerable state of affairs, is it not, my brothers?" General Az'nai said softly.

"What is to be done then, my friends, if we are all in agreement on this matter?" said Bash'tu.

"We must persuade the King of the folly of this misadventure" spat Zu'ghir.

"Which misadventure would that be, my Lord? The impending war with the Ur'gai, or the feted alliance with the Argata?" interjected Til'koi.

"More wine, perhaps, and a moment's deliberation?" Az'nai smiled slyly.

General Bash'tu glowered at the elderly General and grabbed a fresh flagon from the side-table, refilling every man's cup. "A pox on your deliberations, you miserable old bastard, and to Hades and be damned with the Royal Counsel! I speak for myself, if not anyone else at this table. I do not seek a deeper alliance with Persia, much less those treacherous swine south of the Caucasus. We need time to diffuse the present malaise in the east, for winter is coming. We can move this rabble west of the Wol'yi and have them ready for the Ur'gai in the spring."

"I think we are all in agreement with your sentiments, my old friend" General Az'nai mused.

"What is to be done then? The King must be persuaded of his folly?" interjected Zu'ghir.

"What of these recent developments in Nymphaion? Would the Ur'gai be bold enough to attack?" General Til'koi asked the man sat opposite.

"Our intelligence suggests not, at least for the foreseeable future?" replied Nal'gi.

"Could we delay the impending attack against Nymphaion?" asked General Til'koi.

"Not without alerting the Argata, or the Persians, to our change of heart" Bash'tu sighed.

"I fear that we are missing the point, Gentleman?" interjected General Az'nai. "Perhaps our current problem requires a rather more subtle solution?

One that achieves our objectives, yet at the same time invokes the sympathy of our allies, perhaps even our enemies?"

"I cannot conceive of anything that would accomplish such a feat?" Nal'gi sighed lengthily.

General Az'nai sips his wine and turns to General Til'koi directly. "Now, old friend, tell us more of these Royal Princesses? These babes, in whose hands our lawful King entrusts the destiny of our people?"

Mikhouri ladled steaming mint tea into ceramic goblets and laid these on the wooden placemats set for herself and her sister. Alicharia needed neither assistance nor invitation to provision her side-plate with a hunk of freshly baked ryebread, liberally smeared with butter. The Count and Countess shared a bemused glance, for, if the Princesses appetite had returned, then all was well in the world! "I believe we have some visitors?" the elderly Countess directed her question to the two children, who were sat opposite at the table.

"Do you mean the Sauromatae caravan? We met some of their children at the well earlier this afternoon" Mikhouri confessed.

"I hope you welcomed them, for they are our guests, after all?" the grandfather said sternly.

"We were extremely courteous to them, which is more than can be said for some other people!" Mikhouri glanced meaningfully at her younger sister.

"Is there a problem that I ought to be aware of?" the Count looked closely at his two young Granddaughters.

"Some of the local boys decided to be nasty to them. It was nothing more than that, honestly" Mikhouri sighed.

"They were calling them the most horrible names! It seemed like they thought the girls couldn't understand them, but they obviously could?" Alicharia bridled. "Why does everyone hate them so much?"

The Count and Countess glance at one another knowingly. The countess furrowed her brow. "There have been reports, admittedly sketchy, of a significant increase in the threat from the Sauromatae east of the Wol'yi. We have deployed a significant body of additional men to meet this threat over the course of the past six months. Surely you must have learned of this in Mamy'eva?"

"Are we at war with the Sauromatae? If that is so, then why would they even come?" Alicharia pressed, oblivious to the cold glance from her sister.

"We are not a war, my love, for the Sauromatae are not a nation in the sense that we are. They are a disparate aggregate of local tribes, most of whom are far too busy fighting one another."

"So, it is fine to talk with these children?" Mikhouri asked.

"Of course, it is, my love. Why would you ask?" the Count probed.

"One of the boys asked us 'whose side we were on?' that is all?"

"Some of the older youths have been drafted into the new contingents that have been deployed to the east. Their younger brothers and sisters are concerned for their safety, and that is all" the Count soothed.

"Has there been much fighting? Are there many dead?" Alicharia quipped.

"A Princess should not concern herself with the business of men!" the countess admonished her.

"The Sauromatae do not consider warfare to be the exclusive purview of men! Nor do the Ur'gai!" Alicharia spoke sharply. "I do not see why this should not be of concern to me?"

The old Count chuckled. "I would have thought the soldiers in the Royal Palace would know far more about current developments than the Titled Lord of an insignificant backwater in the far northeast of the Duchy. I have heard tale of worrying, even distressing, events, but I do not think the supper table an appropriate place to discuss them" Suddenly, a polite knock came at the door and old Count's most trusted retainer, Ais'ka, entered. "Ah, my old friend, we have finished eating. Perhaps you would care for a small goblet of wod'ki in my private study?"

"That would be most agreeable, my Lord" Ais'ka spoke tonelessly.

"If you would excuse me, my Ladies?" the Count asked respectfully.

"Of course, do we not?" the countess glanced quickly at the children.

"We do, Grandpapa!" the girls chimed.

The old man smiled at the girls and left the room. Something was obviously wrong, for both Mikhouri and Alicharia had sensed a change in their grandfather's spirit as Ais'ka had entered. "Has something happened? Is it to do with the travellers?" Mikhouri asked softly.

"Now, why would you think that? I am sure this has nothing to do with anything that happened earlier at the well, and it is surely nothing you should concern yourself with, my love. It could be about the wheat harvest, or the market price of barley, or anything to do with the community?" the countess soothed.

"They are not welcome here, are they? The boys tried to make that clear to the girls earlier this afternoon. We heard what they were saying, Grandmama, it was horrible!" Mikhouri sighed sadly.

"I think I might know these boys and, if I am right, there were five of them?" The old lady smiled reassuringly. "They have a reputation for being troublesome, you understand. So, I am not in the least surprised they made their feelings known. One or two of them have older brothers and cousins serving in the east, but I doubt it would matter one way or the other. They would be inclined to make these travellers unwelcome, whatever the situation in the east."

"Are things really that bad east of the Wol'yi at the present?" Mikhouri asked.

"I wouldn't know, would I? Not concerning myself with such things. Knowing the lore of the east as I do, for one cannot be immune to it, not even here, I would believe a mere bushel in a wagon-load of wheat travelling west!" the old lady soothed.

"Our visitors have nothing to worry about?" Alicharia beseeched.

"They appear to have made quite an impression on you, young lady, haven't they?"

"I love their clothes; they are very pretty?" Alicharia cooed.

"They sell them, didn't you know? You might enquire as to whether they have winter clothing for sale. Though quite what your mother, much less your grandfather, would make of them? I suspect you would cause quite the stir at the Royal Palace in Mamy'eva."

"We could ask them tomorrow, if you would like?" Mikhouri smiled sweetly at her sister. "We could head over on our way to collect water, after we return from the paddock?"

"Why don't the pair of you run along to your bedchambers and start getting ready for bed, and I shall prepare some warm milk. I think I might be able to stretch to a pinch of nutmeg, as well as a dollop of fresh honey. After all, we can always obtain more nutmeg from our guests. They will be certain to have some."

As Asel'ya led the two girls out into the narrow corridor, Ais'ka morphs from the door on the right, his face creased with worry. Their Grandfather loomed behind him, adorned in an evening cloak. He seemed surprised, even embarrassed, by the unexpected encounter with the two inquisitive girls. "Are you off to bed, my little cherubs? I must head out on a quick errand, but I shall not be long. I promise I shall call in on you to say good-night, after your grandmother has brought your evening milk."

The girls step to one side to allow their grandfather and Ais'ka to pass, then padded along the corridor, turning left at the end, to climb the stairs to the tower, a one-time defensive addition to the property, long-since abandoned, where their bedchambers were situated. Asel'ya bade the children good-night and closed the door to her room. To Mikhouri's astonishment, Alicharia followed her into her bedchamber, her blue eyes twinkling with mischief. She closed the door firmly. "Something is going on, isn't it? Why else would Grandpapa leave the house at this hour to discuss the market price of barley?" Alicharia rolled her eyes.

"You think it is something to do with the travellers? You think they are in danger?" Mikhouri whispered softly.

"If those horrible boys have anything to do it, perhaps they are. You saw the looks we got off some of the villagers when we came back from the well, didn't you? They weren't very friendly." Alicharia noted.

"You think Grandpapa has gone to warn the travellers they might be in danger?" Mikhouri looked worried.

"Maybe he has gone to speak with the villagers? To try and stop them from doing anything rash this night?" Alicharia ventured. "That wouldn't be much use to the travellers, would it? Not, if they were to ignore him. We need to tell the travellers there might be trouble. It would be a simple act of courtesy?"

"Are you serious, Alicharia? We should go and see the travellers, at this hour?" Mikhouri's eyes boggled.

"It isn't even that late, is it? And besides, whatever anyone may think of us, nobody would ever harm us, would they? We are Royal Princesses, after all" the child grinned.

"Spoken like a true Princess, darling sister" Mikhouri grinned. "I suppose you have figured out our escape route, for we can scarcely use the main door, can we?"

"We shall leave through your window, climb down to the roof of the old larder, and then on to the wood-pile" Alicharia grinned.

"You really have thought of everything, haven't you?" Mikhouri smiled brightly at the younger girl. "Now, go and fetch your shawl, for it will be cooler now than it was a few hours ago. And quietly, remember, for we must not alert Asel'ya!" she cautioned in a whisper.

PART THREE

Ten

More than one hundred and twenty of the wealthiest and most influential citizens in Archaeopolis were gathered in the Great Hall of the Royal Palace. It was by now early evening, and the congregation stood in silent obedience, as the Kor'nai announced the arrival of Her Royal Majesty, Queen Lezika, the Crown Prince Mor'kur, the Royal Princes Disch'al and Sea'gir, and their honoured Guests, the Royal Princess Sychoria and Crown Prince Voskar of the Orch'tai Royal House. Queen Lezika waved graciously to her loyal and faithful subjects, and took her seat in the front row, her husband to her right, and Kor'nai to her left. The stage, with its curtains drawn, had been erected some thirty feet away to her front, and a detachment of heavily armed Guards skulked menacingly in the shadows, to the right of the Hall near the kitchens. A few moments after the Royal party had taken their seats, the curtain drew back, and there, in the centre of the stage, stood Daladaeus. He bowed respectfully to the Royal party and addressed the audience.

"My liege Lady, Lords, Ladies, and other notables seated before me, my dear friends! Tonight, my companions and I are honoured to present to our most recent composition. It is a tragedy, dear friends, and one that needs no introduction! So, without further ado, we present for your edification, *The Sceptre and Serpent: A Tragedy of Paris and Helen!* Daladaeus bowed with a flourish, and the curtain fell. A short time later, it parted.

Act One: The Watch Tower

A Guard detail, commanded by Captain Diomanes, is stationed on the South Tower, facing out to the bay. It is a glorious day, without a cloud in the sky, and the omens are good.

First Guard: A fine day, I do declare! Perhaps as fine as any I have ever seen! It is surely a glorious day to be born, for blessed ye will be, in the eyes of gods!

Third Guard: Indeed, it is, young friend! And yet, I thought your sweet wife was not due to labour until the passing of the next Shabbat?

First Guard: Are not such fortunes subject to the whims of gods? I have an inkling, oh dearest friends, and ye may scoff, that a day as glorious as this surely betokens a blessing from the Heavens!

Second Guard: A son? You think that the gods will bestow upon you and your darling wife this very day the glory of a son and heir?

Fourth Guard: He has been bewitched by the Princess Kassandra, I do declare! He may deny it, but I saw them in conversation on the North Wall the day before yesterday! His certitude of proclamation has an almost puppy-like devotion, does it not?

First Guard: The Princess spoke with me, it is true, and her revelations have left me troubled, I cannot deny it, for there is much in what she told me that heralds a darkness yet to pass.

Third Guard: And now my supplicant, ye shall hear a prophecy of things to come? Thy hands to twine, and eyes behold, a vision only mine!

Captain Diomanes: A common soldier's head is a token worthy of the Royal Princesses gifts, is it not? And yet, an idle tongue, or worse a discourteous lyre, would make a fine gift to grace His Majesty's supper table!

Third Guard: I rebuke myself, my Lord, and humbly beg your forgiveness. I accord no disrespect to the Princess Kassandra, or my Liege Lord, our good King Priam, of that I assure you, for my life is forfeit if it were otherwise!

Captain Diomanes: It is a dark art, no greater truth, that unholy matrimony of sun and moon, to presage a future yet to be? And so, my brothers, let us now still our tongues and hear this lamentation?

First Guard: I did not seek out the Princess Kassandra, for she sought me, upon that I duly swear! And so, in duty bound, I did exactly as she bade me in good faith to do. And so, in the days to come, a sun without compare would rise. Yet, despite its glory, would be condemned before the morn had died!

Second Guard: And so, we have the sun! Only gods themselves could curse such a day!

Fourth Guard: We should not speak of such things, my friends! Only gods, in their eternal wisdom, hold sway the fates of cursed winds.

First Guard: Not this day, my friends, of that I was assured. As sure a certainty as the bounty of the harvest lies in the hands of the Sower, the seeds of the cursed winds to come are mans, and mans alone!

Second Guard: And so, we learn the truth. For the gods have fated you a daughter, dear friend. For, you were the Sower, and she the seed, your bounty is revealed!

Third Guard: And yet, you have three daughters, whose light you surely cannot deny, for they have brightened your days since their birth, is that not so?

Second Guard: It is not the blessing of my darling girls, whom I cherish as only a father could, for they are my world, and that is my truth. Yet, cursed was I, a father of girls, kissed at birth with virtues as pure as winter snow, now condemned to an eternity of sleepless nights to keep it so!

First Guard: If that be true, no curse is she! The seed of this day's cloud lies not in the seed of my loins, or in my sins, but in the sins of Troy itself! And yet, within this cloud, I would see a light, bestowed upon me, by gods alone!

Second Guard: A daughter, and a virtuous and dutiful soul she will be, that the gods shall bestow upon thy sweet wife and thee. Only then, will thou truly know the curse of another man's heir!

First Guard: The sweet Princess told me of another truth, a truth so doleful, that it plagues the joy of a first-born true!

Captain Diomanes: A truth shared, however dubious, can surely be borne by counsel of thy brothers? Whatever this truth is, it cannot be shared by you alone, for, as you have intimated, this seed belongs to all of us, as true-born sons of Troy?

First Guard: A vision of an empty vessel, in a form as yet unknown, within which the hopes and dreams of Troy would be forever cast! And yet, if the gods so willed it, within such vessel, could lie the seeds of Troy's eternal doom!

Captain Diomanes: I cannot foresee a future, nor can any mortal, save the Princess Kassandra, yet even she is often discredited. It is not wise to know the fates, and we must instead face the challenges that each day presents.

Third Guard: And yet, we have a beautiful morning, with several hours left, do we not? Perhaps the Princess Kassandra is right, and our friend Chiastos here will be fated with a blessing from the gods, a healthy infant, a girl, or a boy?

Second Guard: By the gods! Captain Diomanes, come, look, and behold! On the horizon, do you see it?

Captain Diomanes: I see it, friend, and fear the worst! Perhaps this is the first truth the Princess foresaw?

First Guard: My prophecy, as revealed to me, now spells the doom of an entire race!

Captain Diomanes: The fault is not yours, for the course of the war has long since fated their coming! But such a sight, I have never beheld, in all my life! This is surely an Armada unprecedented in the annals of mankind!

First Guard: We must tell the King, my Lord, for he must see this with his own eyes?

Captain Diomanes: And he shall, for I will inform His Majesty with haste!

The end of the First Act

Act Two: The West Wall

The Princess Kassandra, fresh from her morning swim, stands in solitary gloom on the walkway of the West Wall, observing the approach of the Greek fleet on the distant horizon of the bay.

Kassandra: Oh, heavenly gods, such a spectacle I never dared to see! The vengeance of Agamemnon, the gloried King of King's, like a baleful storm cloud, now skates gracefully o'er the sea.

A Guard approaches the Princess

Guard: Now, my Lady, the hour of deliverance has surely come? Menelaus, that cursed cuckold, has in impotent fury cast his rage to blind the sun!

Kassandra: Achilles wrath, to Greece the direful spring! Of woes unnumbered, heavenly goddess, sing! The wrath which hurled to Pluto's gloomy reign, the souls of mighty chiefs untimely slain?

Guard: Do not fear, oh Lady fair, they shall not breach these sacred walls! They will land in the bay, and then shall be slaughtered on the gloried plains!

Thy brother Hector, God-like in his wrath, will carry to the field the hopes of all of Troy, and slay the greatest of their champions!

Kassandra: My brother is a useful tool, yet not much more than that! And now, ye shall behold! The greatest Armada in the book of man, a league of all nations, united in hatred of our race, and survey certain doom, in this, the final act!

Guard: This self-styled league of all nations is but a rabble of adventurers! The gods have surely cast their fate to Hades, and they shall fall like ripened fruit from the tree, in the mask of Hector's unchained fury, you will see!

Kassandra: Will you engage them as they land? Shall they taste the fury of immortal Troy, that most blessed race, to curse their blood, which seeps in woeful torrents unto the sand?

Guard: They shall bleed, my Lady, as they have bled before! The Grecian fury, borne of jealousy and hate, shall never triumph, in this most just of wars!

Kassandra: Shall then the Grecians fly! O dire disgrace! And leave unpunished this perfidious race? Shall Troy, shall Priam, and the adulterous spouse, in peace enjoy the fruits of broken vows? And bravest chiefs, in Helen's quarrel slain, lie unrevenged upon yon detested plain?

Guard: This war has cursed a decade of my youth, and it has stolen, like a cursed jackal, souls of many friends and brothers! I was a mere boy at its birth, when that gilded cuckold assembled his unholy tribe, this inglorious horde, with rape and murder in their heart, a collective unrivalled in history, damned above all others.

Kassandra: A thousand schemes the monarch's mind employ! Elate in thought he sacks untaken Troy. Vain as he was, and to the future, blind, nor saw what Jove and secret fate designed. Nor what mighty toils to either host remain? What scenes of grief, and numbers of the slain!

Guard: It cannot be denied, my Lady, it is the gravest threat to the future of our race, this Grecian stain! Proud Agamemnon, accursed soul, who raised a horde, unchaste and untamed, to wreak destruction on the main and plain!

Kassandra: Do you believe our cause is just? That we, sons and daughters of proud Troy, are noble and righteous, blessed by the gods, in whose eternal grace, assured as the new day's sun, our deliverance we trust?

Guard: My own faith in our cause will never be shaken! Not by the deaths of comrades, for so many we have lost, nor by the grinding wheel of fate, that curses sons beneath its weary grate. In this gravest of endeavours, the sinews and the cords that bind our race, are sure to triumph o'er the madness of a cuckold's hate!

Kassandra: 'Tis not for us, but guilty Troy, to dread. Whose crimes sit heavy on her perjured head? Her sons and matrons Greece shall lead in chains, and her dead warriors strew the mournful plains.

Guard: Come, my Lady, you surely cannot believe such truths, nor ever deign to lull a proud Trojan in acceptance of their purity? It is the Greeks, and they alone, who succoured the favour of the dark god and his temptress, cursed Persephone, to wreak upon the earth such treachery!

Kassandra: In Hades shade, I cast my soul, for terror is thy name! A path to ruin all that remains! It was treachery indeed, which sped these winds o'er the main, and in their fury, all innocence was slain! There is no glory in this war, nor ever was! It was a fool's endeavour, an affront to all the gods hold dear, to steal a heart, to unleash such tears!

Guard: Your brother's folly, t'was an innocent act, and Helen's sin, should Cupid's sting redact? I cannot believe all things to pass, that such a passion could be a cause of such distress. I do declare, there is more to this than meets the eye! This Hellenic distemper, this Grecian malice, that has brought ruin to our neighbours and even now, threatens our survival, must now and forever, be disrobed as lie!

Kassandra: Yet come it will, the day decreed by fates! How my heart trembles while my tongue relates! The day when thou, imperial Troy, must bend? And see thy warriors fall, thy glories end. And yet no dire presage so wounds my mind, my mother's death, the ruin of my kind! Not Priam's hoary hairs defiled with gore, not all my brother's gasping on the shore.

Guard: Thy brother Hector, upon whose shoulders all hopes of Troy must rest, and rest assured, the Greeks he'll best. The famed Achilles, scion of gods, will meet his match, as sure as the ferryman must dip his oars!

Kassandra: My darling brother needs no man's counsel on dipping his oar, or whetting his whistle, on this you have my trust! And now, behold, that fairest of maidens to ever grace the earth, sweet Helen, as proud as she is beauteous, as virtuous as sweet, may now survey the harvest of unbridled lust.

Kassandra waves at Helen, and the soldier turns to view her, standing on the balcony of her bedchamber, gazing at the Greek fleet which draws ever closer to the shore.

Guard: Now there is a maid, if ever fair, the gods themselves saw fit to breathe! If Menelaus wants her back, the spears of every Trojan, shall level to his breast!

Kassandra: That is very touching, and how she must yearn, to hear her name peal across the ocean blue to distant lands! For all ye know, yon sons of Troy, how her honour bristled with defiance, when fair Cupid aimed his bow?

Guard: And we do, my Lady, for it could never be other? That fairest of maidens, of a sweetness pure, a slave for all eternity, to Prince Paris' ardour.

The guard bids his leave, and strolls away, leaving a scowling Kassandra still gazing at her brother's lover, a woman she despises with all her heart.

Kassandra: Only the gods themselves, for amusement or scorn, infected mankind with such ridiculous zeal! Was it love, darling brother, who stole your heart, unleashing this horror, for all our sins? I know thy soul, oh gilded tramp, for thou art slave to base desire! Your fate betokens, a once cherished husband's lash, to whip thee naked, moaning like a whore, my beloved city consumed on the pyre!

Kassandra turns back to the sea, and resigns herself to her fate, as Agamemnon's fleet draws ever closer to the shore.

Kassandra: O race perfidious, who delight in war! Already noble deeds ye have performed. A princess raped transcends a navy stormed. In such bold feats your impious might approve, without the assistance, of the fear of Jove. Crimes heaped on crimes, shall bend your glory down, and when in ruins, your flagitious town!

The end of the Second Act

Act Three: The Bedchamber of Helen and Paris

Helen stands on the Balcony, surveying the Greek fleet closing on the horizon, and is plagued with melancholy, for the war has finally reached the city of Troy itself, threatening to consume all that she holds dear. Prince Paris, her consort, has just stepped out of the bath and has slipped into a pearl chiton. He too is fearful of what the next few days will bring.

Helen: Saturnia leads the lash, the coursers fly, and smooth glides the chariot through the liquid sky. Heaven's gates spontaneous open to the powers. Heaven's golden gates, kept by the winged hours, commissioned in alternate watch they stand. The suns bright portals and the skies command, close, or unfold, the eternal gates of day. Bar heaven with clouds or roll those clouds away.

Paris: Come now, my blessed flower, for it breaks the heart to see thee plagued by woe. For, we knew this day would come, did we not? It was fated by the gods, that these infernal Greeks be driven back to the sea before thine own eyes! And that you, sweet Helen, most beauteous and virtuous maid who shall ever live, bears witness to the final folly of proud Menelaus' madness!

Helen: You think my husband mad? By the gods, I knew ye had the wits of a goat, yet now, at the last, do I see what a fool to love I have been. And so, my precious boy, come, look, and behold, a fleet like none will sail again, a magnificent storm that crashes, relentless as remorseless, against our citadel of dreams.

Paris: Till time shall rifle every youthful grace and age discuss her from my cold embrace! In daily labours of the loom employed or doomed to deck the bed she once enjoyed.

Helen: I find your ribaldry quite unsuited to our current travails, my darling Prince! You think this is funny? Have you any conception of the fate my husband plans for me? For you, your father, or that forked-tongued lunatic who swims naked at daybreak without fail, baring her arse to the guards and the gale?

Paris: I think our soldiers more intrigued by Kassandra's front than her rear, is that not so? My darling bud, I do protest, these walls have never breached. Our beloved city and cherished dreams, lie beyond the mad King's reach!

Helen: All heaven beside reveres thy sovereign sway! Thy voice we hear, and thy behests obey. 'Tis hers to offend, and even offending share thy breast, thy counsels, thy distinguished care, so boundless she, and thy so partial grown, well may we deem the wondrous birth thy own!

Paris: Are we still talking about Kassandra? I have heard my sister described in so many colours that I doubt the truth of a rainbow, yet never with such poetic eloquence! My love, you are fretting over nothing, I do declare! Enough, I say, enough, of my unhinged sister's derriere, let us roll around the sheets, and cast caution to the air!

Helen: And, in the hour of truth, will you fight for me, my sweet? Will you stand upon the field of men, shoulder to shoulder with brave Hector, facing down my husband's rage? Or seek sanctuary in the scullery, and frolic naked with the maids?

Paris: Is heaven offended, and a priest profaned? Because my prize, my beauteous maid, I hold, and heavenly charms preferred to proffered gold? A maid unmatched in manners as in face?

Helen: What moves the god who heaven and earth commands, and grasps the thunder in his awful hands? Thus, to convene the whole ethereal state, is Greece and Troy the subject in debate? Already met, the louring hosts appear, and death stands ardent on the edge of war!

Paris: Inglorious slave to interest, ever joined! With fraud, unworthy of a Royal mind! What generous Greek, obedient to my word. Shall form an ambush, or shall lift the sword?

Helen: Loquacious, loud, and turbulent of tongue! Awed by no shame, and no respect controlled. In scandal busy, in reproaches bold, with witty malice studious to defame, scorn all his joy and laughter all his aim.

Paris: And yet, oh sweetest love, let no truth pass untold between us? In our passion, we have been making scandal since the first our eyes met, is that not true? If memory serves, you did not refrain, much less complain, when on all fours, behind closed doors, you gnawed the lash right through?

Helen: You silly boy! How could I have been so blind to my fate? And yet, it is true, for I cannot deny, you set me free, from the prison of a loveless state! Fated was I, by curse of gods, to a marriage stale of lust! Now in woe, all hopes forlorn, where deliverance strides on a hurricanes wind with vengeance to bestow. That raffish charm, and baby's arm, did chain my heart in tow!

Paris: The queen of love, her favoured champion shrouds, (For gods can all things) in a veil of clouds! Raised from the field the panting youth she

269

led, and gently laid him on the bridal bed. With pleasing sweets his fainting sense renews, and all the dome perfumes with heavenly dews.

Helen: Cursed is the man, and void of law and right! Unworthy property, unworthy light, unfit for public rule, and private care! That wretch, that monster, who delights in war! Whose lust is murder, and whose horrid joy, to tear his country, and his kind destroy!

Paris: I fear you mistake me for my brother, oh sweetest light? I am not Hector, the slayer of men, that unrepentant widow-maker, cursed with an unquenchable thirst for blood. For, I am Paris, the pretty one, disrober of babes, God of the sheets, a hymen-shearing stud! Have you forgotten me, oh light of my life, and soul of my pole!

Helen: For Troy, for Troy, shall henceforth be the strife! And the hard contest not for fame, but life? Haste then to Ilion, while the favouring night, detains these terrors, keep that arm from fight. If but the morrow's sun behold us here, that arm, those terrors, we shall feel, not fear! And hearts that now disdain, shall leap with joy, if heaven permit them to enter Troy. Let not my fatal prophecy be true, nor what I tremble, but to think, ensue.

Paris: Disdain, I hear you say? For you did not disdain, nor hold your tongue, when last we frolicked so gaily on the sheets! And now, to bed, my heart's desire, for love, if above all else, life's simple treats!

Helen: You have bewitched me, oh foolish boy, bound fast am I in chains of lust! And ye besmirch me, for my name is tainted, damned to eternity, in pity and disgust! The most beautiful girl in all the world shamelessly traded all comfort with wanton ardour and now hath lost, for I could not keep my hunger trussed!

Paris: You are my world, my darling pearl, of that I do declare! Our shared desire burns like a pyre, for all eternity. Whilst Agamemnon's fury, and a cuckold's scold, will rage, impotent, at these hallowed walls, our gates it shall not breach! And you are mine, as I am yours, our destiny a marital bed. And now, my sweet, lets meet the sheets, where I will tame, and I will shame, until that pillow's shred!

Helen: I do love thee, more than life itself, even though you are a shameless cad!

Paris: And so, my petal, we shall speak no more of your green-eyed husband and his fleet, of my lunatic sister and her prophecies, or my glory-seeking brother upon whom the gods bestowed many gifts, yet a mind was clearly an afterthought, nor of this pestilence that has haunted us for ten long years! To bed, I say, and forget our fears!

Helen: What thou by Jove the female plague designed? Fierce to the feeble race of womankind! The wretched matron feels thy piercing dart, the sex's tyrant, with a tiger's heart! What though tremendous in the woodland chase, thy certain arrows pierce thy savage race? How dares thy rashness on the powers divine, employ those arms, or match thy force with mine!

Paris: We may vanquish in a happier hour, there want not gods to favour us above. But let the business of our life be love, these softer moments let delights employ, and kind embraces snatch the hasty joy!

The end of the Third Act

Act Four: The West Wall

Kassandra stands on the West Wall, gazing at the Greek fleet as it approaches the bay, when her father, King Priam, approaches with Captain Diomanes, who has summoned him from his private chamber to witness the sight. The market is busy with people, yet there is a strange tension in the air. A pair of young lovers, the boy, perhaps no more than fifteen years of age, attired in his combat uniform, stroll hand-in-hand.

Kassandra: Discord! Dire sister of the slaughtering power, small at her birth, but rising every hour! While scarce the skies her horrid head can

271

bound, she stalks on earth, and turns the world around. The nations bleed, wherever her steps she turns, the groan still deepens and the combat burns!

She turns and gazes upon the square below, noting the lovebirds, who are impervious to the impending arrival of the Greek fleet and of the doom it betokens.

Kassandra: With awe divine, the Queen of love! Obeyed the sister and the wife of Jove! And from her fragrant breast, the zone unbraced, with various skill and high embroidery graced, in this was very art, and every charm? To win the wisest, and the coldest warm, found love, the gentle vow, the gay desire, the kind deceit, the still-reviving fire!

Enter Captain Diomanes

Captain Diomanes: My Royal Princess Kassandra, how fares the morn! It is a dark day, to be sure, yet it was fated, was it not? The mad King, plagued by rage, consumed to madness by jealousy, has come to claim his prize, yet begot!

Kassandra: Thus, fly the Greeks (the martial maid begun), thus to their country bear their own disgrace. Shall beauteous Helen still remain unfreed, still unrevenged a thousand heroes bleed!

Captain Diomanes: We are ready, as in duty bound! To defend our walls, our city, and our race, against this pestilence abound! We are proud sons of Troy, and as breath shall grace, we shall not renege these hallowed walls to such a lowly race!

Kassandra: Oh Captain! If you could only know, how my heart peals so, in tune to devotion! And yet, it is not the fate of man, but the will of gods, to accord justice in this gravest motion!

Captain Diomanes: That may be true, my Lady, but is it not equally true that the gods are not merciless? For all our fortunes, our hopes and dreams, the fate of proud Troy itself, is subject to their grace and favour, in duress?

Kassandra: O daughter of that god, whose arm can wield! The avenging bolt and shake the dreadful shield! No more let beings of superior birth, contend with Jove for this low race of earth! Triumphant now, now miserably slain, they breathe or perish as the fates ordain! But Jove's high counsels, full effect shall find! And, ever constant, ever rule mankind.

Captain Diomanes: My Lady, these are things upon which I cannot express an opinion, nor ever be expected to? Of all the fair maidens, those purest of blooms, to flower within these hallowed walls, you alone, sweet Kassandra, are gifted with the sight of fortune true!

Kassandra: I have not Helen's beauty, nor a brother's guileless charm, and not my fathers' ardour, unchained and unrepentant, for I no lover twixt, no offspring have I graced! And yet, for my gifts, oh cruellest bane, to tell the truth, let falsehood be thy name! And, in my sight, the god's purview, a fate lamented, in sin transgressed!

Captain Diomanes: And the gods, in their wisdom and their glory, cast all mere mortals to the fate of chance! I am a loyal Trojan, thy father's faithful hound, and yet I am a man; father and husband, and my devotions, I declare, to that sweetest of all melodies, my wife, and children, I am in trance!

Kassandra: Are you happy with your lot in life, Captain Diomanes?

Captain Diomanes: I am, my Lady, for I have all the gods could gift. Yet now, upon those waves that swell, a turbulence unchained, I am witness to the fury of a lesser god, oh baleful King of King's, to wreak havoc and destruction on my race, and cast my cherished hopes adrift!

Kassandra: Then shalt mourn thou the affront thy madness gave, forced to deplore when impotent to save! Then rage in bitterness of soul to know, this act has made the bravest Greek thy foe!

Captain Diomanes: Is this truly wisdom, a judgment from above? To trove such hatred, bridle it, unleash its terror on distant realms, all in the name of love?

Enter King Priam, with his retinue, surveying the scene in the bay

King Priam: Thus, from the lofty promontory's brow, a swain surveys the gathering storm below! Slow from the main the heavy vapours rise, spread in dim streams, and sail along the skies. Till black as night the swelling tempest shows, the clouds condensing as the west-wind blows.

Kassandra: In me behold the messenger of Jove! He bids thee from forbidden wars! Repair, to thine own deeps, or to the fields of air. This if refused, he bids thee timely weigh, the elder birthright, and superior sway. How shall they rashness stand the dire alarms, if heaven's omnipotence descend in arms?

King Priam: Lament inglorious Greece and beg to die! Oh! Would to all the immortal powers above, Athena, Phoebus, and almighty Jove! Years might again roll back, my youth renew, and give this arm the spring which once it knew!

Captain Diomanes: I would be honoured to serve under your command, Your Majesty, and at your side, shoulder to shoulder, in the cauldron of a battle's fury. I serve you yet, in this gravest of endeavours, against a cruel and hated foe, these bestial Hellenics, who breathe destruction of Troy's noble glory!

Kassandra: (whispers) I fear I am the only rational soul left in this city, for all else have misplaced their wits entirely!

King Priam: Did you speak, my darling child?

Kassandra: I merely stated how it must please your heart to hear our brave Captain speak of you, and of our endeavours, so highly!

King Priam: O parent goddess! Since in early bloom, thy son must fall, by to severe a doom! Sure to so short a race of glory born, great Jove in justice should this span adorn. Honour a fame at least the thundered owed, and ill he pays the promise of a god, if yon proud monarch thus thy son defies, obscures my glories, and resumes my prize.

Kassandra: Bold are the men, and generous is the soil! There shalt thou reign, with power and justice crowned, and rule the tributary realms around. Such are the proffers which this day we bring, such the repentance of a suppliant King.

King Priam: Such glory I did never see, a plague of warships, each bristling with indignity at proud and noble Troy's defiance! I have never seen the hand of the gods so plainly in all my years, and so we must rage against this tyranny with shield and spear! And vanquish forever this unholy alliance!

Captain Diomanes: I live only to serve you, my liege, and proud Troy, for all mortal desire I now disdain! We shall triumph in the siege, my liege, and vanquish in the plain!

King Priam: No empty boasts the sons of Troy repel! Your swords must plunge them to the shades of hell, to seek, beseems the council, but to dare, in glorious action, is the task of war!

Captain Diomanes: My men and I are ready, my liege, and burn with the fury of the gods to avenge the insults of this Grecian horde, and honour the sacrifice of fallen brothers, who bled our cause so free. I say again, my liege, in this our darkest hour, we are thy light, and all proud sons of Troy shall not rest until this heathen race is banished from our night and bled to stain the main and sea.

King Priam: But Heaven its gifts not all at once bestows, these years with wisdom crowns, with action those, the field of combat fits the young and bold! The solemn council best becomes the old, to you, the glorious conflict, I resign, let sage advice, the palm of age, be mine!

Captain Diomanes: I shall convene the Council of War, my liege, with haste and with your blessing!

Exit Captain Diomanes

King Priam: (Turning to face the fleet as it draws ever closer to the shore) The man who suffers, loudly may complain! And rage he may, but he shall rage in vain!

Exit King Priam

Kassandra: And can ye see this righteous chief atone, with guileless blood for vices not his own? To all the gods his constant vows were paid, sure, though he wars for Troy, he claims our aid. Fate wills not this, nor thus can Jove resign, the future father of the Dardan line! The first great ancestor obtained his grace, and still his love descends on all the race. For Priam now, and Priam's faithless kind, at length are odious to the all-seeing mind. On great Aeneas, shall devolve the reign, and sons succeeding sons, the lasting line!

The end of the Fourth Act

INTERMISSION

The curtain falls. General Yas'cal, Commander of Her Majesty's Royal Guard, stepped forward to announce that light refreshments would be served in the Ornate Garden, if guests would care to make their way outside. The congregation stood and respectfully bowed their heads, as Her Majesty, her consort and children, and the esteemed Royal guests, make their way down the central aisle before stepping out in the last light of a glorious evening. The guests filed out of the Great Hall and into the garden, where tables had been set with silver flagons of Hellenic wine and lemon water. The Royal Princess and Crown Prince Voskar were introduced to a coterie of local notables, and soon, happily so, found themselves distanced from Her Royal Majesty and the Crown Prince Mor'kur, in the company of a small group of wealthy merchant families, including one Balabir, a leading importer of silk from the orient, and his comely wife, Jela. The silk trade was growing exponentially with each year, Balabir assured the Royal couple, and the continuing peace would serve to increase demand for silk garments among aspiring families, even as far as the Hellenic colonies of the Pontic. The Crown Prince Mor'kur suddenly appeared and announced, with obvious courtesy, that he wished to introduce the Crown Prince Voskar to an old friend who would be keen to join them on a hunting party scheduled in the next few days. Voskar smiled sweetly at his wife and graciously bade his leave, leaving Sychoria with the merchant and his wife.

"I do hope that Archaeopolis has made a favourable impression, my Lady?" asked Jela.

"Please, you must call me Sychoria, I insist upon it. Archaeopolis is an extremely pleasant city, my Lady, far fairer than Mamy'eva, I do declare!" Sychoria replied.

Jela smiled sweetly at the generous compliment. "And you may call me Jela, I insist! You have surely visited our markets? I would certainly recommend the Royal Market, for my husband is always singing its praises, are you not, my sweet? I have heard you say often enough that it boasts as good a selection as hallowed Babylon itself" she simpered.

"On a far smaller scale, of course, yet some of the garments we have for sale here are finer than any in Babylon!" Balabir declared.

"I was there with my Handmaiden only the other day. We purchased several exceedingly fine garments from the east, made by the Saka, or so I was told" replied Sychoria.

"Have you had time to visit the Jeweller's Quarter? Her Majesty would be most insistent, I don't doubt, for our craftsmanship is renowned, even in Susa itself, is it not, my sweet?" said Jela.

"I did pay a brief visit, after our sojourn to the Royal Market. I was especially keen to see the craft on offer at Mesticrates store. Alas, his premises were closed" Sychoria smiled thinly.

"Such a terrible blow, the poor fellow, I don't suppose it has done much for his custom?" Jela suddenly blushed hotly and looked uneasy. "And the poor sweet child, of course, a terrible business!"

"A truly shocking affair, to be sure, quite untypical for our fair city, I might add. Young Avielle was such a sweet child. Mesticrates is quite beside himself" Balabir said softly.

"Has he left Archaeopolis? Surely nobody in the Royal City seeks to blame him for this most unfortunate tragedy?" Sychoria probed.

The young couple glanced nervously at each other, a gesture that was not lost on Sychoria. "Would you care for another goblet of wine, Your Royal Highness, I fear supply is diminishing rapidly?" Balabir suggested.

"That would be most gracious of you" Sychoria smiled sweetly, draining the last of her goblet. Balabir accepted the proffered goblet, plucked his wife's with a smile, and headed off towards the nearest table. "Do you know Mesticrates personally, Jela?"

"I do, Sychoria, for Mesticrates is loved and respected in the Royal City. All who know him are beset with grief at what happened. He is a good friend of my husband's family and Balabir commissioned him to craft our wedding bands" Jela said, with genuine sincerity. Jela held out her left hand, palm facing downwards, to allow the Sychoria an opportunity to appraise its beauty.

"That is extremely fine work, my Lady. Only the Sauromatae could craft finer" Sychoria replied with suitable grace.

"Mesticrates served his apprenticeship with several Saka craftsmen at a jeweller in Babylon. He then came here, to commission his own designs. He is an impeccable character and there has never been any whiff of underhandedness!"

"A rare trait in a jeweller, wouldn't you say?" Sychoria smile slyly.

"It would appear so, my Lady, but not with Mesticrates."

Balabir returned presently, tailed by a serving-girl bearing a silver platter with three fresh goblets of red wine. He plucked one from the tray and handed this to the Royal Princess, and then a second to his wife. Only then did he take one for himself and sipped it appreciatively. "This is exceedingly good wine, you would agree, my Lady?"

"I would indeed, my Lord, it is Hellenic, likely from Eretria, is it not?" Sychoria flashed her teeth.

"You have an exceptionally fine palate, my Lady, and I would wager that it is. We have had some success in cultivating some vines on the western plains. With time and sufficient care, perhaps we may hope to rival the Hellenics in the wine trade, for there is certainly sufficient land and water here."

"Your darling wife was showing me her wedding band, which is most exquisite, I might add. Jela told me you had the work commissioned privately by Mesticrates?" Sychoria probed deftly.

"I did, my Lady, for I am sure my darling wife informed you that Mesticrates is an old family friend. I would have trusted none other, though the quality of his craftsmanship was the obvious factor in my decision" Balabir smiled sweetly at his wife.

"You would recommend Mesticrates, if I wish to commission a rare token of esteem for my own darling girls?" Sychoria pressed.

"I would indeed, my Lady, for there is no finer or more reputable craftsman in Archaeopolis!" Balabir made the recommendation with obvious sincerity and reverence.

"And where would I find this Mesticrates, if he is not at his store?"

The young couple exchange startled glances, a reaction not lost on the Royal Princess. "You might try him at his home, my Lady. He has an apartment in the northeast of the city, just off the Nineveh Way" Balabir confessed.

Crown Prince Voskar suddenly re-appeared and announced that the play would soon recommence for its final acts. Sychoria thanked the couple for their graciousness, and twirled away, silver goblet in hand, towards Her Majesty and the Royal entourage. Within a few minutes, General Yas'cal loomed in the entrance to the Great Hall and announced to the guests that the performance would begin presently, and that the guests were invited to take their seats before the entrance of the Royal party. The guests drained their goblets and filed back into the Great Hall where, once seated, the General invited them to stand in homage to Her Royal Majesty and her revered Royal Guests, the Crown Prince Voskar and the Royal Princess Sychoria. Once the Royal Party was seated, General Yas'cal took his position at the right of the stage, and duly gave the signal. The curtain rises.

Act Five: A Council of War

King Priam sits on the Great Throne, his sons, Hector, and Paris, are in attendance. His Chief Counsellor, Antimachus, is present, as in Captain Diomanes, and other counsellors.

King Priam: The thunderer spoke, nor durst the Queen reply. A reverent horror silenced all the sky. The feast disturbed, with sorrow Vulcan saw, his mother menaced, and the gods in awe! Peace at his heart, and pleasure his design, thus interposed the architect divine. The wretched quarrels of the mortal state are far unworthy gods of your debate.

Hector: By this I swear! When bleeding Greece again, shall call Achilles, she shall call in vain. When, flushed with slaughter, Hector comes to spread, the purpled shore with mountains of the dead!

King Priam: My proud son, Hector! All here acknowledge you as the greatest mortal Tory has e'er known! Now strains at the lash, to engage the son of gods, in single combat on the loam!

Captain Diomanes: The Grecian army has begun to disembark, Your Majesty! They will almost certainly make camp, a few miles to the south of the Scaean Gate.

King Priam: Now front to front the hostile armies stand. Eager of fight, and only wait command! When, to the van, before the sons of fame, whom Troy sent forth, the beauteous Paris came, in form a god! The Panther's speckled hide flowed o'er his armour with an easy pride, his bended bow across his shoulders flung, his sword beside him negligently hung! Two pointed spears he took with gallant grace and dared the bravest of the Grecian race!

Hector: (whispers to Paris) O wits of man, our father's sense, long since absconded o'er the garden fence! How is thy fair maiden, the comely Helen? Has she been helping you prepare your spear for duty? I hear pray tell, that proud Achilles, has a soft spot for pretty boys with honeyed tongues and a pert booty!

Paris: While Hector idle stands, nor bids the brave! Their wives, their infants, and their altars save? Haste, warrior, haste! Preserve thy threatened state, or one vast burst of all involving fate. Full o'er your towers shall fall, and sweep away, sons, sires, and wives, an undistinguished prey!

Hector: Nice to see that you have conceded the field, oh brother fair, and so shall yield the bride! Sweet Helen's lust, to be tamed and trussed, and no mere boy could break her stride!

Paris: Ye Gods! You know that Helen despises you, do you not? That witless hulk, she names you so, that feckless beast, that porker of pigs, defiler of sheep, seducer of goats, or if not all, that charmless sot!

King Priam: When you have quite finished with your amusing lamentation of our grave plight, I shall be pleased to hear your contribution, for we are all ears! What say ye, Paris, yon hapless oaf? Let us hear your pleas, oh inglorious vanquisher of maids, virgins, and sacred marital oaths!

Paris: Who shall the sovereign of the skies control? Your hearts shall tremble, if our arms we take, and each immortal nerve with horror shake! For thus I speak, and what I speak shall stand, what power so'er provokes our lifted hand? On this our hill no more shall hold this place, cut off, and exiled from the ethereal race!

Hector: Unhappy Paris! But to women brave! So fairly formed, and only to deceive! Oh, had thou died when first thou saw the light, or died at least before thy nuptial rite! A better fate than vainly thus to boast, and fly, the scandal of the Trojan host.

King Priam: Thy power in war with justice none contest, known is thy courage and thy strength confessed, what pity sloth should seize a soul so brave? Or godlike Paris live a woman's slave! My heart weeps blood at what the Trojans say, and hopes thy deeds shall wipe the stain away.

Paris: My pride is stung, oh noble father, by this shameful lore that no man am I, a slave to lust, cursed forever until my bones are dust! And yet, in this our gravest hour, I shall prove myself worthy of the title of your son and take my rightful place in the pantheon of heroes alongside noble Hector, thy will be done!

Hector: Let mutual reverence mutual warmth inspire and catch from breast to breast the noble fire! On valour's side the odds of combat lie, the brave live glorious, or lamented, die. The wretch that trembles in the field of fame, meets death, and worse than that, eternal shame!

King Priam: See, full of Jove, avenging Hector rise! See! Heaven and earth the raging chief defies! What fury in his breast, what lightening in his eyes! He waits but for the morn, to sink in flame, the ships, the Greeks, and all the Grecian name. Heavens! How my country's woes distract my mind, let fate accomplish all his rage designed!

Hector: The war's whole art with wonder he had seen and counted heroes where he counted men. So fought each host, with thirst of glory fired, and crowds on crowds triumphantly expired!

Enter Helen

King Priam: Approach, my child, and grace thy father's side. See on the plain thou Grecian spouse appears, the friends and kindred of thy former years. No crime of thine our present sufferings draws, not thou, but Heavens disposing will, the cause! The gods, these armies and this force employ, the hostile gods conspire the fate of Troy.

Helen: The sceptred rulers lead: the following host. Poured forth by thousands, darkens all the coast. As from some rocky cleft the shepherd sees, clustering in heaps on heaps the driving bees. Rolling and blackening, swarms succeeding swarms, with deeper murmurs and more hoarse alarms! Dusky they spread, a close embodied crowd, and o'er the vale descends the living cloud.

King Priam: Permit thy daughter, gracious Jove, to tell? How this mischance the Cypriat Queen befell, as late she tried with passion to inflame, the tender bosom of a Grecian dame. Allured the fair, with moving thoughts of joy, to quit her country for some youth of Troy?

Helen: O say what heroes, fired by thirst of fame, or urged by wrongs, to Troy's destruction came. To count them all, demands a thousand tongues, a throat of brass, and adamantine lungs.

Paris: Witness thou first, thy greatest force above? All good, all wise, and all-surveying Jove! And mother-earth, and Heaven's revolving light, and ye, fell furies of the realms of night. Who rule the dead, and horrid woes prepare, for perjured King's, and all who falsely swear! The black-eyed maid inviolate removes, pure and unconscious of my manly loves. If this be false, heaven all its vengeance shed, and levelled thunder strike my guilty head!

Hector: Oh! Silly boy, have ye lost yon wits? To trade salvation for a pair of tits! Those noble words, infused with such contrition, won't save our race from Menelaus' perdition! You broke your word, then broke his heart, and chained his bride in binds of lust! And yet, in vanity, ye protest, oh take my head, but spare the rest!

Antimachus: Oh Sire! If I may be permitted, as counsel true, to add my own thoughts, to these worthy few? We must resist and fight to the end, or else counsel compromise, and delegates send? But know this my Liege, as I live and breathe, from proud Agamemnon, no mercy shall ye receive! He came for two prizes, not the one, for they seek fair Helen, and the head of your devoted son!

King Priam: O first and greatest god! By gods adored! We own thy might, thy father, and our lord! But, ah! Permit to pity human state, if not to help, at least lament their fate? From fields forbidden we submiss refrain, with arms unyielding mourn our Argives slain!

Enter Kassandra

Kassandra: Now heaven forsakes the fight: the immortals yield. To human force and human skill the field! Dark showers of javelins flying from foes to foes, now here, now there, the tide of combat flows. While Troy's famed streams, that bound the deathful plain, on either side, run purple to the main.

King Priam: See the long walls extending to the main. No god consulted, and no victim slain! Their fame shall fill the world's remotest ends, wide as the morn her golden beam extends. While old Laeomedons divine abodes, those radiant structures raised by labouring gods. Shall, raised and lost, in the long oblivion sleep, thus spoke the hoary monarch of the deep!

Kassandra: O King! The counsels of my age attend. With thee my cares begin, and with thee must end. Thee, prince! It fits alike to speak and hear, pronounce with judgement, with regard give ear, to see no wholesome motion be withstood, and ratify the best for public good? Nor, thou a meaner give advice, repine! But follow it and make the wisdom thine.

King Priam: Was ever King like me, like me oppressed? With power immense, with justice armed in vain, my glory ravished, and my people slain! To thee my vows were breathed from every shore, what alter smoked not with our victim's gore. With fat of bulls, I fed the constant flame, and asked destruction to the Trojan name!

Antimachus: Oh! Gracious liege, that is the spirit! A sacrifice to gods in heaven shall salve and steel the public merit! For proud Troy, it hope's and dreams burning eternal in your heart, shall never yield, and shall instead stand tall, and triumph o'er this Dorian upstart!

Kassandra: Oh, damned counsel, I must demur, to logic muddled and motive impure! How many sons of Troy would ye sacrifice on the altar of yon naked vice? A blood-geld ye have sworn, all honour now lies shorn! A baseless counsel sold, for a purse of Trojan gold!

Antimachus: You speak scandalously, noble Lady, revealed now is your truth! No indictment from this lunatic, oh shameless font of fortune disbelieved, must pass without reproof! It is I, my noble liege, who doth protest, thine daughter taints me with baseless falsehood, her wits must be distressed?

Kassandra: Amidst the tumult of the routed train, the sons of false Antimachus were slain. He who for bribes his faithless counsels sold, and voted Helen's stay for Paris' gold! Atrides marked, as these their safety sought, and slew the children for their father's fault!

King Priam: My friend, generous is thy care! These toils, my subjects, and my sons might bear, their loyal thoughts and pious love conspire, to ease a sovereign and relieve a sire. But now the last despair surrounds our host, no hour must pass, no moment must be lost. Each single Greek in this conclusive strife, stands on the sharpest edge of death or life!

Kassandra: Beneath the beech-tree's consecrated shades, the Trojan matrons and the Trojan maids, around him flocked, all pressed with pious care, for husbands, brothers, sons, engaged in war. He bids the train in long procession go and seek the gods to avert the impending woe.

King Priam: Thy counsel is of little merit, in this grave moment of truth! For truth, above all else, is the solemn business of a Council of War, its divine remit! Now begone with thee, oh troubled pawn, thy motives winsome, and thy counsel scorned!

Exit Kassandra

Hector: Great Hector saw and raging at the view, pours on the Greeks, the Trojan troops pursue. He fires his hosts with animating cries and brings along the furies of the skies. Mars, stern destroyer, and Bellona dread, flame in the front, and thunder at their head! This swells the tumult, and the rage of fight, that shakes a spear that casts a dreadful light.

Helen: Let reverend Priam in the truce engage and add the sanction of considerable age. His sons are faithless, headlong in debate, and youth itself an empty wavering state!

King Priam: Let sacred heralds sound the solemn call, to bid the sires with hoary honours crowned. And beardless youths, our battlements surround, firm be the guard, while distant lie our powers, and let the matrons hang with lights the towers. Lest, under cover of the midnight shade, the insidious foe the naked town invade.

Helen: Thou mother Earth! And all ye living floods! Infernal furies and Tartarean gods, who rule the dead, and horrid woes prepare, for perjured kings, and all who falsely swear!

King Priam: Troy roused as soon, for on this dreadful day, the fate of fathers, wives, and infants lay. The gates unfolding pour forth all their train, squadrons on squadrons cloud the dusky plain. Commutual death the fate of war confounds, each adverse battle gored with equal wounds!

Hector: Hector's approach in every wind they hear, and Hector's fury every moment fear. He, like a whirlwind, tossed the scattering throng, mingled the troops, and drove the field along!

King Priam: Go, mighty hero! Graced above the rest, in seats of counsel and the sumptuous feast, now hope no more those honours from thy train! Go, less than woman, in the form of man! To scale our walls, to wrap our towers in flames, to lead in exile the fair Phrygian dames!

Paris: What further subterfuge, what hopes remain? What shame, inglorious if I quit the plain? What danger, singly, if I stand the ground, my friends all scattered, all the foes around? Yet, wherever doubtful, let this truth suffice, the brave meets danger, and the coward flies. To die or conquer, proves a heroes heart, and, knowing this, I know a soldiers part!

King Priam: O friends! O heroes! Names forever dear, once suns of mars, and thunderbolts of war! Ah! Yet be mindful of your old renown, your great forefather's virtues and your own. What aids expect you in this utmost strait? What bulwarks rising between you and fate? No aids, no bulwarks, your retreat attend, no friends to help, no city to defend. This spot is all you have, to lose or keep, there stand the Trojans, and here rolls the deep!

Exit Hector, Paris, and Captain Diomanes

King Priam: That wretch, too mean to fall by martial power! The birds shall mangle, and the dogs devour! The monarch spoke, and straight a murmur rose, loud as the surges when the tempest blows.

Antimachus: You have spoken gracefully and wisely, my liege, and all Troy will obey your command. In this our darkest night, you are our sun, and in your glory, we shall make our stand!

Exit Antimachus

King Priam: I brave not Heaven but if the fruits of earth, sustain thy life, and human be thy birth. Bold as thou art, too prodigal of breath, approach, and enter, the dark gates of death!

The end of the Fifth Act

Act Six: A private family supper in the Dining Hall

Helen and Paris sit at the supper table, a coterie of servants conveys food and drink from the kitchen. Paris is in jovial spirits, whereas Helen is plagued with maudlin at the day's events and the King's rallying cry to war.

Paris: Haste, launch thy vessels, fly with speed away! Rule thy own realms with an arbitrary sway. I heed thee not, but prize at equal rate, thy short-lived friendship, and thy groundless hate. Know, if the god the beauteous dame demand, my bark shall waft her to her native land?

Helen: But if from Heaven, celestial, thou descend? Know with immortals we no more contend, not long Lycurgus viewed the golden light, that daring man whom mixed with gods in fight.

Paris: You seem in better spirits that you were earlier, my sweet? Let us not dwell upon the day's events, for the night is young, and tomorrow, as glory promised, shall we reap!

Helen: Where is your sister, yon harpy of the sage? She who doth delight in revelling in weakness, envy, bitterness, and rage! Will she be joining us this night, for how I yearn to learn what gods presage, to a fork-tongued interlocutor with the gift of second sight!

Paris: You may rest your mind, sweet Kassandra no longer enjoys the good King's grace! Her counsel scorned, lamentations belittled, from the annals of proud Troy, she will vanish without trace!

Helen: Aurora now, fair daughter of the dawn, sprinkled with rosy light the dewy lawn. When Jove convened the senate of the skies, where High Olympus' cloudy tops arise! The sire of gods, his awful silence broke, the Heaven's attentive, trembled as he spoke: Celestial states, immortal gods, give ear, hear our decree, and reverence what ye hear! The fixed decree which not all Heaven can move, Thou fate! Fulfil it! And, ye powers, approve!

Paris: The Queen of love with faded charms she found. Pale was her cheek, and livid looked the wound. To mars, who sat remote, they bent their way, far, on the left, with clouds involved he lay.

Helen: Does thy mind embrace a second shade, beyond our folly in the bed we made? Ye Gods! Was there ever born such a fool as I? In my weakness, convinced was I, there were greater depths than met the eye!

Paris: My darling wench, I do declare, if there are truths to be told, let us strip them bare! I told no lies, nor practiced dark deceit, when to my chamber you did sally, starved of love, parched of lust, to chafe upon the sheets!

Helen: 'Tis not in me the vengeance to remove the crimes sufficient that they share my love! Of power superior, why should I complain? Resent I may, but must resent in vain!

Paris: Blessed in kind love, my years shall glide away, content with just hereditary sway. There, deaf forever to the martial strife, enjoy the dear prerogative of life! Life is not to be bought with heaps of gold, not all Apollo's Pythian treasures hold. Or Troy once held, in peace and pride of sway, can bribe the poor possession of a day.

Helen: Pluto, the grisly god, who never spares, who feels no mercy, and who hears no prayers! Lives dark and dreadful in deep hell's abodes, and mortals hate him, as the worst of gods. Great though he be, it fits him to obey, since more than his my years, and no more my sway.

Paris: If only he had seen fit to sink Agamemnon's fleet! And yet, there is meagre consolation in this days' drama, and there is the glee! That muscle-bound lamebrain is champing at the bit to engage Achilles in a tryst of manly honour, to likely die, and my addled sister is estranged from my father's affections, and presumably his legacy, a sweeter day could never be!

Helen: You really are a duplicitous scoundrel, aren't you, my lustful bloom? Our hopes and dreams, of pampered indolence, in ruins they now lie! And yet ye truffle fortune, in a well of certain doom!

Paris: The fate foredoomed, that waited from my birth. There too it waits, before the Trojan wall. Even great and godlike thou art doomed to fall. Hear then, as in my fate and love we join!

Helen: O man unpitying! If of man thy race, be sure thou'st spring, not from soft embrace. Nor ever amorous hero caused thy birth, nor ever

289

tender goddess brought thee forth. Some rigged rock's hard entrails gave thee form, and raging seas produced thee in a storm. A soul well suiting that tempestuous kind, so rough thy manners, so untamed thy mind!

Enter Kassandra

Kassandra: Unhappy coursers of immortal strain. Exempt from age, and deathless, now in vain. Did we your race on mortal man bestow, only, alas! To share in mortal woe? For ah! What is there of inferior birth, that breathes or creeps upon the dust of earth. That wretched creature of what wretched kind, than man more weak, calamitous, and blind? A miserable race, but cease to mourn, for not by you will Priam's son be borne!

Paris: I thought you banished from the supper table, darling sister, for a stench of ordure now taints thy sweet smile? And yet, if you might learn to bridle your tongue, we may tolerate your company, if only for a while!

Kassandra: Oh! Darling brother, can't you see, how blind in mind are thee? Our city doomed beyond the gates of hell, for there is no escaping Agamemnon's spell, and yet ye smirk and confound with silly jests, to impress a tart with average breasts!

Helen: You venomous little harpy! How long have I laboured under your bittersweet glare, suffered your insults, and whispered profanities, ye insolent cur! And how fares thy fortune, muddle-head? Hast thou found a man to grace thy bed? Have the gods illuminated the curse of your distemper, the well of all your hate? To die a blessed virgin, no pillow shall ye grate! No lust could ever flame within thy loins, thy heart a Jailor's gate!

Enter Hector

Hector: Oh! Darling sisters, how dispiriting to see you brought so low! You curse and claw like alley-cats on heat, even as a mad King's fury doth whirl and blow!

Paris: Oh! Hector, light of thy father's eye, his true born son! How could I hope to challenge in my father's grace, for thou art Hector, the people's face, who will vanquish our enemies, in the days to come!

Hector: Do not mock me brother, for your conduct is the cause of Troy's disgrace! To bed another man's wife, 'tis no mere crime, not when she hails from the violet race!

Helen: To Agamemnon's ample tent repair. Bid him in arms draw forth the embattled train, lead all his Grecians to the dusty plain. Declare, even now 'tis given him to destroy. The lofty towers of the wide extended Troy.

Hector: The furies that relentless breast have steeled, and cursed thee with a heart that cannot yield. You think a day will come, when fate's decree, and angry gods shall wreak this wrong on thee. Phoebus and Paris shall avenge my fate and stretch thee here before the Scaean gate.

Helen: Oh generous brother! (if the guilty dame that caused these woes deserves a sisters name!) Would heaven, ere all these dreadful deeds were done, the day that showed me to the golden sun had seen my death! Why did not whirlwinds bear, the fatal infant to the fowls of air?

Kassandra: For I must speak what wisdom would conceal, and truths, invidious to the great, reveal, bold is the task, when subjects, grown too wise, instruct a monarch where his error lies! For though we deem the short-lived fury past, 'tis sure the mighty will revenge at last.

Enter King Priam

King Priam: And what a sight, mine eyes do weep, for all my children, thy glories reap! Oh! Glorious Troy, no greater state! No prouder race, e'er born to rule? Even you, yon Paris, ye feckless tool!

Helen: O daughter of that god, whose arm can wield, the avenging bolt, and shake the sable shield! Now, in this moment of her last despair, shall wretched Greece no more confess her care? Condemned to suffer the full force of fate, and drain the dregs of Heaven's relentless hate? Gods! Shall one raging hand thus level all, what numbers fell! What numbers yet shall fall?

King Priam: When King's advise us to renounce our fame, first let him speak who first has suffered shame? If I oppose thee, prince! Thy wrath behold, the laws of council bid my tongue be bold. Thou first, and thou alone, in fields of fight, durst brand my courage, and defame my might.

Helen: O thou! For ever present in my way, who all my motions, all my toils survey

Safe may we pass beneath the gloomy shade, safe by thy succour to our ships conveyed. And let some deed this signal night adorn, to claim the tears of Trojans yet unborn!

Paris: Of upper heaven to Jove resigned the reign, overwhelmed under the huge mass of earth and main. For strife, I hear, has made the union cease, which held so long that ancient pair in peace? What honour, and what love, shall I obtain? If I compose these fatal feuds again!

King Priam: Whose fates are heaviest in the scales of Jove, tomorrow's light (O haste the glorious morn!). Shall see his bloody spoils in triumph borne, with this keen javelin shall his breast be gored. And prostate heroes bleed around their lord.

Helen: Oh worthy better fate! Oh early slain! Thy country's friend, and virtuous, though in vain, no more the youth shall join his consort's side? At once a virgin, and at once a bride! No more with presents her embraces meet or lay the spoils of conquest at her feet. On whom his passion, lavish of his store, bestowed so much, and promised so much more!

King Priam: Thus, rank on rank, the thick battalions throng. Chief urged on chief, and man drove man along. Far o'er the plains, in dreadful order bright, the brazen arms reflect a beamy light. Full in the blazing van great Hector shined, like mars commission to confound mankind. Before him flaming his enormous shield, like the broad sun, illuminated all the field!

Kassandra: Thou art up shit-creek now, oh silly boy! Our father is now cursed with asinine nobility! Do you think ye truly sired of the gods? Thou art but man-like gristle, void of celestial wisdom, which lives, breathes, bleeds, and dies. No grace from spear or arrows deliverance, in thy duplicity!

Helen: Great Jove has placed, sad spectacle of pain! The bitter dregs of fortune's cup to drain, to fill with scenes of death his closing eyes, and number all his days by miseries! My heroes slain, my bridal bed overturned, my daughters ravished, and my city burned! My bleeding infants dashed against the floor, these I have yet to see, perhaps yet more!

King Priam: My Lady, sweet child, your hands doth tremble! Dwell no more upon such distressing fates, instead of victory, the glorious triumph of our race, awaits!

Kassandra: And now we see there is a first for everything, for it is usually her knees which tremble!

Helen: Shall, ignominious, we with shame retire, no deed performed, to our Olympic sire? Come, prove thy arm! For the first war to wage, suits not my greatness, or superior age. Rash as thou art to prop the Trojan throne, forgetful of my wrongs, and of thy own. And guard the race of proud Laeomedon!

Paris: Nor must thy course lie honoured in the bier, nor spouse, nor mother, graced thee with a tear! Far from our pious rites those dear remains, must feast the vultures on the naked plains.

Helen: Ah suffer that my bones may rest with thine! Together we have lived, together bred. One house received us, and one table fed, that golden urn, thy goddess mother gave, may mix our ashes in one common grave.

Paris: But since the god his hand has pleased to turn and fill thy measure from his bitter urn. What sees the sun, but hapless heroes' falls? War, and the blood of men, surrounds thy walls. What must be, must be! Bear thy lot, nor shed, these unavailing sorrows o'er the dead! Thou canst not call him from the Stygian shore, but thou, alas, may'st live to suffer more?

King Priam: 'Blest is the man who pays the gods above, the constant tribute of respect and love! Those who inhabit the Olympian bower, my son, forget not, in exalted power. And heaven, that every virtue bears in mind, even to the ashes of the just is kind.

Kassandra: O sire! Can no resentment touch thy soul? Can mars rebel, and does no thunder roll? What lawless rage on yon forbidden plain, what rash destruction! And what heroes slain! Venus, and Phoebus, with the dreadful bow, smile on the slaughter, and enjoy my woe! Mad, furious power! Whose unrelenting mind, no god can govern, and no justice bind!

King Priam: To few, and wonderous few, has Jove assigned. A wise, extensive, all considering mind, their guardians these, the nations round confess, and towns and empires for their safety bless.

Helen: Ah, dearest friend! In whom the gods had joined the mildest manners with the bravest mind. Now twice ten years (unhappy years) are o'er, since Paris brought me to the Trojan shore. O, had I perished, ere that form divine, seduced this soft, this easy heart of mine! Yet, it was ne'er my fate, from thee to find, a deed ungentle, or a word unkind.

Paris: But now, O monarch! All thy chiefs advise, nor what they offer, thou thyself despise. Among those counsels, let not mine be vain, in tribes and nations to divide thy train?

King Priam: Rush to the fight, and every foe control! Wake each paternal virtue in thy soul, strength swells thy boiling breast, infused by me, and all thy godlike father breathes in thee!

Kassandra: A lion, not a man, who slaughters wide, in strength of rage, and impotence of pride. Who hastes to murder with a savage joy, invades around, and breathes but to destroy. Shame is not of his soul, nor understood, the greatest evil and the greatest good.

Hector: How proud Achilles glories in his fame! And hopes this day to sink the Trojan name, beneath her ruins! Know, that hope is vain, a thousand woes, a thousand toils remain. Parents and children our just arms employ, and strong and many are the sons of Troy. Great as thou art, even thou may'st stain with gore, these Phrygian fields, and press a foreign shore.

King Priam: And all the gods that round old Saturn dwell, had heard the thunders to the deeps of hell. Well was the crime, and well the vengeance spared, even power immense had found such battle hard. Go thou, my son! The trembling Greeks alarm, shake my brood aegis on thy active arm! Be Godlike Hector thy peculiar care, swell his bold heart, and urge his strength to war!

Kassandra: If Heaven have lodged this virtue in my breast, attend, O Hector! What I judge the best! See, as thou move, on dangers spread, and war's whole fury burns around thy head. Behold! Distressed within yon hostile wall, how many Trojan's yield, disperse, or fall!

Helen: The day shall come, that great avenging day, when Troy's proud power, gloried in the dust shall lay, when Priam's power and Priam's self shall fall, and one prodigious ruin swallow all. I see the god, already from the pole, bare his red arm, and let the thunder roll. I see the eternal all his fury shed, and shake his aegis o'er their guilty head!

Exit Helen (in a fit of tears)

Paris: Swift to her bright apartment she repairs. With skill divine had Vulcan formed the bower, safe from access of each intruding power, touched with her secret key, the doors unfold, self-closed, behind her shut the valves of gold! Here first, she bathes, and round her body pours, soft oils of fragrance, and ambrosial showers, the winds, perfumed, and balmy gale convey, through heaven, through earth, and all the aerial way.

King Priam: You should go after her, my son, for no pride so high, and no shame so low, to lose a treasure sought by Cupid's bow!

295

Paris: Swift from the string the sounding arrow flies! But flies unblessed, no grateful sacrifice, no firstling lambs, unheedful! Didst thou vow, to Phoebus, patron of the shaft and bow? For this, thy well aimed arrow turned aside, erred from the dove, yet cut the cord that tied! Adown the mainmast fell the parted string, and free the bird to heaven displays her wing!

Exit Paris

Kassandra: Thus entering, in the glittering rooms he found, his brother-chief, whose useless arms lay round? His eyes delighting with their splendid show, brightening the shield and polishing the bow, beside him Helen with her virgin's strands, guides their rich labours, and instructs their hands!

Hector: How long, unhappy! Shall thy sorrows flow, and thy heart waste with life consuming woe? Mindless of food, or love, whose pleasing reign, soothes weary life, and softens human pain? O snatch the moments yet within thy power, not long to live, indulge the amorous hour!

King Priam: Which Troy shall, sworn, produce; that injured Greece? May share our wealth and leave our walls in peace! But why this thought? Unarmed if I should go, what hope of mercy from this vengeful foe, but woman-like to fall, and fall without a blow? We greet, not here, as man conversing man, meet at an oak, or journeying o'er a plain. No season now for calm familiar talk, like youths and maidens in an evening walk. War is our business, but to whom, is given to die, or triumph, that, determine heaven!

Kassandra: For I must speak what wisdom would conceal! And truths, invidious to the great, reveal, bold is the task, when subjects, grown too wise, instruct a monarch where his error lies! For though we deem the short-lived fury past, 'Tis sure the mighty will revenge at last!

Hector: If Thetis' son must no distinction know! Then hear, ye gods! The patron of the bow, but Hector only boasts a mortal claim, his birth deriving from a mortal dame! Achilles, of your own ethereal race, springs from a goddess by a man's embrace!

Kassandra: So lies great Hector prostrate on the shore, his slackened hand deserts the lance it bore! His following shield the fallen chief overspread, beneath his helmet dropped his fainting head. His load of armour, sinking to the ground, clanks on the field, a dead and hollow sound. Loud shouts of triumph fill the crowded plain, Greece sees, in hope, Troy's great defender slain!

Exit Kassandra (in a fit of pique)

King Priam: Hear me, and judge, ye sisters of the main! How just a cause has Thetis to complain! How wretched, were I mortal, were my fate! How more than wretched in the immortal state! Sprung from my bed a godlike hero came, the bravest far that ever bore the name!

The end of the Sixth Act

Act Seven: A soliloquy of Fates

Helen stands alone on the balcony to her bedchamber, beset with grief at the fates the gods have dealt her.

Helen: Let me — But oh! Ye gracious powers above, wrath and revenge from men and gods remove. Far, far too dear to every mortal breast, sweet to the soul, as honey to the taste, gathering like vapours of a noxious kind, from fiery blood and darkening all the mind. Me Agamemnon urged to deadly hate, 'Tis past — I quell it, I resign to fate

Paris lies on the bed, overcome with remorse at how his love for Helen, a love which may not last the night, has brought such tragedy to the city of his birth.

Paris: As full-blown poppies, overcharged with rain! Decline the head, and drooping kiss the plain. So sinks the youth, his beauteous head, depressed, beneath his helmet, drops upon his breast!

Kassandra stands alone on the West Wall, gazing out across the bay in the moonlight.

Kassandra: Turn here your steps, and here your eyes employ, ye wretched daughters, and ye sons, of Troy! If e'er ye rushed in crowds, with vast delight, to hail your hero glorious from the fight? Now meet him dead, and let your sorrows flow, your common triumph, and your common woe!

Hector stands on the Watch Tower of the South Wall, gazing down on the plain and the campfires of Agamemnon's army. Despite his optimism, and of the blessing of the gods, he is troubled by Kassandra's prophecy of his certain death in the days to come.

Hector: But let some prophet, or some sacred sage, explore the cause of great Apollo's rage! Or learn the wasteful vengeance to remove, by mystic dreams, for dreams descend from Jove. If broken vows this heavy curse have laid, let altars smoke, and hetacombs be paid.

King Priam stands on the balcony of his bedchamber, gazing out over the bay, and cuff's a tear as he espies his daughter, Kassandra, who does not see him watching her.

King Priam: As when old oceans silent surface sleeps, the waves just heaving on the purple deeps. While yet the expected tempest hangs on high, weighs down the cloud, and blackens the sky. The mass of waters will no wind obey, Jove sends one gust, and bids them roll away!

THE END

The curtain falls. A solemn silence fills the room. Daladaeus and his fellows, all servants of the stage, had done all that could be asked of them, and more. General Yas'cal stepped forward and nodded at Her Majesty. Queen Lezika stood, as did the other members of the Royal Party, followed by the rest of the congregation, then the curtain parted to reveal the actors, arraigned in a semi-circle, Daladaeus at the centre. They bowed respectfully to the Queen and the assembled spectators. The applause is as spontaneous as it was resonant, and the troupe basks in the adulation, for this was their first Royal performance. After the applause had died, the Queen bowed respectfully to the actors, who applauded the Queen with suitable grace, then turned and strolled down the central aisle, followed by the Royal guests, to a crescendo of applause, out into the fading light of the evening where refreshments were to be served. The rest of the audience filed out behind them, to allow tables to be moved and set by the waiting staff, under the watchful eye of General Yas'cal.

Eleven

The actors, led by a blushing Daladaeus, were introduced to Her Majesty and the rest of the Royal Party, who commended the play as '*delightful*', '*inspiring*', and even '*wickedly ingenious*'. Daladaeus, solely credited with its composition, with obvious deference to the great Homer, was positively thrilled by the accolades. The audience were even more flattering, though most of their ilk could scarcely tell Homer from Hades. In due course, General Yas'cal loomed in the entrance of the West Wing and announced that the revellers should make their way to their tables, to be seated before the arrival of the Queen and the honoured guests. The actors waited patiently outside, for they were honoured guests, and would be seated at the High Table with Her Royal Majesty and her esteemed visitors from Mamy'eva. Daladaeus felt honoured indeed, especially when it was disclosed that he and Bella would be sat with the Crown Prince Voskar and Royal Princess Sychoria, whose knowledge of the works of the great Homer, and of Aesop, would make for excellent table chatter. *Fine food, fine wine, and even finer conversation with an esteemed Royal guest; could any thespian, indeed a man, ask for anything more?*

Presently, the Royal party, led by Her Majesty and the Crown Prince Mor'kur, waltzed down the aisle of the Great Hall toward the High Table, set a short distance in front of the stage. Queen Lezika seemed in fine fettle that evening. A great many of the guest's would later remark that this was the most relaxed they had seen her in many moons. Queen and Consort took their place at the centre of the table, flanked on the left by the Crown Prince Voskar and the Royal Princess Sychoria, and on their right by the young Royal Princes, who would be principally entertained by the dwarf, Novaetis, who seemed not in the least offended, just so long as copious quantities of wine were to hand. Despite his delight at the prospect of the Princess Sychoria's company, Daladaeus was quietly troubled by the deliberate short shrift given to Novaetis whom, despite his stature, had given an accomplished, and even lofty, performance as Prince Paris. As the actors were allotted their seating, it became clear that Novaetis had been deliberately seated among the minor actors yet seemed at ease in the company of the young Princes. Daladaeus groaned inwardly as Novaetis drained a silver goblet of wine in a single gulp, before pouring a refill, to the evident delight of the young Princes, who were enchanted by the prospect of an evening in the company of a wine-sodden dwarf!

The fayre was spectacular. The wine was the best the Bordeaux could offer, and the first course included poached swordfish with fresh figs, roast pheasant and stewed plums, and tomatoes stuffed with saffron rice, topped with a crumbly cheese and basil. Daladaeus and Bella chatted animatedly with Voskar and Sychoria, seated across the table, and with Her Majesty and her Counsellors, seated to their left. In contrast to the polite and stimulating conversation at this side of the table, the far end was far livelier, at least judging by the incessant giggling as Novaetis held forth on a range of topics, to the evident delight of the young Princes. As the plates were cleared, Her Majesty smiled sweetly at Daladaeus and rose from her seat, nodding to General Yas'cal, who clapped the room to a respectful silence, before Queen Lezika addressed them.

"My Lords, Ladies, and esteemed Royal Guests, I would greatly please me if everyone would stand and raise your cups to our dearest of friends, this impeccable troupe of Thespians, who are most welcome in our beloved city, now and forever!"

The applause was ecstatic. The actors stood and bowed reverentially to the assembled guests, before retaking their seats. Daladaeus remained

301

standing, to turn and bow to the Queen. "We are truly honoured by your hospitality, and your grace, Your Royal Highness!"

"Hear! Hear!" chirruped the troupe.
"More beer!" Novaetis boomed, to a cacophony of giggles.

"This wine is excellent, don't you agree?" Daladaeus addressed the question to the Crown Prince Voskar.

"It is Gaullish, I believe" Voskar sips his wine. "I am naturally curious as to how you conceived of such a novel adaption of the Iliad. The quotations, the literal ones, were extracted from the epic?"

"They were, indeed, Your Royal Highness. The most famous tragedy in history lends itself all too readily to novel interpretation" Daladaeus replied.
"My tutors in Corinth beleaguered me with Homer, yet I never ranked among the most gifted of their pupils" Queen Lezika confessed.
"With all due respect to your tutors, I fear that Homer's epic is often taught as a study in *style*; a purely academic examination of construction that misconstrues the human theatre of love, lust, fate, and honour" Daladaeus declared.
"You think the Iliad is a paean to the folly of lust, dear Daladaeus?" Sychoria smiled sweetly.
"I think it an important facet of the epic, my Lady. It is primarily a lesson in honour, is it not?" Daladaeus mused. Bella pressed her foot down hard on his own to warn him this was potentially dangerous ground.
"I have often pondered the dilemma of poor King Priam, as I am sure you must have, Princess Sychoria?" the Queen spoke evenly.
"That is surely the real tragedy of the epic, is it not?" mused Crown Prince Mor'kur. "A lesson for future generations of the bane of pride, of a soul torn between what is right, at least in the eyes of others?"
"You think Priam a tormented soul, Prince Mor'kur?" Sychoria chirped.
"Indeed, I do, my Lady! Surely the honourable course was to return Helen to her husband, then deal with his son's folly judiciously."

"Priam should have executed Paris for his foolishness?" Sychoria quipped mischievously.

"It would have satiated Menelaus' burning sense of injustice, and bridled Agamemnon's desire for vengeance against the Trojans."

Sychoria leaned across and smiled sweetly at the prince. "Would you have launched a thousand ships to satiate your injured pride, Prince Mor'kur?" The Crown Prince Voskar shot his wife a warning look, a gesture not lost on Bella and Daladaeus.

"Surely, it was love, not a cuckold's wounded pride, which spirited the fleet across the Aegean?" Daladaeus ventured diplomatically.

"I have always considered Menelaus to be appalling husband material" Bella chirped, drawing a bemused glance from Sychoria.

"Do you think the mistress Helen was unsatisfied in life, my lady?" Queen Lezika asked evenly.

"She was certainly unsatisfied between the sheets, Your Royal Highness, is that not so?" Bella mused without blushing. This time it was Daladaeus' turn to tap a warning on her feet.

"I have always considered the Iliad a tragedy of unrequited love" Daladaeus sighed. "I believe that Lady Helen did once love Menelaus. Yet, over time, a crushing sense of loneliness drove her into the arms of another, one who not only appreciated her beauty, but the passion which coursed through her veins; her virtues, desires, even hunger!"

"You are not in the least disturbed by such unrestrained wantonness in a woman? Polite society expects us to imprison our desires, our hunger, and lust, whilst regaling our virtues like the tail of a peacock" Sychoria mused airily.

"It was precisely those earthly failings in the fair Helen which wrought ruin upon her adopted city?" interjected Voskar. "I felt you explored her torment admirably in the performance" Voskar nodded at Daladaeus.

"And yet, you revelled in your portrayal of Prince Paris as an unspeakable cad? A man governed by his loins, rather than his brains?" Sychoria ventured.

"Is he not forever tainted as a man without a sinew of honour?" ventured Mor'kur.

"And what is this *honour*, this estimable virtue, which men place first above all on such a lofty plinth? The tragedy of Paris is an invaluable lesson to us all, of the folly of allowing your heart reign above reason?" Sychoria's eyes twinkled mischievously.

"Could not the same charge be levelled at the scarlet Helen, Your Royal Highness?" Lezika smiled brightly. "Paris was a fool, both in life, and in love, as many a man is fated to be?"

"I think that might be a fair indictment of you, my love?" Bella grins at Daladaeus, who chuckles wryly.

"I doubt Paris was anybody's fool" Lezika ventured. "His was ruin wrought of selfishness and arrogance. Having rescued Helen from the prison of a loveless marriage, he made her votive and slave to her unbridled lust. In the end, he was simply too proud to let her go."

Voskar coughed lightly to silence any reply from his wife, who was clearly enjoying herself. It was Daladaeus, who answered diplomatically. "I suspect you may be right, on both counts, Your Majesty. Only at the end, did Helen realise her true folly, yet she remained a slave to the sheets."

"An all-too-common failing in many a man, I would hazard? I know of no Pleasure Garden that exists to serve the needs of women?" Sychoria ventured, without blushing.

"And so, we return to honour, do we not?" added Prince Mor'kur.

"I often feel Agamemnon is forever damned as a convenient villain; a man driven to distraction, and destruction, by convention of honour. For vengeance, in of itself, is no matter of necessity, it is a sage lesson to others" the Queen mused. "Perhaps you might explore this issue in a separate production, for we would be honoured if you would consider it worthy of your talents?"

"We would be honoured, Your Majesty, truly so" Daladaeus replied.

"Did you compose the play yourself, Daladaeus, or was this a collaborative undertaking?" the Queen probed.

Daladaeus blushed lightly. "We are a troupe, Your Majesty, and have been together for many years. There is not an actor whose ideas would be lightly dismissed."

"There must surely be a charioteer, driving the idea forward, from inception to completion?" Sychoria beseeched.

"That is true, my Lady. For my sins, in this case that drover was me" Daladaeus confessed. He sipped his wine, his nervousness palpable.

"Have you performed the composition elsewhere, my dear fellow?" Queen Lezika enquired.

"No, Your Majesty, we have not. The script was written in Archaeopolis, soon after our arrival" Daladaeus confessed.

"Then we are truly honoured, my dear fellow! It is a most excellent discourse on the tragedy of Helen and Paris."

"As I have said, Your Majesty, the honour is ours" Daladaeus smiled brightly.

"Yours, surely, for it was your composition? And completed in so short a space of time?" the Queen pressed.

"As I have said, Your Majesty, whilst I must can the credit for composing the play, my mind was receptive to suggestions of my esteemed fellows, for we are a collective."

"If that it so, we are indebted to you all, as a collective" Lezika simpered. "And yet, I fear our dearest Daladaeus may be taking rather more credit than is wise. After all, a man's wife is surely his greatest inspiration?"

"I am honoured, Your Majesty, truly I am" Bella replied softly.

"As we are in your debt, my Lady, of that you may rest assured" the Queen smiled sweetly at Bella, who blushed furiously.

And yet, it was Sychoria whom noted the unease in her husband's eyes.

"How did you become a serious actor?" Prince Disch'al asked Novaetis earnestly.

"Now who would ever claim I was a serious actor, young Prince? Show me this fellow, and I shall soon disavow him of his misconceptions!" the dwarf grinned inanely. "I would not believe all that is whispered about me, certainly not by my companions" Novaetis drained his goblet of wine and promptly poured a refill.

"Aren't dwarves supposed to be figures of fun? They are rarely serious, not from what I have seen" Disch'al pressed.

Novaetis was not insulted by the question, although he was keenly aware that the two Counsellors to his left appeared to be taking a keen interest in their conversation. "You are quite right, Your Royal Highness, with the advancing years I have become rather more serious than I ever aspired to be. When I was younger, that was a different matter entirely!"

The princes giggled. "You joined the stage when you were young?" Sea'gir asked.

"I was seven years old, a little older than you, young Prince. I was born and raised in a flea-bitten hovel a few miles south of Tyre. I was apprenticed as a thief when I was four years old, for a child of such diminutive stature can enter places denied to their peers, is that not so? I was a good thief, I am proud to say, and made a lot of money for my master. One night, I had a close-run call, an event I am in no hurry to repeat!" Novaetis confessed glibly.

The princes were both astounded and more than intrigued by such a glib confession of wayward behaviour. "What happened?" Disch'al whispered.

"I was intercepted by a servant and was lucky to escape with my life. I had a sack full of trinkets, which would sell for a small fortune, for there are always willing buyers for such goods!"

"Were you arrested?" Disch'al pressed.

"No, I was not" Novaetis smiled ruefully, a sipped his wine. "The man tried to impale me upon his dagger. Luckily, I had taken something my master would have considered of little real value, which I had squirreled away in a small pocked within my robe. Fortunately, my prize bore the brunt of the brute's savagery. He was aghast at my unfathomable immortality, yet not so nearly as when I toed him in the plums!" The two princes giggled hysterically, drawing a stern glance from their mother. With typical grace, Novaetis raised a goblet and ceremoniously saluted his host, who smiled back tightly, raising her goblet in salutation to her honoured guest.

"What was it?" Sea'gir asked.

"It was a book. If you would credit such serendipity! As I said, my master would have declared it of little value, yet it was obviously of value to its owner and, from that moment forth, to me!" Novaetis grinned.

"What was the book?" asked Disch'al.

"It was a copy of the Odyssey, by our learned Homer. For quite inexplicable reasons, I had always found books fascinating, despite being a professed illiterate! I escaped with my life, my ill-begotten gains, including the book, which I endeavoured to learn to read. After all, it had saved my life. The rest, as they say, is history!" Novaetis drained his goblet. This was graciously refilled by Prince Disch'al, who was as enchanted by the life story of the dwarf as by his colossal capacity for alcohol.

"You were forced to flee Tyre?" Disch'al probed.

"Indeed, I was, for the neither the authorities, nor the hangman, seemed inclined to clemency. I made my way to Medes, where I had the good fortune to meet our dear friend Daladaeus, who offered me a more profitable vocation" Novaetis replied, without blushing.

"Did Daladaeus tutor you as an actor?" asked Disch'al.

"For his sins, my little Lord, he did. And I have never looked back. In due time, I even started helping him write some of our material. It has been a profitable and enjoyable relationship, and one to which I give daily thanks to the gods."

"Is Daladaeus a good actor, in your opinion?" asked Sea'gir.

"I have yet to meet one finer! I know not what we would ever do without him!" Novaetis said emphatically.

The main course was mouth-wateringly sumptuous, comprising roast lamb, basted with wine, rosemary, and olive oil, roast onions and garlic, and a stewed beef tomato. The wine was a fine as before, and, to Novaetis eternal happiness, jars of rye beer were served to wash it down. Lemon and honey pastries, filled with vine fruits, were served alongside fresh raspberries, and whipped cream. At the end of the meal, Queen Lezika rose to raise her goblet to her guests, the visiting Royals, and the troupe of actors, whom would be extended all courtesy during their stay in Archaeopolis. As the actors climbed aboard their carriages to be ferried back to *The Horn and Crown*, all agreed that this night was the finest of their lives. Only Daladaeus harboured a germ of misgiving, not at Novaetis' conduct with the young princes, but at a specific question Her Majesty had broached. She had been most insistent to clarify the answer to her satisfaction!

Sar'kta Plains, July 493 BC

The air had chilled distinctly in the interval since supper. Mikhouri and Alicharia had wrapped themselves in summer shawls, far lighter than the winter garments. The streets were not regular, as in Mamy'eva or other large conurbations. A central avenue linked the Market Square and Community Hall in the heart of the village, with the paddock and meadow in the far north, yet the course of the beaten tracks which snake from the west and east to meet it were dictated by the density of dwellings, which formed discreet clusters, and by the boundaries of larger properties. The humblest families traditionally inhabited the far north of Sar'kuc, near the vacant lot sequestered by the Sauromatae travellers. The wealthiest families, including the Count and Countess, lived in the south on land that encompassed the rich pastures west of the Illov'ya. The Count owned a sizeable plot of arable fields, lush pasture, and gallery woodland in the far southwest, where the farmstead was sited, in addition to several paddocks, meadows carpeted with wildflowers, an enclosure for his beehives, and woodland for gaming in the far northeast. It was here that the Princesses stabled their mares. The lot occupied by the visiting travellers lay in the far northwest of the village.

Most families would be sitting down to supper, the most important meal of the day, and the winding tracks were eerily deserted, yet the air chimed with the incessant barking of dogs. The two girls took the long route, a beaten path that first coursed east, before heading west between the properties of Su'kir the Baker and Mos'gar the Fishmonger. Soon enough, they reached the Avenue and, checking left and right for any sign of their grandfather or Ais'ka, they cross the lane and continue west, circuiting the dwellings to approach the vacant lot from the rear, via a small stretch of woodland. Neither girl carried a weapon, nor did they expect to be met with hostility, by either the villagers or the travellers. The two girls could smell the smoke from the campfire, long before they reached the edge of the trees, and the traveller's dogs hailed their arrival with a cacophony of barks and snarls. The travellers were gathered around a large central fire, busily eating their evening meal when the two Princesses morphed from the edge of the trees. "What have we here?" a voice, soft and welcoming, hailed the two girls in *Scythiac* as they morphed from the trees, a few yards west of the campsite.

"Good evening, Sir! My name is Mikhouri, and this is my sister, Alicharia" Mikhouri replied politely. "We came to welcome you and apologise for what happened with your children at the well earlier. Those boys should not have behaved the way they did. It was most disagreeable."

"Would you like some mint tea? Or a small wodki, perhaps?" a woman asked.

"Some tea would be lovely" Mikhouri smiled warmly at the woman. She was surrounded by a gaggle of three young children, all of them girls. Mikhouri turned to Alicharia and grins.

"Some wodki would have been nice!" Alicharia muttered sullenly, earning a withering glare from her elder sister.

"Please, come and sit with us. You are our guests" the woman motioned the sisters to a spare patch of ground to the left.

An older girl, who the Princesses recognised from the well, flitted away to the nearest caravan and promptly returned with a heavy flax blanket and two cushions. Mikhouri nodded at Alicharia, and they strolled towards the fire to sit down on the blanket, which had been laid to the side of the group. The Sauromatae children smile shyly at the two sisters. The eldest girl turns to her mother to whisper in *Sarmati*. The kindly woman turned towards the two visitors and flashed her teeth. "My daughter, Azal'ya told me you intervened in their favour at the well earlier? That you stepped in to help when some of the local boys were causing trouble?"

"We behaved with a courtesy we have been taught to extend to all visitors" Mikhouri replied.

"There are others who keenly resent our presence in the village?" the woman pressed.

Mikhouri blushes. It was Alicharia who answered. "Those boys are known trouble-causers. They do not speak for anyone here" Mikhouri gaped at her younger sisters' temerity.

"The rest of the village does not share their animosity?"

"I cannot be certain of that. I am sorry" Mikhouri sighed sadly. "Nevertheless, you are under the protection of Crown Prince Sir'chor. Whilst you remain so, no-one will harm you, I promise."

"If what you say is true, then we have nothing to fear?" the man sitting to the left of the woman, spoke for the first time. "My name is Nai'ka, and this is my wife, Cot'zya. We hail from a village a few weeks trek to the east of the Uruk Mountains. You have already met our daughters, Azal'ya, Nol'yi and Xelia, or so I gather. We are in your debt for the courtesy you showed them."

"That isn't necessary, we assure you" Mikhouri quipped instantly. "As we have said, you are our guests, and we should offer you every courtesy."

"Please, have some mint tea?" Cot'zya proffered a goblet of steaming tea.

310

"Thank you!" the girl smiled brightly. She took the cup and blew on the steaming liquid, before sipping it. The goblet was passed to her sister.

"How long have you been on the road?" Alicharia asked.

"We have been on the road for twenty-two nights" Nai'ka confessed. "My sister, Yaris'ka, gave birth to little Jos'ki three days ago, so we stopped for a few of nights before continuing west. That is her husband, Zi'gan. You met little Nir'ah at the well earlier?"

"I love her kurta and britches! Is it true that you may have some like them for sale?" Alicharia asked eagerly.

"Alicharia? Remember your manners!" her sister implored. "I am sorry, but my little sister can be very persistent. At times she can be inexcusably rude!" Mikhouri glanced sternly at Alicharia, who blushed hotly and bowed her head. The older Sauromatae girls giggled softly.

Cot'zya giggled, as did the three children. "As it happens, we do have garments for sale that were made people in our village a few months ago. We have summer and winter garments if you would care to see them? I could show you tomorrow if you would like?"

"Do you make garments for your own children? We are told it is almost a sacred tradition of the Sauromatae?" Mikhouri sipped the tea and passed the goblet to Alicharia.

"You have learned of such things? I thought the only things the Orch'tai taught their children is that we Sauromatae are cursed with horns and tails. I do, young lady, and it is" Cot'zya smiled brightly.

"They are very pretty kurtas. Far prettier than those most of the children in the village wear, except on special occasions."

"Those garments are often made and sold by communities east of the Uras'ka, young lady" Cot'zya raised an eyebrow mockingly.

"Really?" Alicharia cooed.

"Making clothes is a major source of income for our community, along with wooden goblets, bowls, buckets, and such like. We also harvest band prepare tinctures from plants you cannot obtain here in the west. Those we do not grow for ourselves, but we prepare them from herbs and spices we obtain from communities further east" Cot'zya informed them.

"Will you be heading further west, into the lands of the Nur'gat?" Mikhouri asked interestedly.

"We will be on the road for the next week or so, heading to market in Ry'aia. We intend to stay for a week or so and then return, laden with goods to sell in the east. It is likely that we will return to your village for a night, perhaps two, just as long as it is safe to do so?" Nai'ka informed them.

"Why would you think that it would not be safe to do so?" Mikhouri asked in a puzzled tone. "You obviously thought it would be safe to stay this time?" Alicharia ventured.

"We thought that it would be, as it has these past few summers, but after what happened at the well this afternoon…?" Cot'zya sighed.

"You won't have any further problems with those boys, nor anyone else, for that matter. You are under the Crown Prince's protection, as I have said" Mikhouri quipped.

"Perhaps things have changed?" Nai'ka mused softly. There was an edge to his voice.

The dogs suddenly rouse. Their ears pricked up and they began to bark. Mikhouri and Alicharia glance past the fire and espy a group of men, pacing along the Avenue towards the vacant lot. To a man, they openly sported weapons, mainly agricultural implements, and seemed anything but welcoming! Alicharia shot her elder sister a knowing glance.

Nai'ka stands and eyes the group, perhaps some twelve in number, who now fan out around the far side of the fire, the leader in the centre, facing Nai'ka and the travellers. "If we had known to expect so many guests, we would have prepared a feast?"

"What is your business here?" the leader of the group spoke harshly. He was short and wiry, and hefted a heavy woodsman's axe. Mikhouri recognised the man, yet she could not put a name to him. "You are Sauromatae? If that is so, then you are no longer welcome here! You will leave at first light, if you know what is good for you!"

"Forgive me, friend, but I would never be so presumptuous as to give a stranger advice on how to take care of his family? These are my children, and these are my sisters and their families" Nai'ka indicated the group next to him, and those to his left. The other two Sauromatae men kept their silence.

"You are our guests, are you not?" the villager smiled thinly. "It is up to us to decide whether we extend you the courtesy we would normally extend to friends, is it not?"

"We are not enemies?" Nai'ka said silkily.

"If you are Sauromatae, then you are no friends to the Orch'tai?" another man spoke up. Mikhouri and Alicharia, who had not yet been recognised, exchange meaningful glances. It was the farrier, Za'ku, who worked for their grandfather.

"We are not natural enemies, are we, friend?" Nai'ka said searchingly. "You and I have never met? If you were in distress and needed assistance east of the Wol'yi, our families would not hesitate to come to your aid."

"But we are not east of the Wol'yi, are we? You are here, in our village, on our land?" the leader hissed.

"We stayed here last summer, did we not? We traded with you, profitably and peaceably, and were even invited to attend the village festival. We were led to believe this is vacant land, and belongs to no-one? Have things changed so much since last summer?"

"Everything has changed since last summer! We are now at war!" the leader said icily.

Mikhouri saw the looks of astonishment and fear flicker across travellers' faces. "We are not at war! That is a lie!" Yaris'ka retorted hotly. We would

313

not be here otherwise, would we? We are a peaceful people, just as you are!" The traveller children share bewildered glances.

"We have sons, brothers, and even nephews, who have been conscripted in the past year. They have been sent to the Western Plains of Kazakh'yi to protect our frontier against your people!" hissed another. It was Mos'gar the Fishmonger, whose son was now serving in the east.

"We are not from the Western Plains of Kazakh'yi" Nai'ka spoke softly. "I assure you, my people only desire peace, as you do. We are not aware of increased hostility from the *Altai*, and you may rest assured that we have as much to fear from them as you do? We would not be here if things were otherwise, as my sister has said." There was considerable muttering amongst the villagers.

"There is talk of a Sauromatae Confederacy and aggression against our garrisons in the Signet!" another challenged. It was Nush'ta the Saddler, a large and jovial fellow who had distinguished himself as a Cavalryman in the campaigns against the Nur'gat, many moons before.

"They are old wives' tales, no more than that!" Yaris'ka spat. "Why would we wish to wage war? We are not so different, whatever you may think. We wish for a peaceful and prosperous future for our children, just as you do."

"You will leave tomorrow! Those are our demands. We do not want you here!" the leader spoke coldly.

Alicharia leapt to her feet. "Well, we do! They came as our guests, as we are now theirs! You ought to be ashamed of yourselves!" she bridled.

"What in Hades name?" Za'ku gasped. His astonishment was soon shared by the group as they recognised the child, and the older girl next to her. "What are you doing here? You should be at home in bed?"

Mikhouri now stood, shoulder to shoulder with her younger sister, facing the hostile band of villagers "After what happened at the well, we came to re-assure our guests they were welcome. Now, we find that they are not so. Is this true?" the girl challenged the group icily.

"*You* have welcomed these travellers into *our* village?" the leader hissed defiantly.

"I was not aware you had recently joined the Orch'tai Royal House, Ner'ga the Woodsman? Is it so?" Mikhouri addressed the man with withering disdain.

"I have not, my Lady" Ner'ga gazed furtively at the floor and shuffled his feet.

"I am a Royal Princess, as is my sister!" the girl hissed. "Given we are so, you shall address with the honorific, for I am, and shall forever remain, Your Royal Highness, am I not?" Mikhouri blushed faintly as the travellers gaped in astonishment at the two young girls.

"Of course, Your Royal Highness, the Princess Mikhouri, please forgive me?"

"These visitors are under Royal Protection, from this day forth. They are to be considered as honoured guests, and never enemies, do we understand one another?"

"As you wish, Your Royal Highness" Ner'ga spoke softly, all defiance reneged.

"As we command, my dear fellow" Alicharia quipped, revelling in the affirmation of her regal personhood.

"As you command, Your Royal Highness, the Princess Alicharia."

"And now, we command you to leave us in peace!" Alicharia smiled sweetly.

The group disperse and trudge sullenly into the shadows and the main track back to their homes. Mikhouri turned to the travellers and smiled sadly. "I apologise unreservedly for any offence they may have caused" Mikhouri sighed sadly.

"No offence taken, I can assure you, Your Royal Highness" Nai'ka replied respectfully.

"If that is settled, perhaps I might escort these young ladies, back to their chambers? Their Grandmother would be horrified to learn they were not tucked safely in their beds" a new voice interjected from the shadows of the woodland to the right. It was the Old Count, together with a small detachment of armed retainers.

"Grandfather!" Mikhouri gasped. "How long have you been there?" she blushed.

The old Count chuckled. "Long enough to learn that you are now ready to be a Queen!" The men around him grinned. "Now, let us bid our guests goodnight and get you safely home to bed, before your grandmother skins me alive!"

The Old Count nodded respectfully at Nai'ka and led the two sisters away from the fire toward the central avenue. Mikhouri and Alicharia strolled to the rear of their grandfather, clearly afraid of his ire. "I suppose I am just a stupid little Princess!" Alicharia mused bitterly.

Notwithstanding their recent triumph, the Royal Princesses were roundly scolded for their temerity by their grandmother and Asel'ya the moment they arrived home. Their departure had been discovered almost immediately, for, in their excitement, they had forgotten the warm milk that was to be brought to their bedchambers. The milk was returned to its pot, waiting by the fire, to be re-warmed for the Count when he returned from his discussions with the village Council. Following their chastisement, the two Princesses had been unceremoniously shipped to their chambers, with an explicit command not to re-appear until breakfast. Sometime later, the Count knocked on Mikhouri's bedchamber door, spoken briefly with her, thence with her sister, with whom he returned, and closed the door softly. "I think it might be a good idea to clear the air, don't you think?" the Count said.

"We are sorry, Grandpapa, honestly we are" Mikhouri had sighed remorsefully.

"I think you have been made aware of the potentially disastrous consequences of your actions. I do not think it necessary to tread that path again, if that is fine with you?"

"We are sorry, Grandpapa, truly we are so" the girls chimed.

The old man smiled ruefully. "It may come as a surprise, but I am proud of you, for what you did tonight" the Count sighed.

"You are proud of us!" Mikhouri gaped. Alicharia was stunned to silence.

"Of course, I am" the Count smiled happily. "You behaved with remarkable courage, never lose sight of that, both in your decision to offer your protection to the travellers, and by your conduct in the face of that mob. You were never in any danger, no matter the enmity of some of the villagers toward the travellers. In case you hadn't noticed, they were chastened by the mere sight of you, most of them at least."

"Are we at war with the Sauromatae?" Mikhouri probed. "If we are, our actions this night might be construed as treason, may they not?"

"We are not at war with the Sauromatae, sweet child. On that matter, you may rest your minds completely. There are troubling rumours circulating in the village of a Sauromatae Confederacy, and of a string of recent reversals, marred by heavy losses" the Count confessed.

Alicharia and Mikhouri exchange bewildered glances. "Is there any truth at all to the rumours?" Mikhouri asked earnestly.

"As I am sure you are aware, idle talk of a 'Confederacy', a supra-regional alliance of the various Sauromatae tribes, has become something akin to a folk-tale, especially in the remote regions of the Duchy" the old man sighed exasperatedly.

"Has there been a string of defeats?" Alicharia whispered, scarcely believing the truth of it.

"I suspect there has been fighting, and it is likely we have incurred losses, yet not as serious as the rumours would credit. You would surely have heard word in Mamy'eva if it were true?" the Count probed.

"We have heard nothing" Mikhouri replied instantly. She glanced quickly at her sister. "Alicharia may know far more than I?"

"The soldiers in the Royal Palace have said nothing to me, and I talk to them all the time!" Alicharia chimed.

"I have instructed Ais'ka to take a barge to Mamy'eva tomorrow and discover if there is any truth to the rumour. After all, if there was, we would request the immediate despatch of an armed contingent to safeguard the frontier?"

"The travellers claim the rumours are completely untrue" Mikhouri protested. "They claim we are not at war and that they only desire peace, as we do. Is that not so?"

"I heard their remonstrations, sweet child. For myself, I am inclined to believe them" their grandfather smiled reassuringly. "They have as much to fear from their barbarous ilk from the *Altai* as we do. They would surely not have expected to be treated with courtesy here, had they been aware of increased enmity between our peoples?"

"But there has always been enmity between our peoples, has here not?" Mikhouri chirped.

"Not always, my little dove. Perhaps the history of our peoples is cast as something it never truly was, at least until quite recently. It might surprise you, but I have always considered us to have more in common with the Sauromatae to the east than we do with our allies to the west and south?"

"We are Scythians?" Alicharia protested hotly.

"And who are these mythical Scythia, little dove? And from where did they spring?" the old Count challenged softly. "They certainly did not exist at the height of Assyria, of that much is certain. It is possible that the historic enmity of the Orch'tai and Sauromatae has been overstated, perhaps deliberately so, by those who wish to profit, politically and financially, from the permanent deployment of such a large garrison east of the Wol'yi?"

"But those soldiers serve to protect us!" Alicharia remonstrated hotly. "Without them, we would be conquered by the Sauromatae!"

"Do you truly believe that little dove?" the Count soothed. "Do you have any idea how much it costs to provision the garrisons east of the Wol'yi, even for a single year?"

"I heard Mama talking with Prince Ach'ti about it, just before last winter. I do know he was not happy with the situation at all" Alicharia grinned.

Mikhouri gaped at the girl in bewilderment. "Alicharia? You have been repeatedly warned of the ills of eavesdropping on adult conversations" she remonstrated.

The old man raised a hand to silence his grand-daughter and continued. "Everything the Army consumes must be supplied by our farmers, at a concession, of course. Since the levies were introduced, we provision an even greater force in the east, though our manpower is sorely depleted. This has grave social consequences for every community in the Duchy, though this has eluded the best minds of the King's Counsellors!"

"Is that the real reason why the soldier's stayed?" Alicharia eyed the old man shrewdly.

"The soldiers obeyed the orders of the King, little dove. They came north for your protection" the old man smiled wryly.

"I do not think it so" the child said emphatically. "I think they came to harvest the crops that were ready in the early summer, and to tend those to be harvested in the late summer?"

"I think your mother is blessed with a keener understanding of the land than my own son ever will be" the Count chuckled.

Mikhouri and Alicharia exchange astonished glances. "Mama petitioned Grandfather for his blessing for the soldiers to stay on and help?" the older girl gasped.

"We now must furnish a surplus to feed a larger army, with greatly reduced manpower. That is the real cause of the resentment among the families in this community, and in scores of others throughout the Duchy" the old man confided. "Our surplus can no longer be sold in the markets, either here or abroad, and the shortfall raises the price of grain, fruit, beer, and wodki, all to be borne by own citizens. Yet, there are families in Mamy'eva

319

whose fortunes, in wealth and power, have increased immeasurably since the campaigns of your Great-Grandfather!"

"The majority of our people have grown poorer by the necessity of provisioning such a large army in the east?" Mikhouri ventured.

"Indeed, they have, sweet child. And it has caused much resentment, especially this past year. The poorest in our society must bear even greater hardship" the old man sighed heavily.

"But surely an increase in the size of our army in the east is born of necessity? The King and Royal Council would not sanction incumbent hardship upon our people unless it was justified by necessity of security?" Mikhouri postulated.

"Perhaps there are other motives for the creation of this new army?" the Count turned his gaze towards his youngest granddaughter, much to the astonishment of her elder sister.

Alicharia blushed furiously. "The soldiers in the Palace have not spoken of a new army, at least not to me."

"I would be surprised if they had, for it is not something that would concern you" the Count replied. "There is something deeply troubling afoot, that much is clear, and rumours of a renewed threat from the east, and of recent military reversals, appear to have been deliberately crafted so as to inflame tension with the Sauromatae at the height of the trading season."

"Do you think Ais'ka will learn the truth of the matter?" asked Mikhouri.

"I hope so! If there is any truth to these rumours, the Sauromatae communities east of the Uruk Mountains must be told of these disturbing developments. The security of all caravans travelling through the Duchy depends upon it!"

Mamy'eva, July 493 BC

The light was fading fast when General Til'koi reached the farmstead, a few hours due northwest of Mamy'eva. He was greeted by the old General's manservant, a gruff and scarred rogue named Gish'ri, veteran of the Battle of Gor'khi, before he had even dismounted. The pair embraced warmly, despite their difference in rank, both martial and social. "It has been too long, Sir" the younger man smiled wryly.

"Indeed, it has, my old friend. I take it you are well?" Til'koi smiled warmly at the man he had not seen for several years.

"As you find me, my Lord, yet the old leg wounds now plague in the winter as they rarely did."

"Such is the misfortune of time, my old friend?"

"And carelessness. There is that, is there not?" Gish'ri spat contemptuously.

"I was careful enough, old friend!" Til'koi reproved him half-heartedly. "If anyone asks, I simply came to pay a visit to an old and esteemed friend?"

"I was led to believe you saw the General just the other day, Sir?" Gish'ri said woodenly.

"I meant you, you impertinent prick! Now, where is your master?"

Gish'ri grinned. "I will take you to see him. You are in luck, old friend, for the General is still sober?"

"Not for long, my old friend, I can assure you of that" Til'koi grinned back.

Gish'ri stabled the General's steed at the rear, ensuring fresh forage and water, and led him inside to where his master awaited. As he entered the study, General Zu'ghir simply nodded in acknowledgement of his guest's arrival, before rudely ignoring him to devote his attention to his correspondence. Til'koi smiled thinly, for General Zu'ghir had surely not mellowed with age. Nor had his mind dulled. Zu'ghir wanted Til'koi to presume the correspondence was urgent and pertinent, yet it could just as easily be a letter from one of his daughters, the youngest of whom now resided in Athens with her husband, a wealthy Greek merchant. "Are you going to let the bloody man die of thirst, you insolent rogue!" Zu'ghir growled.

Gish'ri smiled and went to the desk, where a tray was set with a flagon and three goblets. These were filled with Hellenic red, a gift from his son-in-law from his personal vineyards in Thessaly. Zu'ghir finished reading and sipped his wine, his eyes twinkling with mischief. "I trust you were not followed, old friend?" he eyed Til'koi closely.

"And how fare the Grandchildren?" Til'koi mocked.

"You would like that, wouldn't you? To pack me off in ignominy me to that shithole on the far side of the Aegean. You wouldn't be alone; you may rest assured of that!" Zu'ghir growled.

Til'koi stifled a chuckle. "Am I to take it that you too have fallen foul of His Royal Majesty and Counsel?"

"I fear we are doomed! The King has obviously taken leave of what little sense he was born with. The Kor'nai remains in ordure, at so it is rumoured, and the Counsel is bewitched by the melody of that incorrigible buffoon, Mes'khu."

"Surely that is a little harsh on Counsellor Har'juk, and the Kor'nai, for that matter?" Til'koi soothed.

"Would you be surprised to learn that the Kor'nai may not survive the winter? I humbly beseech your discretion, of course."

Til'koi gazed at the General closely and sipped his wine. "The King will retire him to his estates in Kol'yba, with the gracious thanks of a nation. Mes'khu will replace him as Kor'nai, is that it?"

"He will be murdered, for he is too dangerous to be allowed to live" Zu'ghir said evenly.

Til'koi could not hide his astonishment. "You cannot be serious? Is this rumour even credible?"

"The Kor'nai will die mysteriously in his sleep in the next few months. After all, he is no spring lamb, is he?"

"Nor are you and I, old friend. Yet, neither of us would be inclined to conveniently succumb to a sudden bout of fever, would we?" Til'koi mused grimly.

"The man could suffer a tragic fall from his horse, perhaps on a moonlit ride after a few goblets of tainted wine?"

General Til'koi grinned. "The Kor'nai has not been in the saddle in many a moon! Nor is he an especially ardent swimmer, at least not to my knowledge? Is the Kor'nai aware of this threat to his life?"

"And run a risk of getting myself inadvertently disposed of? You really do take me for a fool? How do you like the wine?" General Zu'ghir sighed.

"My appreciation of your hospitality is warmer than your praise for your son-in-law" Til'koi chuckled.

"The man is an insufferable bore! I am eternally grateful that the fates have put such a welcome distance, not to mention the bloody Persians, between us. So, old friend, what are we going to do about this unfortunate predicament?" Zu'ghir brought the conversation to its point.

"Why don't we simply get word to the Kor'nai that his life may be in danger?" Til'koi suggested helpfully.

"An entirely valorous course, yet it would scarcely resolve our deeper problem" Zu'ghir mused brutally.

"I thought the Kor'nai approved the union of Princess Mikhouri and Crown Prince Disch'al?" Til'koi ventured.

"He is not enthused by the marriage of Princess Alicharia to the Crown Prince Sea'gir, or so it is rumoured. That is the root of all our ills, is it not?" Zu'ghir pressed.

"You suspect the King will announce the Princess Sychoria as his rightful heir? Provided she can secure both unions, is that it?"

General Zu'ghir studied the younger man closely. "You agree, as do we all, that such ties with the Royal House of the Argata will ultimately bring disaster to the realm? Notwithstanding the King's imminent folly against the Ur'gai, which will also likely end in disaster!"

"I do, old friend, yet I am at a loss as to how we can prevent it?" Til'koi sighed.

"And there is truth to the rumour that the Princess Alicharia has martial tendencies?"

"It is well known Alicharia is enchanted with the soldiers of the Royal Palace, and that she has a rare mind for military matters, unusual in someone of her birth, sex, and age. She has scandalised her mother by requesting a suit of armour for her next birthday" Til'koi grinned. "Such a child, regardless of her sex, would be a blessing for the Duchy, you agree?"

"Or she could well prove its undoing, if her inclinations, and those of her Counsel, favour our old adversaries in the south? The Princess Mikhouri and her parents are entirely expendable as far as our aims are concerned, for they have acquiesced to the King's folly."

"Whatever the line of succession, we cannot sit idle and allow the Duchy to become supplicant to the whims of the Argata, much less of Persia? We might as well abandon the Signet and the fertile plains of the Uras'ka to the Sauromatae" Til'koi mused bitterly.

"This union must be stopped! And with it, this planned folly against the Ur'gai? We must devise a ploy that will distract the King from his present course. Do you have any suggestions on the matter, General Til'koi?" Zu'ghir raised an eyebrow at the younger man.

Til'koi smiled thinly. "I? Surely there are more competent souls, my Lord?"

"You know full well there are not!" Zu'ghir bridled. "You are the finest strategic thinker in the Duchy. Moreover, you are known to be an unconventional operator. This particular problem requires an unconventional solution."

"Present company excluded of course, my Lord?" Til'koi mocked.

"I want you to think carefully about what might be done, for time is not on our side. We must devise a means of distracting the King's attention and, at one and the same, delay the war with the Ur'gai, at least until the following spring. There is no other to whom we can entrust such a hazardous and pressing mission."

"I understand, old friend, and I am humbled by your confidence in my capabilities. Nonetheless, this would be treason, you do understand that?" Til'koi looked meaningfully at the aged veteran.

"It is only treason if we plan to kill the bastard. No-one is talking about that, not yet at least!" General Zu'ghir mused malevolently.

"Good morning, sleepy head? Where is your sister?" the old Count greets Mikhouri as she plods into the Dining Room. The child was garbed in her sleeping clothes, a simple white kurta with matching britches. It was now some four hours after first light.

"I did knock on her door. She must still be sleeping. Where is Grandmama?"

"She and Asel'ya are discussing matters with the Servants in the Kitchen. They are planning something special for supper tonight. Would you like some mint tea?"

"That would be lovely, thank you. Has Ais'ka left yet?"

The old man passed the child a goblet of mint tea from the bronze cauldron. "He left on the morning passage to Mamy'eva a few hours ago. I am hopeful that he will return in a few days. Are you troubled by last night's events? There is nothing to fear from those villagers."

"I am worried for the safety of the travellers. If these rumours of war have been widely sown, they will be met with hostility wherever they go," Mikhouri sighed sadly.

"And what are your plans for the day? Riding in the meadow with your sister?"

"Would you prefer to let Alicharia loose with a bow and arrow? You know she wishes to learn to shoot" Mikhouri grinned.

"Perhaps your new friends would be more patient tutors? They are famed for their proficiency with the bow, especially on horseback" the old Count smiled mischievously at the child.

Mikhouri was astounded. "You would ask the travellers to teach Alicharia to shoot a bow and arrow from the saddle? This I have to see!" she shrilled gleefully.

"What is the cause of such excitement at such an early hour, young lady?" the countess stood in the doorway with Asel'ya, her tone one of mock severity.

"Grandpa and I were talking about the travellers and their habits. Good morning, Grandmama! Good morning, Asel'ya!" Mikhouri smiled sweetly.

"Their habits, young lady, are not the sort of which your mother would approve" the old lady sighed. "Is there any tea left?"

"There is, my dear, and I can always ask Pas'ka to brew some more?" the Count replied.

"And where is your darling sister, I might ask? I she still sleeping soundly, or has she already left on another adventure?" the woman chided playfully.

"We are sorry, Grandmama" Mikhouri implored. "We only wanted to make sure the travellers were welcomed. We didn't mean to cause any trouble, honestly we didn't."

Alicharia suddenly appeared in the doorway. "And what do you have to say for yourself, young lady?" the countess eyed the child coldly.

"I don't suppose there is any wodki?" Alicharia chirped. Her sister gaped at her in astonishment. The old Count looked down at his goblet and grinned.

"And this, young lady, is why no good will come from learning the customs and habits of Sauromatae travellers! They are notorious drunkards! It starts when they are children!" the old woman clucked disapprovingly.

"We have tea, young lady, if you would like?" the Count smiled warmly at his youngest granddaughter.

"That would be lovely" Alicharia declared. "Do you think we might be permitted to speak with the travellers again? They have the most beautiful kurtas for sale?"

"I do not see why not" the Count replied. "They are our guests, after all. I do not see what harm could come from perusing their goods, do you?"

"And you would have your Granddaughters, Royal Princesses no less, prancing about the village dressed as little Sauromatae whelplings?" the old lady remonstrated playfully. Asel'ya scowled.

"What harm could come of it? It is not like we are asking them to train the girls to shoot a bow and arrow, or to ink their bodies, are we?" the Count grinned at Mikhouri. The girl giggled.

"They can teach me how to shoot a bow and arrow?" Alicharia cooed.

"Sit down and drink your tea, darling sister!" Mikhouri chided. "Grandpapa was only teasing!"

Twelve

Alicharia surveyed the intricate inking's on Zi'gan's arms and legs. She had never seen such wonders, for nobody in the Royal Palace had a tattoo. "Did it hurt?" Alicharia asked innocently. Mikhouri turned away and grinned.

"Not for a man, but a little girl? You would die from the pain! Screaming like a soul condemned to eternal fury. You can beg for mercy, yet you would receive none from a *Scarra*" Zi'gan sneered in mock contempt. "Either that, or you would bleed to death, for girls have not the constitution of men!" He smiled ruefully at the disbelieving child, who stuck her tongue out in disdain.

"Alicharia! Stop that! It is rude and unbecoming!" Mikhouri reproved her.

"So is telling bare-faced untruths! No-one ever dies from a tattoo, do they? And besides, little Sauromatae girls grow to be strong warriors, equal in courage to any man, do they not?"

"I fear you are beaten, darling husband, and by a little girl, no less?" Yaris'ka snickered. She was nursing their new-born son whilst his elder sister, three-year-old Nir'ah, played with a wooden doll.

"How old were you when you had your first tattoo?" Alicharia continued with her interrogation.

"It was a present from my father, for my sixth birthday" Zi'gan replied. His wife rolled her eyes.

"He is quite the story-teller, is young Zi'gan. If you ask him, he will tell you all about his exploits on the campaigns against the Mai'ku!" Nai'ka smiled mischievously.

"Mai'ku? Are they Sauromatae?" Alicharia chirped.

"They are a feral people, only distantly related to us, sweet child" Nai'ka replied. They live on the fringes of the Great Goba, the arid plains to the east of the Al'tai Mountains, many miles away. They are renowned for their savagery, as well as their ris'ka. They are constantly at war with everyone, including the peoples of the great Zan'gou. Yet, when they are not at war, they are a perfectly hospitable people."

"Have you been in many battles?" Alicharia probed.

"I have only been in one real battle. I survived. Many of my comrades did not?" Zi'gan sighed. "Now, if it is war you are interested in, perhaps you should speak to the 'old man' over there?" he nodded towards Nai'ka. "He is a veteran of the last war against the Persians."

"Is that true?" Alicharia cooed.

"There is little to tell, sweet child. It was a long time ago, before you were even born and before I met Cot'zya" Nai'ka sighed. "The Persians were attempting to expand their current frontier further into the plains southeast of the Kas'pa. It was a long campaign, at least it seemed that way. It lasted for three summers."

"Did you beat them?" Alicharia gazed at him intently.

"Perhaps our guests would prefer to talk about something else?" Mikhouri cautioned, earning a winning smile from Cot'zya and Yaris'ka.

"I would not be here had I lost, my Lady. There was little to celebrate, for Persia secured much of the land they coveted north of the Cheli Mountains. There is not much to tell, for there were few real battles" Nai'ka mused gloomily.

"You also coveted the land?" Alicharia quipped unblushingly.

"The land is incredibly fertile, my Lady. It could have been home for a great many of our kin" Nai'ka smiled sadly. "Vast swathes of Central Asia are unsuited to settlement, excepting the Upper Darya and Anu Darya, yet there is little else to the south and the west."

"It is said that the Persians have never been defeated in the field. Is it true?" Alicharia declared.

"Perhaps it is, but then again, perhaps that is what they wish the world to believe" Nai'ka smiled ruefully.

"I do not understand. You lost fertile lands to the Persia, yet still you won the war?" Alicharia frowned.

"We lost the land we had settled but succeeded in thwarting their ambitions to seize the mineral deposits at Ka'Degih and In'Cheh" Nai'ka said proudly. "They also failed to achieve their aim of expanding the frontier further east into the valley of Ai'Temah."

"How many men did they mass in the field? I have heard rumour that Persia can field an army of close to a million men" the girl blushed hotly. "Not that I know how many thousands that is, yet it is impressive, is it not?"

Zi'gan chuckled. "It is a great many thousands, sweet child. Persia could never hope to field an army anywhere close to that size in the plains of Gu'ghan."

"Why could they not do so? Such an army could surely conquer anything before it?" the child remonstrated.

Nai'ka smiled sweetly at the girl. "As I have said, my Lady, the land to the south and west of the upper reaches of the Anu Darya are not conducive to large armies, as the Persians found to their cost! You simply cannot feed them" he smiled grimly. "Their forces can only garrison in concentrations of a few hundred. Such dispositions can be readily lured into traps, especially in the mountains!"

"You could carry food with you, can you not?" Alicharia quipped.

"Of course, but you would need a large body of men to guard the wagons. Like all else made of wood, wagons can be set on fire. Without food, such an army would surely starve."

"So, Persia can be beaten, if their army cannot gain sufficient food?"

"That is true, my Lady, and so they are content to garrison the frontier with sufficient settlements in its immediate rear to sustain such a force" Nai'ka confessed. "And yet, beyond the frontier zone, they have actively

discouraged extensive settlement and cultivation. There is insufficient food
to furnish any large army which breaches the frontier zone."

"What if that army could be provisioned by ships directly across the
Kas'pa?" Alicharia quipped.

"An interesting point, my Lady, yet the Argata and the Orch'tai control
traffic on the Kas'pa? Neither we, nor our kinfolk of the plains, are natural
seafarers!" Nai'ka grinned at the child. The women laughed hysterically.

"You are famed for your horsemanship, are you not?" Mikhouri deftly
changed the subject.

"As are your people, are you not?" said Cot'zya, smiling brightly.

"That is true, for horses are in our blood as much as they are in yours?"
the child quipped.

"And hospitality?" said Cot'zya.

"Of course, for you are our guests, as much as we are now your guests"
Mikhouri smiled sweetly.

"Perhaps some of your kin do not feel the same, in spite of your best
efforts" Nai'ka frowned, and nodded past the two girls.

A small group of men troop along the upper Avenue toward the
travellers. They are led by Ner'ga the Woodsman, accompanied by Za'ku the
Farrier, Su'kir the Baker, and Mos'gar the Fishmonger. A small cart, driven
by a single stout pony, trundled a few yards behind. The two Princesses
are astonished. "Forgive me, Your Royal Highness, the Princess Mikhouri"
Ner'ga blushed, bowing awkwardly. Mikhouri struggled not to laugh as her
sister scowled at the affront to her dignity.

"Why are you here?" Alicharia demanded coldly.

"Hush!" Mikhouri commanded, earning a startled look from her sister.
"You are welcome, as long as you come in friendship?"

"Indeed, we do, my Lady" said Za'ku. "We have brought a cart, with
some tokens of amity for our honoured guests. We have wood, bread, fish,
and a generous offer of any work you require in respect of shooing your
horses, as a gift, you understand?"

Nai'ka smiled. "We have wodki, herbs and spices, and anything else you may require, in lieu of your hospitality?"

"Not sure about the rest of the men, but a small draught of wodki would be most welcome at this hour" said Su'kir the Baker.

"Only a small draught, my friend?" Nai'ka raised an eyebrow.

"A notoriously difficult thing to gauge with precision, is it not? The size of a draught of decent wodki?" the baker smiled broadly.

"As is the love of a good woman, my friends" Nai'ga smiled at the men, and then at Cot'zya, who promptly stood and strolled towards the nearest wagon to fetch flagons and beakers.

Mamy'eva, July 493 BC

Ais'ka arrived at the wharf in Mamy'eva in the mid-morning of the following day and went straight to see his nephew Uh'gui, Captain of the His Majesty's Royal Guard and devoted son of his younger sister, fast approaching the twilight of her fourth decade. Ais'ka enjoyed his regular visits to Mamy'eva, yet they had become rarer these past few summers. His impromptu errand for the Crown Prince furnished a welcome opportunity to check on the health of his sister, no matter the urgency of his mission.

"It is good to see you again, Uncle! I know mother would be delighted to see you again, for it has been too long and we have missed you" Uh'gui embraced his uncle warmly.

"I would have come in the spring, only there were unforeseen problems with the foals" Ais'ka shrugged ruefully.

"We expected you in the late summer. I know mother was deeply disappointed when you had to cancel."

"Our labour is significantly below strength, what with the new levies. It is the same this year, for we have lost too many young men to the Recruiting Officer!" Ais'ka smiled grimly.

"Have you come to petition His Royal Majesty for agricultural levies? I hear some of our lads acquitted themselves commendably during their recent visit?" Uh'gui grinned wryly. "It would be nice to spend some time up north, especially after the last moon before the winter."

"You are certainly in fine fettle to wield a scythe? How are things with your family?" Ais'ka asked earnestly.

"They are well, Uncle, and thank you for asking. I have some news of my own to impart, for you are blessed to become a Great-Uncle" the young Officer beamed proudly.

"That is splendid news, young man! You and Niz'ri must be thrilled, as must your mother?"

"She has already started making swaddling clothes for our new arrival in the late thaw" Uh'gui grinned.

"I am not in the least surprised, for she commenced knitting summer and winter garments as soon as she found she was expecting you" Ais'ka grinned.

"I am due to finish my shift shortly after midday, if you care for a few jars of black rye?"

"Does *The Spring Lamb* still do a decent drop?" Ais'ka asked eagerly.

"It does indeed, but I must warn you. It has become something of a rough-house, what with the increase in recruits and the like" Uh'gui confessed.

"Soldiers are not always the most palatable of drinking partners, eh? I remember it well!"

"We could meet at *The New Moon* if that would suit you? It's on the east side of the Market, near the Arena?" Uh'gui smiled brightly.

"I remember it well, but it has been a long time since I have drunk there. I will first pay a visit to your mother to see how she fares, and then head across and meet you?"

"Splendid! The first round of drinks will be on me, including the wodki chasers. We can't have you going back to Sar'kuc lamenting that our hospitality fell far short of expectations, can we?"

The two embrace and Ais'ka made his way past the Guards to leave the Royal Palace via the Gor'khi Gate. Uh'gui returns to the Guardroom, where he found Commander Zu'ki, sat in a chair, sipping a goblet of mint tea. "I recognised the old man, of course? I never knew you were related. He is Chief Retainer to the Crown Prince in Sar'kuc is he not?"

"That he is, besides being my uncle, of course. You presumably got to know one another during your recent visit with the Royal Princesses?" Uh'gui ventured.

"He is a most commendable soul, as is the Crown Prince. It was a privilege to spend time with them, however briefly" Zu'ki beamed.

"I am meeting him for a couple of jars at *The New Moon*, if you'd like to drop in and say 'Hello'? He was certainly singing your praises, after all of the assistance you gave them!" Uh'gui grinned.

"Do I detect a smirk, Captain? You think routine public duties, including assisting with the rye and barley harvest, are beneath a soldier of the King's Guard?" Zu'ki mocked.

"Not at all, Sir, quite the contrary, as it happens. I think it may be the reason for his impromptu visit to Mamy'eva. They have lost far too many men to the Recruiting Officer, by all accounts" Uh'gui confessed.

"If it is alright with you, I think I will drop in for a quick jar and pay my respects. If the Crown Prince is considering petitioning His Royal Majesty for labour, the support of a few of Officers from the Royal Guard might help, don't you think?" Zu'ki smiled brightly.

The public bar in *The New Moon* was busy when Uh'gui arrived, yet Ais'ka was already seated a table in the far corner, far away from the main door and bar. "I see you have started before me?" Uh'gui grinned at the half empty beaker of rye beer and empty goblet on the table, presumably recently filled with wodki. He waived at the serving wench and beckoned her across. "I take it you would not refuse another round?"

"Thank you! That would be most agreeable. Since when did an Orch'tai refuse another round, especially if someone else is paying?" Ais'ka grinned. "It is nice to be back, after all this time. The place has certainly changed, that is for sure. For the better if you ask me?"

A serving-girl morphed beside the table. "Glad to hear it!" she beamed proudly. "Now, what can I get for you?"

"A couple of large rye beers and wodki chasers" replied Uh'gui.

"A couple of wodki's each, would that be?" the girl smiled mockingly. She could have been no more than twelve years old, for she had not yet developed breasts.

"That is enviably sound logic, sweet child! And I, for one, am sold. After all, he's paying!" Ais'ka smiled happily.

After the drinks had been brought to the table, and froth on the black rye sucked with relish, Uh'gui elected to mention that his Senior Officer would be joining them, sooner rather than later. "From what I hear, you made his lads feel right at home while they were there. They made us as jealous as a cuckold when they regaled us with tales of the countesses' famed honey cakes and berry wine! There was even a rumour the old Count slaughtered and roasted a bullock and a few pigs at a feast in their honour, just before they returned to Mamy'eva?"

"They were a good bunch of lads. As good as any I ever served with in the east. We used to think you Palace boys were a bit limp, but these lads got stuck right in!"

"Not according to the Companions at *The Elysium*! Some of these lads usually do if you take my meaning?" Uh'gui grinned.

"I would advise that you never be too trusting of the Companions at *The Elysium*. I remember a young Officer, not long out of training. They greased him something proper, I can tell you!"

"You never told me stories like this as a child, Uncle?" Uh'gui mocked.

"They charged him double for everything, including the mandatory bathe and complementary towels!" Ais'ka roared. "Your mother would not have approved? Come to think of it, nor would she approve now!"

"Nor would my pregnant wife, which is precisely why I give the place a wide berth!"

"And so, you should, what with a nipper on the way. Not to mention, you are an Officer in His Majesty's Guard, are you not? You wouldn't want to give anyone the wrong impression, would you?" Ais'ka teased.

"What did you make of their Officer? He is a fellow named Zu'ki?" Uh'gui asked interestedly.

"He seems solid enough. He came across as a consummate professional and took a keen interest in the welfare of his lads."

"He recognised you at the Palace. I mentioned we were coming here for a few jars. He said he might pop by for a drink if that is alright with you?" Uh'gui said.

"Bit late in the day, son? There he is, isn't he?" Ais'ka nodded to the far corner of the bar, where Zu'ki had materialised.

"Excuse me, Uncle. I had better go over and let him know where we are sat?" Uh'gui blushed.

Uh'gui returned promptly with a smiling Zu'ki, and a fresh tray of wodki chasers. "It is good to see you again, dear Ais'ka! How is the Crown Prince Sor'chir?"

"He is well, young man! We are busy with preparations for the wheat harvest in a moon or so. We are rather short of men this season" Ais'ka smiled tightly.

"The Recruiting Officers have had a good year of it, have they not?" Zu'ki smiled at Uh'gui.

"And so, they did the last summer, my Lord!" Ais'ka mused gloomily.

"It will likely be so for the next few years, my Lord. The winds are changing" Zu'ki shrugged regrettably.

"Is there any truth to the rumour that a new army has been created to counter increased threats from the Sauromatae tribes to the east of the Signet? Talk in the north is of nothing else, my Lord?" Ais'ka challenged. Uh'gui blinked.

Zu'ki sips his beer and smiles tightly. "That is quite correct, Ais'ka. His Majesty has declared it a matter of urgency to raise and equip a new army to counter the increasingly hostile intent of the Sauromatae" Zu'ki confessed in a low voice. "I should not need to remind you, a seasoned veteran of our previous campaigns, of the guile and ruthlessness of these brutes!"

"Are we at war with the Sauromatae? The caravans arriving from east of the Uras'ka know nothing of these renewed hostilities?" Ais'ka countered.

"Would you expect them to tell the truth? The Sauromatae wish to trade with us, yet they also seek to break the terms of the truce they signed with the last King?" Zu'ki mused.

"Have they broken the truce? There is troubling word of atrocities committed by our sons, not theirs?" Ais'ka pressed.

"And you would credit such rumours?" Zu'ki raised an eyebrow and leaned across the table, lowering his voice to a whisper. "We are aware of the rumours that spread like wildfire throughout the Duchy. Regrettably, as is so often the case, it is difficult to tell fact from fable, such is the scale of the embellishment. What I can tell you, is this. The threat from the east is graver than it has been in more than twenty summers" Zu'ki sighed.

"And yet, we have received no notice of these threats. During the past year, we have lost a great many of our adult sons. Without them, we have limited capacity to defend the frontier against hostile incursions from our enemies east of the Uras'ka?" Ais'ka spoke evenly.

"The threat is from the Western Plains and the Upper Darya, greased by the dark magic of the Queen in Khoda. There is no threat from the Uras'ka. Perhaps your visitors are being truthful, for it is unlikely they would have knowledge of the true situation?" Zu'ki said silkily.

"That could change within a moon!" Ais'ka said testily. "If the Sauromatae did launch an attack across the Uras'ka, perhaps in concert with their kin in the Western Plains, the Duchy would be doomed?" Ais'ka sighed heavily.

"We have no intelligence of any such threat, dear Ais'ka! With due respect, I fear the Crown Prince is troubling himself over nothing. You may rest assured, these new Divisions have successfully stemmed the tide of the Sauromatae threat, at least for the present."

"Nonetheless, my uncle is right, is he not? The northwest frontier is an obvious weakness in our defences?" Uh'gui raised an eyebrow.

"And so, on strength of little real intelligence, we should despatch a significant force to protect the Sama'zka and the Sar'kta, where it may never be required? Until we receive notice of any such danger, we simply cannot justify diverting invaluable manpower from where it is needed most. You must surely understand this?" Zu'ki countered smoothly.

"As a soldier, I would agree that such a deployment at the present time would be wasteful and unnecessary, but the Count must be alerted to the deteriorating security situation?" Ais'ka drains his beer and reaches for a goblet of wodki.

"You think it wise to trouble him about this? What with the pressing issue of the wheat harvest to consider?" Zu'ki frowned.

"Commander Zu'ki has a valid point, Uncle? It might harm any hope of successfully petitioning the Royal Counsel for itinerant labour to assist with the forthcoming harvest?" added Uh'gui

"And what of our duty to protect the lives and property of the travelling caravans? There is also the security of the Royal Princesses to consider?" Ais'ka replied tersely.

"How fares the fearsome Princess Alicharia? You know she quizzed me incessantly during our journey north?" Zu'ki smiled warmly.

"So, I gather, my friend!" Ais'ka chuckled wryly. "She is currently devoted to her riding, but now seems eager to shoot a bow and arrow. The Count is equally determined to dissuade her!" Ais'ka grinned. The three men laughed heartily.

"The paddocks and meadows seem perfect terrain for learning to ride. She will have sufficient confidence to hunt in the woods by the end of the summer, provided she has learned how to shoot?" Zu'ki grinned.

"The countess would not take to such ribaldry. The child is eager to venture further afield, now her proficiency in the saddle improves with each day" Ais'ka confessed.

"It is a beautiful part of the Duchy, is it not? Moreover, it is perfectly safe" added Uh'gui.

"Perhaps it is less safe than in many a previous summer, given what you have told me?" Ais'ka glanced searchingly at Zu'ki. "The Old Count must be told the truth. I cannot lie to him, for the security of the Royal Princesses may depend upon it."

"Of course, it does. And, of course, you must" Zu'ki sighed. "Yet, as I have said, I fear you may be troubling yourself over nothing. Now, if you would excuse me, I need to take a brief sojourn outside."

"When a man needs, a man must" Ais'ka grinned.

Zu'ki stood and made his way around the table, heading for the near door. He stepped outside to relieve himself at the corner wall and was soon joined by a fellow drinker whom he recognised. The man was a colossus, standing over six feet in height, as burly and intimidating as a bear. "It has been a long time, has it not?"

"That it has, Commander" the brute said gruffly. "Is there anything I need be concerned with?"

Zu'ki sighed ruefully. He genuinely liked and respected Ais'ka, and the Old Count, but any petition for an armed detachment, however insignificant, could wreak havoc on their plans. "I fear there is, old friend! I think it best if our friend never made it aboard his return passage."

"It will be done, Commander, upon my honour!" the man spoke softly.

"Make it quick, I implore you? I don't want him to suffer" Zu'ki spoke firmly.

"He won't even know about it, Commander, I promise" the thug smiled grimly.

Uh'gui and Ais'ka weave through the throng of late afternoon shoppers in the Queen's Market, heading south along the Wol'yi Way toward the junction with the Royal Avenue, which continued beyond the imposing south wall of the Royal Palace to the Market Square. Beyond the Market Square, lay the Royal Barracks, in the far southeast of the city. "You don't have to accompany me all the way to the Royal Barracks, Uncle Ais'ka! After all, it is some distance out of your way" Uh'gui implored.

"I have time to kill before the barge sails. And besides, the stroll will do me good. I can burn off most of the alcohol before I fall asleep on the barge!" the older man grinned happily.

"That way Aunt Yal'vya won't berate me for abducting you and getting you drunk the next time we meet."

"There is that, of course" Ais'ka chuckled wryly.

They were fast approaching the Gor'khi Gate; the imposing marble edifice enshrined by the "Warrior King" Mag'kar to commemorate victory over the Nur'gat two decades earlier, and the main entrance to the Royal Palace. "It was good of you to arrange for me to be allowed through and given a tour, especially given my arrival was unannounced. I never thought I would see the day a flea-bitten cavalryman like me would be ushered through the gates of the Royal Palace" Ais'ka marvelled.

"You get used to it, Uncle. After a while, the novelty wears off and it is not much different from anywhere else" Uh'gui grinned.

"It is a world away from a winter camp in the heart of the plains" Ais'ka sighed.

"It has been really good to see you, Uncle Ais'ka. Perhaps we could come and visit you after the next moon. I have some time off, and I know mother would love to come home, at least for a week or so."

"I will speak with the Count as soon as I return. If we can get ahead of things, I am sure I could ask for some time off toward the back end of the wheat harvest. It would be good to have both of you home, if only for a while. You know you are always welcome?" said Ais'ka.

"Take care, Uncle, and have a safe journey home."

The two embraced. Ais'ka turned and headed northwest, back towards Queen Square and, beyond the North Gate, the Docklands and Wharf. He spent a brief time in the Market, perusing the wares on display at the candle-makers and potters for a gift for his wife, Yal'vya, for it would be inconsiderate to return to Sar'kuc without a little something exotic. Ais'ka was not best pleased with the extortionate price of the goods and felt certain he could obtain similar goods for a lower price at the stalls along The Strand at the Wharf. Ais'ka passed through the North Gate and weaved through the throng of shoppers in the Bazaar, ambling towards the warehouses and taverns of the Docklands. As he cleared the Bazaar, he espied a group of men, some six in all, loitering outside the door of *The Old Oak*, a notorious rough house if ever there was. The leader was unusually tall, with broad shoulders, and a large scar on his right cheek, clearly an old war wound. Ais'ka felt a dawning recognition, *a face from his past*! And, with it, came a prickle of fear. Age wearies all men, but it rarely tames the temperament. If it was the man in question, there was nothing to be gained from re-visiting that ancient rivalry!

Ais'ka turned away and strolls west towards Carpenters and Metal-Workers stalls in search of a decent woodsman's axe, without a further glance behind. There was no point, for he was now certain that he had seen the brute and his companions a short while earlier in *The New Moon*. Ais'ka even recalled the brute's name. He was Ja'ghur, a former cavalryman and veteran of the east with a notorious reputation for egregious brutality.

If it were Ja'ghur, there was an outstanding debt of honour which remained unsettled!

Ais'ka selected a heavy woodsman's axe. It had a razor-sharp, oversized head mounted on a two-foot pine handle. He handed two silver pieces to the merchant, who smiled brightly. It was an expensive piece of craftsmanship, yet it would last a lifetime. One of the thugs he had espied outside *The Old Oak* had shadowed him through the Bazaar, yet, as Ais'ka turns, axe in hand, the man darted down the nearest alley, heading for the Warehouse District. Ais'ka knew this part of the city well and had earmarked several locations that would be perfect sites for an ambush. He would avoid these like the plague and would lead his pursuers on a merry dance through the warren of interconnecting lanes and backstreets which led to the wharf. Neither Ja'ghur, nor any of his men, would be foolish enough to openly carry a sword, for they were forbidden in the Royal City, and would instead be armed with daggers and staves. Despite his acquisition, Ais'ka did not relish the prospect of a fight to the death this day, especially against a savage like Ja'ghur! *Yet, if there was blood to be spilled, he could always call upon an old friend.*

Ais'ka continued west along Vol'yar Way until he reached the junction with River Lane, which demarcated the Vintner's District from the Saddler's and Bone Merchants Districts, where he turned right, and continued north towards the Wol'yi. When he reached Morkhant's Wine Shop, he turned right into a backstreet, heading east towards *The Painted Lady*, a fabled brew-house with upstairs rooms for its discerning patrons. Ais'ka passed the entrance to the hostelry and took the next left, heading north again along a narrow alleyway which leads to Wol'yi Street, to the far west of the landing stage. Ais'ka slowed his pace as he approached the end of the alley, hugging the left wall, presuming that any lurking assailant would skulk at the right corner, where they might hope to deliver a murderous lunge with a dagger, or a stunning blow with a stave. As he edged closer to the end of the alley at the junction with Wol'yi Street, Ais'ka stooped and gritted his teeth, the axe raised in his right hand, poised and ready to strike. He coughed lightly.

The attacker swung his stave, aiming for where he suspected his victim's head would be, and Ais'ka felt the air whisper as it whistled past, cracking against the corner of the wall. Ais'ka stepped outside his attacker and thrust the axe-head forward, hoping to slice the man's wrist with the blade. The man hisses as the blade drew blood. Suddenly, a second assailant appeared to the right of the first, grinning evilly, a razor-sharp dagger clasped tightly in his right hand. Ais'ka danced right and, passing the axe to his left hand, he drove a powerful jab into the man's left eye, rocketing his head back. Ais'ka charged the man and, feinting right, he stepped quickly left and around, swinging the axe at the man's skull. The blade bit into its target with a satisfying thud, shattering the man's right cheek and eye-socket in an explosion of blood. The first man screams with impotent rage and attacked, swinging the stave, but Ais'ka parried the blow, both hands gripping the pine handle. Pivoting on the balls of his feet, he smashes the blunt side of the axe head hard into the man's right cheek. The man stepped back and thrust forward with the tip of the stave, yet Ais'ka parried this contemptuously and leapt to attack, feinting right. Ais'ka fells his assailant with a slash to the throat, accompanied by a gruesome vent of arterial blood. He turns to the second man and, retrieving the fallen dagger, he plunged this into his left eye to bury deep into his brain. *Not bad for an old man? Pair of useless twats!*

Another two assailants morphed from the end of the lane at the far side of *The Sheaf and Scythe*, a favourite haunt from many a moon ago! Ais'ka smiled grimly and started towards them, axe held aloft in his right hand, his face a mask of fury. "Come! Let me taste your blood!" Ais'ka roared. "Bring me that slag, Ja'ghur! It is time we settled this, once and for all!" The men turn on their heels and darted back down the alley. Ais'ka sprinted after them, deliberately slowing his pace as he approaches the corner, and quickly stepped outside to avoid a lunge from a waiting assailant. The men had almost reached the end of the lane and would presumably flee to the safety of the Wharf. Ais'ka grinned and turned away, a thin smile playing at his lips as he strode towards the entrance to the tavern. He had earned a draught of wodki! *Sweet Tabiti! It had been an age since he had last killed another man!*

Ais'ka reached the door of *The Sheaf and Scythe* and glanced around, yet there was not a soul in sight. He pushed open the door and stepped inside. As he disappeared inside, two figures loom out of a narrow alley on the opposite side, further to the east. "That has finished things, hasn't it? It is too risky to have another pop at him before he boards the barge" the first sighed ruefully.

"It isn't finished, not by a long chalk. I have a score to settle with this bastard!" Ja'ghur growled. "Let him have his drink, we shall deal with him later."

"The Militia will be here in no time. He will be taken into custody, surely?" said Na'kyr.

"Our friends can handle the Militia. They are no concern of ours. After a couple of draughts of wodki, my old friend Ais'ka will feel an urge to call upon the service of an armourer."

"There are a great many armourers in the Metal Worker's District? At least we know where he is now, don't we?" Na'kyr added helpfully.

"I know exactly which armourer he will go to. The same one I would, if I were him. His name is Saz'jik, and he is an old friend."

"An old friend of yours, is he, this Saz'jik?" the boy asked brightly.

Ja'ghur's eyes burned with hatred. "That pig! That dog! He is no friend of mine!"

Archaeopolis, July 493 BC

"Your Royal Highness" the Kor'nai bowed respectfully as a guard closed the door behind him.

The Queen smiled brightly at her Chief Counsellor. "I trust I find you well, my most faithful Counsel?"

"Indeed, you do, Your Majesty" the Kor'nai smiled thinly. "If I may be so bold, beloved Queen, your streak of mischief remains undimmed with the passage of time."

The Queen smiled wryly. "And so, my most trusted friend, do you have news for me?"

"The populace is enchanted by the performance, and indeed by our guests, for they have gained quite a following in the city this week past."

"Is this sedition?" the Queen pressed.

"It is, Your Majesty, as well you knew. The composition seems to have been carefully crafted to give offence, and yet, to do so in such a way that would seem innocuous to the unlearned" the Kor'nai replied.

"We know who the perpetrators of this outrage are, do we not?" Lezika smiled tightly.

"We do, Your Majesty. The question remains as to what is to be done with them?" the Kor'nai left the question hanging in the air.

"My children were rather taken with the dwarf. He seems a far more serious contender than one would credit, don't you think?" the Queen smiled tightly.

"It was a bravura performance, Your Majesty. And yet, appearances can be deceptive, can they not? Our diminutive friend is both talented and ambitious" the Kor'nai ventured.

"I have it on authority that prior to his epiphany under the watchful eye of our dear Daladaeus, this dwarf was a rather wayward soul. Sadly, blind ambition is an all too common failing, is it not?" the Queen mused.

"It is, Your Majesty. It is all too easy to conceive how such ambition, coupled with a rare talent, might find its expression in baser desires, if it were unsatiated?" the Kor'nai postulated.

"Is it true, Honourable Counsel, that actors are disposed to fits of jealousy, even murder, if their ambition and talents are slighted?" asked the Queen.

"I have heard it whispered, Your Majesty. I think our little friend might be perfectly cast in our own tragedy of ages."

"Can it be done? Discreetly, of course, for there must be a trial?"

"It can be done, Your Majesty! You may rest assured of that" the Kor'nai said emphatically.

Pierl'yi frowned, his eyes unblinking in concentration, as he held the sword in front of him, right arm extended. The blade was far too heavy, and the weight caused the razor-sharp point to waver almost continuously; to the left, to the right, and often to fall. This was not surprising, as Pierl'yi was a boy of only seven years. "If you damage the point, boy, I will use what is left of it on you!" a voice hissed in his ear. The boy yelped in shock and a firm hand reached out with the speed of an asp to seize his wrist and prevent the blade from falling to the floor. The old man took the weapon from the child and held it dangerously in his sword-hand. "What have I told you before, lad? These are weapons of war! They are not toys for little boys; you understand?"

"I was simply training my sword arm, master" the boy whispered softly. "I wish to be a great warrior when I am older, as you once were."

"I was a soldier, boy, and that is the truth of it. In my experience, there are few great warriors. Most of those heralded as such wind up dead in the field, sooner rather than later" Saz'jik looked meaningfully at the boy.

"Was not King Mag'kar a great warrior?" the boy asked quizzically.

It was a dangerous question, yet one which demanded an honest answer. "The old King was a great soldier, that is true, but that is not the same as a great warrior" confessed Saz'jik. "King Mag'kar could inspire men simply by his presence; by exposing himself to the same dangers as the lads. It is true that he was famed for his courage in the face of the enemy, yet he also shared our hardships, even our pain. He was a gifted field commander, with a rare talent for understanding the lie of the land and how best to deploy our strengths in the face of the enemy. He had an even rarer gift for selecting and nurturing excellent Commanders and instilled within them the virtue of leadership by example. Those are hallmarks of a great soldier, not a great warrior, my child."

"I should wish to be a great soldier, rather than a great warrior?" Pierl'yi chirped.

"For the now, you should wish to be a good armourer. Without good armourers, we cannot win any war, do you understand? And, never let it be said too often that a good armourer keeps a tidy floor. Now, away with you for it is time to finish your chores" the old man ruffled the boy's hair with a genuine affection.

"Yes, master" the boy sighed softly.
"Before you sweep the floor, you may join me in a small draught of wodki. Never let it be said too often that a draught of wodki does wonders for a man's spirit in the face of adversity" the grizzled, yet kindly, veteran grinned conspiratorially.
"Yes, master!" Pierl'yi grinned impishly and skipped happily toward the storeroom in the far corner, where the old man kept his wodki barrel.

As the boy disappeared down the aisle between the racks of spears and shields, Saz'jik tested the edge on the weapon, determined it keen enough for sale, and placed it back on the nearest rack. "A dull edge isn't much use in a fight, isn't that so, friend?" a voice spoke up.

Saz'jik turned and appraised the two visitors warily. "Do I know you, friend?"

"You do not, friend, and that is my misfortune. Who in the Royal City has not heard of Saz'jik the Armourer? Your repute for esteemed craftsmanship is widely celebrated. Some say there is none finer in all of Mamy'eva."

"How may I be of service, friend?" Saz'jik asked evenly.

"I require weapons, of course!" the man grinned at his companion. "My name is Ba'chi, and this is Mos'cal. We are retainers to His Royal Highness, The Crown Prince Voskar."

"And how may I be of service to His Royal Highness" Saz'jik smiled brightly.

"It is a delicate matter. Our Master would appreciate your absolute discretion?"

"His Royal Highness may have it." Saz'jik replied.

"Then we have an agreement" Ba'chi sighed happily. "We have an urgent requirement for combat equipment; swords, daggers, spears and shields, sufficient for a body of twenty men. There is also the matter of armour? We prefer Hellenic if you have any in stock?"

"Then I am most definitely at His Royal Highness' service, friend! Such an order will not be cheap? Do you have any requirement for bows and arrows?"

"How forgetful of me, I apologise?" Ba'chi shrugged ruefully. "Perhaps we may look at some of the weaponry if you have sufficient time? As I have said, our assignment is most urgent."

"The swords and daggers you can see before you, the spears and shields are over there" Saz'jik indicated the whereabouts of the weaponry. "I can guarantee sufficient goods for delivery, just as soon as you are ready?"

"That would be today, dear friend" Ba'chi grinned. "We have gold, of course!"

Saz'jik was astounded. "If that is so, then please feel free to browse what we have on offer. The armour may present a problem, if you require a solid breastplate, that is. Corinthian helmets, and our own, of course, we have sufficient for twenty men."

"I think we would prefer Corinthian, is that not so?" Ba'chi turned to Mos'cal, who nodded silently.

Saz'jik turned away and plucked a finely made recurved bow from the shelf to his front. It was an elegant weapon, fashioned from bone, yew, and willow. "This might interest you, my friend, it is the best we have on offer."

Ba'chi smiled ruefully. "My companion is the expert when it comes to the recurved bow."

"Is that so?" Saz'jik nodded respectfully at the man. Mos'cal nodded in silent acknowledgement of the compliment. "Perhaps you might care to peruse the entire shelf? The arrows are stored in the corner."

"Now, these spears you have, I take it that they are military grade?" Ba'chi asked evenly.

"All of our equipment is military grade, for it would be little use if it were not?" Saz'jik grinned at the man. "Now, if you care to follow me, I can show you what we have on the rack over here. I am sure you will find it suited to your requirements."

Saz'jik stepped forward to lead the man across the room when, suddenly, his entire leg seared with unimaginable pain, as the breath literally exploded from his lungs. He glanced down in outrage at the arrowhead protruding grotesquely through the flesh of his outer right thigh. His leg buckled completely, and he hissed with pain as he collapsed to the ground, his right hand moving instinctively to the dagger at his left hip. "I don't think so, friend?" Ba'chi smiled thinly and stooped to pluck the dagger from its sheath.

"Bastard!" Saz'jik hissed. "Stinking, treacherous, filth!"

"This is no robbery, old man! Purely a courtesy visit, for it has been too long, has it not?" a new voice cut the silence like a razor-sharp scythe. "It is good to see you again, Saz'jik? You are now exactly where you belong, on the floor, like the vermin you are!" the newcomer sneered.

Saz'jik turned to face the brute, wincing with pain. Yet, his eyes burned with hate like the fires of Hades as he recognised his tormentor! "There is no vermin more vile, murderous, or treacherous, as you, Ja'ghur! You are a man without honour, now and forever!"

Ais'ka strolled breezily along the Foundry Lane, the main thoroughfare of the Metal Workers District to the far west, a short distance from the Promenade and Wharf. Despite the peril of his predicament, Ais'ka was in fine spirits, fortified by his recent exploits and a few generous draughts of apricot wodki at *The Sheaf and Scythe*. The Metal Workers District was largely deserted, and most of the foundries had closed for the day, yet there were still signs of life at nearly all premises. With the sole exception of Saz'jik the Armourer, whose heavy gates were inexplicably shuttered! Ais'ka tried the gate, found it unbolted, and, after first checking the street and nearby gates for anything untoward, he opened the left gate slightly and slipped into the yard. A cart was parked in the far corner of the yard, fixed to two elderly ponies. Saz'jik was presumably still on site, yet there was something clearly amiss. Ais'ka felt the hairs prick at the nape of his neck. He smiled grimly. *Death had laid its icy hand upon his shoulders, and he must face it down, no matter the cost*!

Ais'ka approached the door and tried the handle; it was unlocked. He pushed the door ajar, stepped inside, and closed it firmly behind him. He padded through the workshop, past the furnaces and workbenches, with their array of metal-working tools, all neatly arraigned, until he reached the far end, with its rows of finished articles. There he found Saz'jik, prone on the floor in a pool of blood, his throat slashed almost to the bone. Ais'ka knelt beside him and stifled an urge to vomit, for the eyes had been brutally gouged, the ears removed, and the tongue carefully slit and then drawn through the gaping wound in the throat, to hang on the upper chest. He had seen this before, in a different place, and a different time. There was a message in the defilement of Saz'jik's corpse, Ais'ka was sure of it! Ais'ka reached down and slipped his fingers around the wrist; the body was still warm. He glanced quickly around the store, eerily deserted, and then down at the lifeless body of his comrade. As his eyes scanned the empty rack to his front, they fixed on something that caused his jaw to sag in bewilderment!

Ais'ka's eyes narrowed as he studied the trinket. It was a rare thing of beauty which seemed so obviously out of place, here among the instruments of war. The pendant dangled from an iron nail that had been hammered into an oak frame to mount a weapon for display, a bow in this case. It had obviously been deliberately placed. Ais'ka stood and stepped around the body, to pluck the trinket from its hook. He examined it closely. The pendant was fashioned to be worn around the neck, and comprised a cord of woven silk, around which a series of highly polished oval beads of the purest sapphire, perforated in the centre, had been strung. Ais'ka had seen it before, many moons ago, and as he gazed upon it afresh it rekindled vivid memories of his youth: of an unblemished beauty and of a base ugliness; of honour, fidelity, and courage, and of wickedness, dishonour, and injustice. Ais'ka turned the trinket over and over, as tears well in his eyes. "It is good to see you again, Ais'ka!" a voice spoke softly from behind.

Ais'ka spun, pivoting lithely on the balls of his feet, the axe clasped firmly in his two hands, and faced down the sneering colossus who stood twenty feet away, armed with a heavy iron sword, a mocking look in his eyes. Ais'ka pointed to the body of his comrade. "Is this your handiwork, Ja'ghur?" Ais'ka spoke evenly. "Of course, it was! Just as it was all those summer's ago? Even then, you were a nothing but a degenerate animal! A man without a sinew of honour, is that not so?"

"Saz'jik the Armourer was foolish enough to press the allegation once more. You can see how far it got him?" Ja'ghur sneered.

"How else do you explain this?" Ais'ka held aloft the pendant in his left hand. "It wasn't all you took from her, was it? You shit-pig!" he glowered at the brute.

"She was a whore! It is all she was ever born to be. Have you conveniently forgotten that fact, old comrade?" Ja'ghur hissed. "She was a Sauromatae whore! A filthy, stinking, ill-bred heathen whore!"

"Is that how you remember her, Ja'ghur? Is that what drove you to defile her? Did she bewitch you to a lustful fury with her repulsiveness? Is that that how you justify, even to this day, what you did to her?" Ais'ka hissed.

"She was a whore! She and her sister were nothing but whores!" Ja'ghur raged, his voice echoing around the room.

"They were *children*, you heathen bastard!" Ais'ka glanced again at the pendant and spat on the ground. She was only eleven-years-old when you abducted, raped, and murdered her!"

She was named *Caealla*, and she had been beautiful beyond compare, even at such a tender age. Caealla was strikingly tall for her age, blessed with long, slender limbs and pale skin. Her hair was a most captivating red, her eyes the purest emerald which twinkled when she smiled. She had been born to a *Caravan*; a travelling community of related families, bound by blood and honour, who were fleeing a band of marauding renegades on the plains when they had chanced on an Orch'tai Cavalry Brigade, Commanded by Kour'zan Az'nai. The brigade ranked among its members the living Ais'ka and Ja'ghur, and the recently murdered Saz'jik! Despite their historic enmity, the Caravan was placed under the protection of Kour'zan Az'nai! They were to be afforded all courtesy, upon his Honour, and were not to be harmed. Caealla, and her sister Menoria, aged seven-and-a-half years, were the only girls among a dozen children, and their desperate plight had touched the hearts of all men, who would have willingly sacrificed their lives to protect them. Then, early one morning, the pair had vanished, seemingly without trace. Patrols were sent into the immediate hills to scour for them, until they were eventually found. They had been violently raped, likely by several assailants, and then brutally murdered. *Their eyes had been gouged, ears excised, their tongues drawn through their throats; a ritual defilement of the Sauromatae!*

Suspicion had fallen on a small band of tightly knit, ill-disciplined, and brutish teens, hailing from the same troop, among whom the titanic Ja'ghur, an orphan from the streets of Mamy'eva, had a fearsome repute for unbridled barbarism. The spirits of the men had never been darker. One night, after a bout of heavy drinking, a young Cavalry Officer named Ai'kan had publicly charged Ja'ghur and his peers with the abduction and defilement of the innocents. The fight had been quickly broken up, yet Ja'ghur had sworn vengeance, demanding the slight against his honour be satisfied. The investigations into the murders provided no evidence as to the guilt of the suspects, and not trace was ever found of Caealla's missing pendant necklace, a gift from her grandmother, bestowed a few months before her death. *The same necklace Ais'ka now held in his hand, twenty-five years later!* Kour'zan Az'nai yielded to the demand that, in the absence of evidence of guilt, the slur against Ja'ghur and his comrades be withdrawn. The young Officer, barely beyond his teens, stubbornly refused. Ja'ghur demanded satisfaction by duel of mortal combat. It was a matter of honour, yet there could only ever be one winner. Ai'kan had died on his knees, his belly slit open, cradling his guts in his hands, as a triumphant Ja'ghur mercilessly plunged a dagger through both eyes! *The spectacle of Ai'kan's death had, in the minds of most onlookers, been as dishonourable as the rape and murder of the two girls.*

"Where are the rest of your rapist friends, cunt-face?" Ais'ka traced an index finger across his right cheek, mercilessly mocking the scar on his hated enemy's face.

Ja'ghur glowered at the man, his shoulders trembling violently, as he struggled to contain his fury. "You will pay for that, fuck-pig! I swear it before the Gods!"

"What were their names? Ba'chi? Mos'cal?" Ais'ka sneered contemptuously. "What happened to that other shite-hawk, Vist'ari? You have no idea how much it pleased me to learn of his demise. I heard whisper he caught the deathly pox from your rancid mother!"

Ja'ghur exploded like a volcano. He bellowed incoherently and charged, roaring his battle-cry, yet Ais'ka remained strangely impassive to his fate. Ja'ghur did not get far, for Ais'ka danced to his right, skipping over Saz'jik's corpse, to hurl the axe at the oncoming brute, who desperately tried to side-step the danger, his eyes gleaming with triumph at his hated enemy's foolhardiness. The axe struck true, biting deep into the outer flesh of Ja'ghur's left thigh. His leg buckled, and he collapsed, sprawling ungainly on the floor, screaming like a stuck pig, as his sword skittered towards the Saz'jik's corpse. Ais'ka plucked the weapon from the floor and advanced upon his nemesis, sword in his right hand, pendant clenched in his left, his face a mask of righteous fury. "Now, you murderous piece of dogshit, this will end!" he seethed. Ja'ghur's eyes widened with terror, as the last of his defiance seeped away, and he raised his arms in futile defence of his eyes. As Ais'ka readied the blade to plunge deep into Ja'ghur's throat, two arrows thudded into his back and dropped him to the floor. He twitches briefly, and then stills forever.

"Are you alright, Boss!" Mos'cal asked earnestly. He knelt quickly beside the groaning brute and examined the wound to his outer thigh.

"Do I look alright to you, dickhead?" Ja'ghur hissed with pain. "I need a surgeon, you plank! This fucking wound will be the death of me if it starts to fester!"

Ja'ghur was aided to his feet; hissing and cursing with pain, by Mos'cal and Ba'chi and ferried to the waiting cart, to be driven away by Na'kyr, eldest son of the lately departed Vist'ari. The cart left with undue haste, heading for a trusted Surgeon who would, for a price, brook no questions.

Back at the deserted workshop, Pierl'yi wept solemnly over his master's corpse. In the two years since he had started his apprenticeship, he had grown to love Saz'jik, who had become almost a surrogate father. Pierl'yi did not weep for the other man, for he did not know him. Yet, from the safety of his hiding-place in the storeroom, he had overheard everything, including the names of the perpetrators. Pierl'yi glanced down forlornly and espied the pendant, still clenched tightly in the left hand of the dead stranger whose name was Ais'ka, and who had once been a friend and comrade of his master. He plucked it from the dead man's fingers and stashed it in his pocket, before turning on his heels and padding solemnly to the entrance. He would not go to the Militia. If soldiers were involved, it was simply too dangerous.

Young Pierl'yi, aged only seven-years-old, had a widowed mother and three-year-old sister to worry about!

Thirteen

Novaetis had woken suddenly. He felt nauseous and immediately resisted an urge to vomit. He desperately needed fresh air, and so slipped silently out of bed, leaving the naked Charaen blissfully ensconced in her dreams, and left the room, closing the door behind him. He padded down the corridor, past Daladaeus and Bella's room, then down the steps and through the bar towards the back door. The door was closed, yet never locked, for there was a night watchman on duty in the main bar, a young and pleasant character named Ru'chak. Strangely, Ru'chak was nowhere to be seen. Perhaps he had stepped briefly out into the stable yard for some fresh air? The night was cool, for the day had been excessively hot, not unusual for the height of summer. Novaetis closed the door, took several gulps of air, and felt immediately better, for his nausea had dispelled. Perhaps a cheeky draught of rye would be in order, for the generosity of the kindly Ru'chak could be counted on, at any hour of the night.

The troupe was due to leave Archaeopolis later in the morning, with hopes to return a few months later. Despite the assurances of Her Royal Majesty that they were welcome to stay, Daladaeus had procured a lucrative contract for an autumnal and residence in Babylon, and so the troupe would begin the long overland journey to Diaeni, situated on the northern reaches of the Euphrates, and sail south by barge. The wagons were stationed at the far left, adjacent to the stables, and had been readied the previous night. Novaetis no longer felt tired and so strolled toward the wagons, for there were several flagons of apricot wodki squirreled in the cabins. He would, of course, take great care to ensure he drank from a flagon in a vehicle he did not intend to travel in. It was a wise decision, and one that ultimately saved his life.

The wagons were arraigned in two files, three vehicles deep, ready for departure in a few short hours. Novaetis sidled along the far side, nearest to the stables, until he reached the rearmost wagon, cloaked in the shadows of the corner wall. He truffled for a flagon and peeled away the wax seal with a knife, before drinking greedily, grimacing as the liquor reached his stomach. The rear door of the hostelry suddenly opened, and several men emerge, closing the door behind them. There was a scurry of feet to his left, from the vicinity of the far side of the next wagon, and Novaetis felt a prickle of fear course his spine. He drops to one knee, shielded by the front wheel, and laid the flagon on the ground, slipping his knife from his belt. He sensed intuitively that something was wrong. "Is it done?" a voice hissed from the opposite side of the wagon. It was Ru'chak.

"It is done! Her Majesty is in your gratitude, now and forever" a voice replied.

"What will happen next?" Ru'chak asked nervously.

"There will be a trial, followed by a hanging! You will testify that no-one entered or left after you closed for the night. Are we clear on that? All evidence will point to the dwarf. You know what these acting types are like? They are forever killing one another with their petty rivalries!" the man sneered. Novaetis stifled an urge to vomit. Whatever evil had transpired this night, it had been perpetrated to ensure a swift trial, a guilty verdict, and his execution. He must inform the others, for they must leave immediately.

"We shall be on or way if that's alright with you? You go back to your desk and say nothing to nobody, do you understand? Not even to Cenarius, do you hear?" the voice hissed menacingly.

The four men slipped past the brooding Ru'chak and left the yard through the back gate. Ru'chak took a few paces forward, clearing the front wagon, and then paused to drain the remaining wodki in his flagon. He was scared, and with good reason, for if the truth were ever discovered, he would surely hang. Novaetis reached for a heavy oak stave, conveniently placed in the foot well of the cabin, his fingers curling lovingly around its handle. He moved stealthily forward, cloaked in the shadows of the stables, careful not to arouse the attention of the horses, and waited to strike. Ru'chak burped and padded towards the rear door of *The Horn and Crown*, oblivious to danger, and, almost as he reached it, Novaetis scurried out of cover and brought the stave down on the back of his head. Ru'chak's legs buckled comically, and his unconscious body slumped to the dirt. Incensed by a righteous fury, Novaetis brought the stave down several more times, until the boy had ceased breathing. He opened the door and strode swiftly across the bar to the stairway in the far corner, bloodied stave in his right hand, knife in his left, and climbed the stairs to the guest rooms on the first floor.

Novaetis paused outside Daladaeus and Bella's bedchamber and knocked lightly, yet no answer came. He knocked again, and, when no reply was forthcoming, he tried the door. It was locked. He stooped to peer through the keyhole, noting that no key was inserted on the inside. Novaetis fished inside his robe for the spare key he had commissioned, without the knowledge of the Hosteller, yet with Daladaeus' approval, and inserted this into the lock. He turned it twice to the right, slipping the iron bar out of its close, and withdrew the key. Novaetis pushed the door ajar and slipped inside, closing it firmly. Daladaeus and Bella lay motionless on the bed; its sheets seeped with crimson, for their throats had been cruelly slashed. Novaetis blinked back the tears, for he had loved them dearly, yet there was nothing that could be done for them now. If the troupe were to survive, they must leave Archaeopolis immediately. Novaetis was nobody's fool, and he had seen enough evil in this world to know the truth of it. This was the Queen's handiwork, he felt sure of it. He padded morosely around the bed to where Bella lay, kissing her lightly on the head, before retrieving the key to the trunk out of the secret pocket in her cloak, which hung from a peg on the near wall. Novaetis padded across to the trunk and unlocked it, fishing the cloth sack of gold from within. He turned back towards the bed, bitter tears coursing down his cheeks, and left the room, closing the door firmly.

Novaetis woke Charaen from her slumber and ordered her to dress and be ready to leave within the next few minutes. He silenced the girls' hysteria, comforting her as she wept inconsolably, and implored her to head along the corridor the rouse Maja, otherwise known as Kassandra, who shared a room with Cerrae, for he would wake the others. There was nothing to be gained from staying in Archaeopolis; for they would be damned if they did. The girl dressed quickly and left the room, leaving the door ajar. Novaetis made sure that the gold was securely stashed inside his trunk. When an ashen Charaen returned, Novaetis left to wake Meridonis and Menaeus, or Hector and Antimachus as they were cast, and finally the remaining minor actors, to break the devastating news of Daladaeus' and Bella's murders. "If they catch us, Novaetis, we will all hang!" Meridonis mused gloomily.

"Then we shall give them more than a run for their lucre, shall we not? They will expect us to make for Diaeni, for it is the quickest and surest route of escape."

"We are not going to Babylon, are we?" Menaeus looked miserable.

"They will surely come after us if we do? Instead, we will head southeast to Argishtikhinili, for they would not dare venture into Armenia without an army, and we are not worth the effort" Novaetis proclaimed with an uneasy confidence.

Charaen appeared in the doorway and informed the men that the ladies were ready to go. "We will leave immediately, heading southwest, and within a few hours, we will all be safe!" Novaetis assured the terrified girl and her companions, arraigned behind her. Within a matter of minutes, the horses were fastened to the first of the wagons in the yard, and soon those to the rear. Soon enough, the baggage train trotted out of the yard of *The Horn and Crown* and headed south toward the outskirts of the city. Novaetis hoped it would be several hours yet before the bodies of Daladaeus and Bellatae were discovered and, if the Gods favoured justice, a few more before the first riders ventured south to intercept them. As fate would have it, the Gods were smiling upon our merry band of fugitives, for he was correct, on both counts. It would be five hours before a posse of riders, led by a grim-faced and determined Captain Galligalcix, gallop through the South Gate, heading due southeast towards Diaeni and the Euphrates!

Mamy'eva, July 493 BC

The grim discovery was made by a neighbouring merchant, himself a veteran of the war with the Nur'gat, early the following morning. A rider was sent to the gates of the Royal Palace to inform the Guards, who despatched a detachment to secure the yard and workshop. News of the atrocity spread quickly through the taverns, for Saz'jik was universally admired and respected, and there was talk of dark deeds, for the bodies of two others had been discovered the evening before in the vicinity of *The Sheaf and Scythe*, though no witnesses would ever likely be forthcoming. The men were identified as mere thugs, each with a litany of arrests for theft and violent affray, and their demise was an inconvenience, rather than an injustice. The identity of the second victim in the Metal Worker's District, shot through the back by two assailants, was a mystery, yet the man was obviously of some status, judging by his attire.

The first clue was the axe, clearly one of Mir'gul's wares, which appeared to be very new. Subsequent inquiries confirmed that the merchant had sold the axe to a visitor from the north the previous evening, only a few hours before he was brutally slain. The visitor imparted a crucial piece of information; that he was destined to return to Sar'kuc that evening by barge, and word was circulated among the Officers of the Guard with a view to identifying anyone with ties to the Sar'kta Plains who might recognise the man. It was with heavy heart that Uh'gui ventured forth to the City Mortuary, having been informed of the news and, fearing the worst, tearfully identified his Uncle Ais'ka. A visibly ashen Uh'gui had then reported the news to his Superior Officer, Commander Zu'ki, who seemed genuinely distressed by the revelation.

"This is a truly shocking business, brother, and it will not go unchallenged. I swear it, by all the Gods! We will discover the identities of the perpetrators; I assure you of it!" Zu'ki had stressed. "They will be dealt with, quickly and severely, by the King's Justice!"

"My aunt Yal'vya will have to be informed, as will Crown Prince Sor'chir. With your permission, my Lord, I will undertake that duty myself, just as soon as I have informed my mother."

"Of course, you must go. Take as much time as you need to comfort your aunt. Perhaps your mother would wish to accompany you? I will send a rider to the Wharf and arrange everything, at no cost to yourself, you understand?"

"Thank you, my Lord, I don't know how to every repay your kindness" Uh'gui blushed.

"We are brothers, are we not?" Zu'ki smiled sadly. "We will pursue our enquiries into this outrage with undue haste. There will be no stone unturned, you have my assurances on that. The perpetrators of this wicked act will be brought to justice!"

"Thank you, Commander, for honour demands that it be so!"

Ja'ghur had been in a vile mood for most of the morning, despite the copious quantity of poppy oil he had ingested. He reached for the wine flagon at the side of the bed and found it empty, much to his disgust. "Child!" he barked at the half-open doorway. Moments later, a girl of no more than six years, with hazel eyes and chocolate curls, peers nervously around the door. "So, you are not deaf then?"

"No" the girl replied softly.

Ja'ghur glowered at the child. "You are supposed to be looking after me, aren't you?"

"Yes" said the girl.

"What is your name? I was told it yesterday but seem to have forgotten."

"I am called Au'vihn, as you are called Ja'ghur, is that not so?" the girl quipped.

"I can remember my own name, you half-wit!" Ja'ghur growled, wincing with the pain. "Are you a simpleton? Is that what you are?"

"No" Au'vihn answered coldly.

"The flagon is empty, Au'vihn? Do you understand what that means?" he sighed heavily.

"Would you like me to fetch you some water?" the girl smiled sweetly.

"I don't drink water! I drink wine! The flagon was full of berry wine a few short hours ago, but now it is empty?"

"And now you would like me to fill it? What would you prefer? We have water, milk, some beer, or berry wine?" Au'vihn chirruped.

Ja'ghur was seething. The girl was either simple, or else she was simply playing so to amuse herself at his expense. Either way, he wanted to strangle the bitch. "What did I just say, you insolent cur! Fetch me more wine!" he barked. Au'vihn ignored the man's pique and strolled to the table to retrieve the flagon, before pacing away without a further glance at the miserable bastard! *Perhaps she could pee in the flagon before she replenished it with wine?*

Na'kyr loomed in the doorway. He looked pale and nervous. "We have a visitor, master?" he nodded respectfully.

"That idiot sister of yours is playing me for a cunt!" Ja'ghur hissed.

"I will speak with her, I promise you. It is just her way. She does not like strange men. Well, all men, actually" he shrugged apologetically.

"She hopes to be a rug-muncher when she's older, does she?" Ja'ghur mocked snidely, enjoying the flash of anger in the young man's eyes. Na'kyr turned away and padded along the corridor.

Ja'ghur got the shock of his life when Commander Zu'ki strolled through the door, ferrying a tray with two flagons of berry wine and two goblets. Zu'ki appraised the brute and raised an eyebrow mockingly. "You should thank Tabiti for your blessings, old friend? You are lucky to be alive, from what I hear?"

"That is just what I need right now, another fucking jester? I get more than enough from that insolent little bitch" he sighed irritably.

"I am beginning to wonder if you are the up to the job we hired you for, Ja'ghur?" Zu'ki smiled thinly. "You will take a drink, of course?"

"Thank you, my Lord, and forgive me" Ja'ghur spoke contritely. "I misjudged the old bastard, nothing more. I let him provoke me, and that was foolish."

Zu'ki eyed him coldly. "Why did you murder Saz'jik? I never authorised you to do so?"

"Two of my men tried to jump Ais'ka earlier on. He killed them. I decided to exercise my own judgement in the matter, my Lord" Ja'ghur replied warily.

"Is that so? Well, here we are! We have a double murder in the Royal City, where one victim was much admired and, soon enough, we will have the ire of Crown Prince Sor'chir to contend with" Zu'ki spoke icily. "I think we have a problem, don't we?"

"There were no witnesses, I assure you?" Ja'ghur spoke softly.

"Not even the young apprentice?" Zu'ki smiled thinly, enjoying the bewilderment in the older man's eyes. "You did know old Saz'jik had an apprentice, did you not?"

"We searched the place, thoroughly, I swear it! There was no-one else present!" Ja'ghur spoke hoarsely.

"Our own investigations have not yet discovered the boy's whereabouts. I can tell you that, of course" Zu'ki smiled tightly. "It is entirely possible that he had already left before your men arrived. We have a name, for the boy was known to the neighbouring traders, yet he now appears to have vanished. As has his mother and younger sister. Strange, you might think, that the boy did not turn up for work this morning?"

"We will find him, and silence him! You have my word on that" Ja'ghur hissed.

"Another series of slayings, is that your solution?" Zu'ki clipped tersely. "As I said earlier, I am beginning to wonder if you are the right man to lead our little foray in the north, especially in light of your condition. Would you agree?"

"I shall be right as rain in a week or so, I promise you?" Ja'ghur was plainly worried.

"Perhaps another solution to this troubling matter might be devised? With that in mind, you may yet be of some use, Ja'ghur. If we could pin the murders elsewhere, justice would be seen to be done, would it not?" Zu'ki mused brightly.

"And what will you do about the boy and his family?" Ja'ghur ventured quickly.

"I doubt anyone would take the word of a boy over the King's Justice, do you?" Zu'ki mocked.

Ja'ghur drained his goblet and accepted a refill from his guest. "You require a name, of course?"

"Someone reliable, don't you think?" Zu'ki spoke softly. "We can't very well pin this on a gang of unruly kids? We require a group of individuals, preferably of some notoriety, whose guilt the public could be readily convinced, you would agree?"

"If this goes tits up, and certain people find out I was involved, I am a dead man walking. You do know that?" Ja'ghur remonstrated.

"As I have already said, I am beginning to see you as more of a liability, rather than an asset, old friend. You are entirely disposable, as is your entire fucking tribe!" Zu'ki hissed.

"I understand" Ja'ghur sighed gloomily. He drained his goblet. "Guh'lac and his mob, will they do? You will find them at the Tanner's yard, along from *The Silver Ingot*. You know the place?"

"I know the place, and the name, as I know yours, friend" Zu'ki smiled thinly.

"Guh'lac and his gang have been a plague on this city for a decade and more! They are a right pack of bastards, and the world will be a better place without them!" Ja'ghur spat belligerently.

"The King's Justice will be done! And we will speak no more of it? I take it you and I have an understanding on this matter?"

The brute nodded sullenly. Zu'ki drained his goblet and left the room.

"What a wanker!" Ja'ghur spat feelingly.

Du'byka, July 493 BC

The following morning, a few hours shy of noon, a passenger barge dropped anchor at the Wharf of the picturesque promontory of Du'byka, located on the west bank of the Wol'yi, eleven miles due southwest of the village of Sar'kuc. As a group of Stevedores approached the gangplank, the captain turned to the passengers and gave the signal to leave. A gaunt woman, slim and pale, with long golden hair was assisted by her dutiful son as she treaded the gangplank to safety of the Wharf. Uh'gui escorted his mother to a waiting carriage and supervised the loading of their luggage on to the back. He paid the driver with a handful of copper coins, minted in the reign of King Mag'kar, and climbed aboard the cabin, to sit beside his mother. "We are going to the home of Ais'ka, Chief Retainer to Crown Prince Sor'chir in Sar'kuc. Do you know the place?" Uh'gui spoke cheerily, despite his grief.

The driver grinned. "I know the place, and the man! Who does not know of Ais'ka in these parts? He is a fine fellow!"

Uh'gui glanced quickly at his mother. "That he is, my friend, there is none finer" he replied.

"It has been a while since you were last here, is it not? You are Ais'ka's sister, Ishoria? And you were a youth the last we met!" he grinned at the Captain of His Majesty's Royal Guard. "I was sorry to hear about the passing of your dear husband, my Lady."

The driver whipped the horses and the cart headed north along the main street of the hamlet of Du'byka, once a tiny fishing village, and now a thriving centre boasting innumerable hostelries and guesthouses, moneylenders, a bustling market, and several granaries to the far north. The driver turned right at a junction on the outskirts of the settlement and headed north along a dusty track. It had been several moons since the thaw and the track was parched from the endless summer heat. Soon enough, the winds would change, and the snow would fall, for winter lasted seven-and-a-half months in this part of the world. The track veers west, following the course of a stream, bordered to the north by an escarpment cloaked with dense woodland. To the south, lay rich pasture and grain-fields. After half a mile or so, the escarpment gave rise to a vast expanse of plain, all belonging to the Counts of Try'voye. "The place has changed little since last I was here?" Uh'gui remarked.

"Nothing ever changes here, Sir, does it? We could not imagine a world with change. It would be unthinkable!" the driver chuckled.

"Are the villagers still so superstitious?" Uh'gui remarked.

"As I have said, nothing ever changes" the driver guffawed. "They like their winds of change to be predictable, and that is the way of it."

"We cannot stop the world from changing, my friend. It is the way of the world, is it not?"

"Perhaps in the Royal City, it is. But we wouldn't want to disturb the villagers, would we?"

An hour-and-a-half later, the cart trundled into the northwest outskirts of the village, flanked on its eastern side by dense, coniferous woodland, rich hunting pastures, with its deer, bears, rabbits, and copious birdlife. Uh'gui espied the Caravan, with its three covered wagons. The travellers were engaged in routine daily chores. "I see we have visitors?" Uh'gui remarked.

"That we do. We also have the blessing of Royalty!" the driver pointed to the meadow, where the Royal Princesses were gaily riding their steeds, seemingly without a care in the world. Uh'gui espied the Crown Prince, or the "Old Count", as he was affectionately known, for the old man detested the honorific. Uh'gui gently squeezed his mother's hand, a gesture not lost on the driver. "Perhaps you might alight here, young Sir, and pay your respects in person to the Old Count?"

"That I shall, old friend. Please escort my mother to her brother's house. I will follow on later."

The driver chided the train to a stop and Uh'gui quickly alighted and nodded solemnly at his mother, a further gesture that was keenly noted by the driver. *Something was obviously wrong!*

Uh'gui strolls across the meadow to the Count, who having recognised him, despite the passing of the summers, now paced to greet him. "It is good to see you again, young Uh'gui! I was deeply sorry to hear the news of the loss of your father" the Count looked uneasy.

"Thank you, my Lord. I am a harbinger of other distressing news, I am afraid."

"I had expected your dear Uncle to return on the early morning barge, yet he was not aboard. Now, I fear he will never return from Mamy'eva?" the old man sighed sadly.

"No, my Lord, he will not be returning, at least not in the flesh."

The Old Count blinked back the tears. "He only went to the Royal City on my instruction, as a matter of grave urgency. What happened? Was it an accident of some kind?"

"It was no accident, my Lord! Poor Ais'ka has been brutally murdered, along with Saz'jik the Armourer. They were old comrades, from the campaigns east of the Wol'yi."

"Tell me everything? There is something deeply troubling in all of this?" said the Count.

Kour'zan Ni'jal, Commander-in-Chief of the His Majesty's Royal Guard, reclined lazily in his chair and sipped his wodki. He eyed the young officer, perched rigidly erect in his chair on the opposite side of the desk, with justified cynicism. "Are we quite certain as to the reliability of this witness, Commander?" he spoke icily.

"Our source is unimpeachable, my Lord. They would forfeit their life otherwise" Zu'ki smiled tightly.

"We are dealing with a fellow criminal, I take it. And who is this source, may I ask? Is he a petty thief, a racketeer, a murderer for hire, even?" Ni'jal probed acidly.

"Alas, my Lord, I cannot reveal his name. To do so, it would surely endanger his life" Zu'ki said silkily. "Suffice it to say, the man is a veteran of some repute, who has sadly fallen on hard times. It is true, my Lord, that he is a known criminal, but I assure you he is no murderer."

"And this fellow, in the company of a group of like-minded souls, witnessed this brutal slaying, and did nothing?" Ni'jal clipped icily.

"Alas, my Lord, he did not" Zu'ki shuffled himself uncomfortably. "My source claims to have met Guh'lac, whose notoriety is versed among the criminal classes, at an old warehouse near the Wharf" Zu'ki said evenly.

"Presumably with a view to engaging in a criminal offence, prescribed by the King's law, is that not so?" Kour'zan Ni'jal interjected.

"That is true, my Lord" Zu'ki replied quickly. "It was to be a transaction involving a cargo of stolen armaments, originally destined for the front."

"A consignment of weaponry, destined for our troops in the east, which had been unlawfully appropriated from a nearby repository. Is that not treason?" the Kour'zan was outraged.

Zu'ki blushed. "My Lord, our informant was not aware that these weapons were destined for our troops. He was told this was decommissioned weaponry."

"Decommissioned weaponry is still capable of inflicting catastrophic damage, young man! Potentially upon our own Royal Guard!" Ni'jal rapped icily.

"Most of our citizens own at a keepsake from our old wars, do they not? I learned to hunt with an old military bow, as I am sure most of my comrades did?" Zu'ki smiled brightly.

"There is that, but such trinkets are scarcely of concern to professional criminals? The weaponry stolen from Saz'jik's premises was new!" the Kour'zan remonstrated.

"That was always our presumption, my Lord. The witness confirms it" Zu'ki confessed.

"And you believe him, Commander Zu'ki?" Ni'jal seemed unconvinced.

"Indeed, I do, my Lord. He has told me Guh'lac boasted of killing Saz'jik the Armourer and a visitor to the Royal City, a few hours earlier. This was a robbery which went horribly wrong!"

"There are other witnesses to this confession, I presume?" the Kour'zan probed.

"There is, my Lord. Once our informant learned of the killings, he wanted nothing to do with Guh'lac or the stolen merchandise!" Zu'ki smiled wryly.

"How public spirited of him!" Ni'jal remarked breezily. "I am curious why Guh'lac saw fit to approach this fellow in the first place, much less confess his crimes. This is, after all, a capital offence!"

"The point was forcefully pressed by our informant, in front of witnesses, I might add!"

"At which point, Guh'lac proceeded with a practical demonstration of the effectiveness of this stolen weaponry, purely as a courtesy, I presume?" Ni'jal sighed irritably. "Will these fellows testify in open Court?"

"I very much doubt it, my Lord, for they would be marked for death, would they not?"

"You wish to instigate an armed search, acting in the name of the King's Peace, at the known address of Guh'lac and his brethren?"

"That is so, my Lord. We plan to arrest them this very evening?" confirmed Zu'ki.

"There is still no word on the whereabouts of the elusive apprentice, his mother, and sister?" the Kour'zan sighed irritably.

"Alas, there is not, my Lord. They could be anywhere?" Zu'ki confessed.

"In the interests of the King's Justice, we must endeavour to discover their whereabouts. Until such time, I cannot see how we can put the alleged perpetrators on trial, not without disclosing the identity of our source in open court?"

"It will be done, my Lord, you have my assurances on that. We are not expecting any resistance from this Guh'lac, or his minions, yet we will prepare accordingly" Zu'ki smiled brightly.

"See that you do, Commander, for it is likely that these criminals will be armed with military-grade weaponry" the Kour'zan sighed.

"We will take all due precautions, my Lord, and effect the detention of these persons with the minimum of fuss. It will be over in minutes, I assure you of that, Sir!" Zu'ki quipped.

"Very well, Commander, I shall leave the matter in your capable hands. Execute your warrant and bring this slime to heel, with a bare minimum of fuss" Ni'jal sighed resignedly.

Prince Mor'kur slugged from the flagon and sighed happily. He gazed at the landscape, almost as if he were breathing its majestic beauty. To the north, the imposing snow-peaked caps of the mountains dominate the horizon and, to the west, lay the forest of Kur'zu. "It is a fine day for a hunt, is it not?" he declared.

"Indeed, it is, my Lord. Judging by the clouds, I suspect we may be in for rain later" Prince Voskar appraised the ominous grey which gathered on the horizon.

"You do not strike me as a man afraid of a little rain, my friend?" Mor'kur raised an eyebrow mockingly.

"I am not afraid of a little rain. We Orch'tai are fashioned from far hardier matter, you may rest assured of that" Voskar smiled tightly. "A spot of rain will do wonders for the vegetation, before the height of summer."

"You are thinking of home, is that it?" Mor'kur pressed.

"I miss my children, of course. They will be having a rare time in Sar'kta."

Mor'kur smiled at the younger man with affection, for they had become close during the past few weeks, despite the obvious coolness of their respective spouses, more evident than ever after the unpleasant incident at *The Horn and Crown*. "We still have much to discuss, do we not? For myself, I welcome the union between our children for no other reason than I have a great respect and affection for you, as a man, a husband, and a father. Your daughters are a credit to you and your wife, and I have no reservations in asserting that the Royal Princess Mikhouri will make a fine future Queen."

"If we are being truly honest, as men are bound by honour to be, do you value your eldest son and heir more than the Prince Sea'gir?" Voskar probed.

"As a man, and a father, I do not. Nonetheless, we are both men of the world, Voskar? We both know how these things work. Disch'al is the heir to the Crown, the future of our people, in a world which grows ever more uncertain with the cycles of the moon!" Mor'kur sighed.

Voskar grinned. "Indeed, it does, my friend. If only I had been born a century earlier!"

Mor'kur laughed loudly. "I think we all feel the same, friend, for the world was far saner back then!"

The afternoon hunt was memorable, for the group of some twenty strong encountered a pride of lions, which were driven off with arrows. To Voskar's surprise, these were fired with no intention of killing. He had heard much of the threat from lions and leopards in his brief time in Archaeopolis, yet he had never seen a lion in the flesh. He was all too familiar with the threat from bears, boars, and wolverines, and had heard tale of an even fiercer beast that stalked the lands of the Sauromatae to the east of the Uruk Mountains, the fabled tiger. "Why do you not kill them?" Voskar asked Mor'kur, as the party rested to skin the rabbits and pheasants they had bagged.

"They are not natural enemies, my friend, despite what you may have heard. Lions are not pests, in the way that wolves and jackals are, and are to be treated accordingly" replied Mor'kur.

"Surely a man cannot share his lands with such a pestilence. They are killers, are they not?"

"That is true, but a lion only kills what it needs to survive. They are not, by nature, merciless. They have a natural fear of men and will avoid them if they can."

"Is it not true that travelling caravans are often preyed upon by lions?" Voskar pressed.

"That is true, and they are especially vulnerable at night, but only if the lions struggle to find alternative food. It is more of an issue in the summer, for that is when the cubs are born, as you have seen."

"You actually encourage them to live amongst you?" Voskar was astounded by the reasoning.

Mor'kur smiled brightly. "We cannot rid ourselves of them. If they choose to, they can simply vanish into the hills and forests, avoiding our hunting parties. With that in mind, we seek to manage their presence in the environment."

Voskar was astounded by the largesse afforded to such dangerous beasts. "If left unchecked, their numbers would surely increase, to the danger of the populace? It is the way of things, is it not?"

Mor'kur shrugged his shoulders and smiled wryly. "If their numbers increase, they go hungry, and then cause problems for the surrounding villages and farmsteads, preying on their animals and even on people. This invariably leads to increased vigilance and retribution, for a pride must have its place in a landscape and cannot survive if too many of its females are killed, no matter how powerful the male is. A lion may be the true King of the Plain, yet it is females who wield real power, as in so many other realms" Mor'kur smiled ruefully.

"Indeed, they do!" Voskar chuckled wryly. "They do not kill indiscriminately?"

"They do not, I assure you of that. A lion, or a lioness, will move the Heavens and the Earth to protect their cubs from harm. They kill only to defend their pride and hunting grounds, and to feed, of course! Despite their deserved repute for unbridled ferocity, even majesty, they are not, by nature, cruel beasts!"

"They are not like us, is that what you are saying?" Voskar chuckled.

"They do not have a Kingdom to rule, or a people to protect from enemies, sworn or no!" Mor'kur smiled thinly. "A lion does not choose which of his sons succeeds him as head of the pride, for succession is not anointed at birth. And yet, it is likely they have the same fears, perhaps even the same hopes, for their offspring as we, for they are fathers too, are they not?"

"That most difficult of vocations, for which there is no training regimen" Voskar noted.

"I would heartily agree with you. As fathers, we must do what is in the best interests of our children, always with an eye to their future, yet we may not always be comfortable with the methods we must employ?" Mor'kur ventured.

"All in the name of land, my friend, for it could never be anything other."

"How much land does a man truly need? I have often found that large family estates are more of a burden than a blessing?" Mor'kur smiled brightly.

"Especially so, if the estate is overrun by a marauding pride of hungry lions, you would agree? Thankfully, that is not a problem we encounter too often in Sar'kta" Voskar noted cynically.

"These are the estates which your children will one day inherit?" Mor'kur spoke evenly.

"That is true, my friend, as your children will inherit your own estates, ancestral or not?"

"As will any beloved Grandchildren, born in the not-too-distant future?" the Crown Prince Mor'kur noted soothingly. The Crown Prince Voskar smiled tightly, for therein lay the resolution to the current impasse. It was not a transfer of title, was it? All land would remain in Orch'tai hands. The estates in question were mere security, an income for any child sired of the marriages of Disch'al and Mikhouri, on the one hand, and of Sea'gir and Alicharia, on the other.

Voskar nodded. "I think you and I have an understanding, my friend?"

All that remained was persuade his wife, and his irascible father-in-law, to acquiesce to the revised terms!

"This is a terrible business" the old Count sighed mournfully, upon hearing details of Ais'ka's murder. "Shot in the back. He did not deserve such an ignominious end?" The old Count respectfully replenished Uh'gui's cup with fine Hellenic red.

"I agree, my Lord, it was not a noble death for such an upstanding soul" Uh'gui replied softly.

The pair sat facing one another in the Crown Prince's private study. The Princesses were in a room across the corridor, learning their letters with Asel'ya, with strict instruction to be obedient. "You mentioned a trail of blood leading to the front entrance of the workshop. This could not have come from either victim, unless they were killed elsewhere?" the Old Count ventured.

"My regret, my Lord, is that I did not visit the scene" the young man blushed. The Count raised a hand to quell any misplaced sense of duty.

"I presume the workshop was secured by the Royal Guard?" the old man probed.

"It was, my Lord. According to the men who did, at least one of Ais'ka's attackers may have been gravely wounded. There is additional evidence from the axe, which bore traces of fresh blood, especially on the upper handle."

"We have a wounded assailant, and two or more compatriots, skulking unseen in the shadows. Poor Ais'ka never stood a chance, did he?" the Count sighed morosely.

"It is probable, my Lord, that he acquitted himself commendably" Uh'gui said proudly.

"I presume the Royal Guard is speaking with all the registered Surgeons in the Mamy'eva. Any gravely wounded man would require the immediate attention of a Surgeon?" said the Count.

"We also have the mystery of the apprentice, now seemingly vanished, together with his family" said Uh'gui.

"There is the possibility the child may be a material witness. He may have seen, or, most likely overheard, something which could verify the identity of the killers" the old Count postulated.

"My Uncle was vague about his reasons for visiting Mamy'eva. He did ask a lot of questions about the current situation east of the Wol'yi?" said Uh'gui.

"That is why I sent him, young man" the old Count confessed. "There are troubling rumours that we are at war with the Sauromatae. If that is so, the entire security of the region, and the safety of the Royal Princesses, could be at risk."

"I spoke with a Senior Officer, Commander Zu'ki? You know of him, of course?"

"Indeed, I do! He is a fine man!" the Count exclaimed warmly. "He and his men were sorely missed when they departed, not least by the Princess Alicharia."

"We are all exceptionally fond of the young Princess" Uh'gui grinned.

"Are we at war with the Sauromatae, Captain Uh'gui?" the Count asked bluntly.

"No, my Lord, we are not? If so, my men would be busy preparing forward defensive positions on the east bank of the Wol'yi. I have heard something of these rumours, and they are deeply troubling."

"How so?" asked the Count.

"There is talk of atrocities, my Lord. Grave crimes committed by our forces against defenceless communities in the plains. If this is true, these men would be a disgrace to the uniform!" Uh'gui spat feelingly.

The old Count grimaced. He sipped his wodki. "From my experience, there is no such thing as a defenceless community, not in the plains. Yet, these people are scarcely equipped for war. They pose little threat to the Signet, or any of our forward units."

"There is much dissatisfaction with the quality of these new troops, from what I hear. They are ill-equipped for the rigours of the front" Uh'gui ventured.

"All men are, until they serve there" the old Count softened any sting of reproof with a smile. "Is there any particular reason why we have seen fit to deploy several new divisions to the east?"

Uh'gui was momentarily startled, yet quickly recovered. "These are not mere divisions, my Lord, this is a new army!"

"What?" the Count gasped in horror.

"Surely you were told. Given the significance of this region to logistics effort?" Uh'gui blushed hotly.

"I most certainly was not! What in Hades name is going on?" the Count spoke angrily. "No wonder we have lost so many able sons to the Recruiting Officers. How does the King intend to provision such an army?"

"Perhaps that is the root of the problem, my Lord? We have not the supplies to provision this new army, and so must take from the land" Uh'gui hypothesised.

"Either by force of arms, or by threat of such force!" the Count scowled. "If that is so, there may be more than a morsel of truth in these rumoured atrocities. This could well sting the Sauromatae to fury and invite war in the east!"

"Surely, my Lord, you do not suggest that my uncle's murder is in some way connected with events in the east?" Uh'gui was deeply troubled.

"In light of these revelations, I am no longer certain of anything" the Count confessed sadly. "It is quite clear that His Majesty and his Counsel have not been entirely truthful in their dealings with us. Ais'ka must have stumbled upon something, I am certain of it, for there can be no other justification for his murder. We must make all efforts to find this boy, this apprentice. Everything depends upon it!"

Two covered wagons, adorned with the insignia of His Majesty's Royal Guard, clatter north along a backstreet which runs parallel to Grocer's Lane. The lead driver reined to a halt outside a two-storey apartment block which overlooked the old Tanner's Yard, a short distance along from *The Silver Ingot*. The two drivers, attired in military uniform, including weaponry, leap from their cabins and pace to the rear of the wagons, hissing orders. A few moments later, two teams of archers race up the stairs to the Reception Hall, located on the second floor, to secure the stairwells which lead to the flat roof. Soon enough, they were safely in position, a few metres from the parapet which skirts the perimeter. The street is largely deserted, for the market had long since closed for business, and the sounds of revelry chime from *The Silver Ingot* on a faint breeze. A cavalry detachment of fifty men, comprising two teams, were fast approaching the lane and would secure both ends, before an infantry detachment of sixty men would follow to secure the entrance to the tavern and adjacent stables. It would be the infantry, not the cavalry, who would move into position and enforce the arrest of an unsavoury gang of criminals whom, blissfully unaware of their impending arrest, were happily demolishing a consignment of wine stolen the previous evening from a Merchant's Yard. The men of the Royal Guard had been carefully briefed by Commander Zu'ki. To a man, they understood they were now dealing with dangerous and even desperate men, to whom murder was instinctive. These were likely to be armed with military weaponry every inch as deadly as theirs. *In the event of resistance, the order was to engage the offenders with lethal force!*

The first sub-detachment, Commanded by Gal'mur, trots past entrance to *The Silver Ingot*, thence the old Tiler's Yard, warily noting any signs of human activity, and proceeded on to secure the south end of the street. The second team trotted into the stable yard of the Inn and dismounted, leisurely stretching their limbs, as they awaited the arrival of the infantry. From his vantage of the roof, Commander Ner'ku was the first to note the infantry turning the corner at the north end of the street. He smiled tightly as the cavalry began buzzing about the stable yard, splitting into two teams. As the infantry passed by, twenty men climb into their saddles and trot out to seal the north end of Grocer's Lane. The infantry march past the entrance to *The Silver Ingot*. The inn had been secured by armed soldiers who barged through the doors and quickly quelled the revellers to silence, as their comrades march south until they reached the gates of the old Tiler's Yard. It was then, that a lone figure morphed from behind a row of kegs in the far corner, to stare wild-eyed at the party assembled outside the gate. The man turns to yell a warning to his comrades inside, when he is downed by two arrows, fired from the rooftop opposite. The man falls and stills.

"Guh'lac! Guh'lac! We have a warrant in the name of the King!" bawled the Infantry Officer, Commander Du'ma.

Inside the building, Guh'lac had been enjoying the virtue of a gamely prostitute, the thirteen-year-old Namelya, when his name was bellowed by an Officer of the King's Guard. "Fuck this! I'm out of here!" he spat indignantly. "Put your kurta back on petal, and an alluring smile, for you might be busy for the rest of the evening!"

"What the fuck have you done now?" Namelya gaped. "You haven't even paid me!"

"What's wrong with you?" Guh'lac fumed. "Is that all you can think about at a time like this? Get your fucking clobber on!"

"What the fuck are we going do, Boss? There are dozens of the bastards!" a breathless Nis'ric, his trusty lieutenant, looms in the doorway.

"Where's the rest of the mob?" Guh'lac smiled brightly.

"Trying to make a run for it, or trying to hide?"

"They're a pack of useless cunts!" Guh'lac spat feelingly. "I don't want anyone playing silly buggers, you understand. We will try and make a run for it, because I for one do not intend to spend a term in their plush new nick? But, if they catch you, do not offer any resistance, got it? They will only add it to whatever else they've obviously got against us, won't they?"

The grim silence was shattered by a litany of insults to auditory nerve. A series of ear-deafening bangs soon gave way to a crisp interlude of splintering wood, followed swiftly by a drumbeat of authoritative bawl, lasting a mere matter of seconds, and, finally, the high-pitched screams of a hysterical woman and babe-in-arms. Guh'lac scowls and spits on the tiled floor in contempt at the unwelcome intrusion of the Royal Guards. "That is all I need, isn't it? A new fucking door! On top of Loy'la and a screaming baby" he sighed despairingly.

"I'm making a run for it, Boss!" Nis'ric smiled grimly.

"Fuck off then, there's a good chap? I had better find out what these dickheads want."

Guh'lac sauntered cockily down the corridor, paying little attention to Nis'ric or Namelya. Two soldiers appeared at the end of the corridor and roar at him to get down on his knees. The career criminal responded to the command with a wry smile and rueful shrug of his shoulders. He padded towards them. "Stay where you are?" a soldier yelled.

"Now look here, matey! That is my missus bawling like a stuck pig, not to mention the little 'un, and a new fucking door you owe me, by the way!"

"Insolent cunt!" the senior soldier scowled, then drew his sword and plunged the point into Guh'lac's outer thigh.

"Fuck me! There's no need for that!" Guh'lac remonstrated, as his leg gave way and he slumped to the ground. A foot lashed out and caught him squarely on the jaw, causing stars to dance before his eyes.

"Shut your fucking mouth, twat!" the soldier roared. He quickly checked the prisoner and found the dagger at his hip, which was taken. "Nice! What were you thinking of doing with this?"

Guh'lac was roughly manhandled down the corridor towards the front door, where Loy'la was screaming. "Hey! You can see that's a woman with a baby, can't you?"

"Shut your fucking mouth!" the senior soldier roared, slamming Guh'lac's head against the wall.

For the first time in his life, Guh'lac was scared, for there was something deeply wrong in all of this. He had been on the receiving end of a 'talking to' by the Palace Guards, ever since he was a kid, but there was something chilling about the brutality meted out by these bastards. "Leave him alone? Leave him alone?" Loy'la wailed pitifully, as her lover was dragged towards her. She was still cradling the infant, the five-month-old Ischalla, in her right arm.

"Was he armed?" Du'ma asked softly.

"Only with this" the soldier held aloft the dagger.

"Doesn't look much? Then again, in the wrong hands, who knows?" Du'ma smiled chillingly.

Guh'lac was powerless to prevent what happened next. His beautiful baby girl, the blonde-haired and blue-eyed Ischalla, the 'apple of her daddy's eye', was cruelly snatched from her wailing mother and handed to one of the soldiers. The dagger was then passed to Nis'gri, a hulking brute of a man, who manhandled the sobbing Loy'la, little more than a child herself, and drew the blade quickly across her throat, showering her horrified husband with a sickening font of arterial blood. "That's how we deal with your kind, you murderous scrap of filth!" Du'ma hissed chillingly. "Get him outside!" He turned to the soldier holding the infant Ischalla. The gurgling infant was mercifully unaware of the horror inflicted upon her mother. "Take that little fucker somewhere and end it!"

"You murderous pack of cunts!" Guh'lac roared, the tears streaming freely.

"You and I have a lot in common, don't we? Move your arse, scumbag!" Du'ma smiled thinly.

Guh'lac was dragged out of the building and down the steps, past the bodies of four of his gang, one of them barely a teenager, who had been stupid enough to try and make a break for it. In truth, they had been trying to surrender when they had been cut down in a hail of arrows fired from the roof across the street. On the roof, three more daring escapees had been casually despatched (*"just like shooting pheasants, wasn't it?"*), and the teenage identical twins, Gi'la and Gru'la, were dragged from their hiding place in a vacant upstairs room and stabbed in the throat. The sweet and enchanting Namelya had found the soldiers depressingly unresponsive to her overtures and, instead of a good night's shagging and a shower of silver she was roughly escorted down the corridor to the kitchen, where a knife had been driven through both eyes.

The baby Ischalla had been dunked until drowned in a barrel of Hellenic red before her lifeless form was conveyed upstairs and flung through an attic window into the yard below. The soldiers toasted her passing with a goblet of wine from the barrel in which she had been drowned! At the end of the foray, Guh'lac and three survivors, including Nis'rac, were thrown into the back of a waiting wagon and driven to the Central Square, to be summarily hanged. The guardians of justice in the Royal City of Mamy'eva were not inclined to mercy when faced with such egregious lawbreaking.

News of the arrests and executions spread like wildfire among the populace, who were outraged and saddened in equal measure by the apparent murder of a defenceless young mother and her baby (*"Animals, they were, just animals! Who could do such a thing?"*), the pretty teenage waif (*"Such a shame, for she was a lovely lass, wasn't she? She just fell in with a bad crowd, didn't she? Now see what has become of her!"*), but, for the demise of Guh'lac and his gang, who had apparently tried to kill the Guardsmen sent to apprehend them, there was none. *Murdering scum! They had gotten what they deserved! Hanging was too good for them! The soldiers should have drowned the bastards in the river, just like that toerag had done to his own poor baby!*

PART FOUR

Fourteen

"You wished to speak with me, Voskar?" said the Crown Prince Mor'kur.

Voskar glances up from his half-empty goblet of wine and raises a hand in greeting to a smiling Prince Mor'kur, who stands framed in the doorway of the Regimental Mess of the Argata Royal Guard, sited in the bowels of the Southwest Tower. The Mess was deserted at this hour of the day, save for its Chief Steward, Callitrix, a grizzled and thick-bearded Celtic veteran hailing from the wilds of the Atlantic coast. Mor'kur nods in greeting to the Steward and took a chair at the occupied table in the near corner of the room, facing the bar. Mor'kur was in a breezy and business-like mood. He reaches for the flagon and pours himself a goblet, courteously re-filling Voskar's own. "You seem troubled, my friend? I do hope the Lady Sychoria is not plagued by sickness?" he smiled wryly.

"My wife has arranged to meet Her Majesty tomorrow?" Voskar replied woodenly. He sips his wine.

"I am aware of that. Is there some problem I ought to be aware of?" Mor'kur seemed bemused by the unspoken confession that the younger man was unsettled.

"If there is, it may be more of a problem for you, than for me" Voskar smiled tightly.

Mor'kur raised an eyebrow. "I think you are in danger of overstating a problem that does not exist. Her Royal Highness and I are in complete agreement on this matter. Our terms are non-negotiable, and I have intimated for several weeks, have I not?"

"My wife has several concerns, and she would prefer to address these with Her Majesty directly. It is we, rather than the Argata Royal House, who must pay heed to any political consequences of the settlement" Voskar sighed.

Mor'kur's eyes twinkled with mischief. "We are now allies, are we not? Our two Royal Houses, and the fate of our great nations, will be forever betwixt. I understand your darling wife has concerns, of course I do. Nonetheless, the settlement upon which my wife and I are at one is not ungenerous, in either its terms, or spirit. We have asked for nothing more than we might expect from a professed ally, nor anything less, for that matter."

"You demand a dowry of five hundred Persian gold pieces in exchange for the hand of each of my daughters, in addition to land, titles, and an annual tribute of one hundred pieces per annum. This tribute would not be subject to a levy?" Vos'kar eyed the Crown Prince steadily.

Mor'kur sipped his wine and sighed lengthily. "Those are the just terms of the Argata people, dear friend. I can assure you that they were never intended to be construed as an insult."

"There is a distinct possibility that His Majesty's Counsel, not to mention the King, will see matters differently. We must look to the future, rather than the past?" Voskar spoke evenly.

"Am I to take it that you now construe our settlement to be tantamount to reparations against the Orch'tai realm? A penalty, if you will, for the various crimes committed against our people during the last war?" Mor'kur said airily.

Voskar's eyes flash with anger at the thinly veiled insinuation. *And yet, that was exactly how the settlement would be construed in Mamy'eva!* "I have intimated no such thing. I merely suggest there may be unintended political consequences in the event the dowries were perceived to be excessive, even punitive. There is the small matter of the Royal Army to consider, after all?"

"The Royal Army takes its orders from the King, does it not? If King Tagar, in good faith and good grace, acquiesces to these marriages, surely that should suffice to assuage the concerns of the army?" Mor'kur noted.

"That is a matter for the Royal Army, my friend. Sadly, I regret to inform you that the resolution of the matter is now firmly in the hands of the Royal Princess Sychoria" Voskar smiled thinly.

Mamy'eva, August 493 BC

Commander Zu'ki arrived at the villa just after nightfall. He stabled his horse and was greeted on the porch by Ny'azmi, who escorted him to the General's Private study. "You may go in, they have been expecting you, Commander" Ny'azmi spoke evenly. Zu'ki felt the blood chill in his veins as he opens the door and steps inside. He was astounded by the calibre of the General's visitors this night, for they included, in addition to Az'nai himself, General Nal'gi of His Majesty's Royal Guard, General Zu'ghir, and General Til'koi.

"Good of you to join us, Commander Zu'ki?" said Az'nai evenly.

"I thought it was prudent to wait until nightfall, my Lord" said Zu'ki respectfully.

"It is a great pity that you did not exercise such prudence in your escapades yesterday evening!" Az'nai said icily.

"With all due respect, my Lord, I was presented with a vexing problem which required immediate resolution" Zu'ki smiled thinly. "As far as the populace is concerned, a notorious and ruthless gang of violent criminals have been duly served with the King's Justice."

"You are not in the least perturbed by the brutal slaying of a young mother and her babe-in-arms?" Az'nai challenged.

"Their deaths are most regrettable, my Lord. I have spoken with the Senior Officer to express my displeasure. Nonetheless, it is my belief that the populace can be readily gulled to believing their demise came at the hands of their kin."

"I have heard that certain members of His Majesty's Counsel will seek to pressure Kour'zan Ni'jal into convening an inquiry into the matter" General Nal'gi sighed.

"If he did, what would any inquiry accomplish? The men will not talk. You may rest assured of that" Zu'ki said airily.

"What of this elusive apprentice? Have you considered the importance of his testimony; in the event he did witness something?" Az'nai spoke evenly.

"We are making enquires in the neighbourhood where the boy and his mother lived. There is a sister, I believe?" Zu'ki confessed.

"When you do eventually find them, is it your intention to deal as ruthlessly with them as you did this gang of reprobates?" General Nal'gi interjected "I have serious concerns about committing His Majesty's Royal Guard to such disreputable ends."

"There is also the pressing matter of this Ja'ghur creature!" General Zu'ghir spoke for the first time. General Az'nai eyed the young Commander closely. "I am firmly of the opinion that this unruly brute has long since served his purpose. He is now a liability, not an asset, to our plans!"

"Ja'ghur and his band are unconventional allies, to say the least. Nonetheless, they are entirely expendable, is that not so?" Zu'ki said brightly.

"There is that, of course. Nevertheless, in a matter as delicate as this, I am no longer certain this band of cut-throats is suited to the delicate task ahead" Zu'ghir sighed.

"We need killers, not Handmaidens!" General Az'nai bridled. "I would be greatly interested in your own thoughts on the matter, General Til'koi?"

"Ja'ghur may be an untamed brute, but this mission was never for the faint-hearted" General Til'koi smiled grimly. "We need reliable men with martial experience who can handle themselves in a fight, as necessity arises. These men can handle themselves, can't they?"

"The bugger scarcely covered himself with glory the other night, did he?" Zu'ghir noted acidly.

"A regrettable error of judgment, nothing more than that" Zu'ki replied. "Ja'ghur has given me assurances that he has selected the right men for the mission. His own life is forfeit upon failure to deliver."

"How soon could they move?" asked General Az'nai.

"Ja'ghur is injured, but his wounds should heal within a week. I can instruct him to move north after the next Shabbat. If would be acceptable to all present?"

"In the interval, we run a grave risk of discovery of the whereabouts of this apprentice whose testimony, and we must consider the possibility, may directly incriminate Ja'ghur and his thugs in a double murder" interjected General Nal'gi. "I think it might be wiser if this creature and his ilk simply disappeared, sooner rather than later."

"You would prefer it if Ja'ghur recuperated in the north, my Lord?" Zu'ki raised an eyebrow.

"I think that would be the safest course, don't you, Gentlemen?" General Az'nai drained his goblet. "I also have reservations as to the suitability of this animal to lead such a delicate mission. We require a commanding figure whose capabilities are beyond reproach, and in whom we can place our complete trust and confidence."

"Who did you have in mind, General Az'nai?" General Til'koi broke the uncomfortable silence.

"I think our dashing young Commander would do splendidly. After all, you are known to the two Princesses, are you not?" Az'nai's eyes twinkled mischievously.

Zu'ki was aghast. "I am honoured by your trust in me, My Lord, but surely we should appoint a non-serving Officer. There is a grave risk?"

"In an undertaking such as this, there is always a grave risk!" the General hissed. "And besides, in the event of an inquiry into this night's affair, you will be suspended from your current duties at the Royal Palace, is that not so?"

"I think we could arrange a transfer, to a front-line Division, in any such event" General Til'koi smiled ruefully at the visibly unnerved Commander.

"You would have me transferred to a Detachment in the Signet?" Zu'ki gaped in horror. "The King himself would have to approve such an appointment?"

"As luck would have it, Commander Zu'ki, such an accommodation requires only the blessing of your Senior Commander, who has already consented" General Az'nai glanced at Nal'gi, then back at the young Commander.

Zu'ki turned and eyed General Nal'gi coldly. "Is that so, my Lord?"

It was Az'nai who answered. "It is so ordered, Commander Zu'ki. You will leave the city with General Til'koi early tomorrow, for his time here is done. That should give sufficient time to pass instruction to Ja'ghur and his men to move with haste to the farmstead at Zi'gursk. I am certain they will find it accommodating to their needs."

"Very well, my Lord" Zu'ki said respectfully. "I shall break the news to Ja'ghur immediately."

Sar'kta Plains, August 493 BC

Alicharia reached into the pail to grab a handful of rye. She threw it idly towards the chickens, ensuring it landed far enough away to cause a flurry of excitement from the birds as they race to peck at it furiously. The girl reached inside the pail and threw another handful to the birds. "I have never seen Grandpapa so miserable! I wish there were something we could do to make him smile?" the child sighed.

"I doubt there is anything we can do, certainly not at this moment. I think Grandfather blames himself, at least a little, for what happened to poor Ais'ka" Mikhouri postulated.

"That is silly, isn't it? Ais'ka was murdered, or so it is said. Grandpapa didn't kill him, did he?"

"I think it's a little more complicated than that, don't you? It was Grandpapa who instructed Ais'ka to go to Mamy'eva. Had he not done so, poor Ais'ka would still be alive" Mikhouri said.

"If I asked you to go and hunt me a bear, which you ought to, and the bear killed and ate you, it would all be my fault? That doesn't make any sense?"

Mikhouri giggled. "Firstly, darling sister, I would throw you to the bear, for that goes without saying!" she grinned. "Secondly, we would have wilfully exposed ourselves to the danger of being killed and eaten by your bear? If Grandpapa had not despatched Ais'ka to Mamy'eva, he would not have been in the Armourer's store, which is where he was killed."

"I still think you should kill a bear for me?" Alicharia snickered. "I think it would bring a smile to Grandpapa's face, don't you?"

"What, my being killed and eaten by this bear of yours?" Mikhouri snickered.

"It would certainly make me smile, darling sister! I could seize the Argata throne for myself! I could also avoid marrying that dreary little whelp!"

"You would be free to marry his older brother instead, would you not? And besides, perhaps you are not as clever as you think? Do you really believe that all Sauromatae men must undergo a trial of killing a bear, alone in the woods, armed only with spear?" Mikhouri snorted.

"Perhaps I could marry both at the same ceremony, for a Queen is allowed more than one husband, is she not? Why would the travellers lie to us? If they say they have killed a bear, I would be inclined to believe them" declared the younger girl.

"You are a strange child, darling sister, of that there can be little doubt. Firstly, you say you do not wish to marry Prince Sea'gir, yet now you want to marry his brother as well!"

"Speaking of wells, perhaps we could fetch water for Grandmama? That might make Grandpapa smile, don't you think?" suggested Alicharia.

Mikhouri gazed at her younger sister for some time, wondering if she was serious. "I think that would be a splendid idea. Maybe we could help more around the house, at least for the next few days? That might make Grandpapa smile?"

"We could bake honey cakes for Ais'ka's widow, couldn't we? That might make her feel better, for everyone feels happier after eating a honey cake" Alicharia chirped.

"I don't know what to make of you some days, darling sister, I truly don't? I think that is an excellent idea. We should speak to Grandmama when we return from the well."

A brief while later, the sister's gathered pails from the pantry and trooped along the Avenue toward the well. When they got there, only a few local villagers were congregated, all of whom nodded a polite greeting to the girls. A girl, aged several years younger than Alicharia, with long blonde hair, was quietly picking daisies from a patch a little further away. "Hello!" Alicharia greeted the girl, who said nothing in reply. Presently, a cart reins in and the driver leapt from the cabin to assist the women to load their pails into a barrel on to the back. They were obviously from the far south of the village, beyond the Meeting House and Armoury. To the surprise of her sister, Alicharia laid her pail down on the grass and strolled across to the young girl. "They are very pretty flowers, don't you think?"

Again, the child said nothing, and looked apprehensively past the older girl towards a young woman, aged in her early twenties, who was busy chatting by the cart. "You can speak, can't you?" Alicharia challenged the girl, who promptly burst into tears and raced to the woman for comfort.

Mikhouri blushed hotly. "I am sorry, please forgive my sister, she has no manners!"

"I was only being friendly! She doesn't even speak?" Alicharia protested.

The woman eyed the girls coldly. "You should not frighten her, for she is easily startled."

"I am sorry" Alicharia spoke softly.

"Come on, Nurialla, let us go home" the woman soothed the child.

"I thought we could never go home?" the child spoke in barely a whisper.

"Our new home, my love, that is what I meant" the woman ruffled her head affectionately. She gave Alicharia a withering glance and lifted the little girl aboard the wagon.

"You do have a way with people, don't you, darling sister?" Mikhouri mocked.

"I didn't even do anything!" Alicharia spat defensively. "She is very *peculiar?*" she whispered.

As the wagon pulled away, the two Princesses filled their buckets with water and then watched the wagon disappear along the main track of the village.

Mikhouri had to admit it, the behaviour of little girl, and her mother, had been most peculiar!

"It is good of you to join me, Your Royal Highness, for it is always a pleasure! Would you care for some mint tea?" Queen Lezika greeted her guest. She was perched at a table in the Ornate Garden, far away from prying ears. Sychoria was nobody's fool, and she was certain that at least one of the Queen's Counsellors would be skulking in the shadows of the Balcony of the Throne Room, overlooking the garden.

"When did you guess that I was pregnant, Your Royal Highness?" Sychoria smiled sweetly at the woman she had grown to despise.

"My suspicions were confirmed at supper after the performance, for you barely touched a drop of wine. I would wager you are at least two moons gone by now?" Lezika smiled thinly.

Sychoria smiled thinly. "Three, if you must know. I did not wish to burden my husband with the added worry on the journey. You know only too well how fretful men can be?"

"They are a weaker vessel, to be sure, yet would we have it any other way?" the Queen smiled brightly.

"I informed my husband of the pregnancy, just before the performance" Sychoria confessed unashamedly.

"I have been reliably informed that you harbour reservations in regard to the precise terms of the marriage settlement?" the Queen asked coolly.

"I freely admit, Lady Lezika, but I am somewhat curious as to why you acquiesced to the unions in the first place? There must be other suitable brides, surely, for the Royal Princes are still young. Queen Illir'ya may yet bear a daughter, and the Princess Laeschalla would make an exemplary match, as would any future daughter of the Persian Royal House. Prince Xerxes cannot avoid the trappings of marriage forever?" Sychoria smiled sweetly.

Lezika frowned, yet her eyes betrayed her anger. "You consider a dowry of five hundred gold pieces to secure the future happiness of your beloved daughters to be unduly excessive?"

"I would move the Heavens and the Earth to protect my children, as you would, my Lady" Sychoria replied evenly. "Their future happiness is all I desire, and I have no doubts of the suitability of the Royal Princes as husbands. There is the issue of land, not to mention the annual income, is there not? This is a most unusual departure from accepted convention, you would agree?"

"I simply wish to ensure security for my future grandchildren. I am sure you understand. After all, you never tire of mentioning how devoted you are to your darling girls" Lezika noted acidly.

Sychoria smiled tightly, yet her eyes betrayed her amusement at the jibe. "I assure you, Your Majesty, in this matter, my determination is resolute. You surprise me, for your talent for statecraft is universally renowned? And yet, you would run the risk of bestowing the contempt of the Orch'tai people, not to mention the Royal Army, upon your unborn grandchildren?"

"It would be most remiss of me not to impart that I am equally determined in this matter. The settlement is neither excessive, nor punitive?" the Queen declared.

"On the contrary, Your Majesty, it is both!" Sychoria snapped, momentarily startling the older woman. "Moreover, it appears to have been crafted, perhaps deliberately so, to lend itself readily to such an interpretation. I have a counteroffer, Your Majesty, and it is this. The bridal purse shall be two-hundred-and-fifty Persian gold pieces, no more, no less. I do suggest you take appropriate time to consider it. It is my final offer, and it issued in the authority of the Orch'tai Crown."

"I see" said the Queen simply.

"Touching on the issue of conferred estates, I have a suggestion. I am sure you are aware that I inherited land to the west of the Wol'yi from my grandfather, in addition to a small estate to the south of Sar'kta."

"I am well aware of this, my Lady?" the Queen smiled thinly.

"The lands do not confer a title, but ay such conferment would be the purview of the King. The lands provide a generous annual income. In a good year, it may be as high as three hundred gold pieces. The revenue is not subject to a levy, naturally."

"And you are prepared to gift these estates to any future grandchildren?" Queen Lezika pressed.

"They will be conferred upon the second-born child of either union. As you freely admit, our 'runts' do not often fare well?" Sychoria smiled sweetly.

"And this counter-offer would be honoured?" the Queen sipped her tea.

Sychoria scowled. "Upon my honour, Your Majesty, and you may rest assured of that. Moreover, I cannot foresee any issues with these terms in respect to either the populace, or the Royal Army, for these lands are within my power to grace, are they not?"

"I cannot speak for my husband in such matters, of course?" the Queen smiled thinly.

"We are both women of the world. Your husband will be persuaded by your reason, will he not? After all, you have paid little heed to the opinions of men ever since you were a child?"

The Queen eyed the woman icily. "Three hundred gold pieces would be an acceptable price?"

"That I cannot do, my Lady, and, as I have already stated, my offer is final. Two-hundred-and-fifty pieces is a more generous settlement than your own father ventured in your first marriage, was it not?"

The Royal Princess drained her tea and bade her leave, a satisfied smile playing at her lips as she strolled across the garden towards the Palace. She felt sure that the matter was now settled, and that honour had been satisfied.

Two men, garbed in military uniform, armed with heavy iron swords, stand aloof from the throng of eager passengers waiting patiently at the passenger wharf. A team of Stevedores were busy loading the remaining luggage into the hold, as the last of the passengers readied to board. General Til'koi nods at the skulking figure that limps heavily up the gangplank, his face a picture of misery. "He doesn't look very happy, does he?"

"Ja'ghur is not a natural water-baby, my Lord. Or so I have been told" Zu'ki grinned.

"He will really be in the shit if the barge sinks, won't he?" Til'koi mused brutally.

"The point was certainly not lost on him when I informed him of the change of plan" Zu'ki confessed in a bemused tone.

"I take it their equipment will find its way upriver in the next few days?" the General smiled thinly.

"It has been packed into cases and will be on route to Ky'rovka in three days' time. A reliable charter, of course, given the price we paid."

The two men turn away from the Wharf and stroll towards the awaiting carriage and its cavalry detail of twenty men, commanded by a junior Officer, Or'kuh. "I doubt you have ever travelled in such luxury before,

Commander?" the General teased as they climb aboard. The carriage was driven by a team of four thoroughbreds and hoped to cover the distance to the Signet in six days.

"Certainly not in the Royal Guard, my Lord!" Zu'ki grinned.

"Well, let's see what we have, shall we?" said the General, reaching into a large knapsack at his side. "We have fresh bread, cheese, cured meat, and a couple of flagons of wodki. I do have a rare treat for a lowly officer of His Majesty's Guard, a decent flagon of Gaulish red!"

"I am honoured, my Lord" Zu'ki sighed happily.

"It is good to see you smile, Commander! Your face was quite the picture when that old bastard blindsided you with your new assignment" Til'koi mused.

"I am truly honoured, my Lord, albeit a little overwhelmed, if I may be candid" Zu'ki confessed.

"You would do well to be so, Commander. They will hang you if this goes tits up." the General mused grimly.

"I won't fail you, my Lord. You have my word, upon my honour."

"Spoken like a true Officer of His Majesty's Royal Guard. I am afraid you will learn that honour is a rare commodity, especially east of the Wol'yi" the General sighed.

"You have reservations about the calibre of the men recruited by Ja'ghur?" Zu'ki probed.

"On the contrary, Commander, they are all good men, or at least they once were" the General mused. "They all know how to handle themselves in a fight, some more than others. Just make sure you keep them off the drink, at least in the few days before the raid."

"Have we truly considered what will happen next?" Zu'ki sighed. "Whilst the raid itself is a simple enough proposition, and I do not expect to encounter any resistance, we have no real idea how things will play out, do we? Do you really expect the King and Counsel to capitulate to our demands so readily?"

"We have winter on our side. Given the gravity of the situation, the King will be advised by his Generals, rather than his Counsellors" the General said.

"Have we even considered the prospect of a purge? How many good men in Mamy'eva may die in the days and weeks which follow in retaliation for our actions?" Zu'ki pressed.

"I am reliably assured that elements of the Royal Guard will be poised to strike in the event of any hostile reaction against the Army. It is not something which should trouble your mind. Now, young man, how about a drop of the wine, eh?" the General smiled brightly.

The two officers sip the wine in silence, enjoying the placid beauty of the landscape immediately east of the river, with its generous tills and bountiful forests. Within a few hours, the landscape became increasingly bare; an almost boundless monotony of shrub, broken only by the rugged profile of the uplands. It was General Til'koi, who eventually broke the silence. "You do know why this has to happen, don't you, Commander?"

"This madness of the King's Counsellors is infectious, my Lord. There is no other way, is there? His Majesty will not listen to reason" Zu'ki spoke softly.

"Do you have any opinions concerning the forthcoming campaign against the Ur'gai?"

"Only that it is an act of supreme folly to start a war so late in the summer, my Lord" Zu'ki sighed exasperatedly. "From what I have heard, the Ur'gai Household Division, some twenty thousand strong, is within striking distance of Panticapaeum and Nymphaion. They are good soldiers, as good as any we can muster, yet we have no plans to engage our best Divisions. I fear the Argata may not hold their promise, and, even if they do, there are few locations on the southern coast of the peninsula where they could land such a force."

"This plan will fail! I have little doubt of that. Any attack against Rost'eya at this time of year could run in to all manner of difficulties! Even if we make it to the city walls, we could find them far better defended than some would have us believe" Til'koi mused grimly.

"Leaving our army stranded in the steppe throughout the winter, without adequate supplies" Zu'ki added gloomily.

"We should have attacked two moons ago, the moment our sources reported that the Queen had left for the Saiga Plains" the General spoke harshly.

"Does this entire endeavour hinge upon the capture of the Queen herself, or at least, her ready capitulation?" Zu'ki appeared bewildered by the assumption.

"It is primarily reliant on a change of Governance, a shift in sympathies in Panticapaeum and Nymphaion, and the large-scale landings of the Argata" the General confided.

"And yet, the Argata could not have readied their forces until now?" Zu'ki spat contemptuously.

The General smiled wryly and sipped his wine. "The Ur'gai have infested every large settlement in the Pontic with their spies, including Archaeopolis. Our agents in Panticapaeum relay news of an inchoate plot to assassinate Illir'ya during a planned visit to Chersonesus" the General smiled tightly.

Zu'ki was astounded. "The Queen's position is weak. Killing her would strengthen the resolve of her loyalists, surely?"

"In the event of Illir'ya's demise, the Crown Prince Sag'ra may prove a more malleable ruler!"

'Sag'ra can be persuaded of the virtue of abandoning the Crimea?" Zu'ki seemed unconvinced.

"If our recent despatches are accurate, I very much doubt this febrile plot to usurp the Ur'gai Crown will succeed" the General mused darkly. "Our agents in the peninsula have relayed tale of a grisly series of events that transpired in Nymphaion during the past week. The Ur'gai may be poised to strike at its Administration at any given moment!"

"What on earth happened in Nymphaion?" Zu'ki was startled by the revelation.

"A series of murders, including two young girls, reputed to be the Queen's Handmaidens. Some fool thought it wise to involve those bastard

Celts in the hunt for this elusive 'Gold Witch', with entirely predictable consequences" Til'koi spat contemptuously.

"The Celts murdered two of Illir'ya's Handmaidens? These were children?" Zu'ki was aghast.

"The Celts were subsequently slaughtered by a vengeful mob" the General seemed unduly pleased at the news. "Ur'gai sympathisers responded with alarming speed and brutality. The Chief Persian agent in Nymphaion was murdered, along with a Commandant of the Civis Militia. Nichassor of Pasargadae was lucky to escape with his life!"

Zu'ki gaped at the General in wide-eyed disbelief. "The Ur'gai have learned of the existence of the Celts in Panticapaeum?"

"I would wager heavily upon it" Til'koi said breezily. "The web of Ur'gai sympathisers in the Crimea is far more intricate than we could ever have imagined."

"With the Ur'gai Household Division now at a heightened state of readiness, this would surely scupper plans for a surprise offensive?"

"I would say so! The King's face must be a sight to behold!" Til'koi grinned broadly.

"This entire endeavour is doomed. It would surely be safest to presume the Ur'gai have learned of the planned landings of the Argata on the Southern Coast."

"The Argata may get more than they bargained for, if they are foolish enough to attempt any such landing" the General smiled tightly.

"What of the fate of our own troops, my Lord? Are they to be sacrificed upon the altar of this folly?" Zu'ki hissed.

"The King will be forced to abandon the entire endeavour. If the Ur'gai Queen has learned of our plans, and we must now consider that possibility, we will be at war within the moon!"

"Not if the King abandons all hope of closer ties with the Argata Royal House?" Zu'ki ventured.

"And that, Commander, is where you and your little band of patriots come in?"

A group of boys close menacingly around a younger boy, only recently arrived in Sar'kuc. One of them seizes the boy by his collar and raises his fist. "I asked you a fucking question, didn't I? You will answer me, you little scrote? If you do not, then I shall beat your face to a pulp and feed what's left of you to the pigs!" the boy snarled.

"Why don't you leave me alone? I haven't even done anything!" the younger boy protested.

"You were making eyes at my sister? We saw you, didn't we?" challenged Amas'ki. His two companions, Tiz'ga and Ni'ku, nodded in agreement.

"I don't even know who your sister is, do I?" the younger boy remonstrated.

"You're a liar! That is what you are? You saw Chyra at the Bakers earlier? She came home in tears, didn't she? She said you were drooling over her!"

A few of the villagers stood watching the scene with interest, yet none would intervene to help the younger boy. It was not that they wished him harm, but if he had insulted Chyra, it was right and proper that he account for it, for honour demanded it so. "There were lots of girls at the Bakery! How would I know who she is? Are you with the travellers from the north of the village?"

"You cheeky little orphan bastard! Do we look like fucking Sauromatae travellers to you? I will give you a slap if you don't mind that heathen tongue! I owe you one as it is, for the insult to my sister!" hissed Amas'ki.

"I only meant that I saw a few of the traveller girls at the Bakery this morning, and that is all. I nodded a "Hello" to them, nothing more. I certainly never meant to offend anyone" the boy protested.

"Well, you offended my sister, or so she says!" said Amas'ki.

"Perhaps you are someone who revels in being easily offended, not to mention, offensive?" a stranger interjected. He had just emerged from the Ironmonger's shop.

"And who might you be, mister?" Ni'ku demanded. "This is none of your business!" he spat in the dirt with contempt.

"Who I am, little cur, is no concern of yours? Like the young fellow here, I am a visitor to your community, and I have always been welcomed" the stranger confided.

"He offended my sister!" Amas'ki protested, albeit unsurely, this time.

The stranger was nobody's fool, and nor would he be fooled by this obvious charade. "If that is so, then the boy should answer for his indiscretion, yet not to you, little man! Perhaps your sister will corroborate the charge? If there is a germ of truth in it, the boy should apologise for the insult, rather than being beaten to a pulp by you and your friends?"

"I don't even know who his sister is! I am a stranger here, just like you?" the boy said meekly. "Why would I deliberately insult his sister, who I cannot be certain I have even met? My mother would surely box my ears blue if I did so. I have a little sister too."

"Would you be prepared to ask your sister to join us? After all, it is her honour, not yours, that is aggrieved?"

"My sister is helping mother with the washing?" Amas'ki replied sullenly.

"You sister is obviously dutiful and virtuous? Perhaps you might learn a lesson from her?"

"We are not finished with you, little cur! We will sort this out another time!" hissed Tiz'ga.

"You will do no such thing!" a new voice interjected with a chilling certainty. Mikhouri and Alicharia had been shopping at the Fishmongers, a short distance away, and had eyed the developing scene with barely concealed disapproval.

"I am sorry, Your Royal Highness, the Princess Mikhouri, please forgive me" Tiz'ga said contritely.

The younger boy was astounded and gaped at the two girls. Alicharia stifled a giggle, earning a stern askance from her sister. "Hello!" Alicharia quipped, blithely ignoring her sister's reproof.

"Hello" the boy replied nervously. "I mean, Your Royal Highnesses!" the boy flushed crimson.

"Where are you going? We can walk with you if you'd like us to?" Mikhouri smiled sweetly.

"I will be fine. Thank-you for your courtesy" said the boy.

"It isn't a problem, we assure you. It would be nice to stretch our legs" Mikhouri smiled encouragingly. "We too are strangers, even though we have been coming here every summer since we were little. We have always been made to feel welcome."

"Have you recently come from Mamy'eva?" Alicharia asked innocently.

The boy's reaction was as unexpected as it was inexplicable. He gaped wide-eyed at the Princess, then turned on the balls of his feet and darted away, racing down the street, right into the path of an oncoming cart! The boy saw the vehicle, and weaved left, almost careering into two women as they emerged from the Potter's shop. He instinctively weaved left, tripped on a stone, and was propelled violently forward, cracking his forehead sickeningly against the axle boss of the wheel. He collapsed in the dirt and was still. The women shrieked in horror, and, as the cart passed by, the Princesses and the stranger caught sight of the boy lying prone in the dirt. The stranger ran towards him, followed by the Princesses, minus their baskets of fish. The boy was unconscious yet was mercifully still breathing. He had sustained a large cut to his forehead, which now bled profusely.

"He needs to see a Surgeon, Your Royal Highness" the man said simply.

"We will take him back to Grandpapa's. He will send for a Surgeon. Can you give us a ride?" Mikhouri asked earnestly.

The man lifts the unconscious boy with a surprising tenderness to carry him across the street to the wagon, followed by Mikhouri and Alicharia, who collected their baskets and climbed aboard, assisted by the stranger. "I suppose this is my fault as well, isn't it?" Alicharia sighed despondently.

⌇

The Count closed the study door and smiled sadly at his youngest Granddaughter, who sat chastened in one of the cushioned chairs. "I would like you to tell me what happened? Nobody is blaming you. This was not your fault. I just want to know exactly what transpired between you and the boy?" the Count sighed.

"Mikhouri witnessed everything! If you do not believe me, why don't you ask her?" Alicharia spat defensively.

"I have already spoken with your sister. She has told me what she recalls of the incident. I have also spoken with Zarrigal, whose recollection of events is a little broader, yet is consistent with Mikhouri's."

"The boy was being picked on by Amas'ki, Ni'ku and that other little runt, Tiz'ga!" Alicharia sighed. "They were accusing him of insulting Amas'ki's sister, at least that is what appeared to be the cause of their quarrel when we arrived. Zarrigal had already intervened by then. They would not have hurt the boy, for Zarrigal would have made sure of that. Who is Zarrigal, by the way?"

"Zarrigal is a Mede. He is a long way from home, sweet child. He has been a regular visitor here for years, for he has business interests in Sama'zka, and even further afield."

"Are you friends, you and he?" Alicharia asked interestedly.

"I would like to think we are, for I have always found him to be both honest and agreeable. Now, young lady, what happened after you arrived?" the old Count pressed.

"Mikhouri told them to mind their manners, for you know what she can be like? I said "Hello" to the boy, and he said "Hello" back. He seemed to be acting strange, especially when he found out who we were."

"In what way, was his behaviour strange?" the Count probed.

"He seemed scared. I do not know why? I am not that scary, am I?" Alicharia asked earnestly.

The Count grinned. "Sometimes, my little dove, but only sometimes? He may have been a little humbled by your regal status, nothing more."

"No, he was scared! I could see it in his eyes. No wonder he seemed reluctant to accept our offer to escort him home" the girl confessed.

"And you re-iterated the offer to escort him home?"

"Yes, Mikhouri did" Alicharia confirmed. "It was then that I asked whether he had recently arrived from Mamy'eva. He was terrified, that was when he ran! I have never seen such strange behaviour before. That is when he was hit by the cart. I did not mean to upset him, truly I did not! I certainly didn't want him to get hurt. Will he be alright?" the child implored.

"The Surgeon seems to think so" the old man smiled reassuringly. "It is just a flesh wound, but it will require closing with a needle and silk thread!" the Count confirmed.

"Do you believe that it was not my fault? I am sure Mikhouri blames me!"

"No, my little dove, she does not? You should never be so presumptuous in the matter of your sister's virtue. You do yourself no credit, my sweet."

"She is always reprimanding me for speaking my mind, even when I do not mean any harm to anyone. Just like the other day at the well." the child seemed hurt.

"What happened the other day at the well? Did this concern the Sauromatae children?" the Count seemed genuinely troubled.

"No. There was a little girl, younger than I. She was picking wild-flowers at the side of the well and I simply said "Hello" to her, but she didn't answer" Alicharia confessed. "I thought she was simple, either that or simply rude, so I walked across and told her I thought the flowers she had collected were pretty. She looked scared and started crying. She ran to her mother who told me that I was being horrible to her, saying that she couldn't speak, when clearly she could!"

The old Count was puzzled. "Why would you think that she did not speak?"

"There are people who do not speak, are there not? I wondered if she was one of those when she did not answer. I was only being friendly, after all" the girl protested.

"How do you know that she is not a mute? Perhaps she could not hear or understand you?"

"She understood everything I said, she must have done" Alicharia countered.

"How can you be so certain?" the Count probed.

"Because her mother told her that they were going home. She certainly understood that. And she replied that she thought they could never go home."

The old Count's eyes narrowed. He gazed steadily at his Granddaughter. "Are you certain that is what the little girl said, Alicharia?"

"I am quite certain, and if you don't believe me, ask Mikhouri? They are a most peculiar family! Even their mother was behaving awkwardly. We are strangers here, just like them, yet Mikhouri and I do not behave like them, do we?"

"You think the little girl and the injured boy are related?" the Count felt an icy tingle at the nape of his neck.

"We heard him say he had a little sister. Both Mikhouri and I thought the girl in question is the one we met at the well. They are peculiar people, as I have already said."

"Either that, or they are very scared, little dove. And with damned good reason to be so!" the Count smiled grimly.

Archaeopolis, August 493 BC

Sychoria saunters through the door and smiled brightly at the Queen. "You wanted to see me, Your Royal Highness? You will forgive me if I don't curtsy" she smiled mockingly.

"Given your condition, my Lady, I think we can dispense with the protocol on this occasion" Queen Lezika sighed irritably. "How are you feeling? Is there anything you need?"

"Have you considered my offer, Your Majesty? Time is of the essence, is it not?"

"My husband and I have considered the amendments to the settlement, and we are in agreement" the Queen said briskly. "The terms are these, my Lady, and you may take them or leave them. The dowry for the Royal Princess Mikhouri, who will one day be the future Queen of this realm, is set at three hundred pieces. In the case of your younger daughter, we would be prepared to accept a revision of two hundred pieces. We agree to the terms of the settlement in respect of the estates, to be transferred to any second born children sired of the union at birth. I will leave the matter of titles to your father and his counsel. Is that acceptable, my Lady?"

"Then we agree, Your Majesty. I have little doubt the King will grant his blessing to the union of our two Royal Houses" Sychoria replied firmly.

"What of the Royal Army, my Lady? Will they acquiesce to these revised terms?" the Queen asked pointedly.

"The Royal Army will obey their oath to their King, no more, no less" Sychoria replied coldly.

"Are you quite certain of that, my Lady? Our agents in 'the lands between the seas' suggest there is some reluctance, perhaps even hostility, to the union of our beloved children."

Sychoria was astonished. "These are matters for the Orch'tai King and Counsel, are they not?"

"Yet, we are allies, are we not, my Lady?" Lezika smiled sweetly at the younger woman.

"And allies spy upon one another nowadays?" Sychoria charged testily.

The Queen appraised the younger woman with amusement. "Come, my Lady, for we are both women of the world? I simply refuse to believe that a woman of your reputed intellect could be so naïve. You have been secretly gathering intelligence on the political situation here in Archaeopolis ever since your arrival! Do you deny it?"

"I haven't the faintest idea to what you refer, Your Majesty?" Sychoria smiled tightly.

"Ever since you arrived in Archaeopolis, you have been at pains to uncover evidence pertaining to the grisly murder of a girl, once in the employ of an eminent goldsmith named Mesticrates, is that not so?" the Queen's eyes flashed dangerously.

"I merely wished to engage Mesticrates in designing a gift for each of my daughters. There was no ulterior motive, I assure you of that" Sychoria replied quickly.

"You even sent emissaries to the man's home, with little concern for his grief, did you not?"

"I was not aware the master and his slave were so close, my Lady? She was not his child, was she?" Sychoria replied softly.

"What do you know of the girl, and of the details surrounding her untimely demise, my Lady?" the Queen probed.

"Only what I have heard whispered in the city, for you cannot still every wagging tongue, Your Majesty?" Sychoria mused.

"I might, my Lady, if it were to become necessary!" the Queen replied cruelly.

Sychoria was startled. "You would justify the indiscriminate slaughter of your own people, all because your son became friendly with a slave girl? The girl in question was a sweet child, or so it is rumoured, who seemingly captured the young Prince's heart!"

"You have much to learn, my Lady, if you ever wish to be a Queen" Lezika spoke evenly.

"I should model my conduct, and my persona, on your own! Is that it, Your Majesty?"

"Just in case you have failed to grasp the nettle, for you are exceptionally fond of the lore's of Aesop, we are a small state, surrounded by powerful enemies, civilised or no! It is one thing to win a crown, my Lady, even over the claim of more rightful heirs, yet it is another thing entirely to keep the head which sports it!" the Queen smiled wryly.

"As you once did, Lezika, if my memory serves?" Sychoria quipped insolently.

"As you intend to, my Lady, for my agents have been quite thorough, I assure you of that. As I have intimated more than once, you have much to learn. I can only pray you do so before that child of yours is born!" the Queen clipped icily.

"Are you threatening me, Your Majesty?" Sychoria hissed.

"Not at all, my Lady, for you and the Crown Prince are honoured guests and valued allies, is that not so? As you are so, I shall impart to you a sage piece of wisdom that you would do well to remember. No matter how sweet, or generous, her natural disposition, a Queen must never let an insult go unchallenged. I can only pray you learn this before others do. Those with more rightful claims to the Orch'tai crown, and their supporters, for there will always be traitors and dissidents to contend with."

The boy's mother, Mae'va, barely in her middling twenties, had wept at the sight of her injured son, now sleeping soundly on a bed in a spare bedchamber, and had graciously accepted the countess' offer that the Surgeon's bill would be taken care of privately. Mae'va had brought the little girl, Nurialla, who barely spoke, even when directly addressed by the countess, yet she too had been distressed at the sight of her injured brother and had wept softly. "It might be best if the boy spent the night here. He will be looked after, and, if he requires further attention from the Surgeon, this can be easily arranged" the countess had made the gracious accommodation. "And of course, there would be a spare bed available for you and the little girl, in addition to a plate of food, and anything else the family required."

Mikhouri and Alicharia had been banished to the meadow, with explicit instruction not to return until supper. Mae'va had accepted an offer of a goblet of mint tea, taken in the Count's private study. And so, in the mid-afternoon, the woman and her daughter, whose behaviour had startled the countess, was ushered through the door where the Count, or Crown Prince Sor'chir, as he had been introduced, eagerly awaited their arrival. "Please, my Lady, sit down. We have tea, or something stronger, if you prefer?" the Count asked his visitor.

"Tea would be fine, my Lord" the woman smiled nervously.
"I was going to have a small draught of wodki? Are you sure you would not take one? I might help to soothe your frayed nerves?"

Mae'va accepted the offer a medicinal goblet of liquor with a polite nod. The Count attempted to engage the child in conversation, but the little girl said nothing. "She rarely speaks, my Lord, though she is not a mute."

"A distressing business, my Lady, and I extend sincere apologies for the unfortunate accident that befell your son. I assure you that my youngest Granddaughter will be disciplined for her lack of manners!" the Count said sternly.

"Children are children, are they not?" Mae'va replied quickly. "I do not think the girl should be treated too harshly, especially after what I learned of the incident. We are newcomers, and I do not wish to cause unnecessary trouble."

"When did you arrive in the village?" the Count asked softly.

"It was a week or so ago, we came down by barge from Du'brya. My sister lives here, with her husband and their family. Things have been hard these past few months, ever since my husband passed" confessed Mae'va.

"I am truly sorry for your loss, my Lady, and with two young children to care for" the old Count sighed, his remorse genuine. "If there is anything you require, anything at all, you only have to ask. We are well known for our hospitality, especially to those unfortunate souls who so desperately need a helping hand."

"Thank you, my Lord. You are most gracious. I do not think that I will ever be able to repay you."

"That is not necessary, I assure you. I am sure my wife has already told you that the Surgeon feels your son will make a full and speedy recovery. His injuries will not adversely affect his ability to work."

"Yes, my Lord, and thank you" Mae'va said simply.

"Does the young fellow have a trade? Was he apprenticed in Du'brya? I am sure in due course a suitable vacancy would arise here. I certainly would not pay heed to the unfortunate dispute with these other boys."

"As I have said, my Lord, children will be children, will they not? My son had hopes of an apprenticeship with an Ironmonger, but it would have meant moving to Mamy'eva. Sadly, the untimely death of his father affected him deeply and he felt he could not leave, at least for the foreseeable future. In that event, he had to settle for something less" Mae'va confessed sadly.

"An Ironmonger is a good trade, especially in the present climate" the Count smiled brightly. "We have a far greater need for weapons than we once did, what with the increase in the size of the army east of the Wol'yi."

"It is a good trade, but the hope was that he could find something other than the tools of war to apply his devotions" Mae'va spoke softly.

"I agree, my Lady, for I was fortunate enough to come of age during the interlude of peace. I too lost my father, and then inherited the duties of the estate and its community" the Count sighed softly.

"It is your birth right, my Lord. I have heard it said that you are much loved in the community" Mae'va ventured, blushing lightly.

"I try my best, my Lady. What else can a man do? I have been most fortunate in my retainers, until very recently, that is. Alas, my Chief Retainer, Ais'ka, was brutally murdered in Mamy'eva only a few days ago. A terrible business" the old Count saw a flicker of distress, followed by terror, in the eyes of the woman seated opposite.

"I am sorry for your loss, my Lord. Ais'ka was highly spoken of in the Community. They all grieve his loss" Mae'va said softly.

"Poor Saz'jik the Armourer, also brutally slain, was held in equal esteem in his community, both martial and civil. I am certain, if he were alive, that he would speak highly of your son, Pierl'yi, his most recent apprentice" the Count smiled tightly.

The Count watched closely as all colour drained from the woman's face. She bowed her head and broke down, sobbing softly, her shoulders heaving rhythmically. "Forgive me, my Lord. I am so ashamed!"

"I am truly sorry for your pain, my Lady, but my instincts tell me your son knows far more than he perhaps should about this grisly affair" he spoke softly, and with compassion.

It was the little girl who broke the awkward silence. "Please don't cry, Mama? We can trust him! I know we can trust him!" the little girl chirped.

"And trust me you must, my Lady. I may be the only person who can save you from the men who are currently hunting you?" said the Count softly.

Fifteen

Sar'kta Plains, August 493 BC

"It is good of you to come, young man" the Count exclaimed breezily, as Uh'gui was ushered into the study by the countess. "I thought it best if we spoke privately, you understand?"

Uh'gui, who had no inkling of the motive behind his impromptu summons, could not hide his surprise. "Please forgive me, my Lord. Your servant told me nothing beyond that you wished to speak with me as a matter of urgency."

"What I have to say to you cannot leave this room" the Count said briskly. "As will become clear, I have not yet had an opportunity to corroborate what I learned this afternoon, although the source of the information has no reason to lie. Please, sit down and help yourself to a drink. We have wine and wodki."

"Thank you, my Lord. That is most gracious of you. I take this new information pertains to the murder of my uncle and Saz'jik the Armourer?" asked Uh'gui expectantly.

"It does, young man. How long have you served in His Majesty's Royal Guard in Mamy'eva?" the Count asked.

"I joined six years ago as a junior Officer. Prior to that, I spent five years in a cavalry division stationed east of the Wol'yi. We undertook regular patrols of the Western and Central Plains."

"You are familiar with the criminal fraternity in Mamy'eva, particularly its brutish elements?"

"I am all too familiar with them, my Lord. As I am sure you are aware, in addition to guarding the Palace and the Royal Household, our function is to enforce His Majesty's peace within the city" Uh'gui confessed.

"Are you familiar with the name, Ja'ghur, Commander?"

The Commander's eyes narrow. "Few in Mamy'eva do not know of Ja'ghur! He is a notorious criminal with a well-deserved reputation for brutality. His gang are a plague upon the city. I have heard it said, though I am not sure I believe it, that he was once a soldier of repute."

"Disrepute might be a more apt description, I would venture!" the Count said sourly. "Did your Uncle Ais'ka ever speak of him?"

Uh'gui was astonished. "Why in Hades name would Uncle Ais'ka speak to me about a notorious criminal from Mamy'eva?"

"They served together, once upon a time. They were stationed east of the Wol'yi, as you once were. His name was one which your uncle would have struggled to forget, I am certain of that!"

"My Uncle never spoke of him, my Lord. I am certain of it. Why would you ask?"

"As fortune would have it, a widow and two young children, boy and girl, came to the village a few days ago" the Count continued. "They reside with a relative in the south, beyond the Community Hall. You may have heard something of the incident earlier today?"

"Is it the elusive apprentice and his family?" Uh'gui gasped.

"Indeed, it is, young man. The boy, Pierl'yi, is sleeping soundly down the corridor. He is quite safe. I spoke with his mother and sister at length this afternoon."

"Ja'ghur and his gang were involved in my uncle's slaying?" Uh'gui's eyes blaze with fury.

"Ja'ghur is ultimately responsible for the deaths of both men, though I suspect he did not strike the fatal blows to your dear Uncle. From what I learned, he may not have been in any fit state to, not after Ais'ka had dealt with him!" the Count mused drily.

"And this boy, Pierl'yi, witnessed all of this?" Uh'gui could not hide his distaste.

"Do not be too hard on him, young man" the Count reproved the Commander gently. "The boy overheard much of what transpired that evening, though I have not had chance to speak with him directly. He is, quite naturally, terrified. So too is his family, I might add."

"They have damn good reason to be so, my Lord!" Uh'gui grimaced. "Ja'ghur and his ilk rank among the most ruthless criminals in the city. They have never been prosecuted, largely due to a failure of witnesses to testify. Or to live long enough to make it to trial if they did!" he mused bitterly.

"Are the identities of his gang equally well-known? I have one, for the boy overheard the name "Vist'ari"? Is that a name of any significance?"

Uh'gui blinked. "Vist'ari is dead, my Lord, He died three summers past, leaving a widow and several children. The boy must be mistaken?"

"I suspect not, for there is something deeply troubling about this entire affair, if the boy's account to his mother is to be credited" the Count confessed. "Pierl'yi overheard what appears to have been a heated conversation between two men, one of whom was surely Ja'ghur, relating to the abduction, rape, and murder of two Sauromatae girls. This happened decades ago, in the Central Plains of Kazakh'yi."

"And you think the other party to this dispute was Uncle Ais'ka, my Lord?"

"I am certain of it" the Count said sadly.

"With all due respect, my Lord, but how can you be so certain?" Uh'gui seemed dubious.

"Because, young man, old Saz'jik the Armourer, who served with your Uncle Ais'ka in the east, had argued heatedly with the same man, about the same event, just before he died."

"The boy confessed this to his mother?" Uh'gui probed.

"The moment he returned home. Poor Ais'ka arrived soon after Saz'jik was killed and stumbled upon his body. He was confronted by Ja'ghur, and they exchanged words about the same grisly crime."

"Whatever transpired all those years ago must be of significance. More to the point, it must have directly involved Ais'ka, Saz'jik and Ja'ghur?" ventured Uh'gui.

"They served in the same cavalry Division, commanded by the now-retired General Az'nai" the Count recalled. "Your Uncle rarely spoke of his years of service, which surprised me, as most old soldiers do little else, but I think I now understand why?"

"I am not sure that I follow, my Lord?"

"One of my former duties, as Count of the Duchy, was to serve as a Jurist in matters relating to crimes committed by serving soldiers" the Count confessed.

The Commander smiled tightly. "I am aware of such Courts, my Lord, but have never had any experience of them."

"Thankfully, they are far rarer today than they once were. In most cases, these were convened to investigate allegations of atrocities committed against the communities of the plains."

Uh'gui was incredulous. "We tried our own soldiers for alleged crimes against the Sauromatae?"

"Old King Mag'kar was most insistent we do so. On the few occasions where the perpetrators were convicted, on strength of compelling evidence, I hasten to add, they were hanged in front of their comrades."

"Begging your grace, my Lord, are you seriously insinuating that Uncle Ais'ka was murdered because he knew something of a crime committed decades ago in the Central Plains?" Uh'gui was bewildered.

"Does it seem so far-fetched?" the Count smiled wryly. "The boy's mother told me her son overheard two separate arguments, involving a single antagonist, undoubtedly Ja'ghur, with Saz'jik and Ais'ka, just before they died. In both cases, the argument concerned the same historic crime. The crime was the abduction, rape, and murder of two young sisters. It must be of significance? It cannot be otherwise!"

"If that is true, then the family are in grave danger. We have no idea who may be involved, in the crime itself, or in any subsequent ploy to shield the perpetrators from the King's justice" Uh'gui ventured.

"That is quite true, Commander. This Ja'ghur creature remains at liberty, wounded or no. In my experience, a wounded animal is the most dangerous animal of all!"

Ky'rovka (East bank of the Wol'yi), August 493 BC

Quite regardless of his habitual distemper, the wounded animal in question made for a sorry spectacle as he hobbled gingerly down the gangplank to the wharf at Ky'rovka a few hours later. It was fast approaching last light, and the journey north along the Wol'yi had been a trying two days. Ja'ghur's mood had not been helped by a lack of liquor, for their supplies were drained during the first day. A handful of flagons of apple blossom wodki had been procured at Lu'vaya, a large fishing village on the west bank of the Wol'yi the previous afternoon, yet the exorbitant cost had only darkened the brute's mood even further. The nine adventurers waited patiently at the wharf as their steeds and luggage was unloaded by a team of Stevedores. The baggage cases, containing hunting weapons and clothing, were stored on to the back of a waiting cart, ready for departure. Ja'ghur glowered at the Chief Stevedore as he approached the group for payment, yet it was the ever-diplomatic Mos'cal who took care of the matter. He stepped forward, graciously shook the man's hand, and thanked him for his service, before handing over two bronze disks. Mos'cal turned to the rest of the party and grinned. "I have it on authority there is a fine hostel in the village called *The Maple Leaf.* They do a decent drop of the local rye, by all accounts!" he said cheerily.

"I could drink a fucking barrel of the stuff! By the Gods, I am glad to be off that bastard boat!" Ja'ghur spat sullenly. The rest of the group laughed.

"You can ride aboard the wagon, old friend!" Mos'cal nodded towards the waiting cart. "I will bring your steed!"

"Just remember one thing, sunshine? This is my outfit, not yours, no matter my condition. Do we understand one another?" Ja'ghur hissed menacingly.

"Just get aboard the wagon, you miserable bastard! We have a night of drinking ahead of us?" Mos'cal grinned. The group laughed heartily. Even Ja'ghur managed to crack a smile.

A few hours after first light the following morning, before the heat became almost unbearable, the party of nine riders, accompanied by the wagon and a sleeping Ja'ghur, began the trek northwest to the farmstead at Zi'gursk, a journey of some forty miles along a dusty track skirting lush pastures and golden-brown fields of wheat and rye. This was some of the richest land in the Orch'tai Duchy and was, at least according to legend, once home to the humble warrior-daughter K'ouhr, first Queen of the Orch'tai Royal House. A party of four outriders, including Mos'cal, rode ahead whilst the remaining members of the party ambled alongside the wagon and its precious cargo. Mercifully, Ja'ghur slept for most of the journey.

Sometime later, the cart ambled through the hamlet of Bai'vych, the ancestral see of the Counts of Kran'ye, who ranked amongst the wealthiest families in the entire Duchy. By now, Ja'ghur had awoken, and was perched next to the driver in the cabin, slugging a flagon of elderflower wodki, a speciality of the region. The brute gaped in wide-eyed astonishment at the fortified walls of the Count's Khur'yi, scarcely believing such ostentatious wealth could exist in such a remote place. "Now there is a flower worth plucking, wouldn't you say?" he grinned at Hai'mur, who rode beside him. To the north, lay dense orchards of apple, pear, and plum trees.

"The Count is well liked in this part of the world, if you take my meaning, friend?" the driver warned. Ja'ghur shot the man a withering glare of contempt.

"A place like that must be well guarded, surely? A place that size could house a detachment of a hundred cavalry, I would venture?" Hai'mur mused.

"There is no need, friend. The garrison at Vy'khu is less than an hour's ride to the south. There are close to six hundred men stationed there!" the driver confessed.

A bewildered Ja'ghur nearly fell from the cabin. Hai'mur glanced quickly at the ground and scowled. Neither man had been informed of the garrison, which posed an obvious security risk to their escape. "I thought the garrisons had been abandoned after the end of the war with the Nur'gat?"

"Most of the garrisons have long gone, but they retain Vy'khu as a Militia Force, just to keep the peace. There is occasional trouble, mostly involving travelling malcontents from Mamy'eva!" the driver smiled tightly. Ja'ghur glowered evilly at the man. The rest of the party laughed.

"You will have no trouble from us. We are here to help with the harvest!" Hai'mur quipped.

Soon enough, the driver espied the small party of outriders congregating at a fork in the road, a mile or so ahead of them. On the left of the road, small track veered northwards towards an isolated farmstead, surrounded by nothing but fields, and bordered further north by an escarpment of dense woodland. Ja'ghur rubbed his bloodshot eyes and gaped in disbelief. "Is this the fucking place? It looks like a right shithole!"

"As good a place as any to put idle hands to good work, friend?" the driver mused.

Ja'ghur flushed with rage at the insult. Hai'mur chuckled ruefully. "These hands won't be idle beyond the morrow, good Sir!"

"Please, help yourself to some food? We have hard-boiled eggs, fresh bread, and salted fish. We have plenty of mint tea and a flagon of wodki" the Count pointed to the spread of food on the dining room table.

"Thank you, my Lord. I don't think I shall ever be able to repay the kindness you have shown to us" said Mae'va.

"Perhaps I may be in need of an Ironmonger one day?" the Count smiled warmly. "I checked on your son earlier and took him a cup of mint tea. He seems to be recovering well."

"Did you say anything to him? About that matter of which we talked yesterday?" the woman blushed.

"I did not, my Lady, just as I promised. Perhaps I should call Pierl'yi to breakfast. We can talk after we eat. Where is your daughter?"

"Nurialla has been seized by the Princess Alicharia, who is also an early riser! They are in the yard feeding the chickens" the countess entered the room and smiled warmly at Mae'va. "Do not worry, my Lady, they are being watched by the Princess Mikhouri. I promised that we would save them a plate of food."

"Perhaps you would like to fetch your son, my Lady" the Count said softly.

After breakfast, whilst the girls played in the yard, the Count, Mae'va, and a pale and visibly worried Pierl'yi, were ensconced in the Count's study, the obligatory flagon of wodki and goblets of mint tea on the table. "How are you feeling, young man?" asked the Count. The scar on the boy's forehead was large, requiring six stitches in all, yet the Surgeon assured a plainly worried Mae'va it would fade to become almost imperceptible with the passing of time.

"I am well, my Lord, and thank you. I am in your debt, now and forever" the boy said meekly.

"That is not necessary, young man, I assure you. As I said to your mother earlier, I may have need of an Ironmonger one day" the Count grinned.

"You know of my apprenticeship, my Lord" the boy was troubled. He fiddled with his fingers.

"I am afraid there is little that I do not know about you, young man. You are not in any trouble, certainly not with me or the authorities, do you understand?" the Old Count soothed.

"If they find us, they will kill us all!" the boy sobbed.

"Not here, they won't, I promise you. Not whilst your family are under my protection. You have my word on that, upon my honour" the Count said evenly.

"They are killers, my Lord! They are amongst the worst of their kind in Mamy'eva!" protested Pierl'yi.

"You are wise beyond your years, young man? How is it that an innocent child is no innocent to the wickedness of men?"

"I had a good tutor, my Lord" the boy replied simply.

"You were incredibly fond of Saz'jik the Armourer, were you not?"

"He was good to me, my Lord. He was kind and always treated me well. He encouraged me and was not overly harsh when I failed at something, which was often" the boy confessed.

"An Ironmongers trade is not easy to learn, my child" the Count soothed.

The boy was pained. "I am no Ironmonger, my Lord. I was apprenticed to Saz'jik as a swordsmith" protested Pierl'yi, "I wanted to be every bit as good as old Saz'jik himself. At least until I am old enough to be a warrior, just as he was."

"So was the other man who was murdered, young man. I suspect you already know this?" the Count probed.

"I didn't see anything, my Lord. Honestly, I didn't. I heard everything that was said, before and after they died!" Pierl'yi confessed.

"What happened to Saz'jik the Armourer? What can you tell us?"

"I left the workshop to sweep the storeroom, just before the men arrived. There were only two of them at first. I heard them talking with Saz'jik. They had an urgent requirement for weapons; swords, spears, and armour, in addition to bows and arrows!"

"That is a sizeable order, wouldn't you say?" the Count pressed.

"Saz'jik couldn't believe his luck! I could hear it in his voice. They had a requirement for twenty men! It would have cost a small fortune."

The old Count was startled by the revelation. "Indeed, it would. Are you quite certain of this?"

"As certain as I am sitting here now, with this scar on my head!" the boy chirruped.

The Count smiled wryly. "Was one of these men called Ja'ghur, is that what you remember?"

"Ja'ghur arrived later. After I heard Saz'jik cry out and fall to the ground. I wanted to go and help him, honestly I did, but I was so scared."

"What happened next, can you tell us?" the Count pressed.

The boy glanced at his mother, who nodded her encouragement. "You can trust him, my son."

The boy continued. "This Ja'ghur fellow and Saz'jik served in the army together, many moons ago. They started arguing with one another, well, Saz'jik did most of the talking, if you must know. He was calling the other men, all three of them, for it turned out that he also knew the other two, also from the army, but he didn't recognise them when they first came in. He was calling them the most horrible names. I won't repeat them, for my mother would surely box my ears, but I understood nearly everything that was said."

"Soldiers are not the gentlest of creatures, my child, especially with their tongues!" the Count smiled thinly. "Please, carry on?"

"Saz'jik accused them of taking two Sauromatae traveller girls who had sought their protection and killing them in the hills. He said that they were dishonourable and were not fit to wear the King's uniform, Ja'ghur especially so. Saz'jik seemed to hate him."

"This happened a long time ago, did it not?" the Count smiled tightly.

"It did, it was about twenty years ago, for they were young men then. Ja'ghur and these men were arrested and questioned about the incident, but they couldn't prove they did it. Ja'ghur thought that was funny."

The Count was naturally intrigued. "Why was Ja'ghur so bemused? Did you hear him confess to the crime? Please, my child, think very carefully about what you say next, for a man's life hangs in the balance?"

"But he killed Saz'jik, the murdering bastard!" the boy protested, earning a reproving hiss from his mother for the obscenity. "It was Ja'ghur who killed him! I heard him say he was going to do it. Then, I heard old Saz'jik scream. It was terrible! I don't ever want to hear the like again." The boy was sobbing uncontrollably now.

The old Count refilled the empty wodki goblets and waited for the boy to finish crying. "I am sorry, my child, truly I am. No-one of your tender years should ever have to witness what you did. I must ask you again, did you hear Ja'ghur, or anyone else, confess to the killing of the two Sauromatae girls?"

"Yes, I did. He said he did it to Saz'jik and to the other man" Pierl'yi replied quickly.

"You are quite sure of this? It was the same man, on both occasions?" the Count probed.

"It was, my Lord, upon my life. He said he killed the girls, and he was happy that he had. But Saz'jik accused all of them, including someone called Vist'ari. I am sorry, my Lord, but I never met the other man before, the one they killed next. I didn't know him."

"Would you sign a sworn statement to that effect? That you heard Ja'ghur confess that he and his accomplices abducted, and then murdered, the two Sauromatae girls all those years ago? In a case such as this, there is a record of the incident that will name the suspects, dead or alive, do you understand?" the Count spoke evenly.

"The records have been destroyed. Ja'ghur said he knew this, which is why he was happy to admit it. He said he knew they could never touch him, not after his friends had destroyed the records" the boy said sadly.

The Count blinked. "Did Ja'ghur mention the name of the person he claims destroyed the records? This is most important, young man?" he encouraged.

"I honestly can't remember, my Lord, there were so many names. I only remember a few of them. I do know that he is, or was, a General" confessed Pierl'yi.

"Are you quite certain of this?" the Count was astonished.

"I am, my Lord. As I have said, there were so many names. I didn't know any of them, apart from one. He was the person who wanted the weapons" the boy smiled brightly.

"And whom might that be, young man?" the Count eyed the boy shrewdly.

"The Crown Prince Voskar, my Lord. He wanted the weapons, or so they said. Everyone knows who the Crown Prince is, don't they?"

The old Count gaped at the boy, as did his mother. "I can't believe I'm hearing this?" the Count exploded.

"It's true, I swear it! His name was mentioned by one of the men who first came in. The men who came looking in the storeroom after Saz'jik had been killed. They mentioned the Crown Prince by name and told Saz'jik they worked for him."

"The Crown Prince Voskar is my son, young man. Those two girls playing in the yard with your sister are his daughters" the Count exclaimed. "Did you see the two men, when they came into the store?"

"I saw one of them, and I know his name. He was called Mos'cal! I did not see the other clearly, I just heard him. He seemed to be giving the orders, or so it seemed to me!"

"Is there anything else that you remember? Anything at all that is important?"

The boy looked sheepish, and his cheeks burned hotly. "One of the Sauromatae girls who was murdered, the older girl, she was called Caealla. I have her necklace. The other man was holding it in his hand when they killed him. When they left, carrying that Ja'ghur bastard because he could not walk, they forgot to take it."

"So Ais'ka, the second man who died, for that was his name, he found this necklace?"

"Ja'ghur wanted him to find it. He wanted to remind him of what he had done all those years ago!" the boy confirmed.

Mamy'eva, August 493 BC

Three days later, as the sun approached its zenith, His Majesty's Kor'nai, Counsellor Kol'cha, met an Officer of His Majesty's Royal Guard in his private chambers at the Royal Palace. He bade the Commander to a vacant chair, politely offered him refreshment, before seating himself opposite. "It is good of you to see me, my Lord, without a prior invitation" Uh'gui beseeched.

"Such a terrible business, Commander, there is no other description. The King himself is deeply sorrowed by the senseless murders of your Uncle Ais'ka and poor Saz'jik."

"I am touched by His Majesty's condolences, my Lord. I shall endeavour to pass on the King's condolences to my Aunt Yal'vya, and my mother, of course." Uh'gui replied.

"You have come at the behest of the Crown Prince Sor'chir, is that true?" the Kor'nai brought the meeting swiftly to its point.

"I do indeed, my Lord. The Crown Prince considers this matter to be sufficiently grave as to warrant the attention of His Majesty and Counsel."

"You are surely aware that the perpetrators of these grave crimes have already been subject to the King's Justice?" the Kor'nai smiled thinly.

"With all due respect, my Lord, they have not" Uh'gui sighed sadly. He had been dumbfounded by the news of the apprehension and execution of Guh'lac and his gang.

The Kor'nai eyed the young Commander warily. "Are you quite certain of that, Commander?"

"With the evidence I have at hand, my Lord, I am quite certain. Is it true you once served as the King's Jurist, on a special Council, pertaining to matters of a sensitive nature in the east?"

"As did Crown Prince Sor'chir, though neither of us bore the lofty honorific of State back then" the Kor'nai chuckled. "I am sure you are aware, such tribunals were common during the reign of King Mag'kar before the construction of the Signet. Am I to take it your evidence in respect of this present crime is, in some way, connected with a more ancient one?"

"The Crown Prince believes it so, my Lord. The case is one which the Crown Prince remembers with unusual clarity?" Uh'gui ventured hesitantly, blushing furiously.

"The Crown Prince has concerns as to the voracity of my mind, is that it?" the Kor'nai smiled sardonically.

"Of course not, my Lord, I humbly beg your pardon for any offence I may have given."

"That is not necessary, I assure you, Commander" the Kor'nai chuckled. "There were several cases where the material facts of the allegations were of such malevolence they may haunt a man, even to this day."

"The case involved the alleged abduction, rape, and murder of two Sauromatae children who were, at the time, under the protection of a senior Commander" Uh'gui spoke evenly.

The Kor'nai sipped his wodki and closed his eyes. "I remember the case well, although the precise details, names and the like, may escape me. Still, they will be in the official record, of course."

Uh'gui sipped his wodki. "What if the official record no longer exists, my Lord? What if they have been wilfully destroyed, at the behest of those who might wish to protect the guilt of the alleged offenders?"

"These are very serious allegations, Commander, you do understand?" the Kor'nai eyed the younger man coldly. "It would not matter if they had. Though I cannot, in all good faith, entertain such a fancy. Did the Crown Prince appear to have a firm grasp of the minutiae of the case, even after all these years?"

Uh'gui nodded. "Yes, my Lord. He could recall the name of every alleged perpetrator, even after all this time. I freely admit, I was rather awed by the Count's clarity of recollection."

"The bugger still likes to play his little games, does he? I don't suppose that will ever change!" the Kor'nai chuckled.

Uh'gui was puzzled. "Forgive me, my Lord, I don't understand?"

"The Jurists were encouraged by His Majesty to keep a private journal in each of the cases they served on" the Kor'nai confessed. "The Count was teasing you, young man. He could remember the details of the case with such clarity because he had perused his notes beforehand. I still have mine, Commander, in case you are wondering. They are quite safe, I assure you?"

"The killers of Ais'ka and Saz'jik remain at large, my Lord. Moreover, it is the Crown Prince's belief, one which I share, that if the true perpetrators are not brought to justice swiftly, then other innocents may be in peril."

"I see, Commander!" the Kor'nai stroked his beard. "Am I to take it that this is a matter of evidence?"

"It is, my Lord, though I cannot speak of this any further, upon my honour!"

"Perhaps it is time the Count and I renewed our acquaintance? It has been many a moon since I last visited the Sar'kta?" the Kor'nai sighed happily.

"The Crown Prince intimated he would be happy to visit Mamy'eva, my Lord."

"If that is true, then my old friend may not be as sharp in mind as you credit, young man" the Kor'nai smiled thinly. "In this place, and at this time, treachery abounds!"

Archaeopolis, August 493 BC

The Crown Prince Voskar and the Royal Princess Sychoria were respectfully ushered through the doors of the Throne Room by General Yas'cal, where Her Royal Majesty, Crown Prince Mor'kur, and Her Majesty's Counsel were assembled. The Royal visitors were scheduled to leave Archaeopolis within the hour and hoped to reach the garrison outpost at Veryn before nightfall. Her Majesty was taking no chances on this occasion, and the Royal Train would travel in the company of a detachment of two hundred Royal Guardsmen, who would escort the Royal Train as far as Neh'ma, some two-hundred-and-eighty miles to the east. To Sychoria's surprise, it was Her Majesty's Kor'nai, the Honourable Counsellor Miris'kar, who addressed them on the Queen's behalf. "We are truly honoured, Your Royal Highness, that you consent to this blessed union of our two Royal Houses."

"The Honour is ours, Your Royal Majesty. You and your husband, the Crown Prince Mor'kur, have raised two splendid sons and they do you credit" Sychoria addressed Lezika directly. "My husband and I feel they will make fine husbands for our beloved daughters."

"As your daughters would make dutiful wives, I would venture" Queen Lezika smiled tightly.

Sychoria ignored the barbed reproof. "We are honoured that Your Royal Majesty has graciously accepted the revised terms of the settlement, and we have every intention to honour our obligations to the proposed union. On that, you may rest assured"

"As we have every intention of honouring our obligations, you may equally rest assured, my Lady" the Queen replied evenly.

"I will speak with my father as soon as I return, Your Majesty, and am certain he will graciously acquiesce to the unions and the agreed terms" Sychoria affirmed.

"You intend to announce the unions publicly within a day of your return?" the Queen pressed.

The Crown Prince Voskar was startled by the question, whereas Sychoria was visibly irritated. "We would like to speak with our children first, naturally" she smiled tightly. "They are staying with their Grandparents in Sar'kta, so a public announcement would have to be delayed, at least until you have received formal entreaty from His Majesty the King."

"Perhaps we could agree to a mutually desirable date in advance, Your Royal Highness?" the Kor'nai suggested helpfully. "There is a full moon upon us. The following day would seem appropriate, would it not?"

"We would be amenable to such an accommodation" Voskar spoke for the first time. "As you must surely understand, it is our youngest daughter's reaction that worries us, for she is only seven-years-old."

"Perhaps it is time your youngest daughter learned to behave in accordance with her expected station?" Lezika smiled mischievously.

Voskar frowned. Sychoria struggled to contain her fury. "And what would that be, Your Royal Majesty, if I may be so bold?" she spoke icily.

"Merely to do what is expected of her, my Lady. Which is to be a noble and faithful wife, is that not so?"

"I have no doubts as to my daughter's virtues, Your Majesty, despite her tender years. She will be formally schooled, my Lady, as you once were" Sychoria spoke evenly.

"I will insist upon it, my Lady, you may rest assured of that. And now, my dear friends, it is time for you to begin your long journey to Buk'hu? I can only pray for the safety and security of both of you, for we are now family, are we not?"

"Thank you, Your Majesty, for your grace, favour, and hospitality. I hope that we can return the favour, in the not-too-distant future?" Voskar said firmly.

"You will forgive me if I do not curtsy, Your Majesty? My condition, you understand?" Sychoria said pointedly.

Three days following Uh'gui's return to the village of Sar'kuc, the old Count ushers his visitor into the Sitting Room which served as his private study. It had been many years since the two had last met, and the Count had been surprised at how the old fox had aged. Yet, not in the mind, for there were few in the Kingdom who could best the wits of Count Kol'cha, Kor'nai to His Royal Majesty, King Tagar, especially in the dark arts of treachery and subterfuge. "It is good of you to come, old friend. I would have visited you in Mamy'eva, you understand?"

"Under the circumstances, I felt it wiser to meet here, my Lord" the Kor'nai's eyes twinkled like diamonds.

The Count frowned. "A lifetime of sniffing out traitors does nothing for a man's opinion of his fellows?"

"Nor women, for that matter. They are not so different than us, are they?" the Kor'nai smiled tightly.

"No, my old friend, they are not. Concerning the distressing matter in question, have you given it much thought?" the Count brought the conversation deftly to the matter at hand.

"It is a bad business, to be sure. I have been able to recollect many details of the case. However, despite the passing of the years, my judgement of the material facts remains as it was during the tribunal" the Kor'nai sighed irritably.

"We knew they were guilty, each and every man, yet we could not prove otherwise!" the Count sighed regretfully.

"Then they are *innocent*, for how could they be otherwise?" the Kor'nai mused. "I am curious as to why you seem certain of the involvement of the suspects accused of that historic crime, those still alive, in these ghastly murders in Mamy'eva? I am deeply sorry for the death of your dear friend, Ais'ka."

"Thank you, old friend. I will pass your condolences to his wife. The victims were known to the suspects arraigned for the abduction, rape, and murder of two Sauromatae girls. The crime took place in the Central Plains, twenty-one years ago this summer" said the Count.

"That is pure happenstance. It is assuredly not evidence of complicity" replied the Kor'nai.

"When I perused my notes, for I still retain them, I found an allusion to a necklace. This trinket, to be more accurate, had been worn by the eldest girl since her last birthday. It was, or so my notes say, a gift from her grandmother. It was not found on her body, nor recovered from the immediate vicinity" the Count revealed.

"Had it been found in the possession of any one of the arraigned suspects, it would surely have damned them all" the Kor'nai smiled thinly. "If my memory serves, it was worth nothing of any material value, for the stones were not gems, were they?"

"That is quite correct, my Lord. There would be no reason to take it, unless the perpetrators of the crime, one of them at least, intended it as a trophy?"

"That seemed to be the consensus of the panel of jurists at the time, was it not? Yet, none of the suspects had it in their possession, did they?" the Kor'nai sighed. He sipped his drink.

"No, my Lord, they did not. However, just because we did not find it, does not mean it was not, in fact, taken by one of the suspects, almost certainly with the knowledge of his accomplices" the Count ventured.

"That is true, my friend. And yet, in absence of the trinket itself, it is pure speculation. Have you finally recovered the pendant, old friend? Is that your link between the two cases?"

The Count fished in a pocket and retrieved the necklace. He passed it to the man sat opposite. "The pendant you are holding in your hands clearly matches the descriptions we were given by the parents of the murdered girls?"

"How did you come by this, if I may ask?" the Kor'nai raise an eyebrow.

"If the description of the item that I have in my notes matched that keepsake you hold in your hands, would you concur they are one and the same?" the Count probed.

"I would not, my Lord. We have no witnesses to verify the fact, do we?" the Kor'nai smiled tightly.

"That is true, my Lord, yet we have a material witness to the murders of Saz'jik and Ais'ka, who would testify, in the event of a trial, that he overheard both victims discussing the same historic event, the violation of two traveller girls, with the same man, just before they were murdered?" the Count confessed.

"This man would be Ja'ghur? He remains as repugnant to polite sensibilities as ever. The man is a notorious criminal" the Kor'nai mused.

"It would be, my Lord, and I am well briefed on Ja'ghur's criminal tendencies."

"You have located the missing boy, this elusive apprentice, is that it?" the Kor'nai smiled tightly.

"We have, my Lord, though I am not at liberty to reveal his whereabouts, you understand?" the Count smiled tightly.

"And this boy found the pendant after the murderers departed?"

"He did, my Lord. He will swear that he has never laid eyes on it before in his life?" the Count insisted.

"Will he now!" the Kor'nai mused, shocking the older man. "I am sorry, old friend, I truly am. Surely, you must accept that the pendant cannot be verified as the personal property of the historic victim. It is not enough to arraign the suspects again, not unless they could be made to confess."

"The pendant could establish the boy's presence in the workshop at the time that Saz'jik and Ais'ka were murdered?" the Count ventured. "In that event, his testimony would be crucial in arresting the suspects and arraigning them for murder?"

"I am not saying that I doubt the boy's integrity, but it is entirely possible he could have stumbled across the bodies and the pendant sometime after the slayings?" the Kor'nai sighed heavily. "My point is this. The pendant, taken by itself, or in conjunction with anything else, does not substantiate a connection between the perpetrators of the historic crime and the recent killings. Not unless we can produce a witness, or several such souls, who will testify this pendant belonged to the murdered Sauromatae girl."

"I have spoken at length with the boy, and he claims to have overheard two separate arguments, involving a single, unseen antagonist, identified as Ja'ghur by both victims, shortly before their violent deaths" the Count pressed.

"And he would testify this under oath?" the Kor'nai pressed.

"He would, my Lord. He also remembers the names of others who were mentioned during the argument. These are men he has never met, one of whom is now deceased."

"And these names correspond with the suspects arraigned for this historic crime?" the Kor'nai quipped.

"In some instances, yes, but I have not, as yet, had the opportunity to present to the boy the names of the suspects listed in my notes" confessed the Count.

"May I ask why, my Lord?" the Kor'nai seemed suspicious.

"I thought it wise to discuss the matter with you first, my Lord. When I do reveal the names to the boy, I will do so in the presence of several independent witnesses."

"That would be the wisest course, to be sure. It is possible that the names overheard by the boy, those of strangers, are not in fact the historic suspects, excepting Ja'ghur, of course?" ventured the Kor'nai.

"You are quite right, my Lord. There is one name the boy clearly remembers. This was disclosed as vouchsafe for the purchase of a large supply of armour and armaments, sufficient for a party of twenty men."

"This would be the missing stock from Saz'jik's store? I presume this boy intimated the name to you, in front of witnesses?" the Kor'nai probed.

"Indeed, he did, my Lord, in front of his mother and my wife. The weapons were requested by the Crown Prince Voskar"

"You surely cannot be serious?" gasped the Kor'nai.

"There is something else, old friend. The boy claims to have overheard Ja'ghur confess to the murder of the two Sauromatae girls. He even knew the name of the older girl, to whom the pendant belonged. He ventured the name without prompting. She was called Caealla, as I am certain you recall?"

"And why, after all these years, should Ja'ghur confess willingly to such a barbarous crime he committed all those years ago?" the Kor'nai asked evenly.

"Firstly, he intended to kill both victims, for they could never be allowed to live" the Crown Prince mused drily. "Perhaps he confessed to taunt his victims, for we are both aware of the unsavoury incident that transpired thereafter, sanctioned by a now retired senior Officer."

"That is pure speculation, old friend! It would not stand up in Court" the Kor'nai said coldly.

429

"I would concur with that reasoning, of course" the Count said mildly. "Secondly, according to the boy, Ja'ghur has no reason to fear the King's Justice because all records of the crime, including its prosecution, were subsequently destroyed on the instruction of a senior Army officer."

"I see" said the Kor'nai simply. "And you believe the word of this boy, do you?"

The Count eyed the Kor'nai steadily. "The boy has no reason to perjure his soul, my Lord. I specifically instructed Uh'gui to disclose this when you met with him in Mamy'eva. Perhaps you know the answer to the riddle, even the identity of the General in question?"

The Kor'nai smiled grimly. "I regret to inform you that all official records relating to the case have gone missing. I have firm grounds to believe they were removed, and then destroyed, on the instructions of General Az'nai."

"There is far more to this than meets the eye, is there not, my old friend?" sighed the Count.

General Nal'gi afforded himself a rueful smile as he was ushered through the door to the General's study. His temerity was rewarded with a half-hearted scowl from a seated General Az'nai. "You had better sit down, old friend. I trust you are the bearer of bad news!"

"A calling to which I seem naturally suited, my Lord" General Nal'gi chuckled.

"You will join me for a drink?" The younger General nodded his assent. Az'nai turned to Ny'azmi. "Get a couple of flagons of our best apricot wodki if you would? Bring three goblets, the finest silver. I would like you to join us, old friend." Ny'azmi bowed respectfully, and left the room, closing the door. General Az'nai turned to his visitor. "You do not object, old friend?"

"I do not, my Lord" Nal'gi replied.

"We shall wait for Ny'azmi to return. I suspect your visit concerns that unsavoury little incident in the Warehouse District?"

"It would, my Lord. I regret to inform you that things have taken a turn for the worse" Nal'gi spoke evenly.

"Has that cantankerous old bastard in Sar'kuc been stirring things up?" Az'nai smiled ruefully. "Not that I am in the least surprised! That skulking ape may have compromised our best laid plans!" A knock came at the door. "Would you be so kind, old friend?"

Moments later, the three men sat together, a table set between them bearing a silver tray with two ceramic flagons. General Az'nai sipped his wodki and sighs happily. "What news regales us from the dungeons of the Royal Palace?" he chortled.

"The Kor'nai met with an impromptu visitor several days ago. It was Commander Uh'gui, a nephew of Ais'ka. The Commander is on compassionate leave with his mother in Sar'kuc and has not yet returned to duty" Nal'gi confessed.

"Perhaps the old Count wished for an update on the ongoing investigation? The Kor'nai and the Crown Prince are old friends. Perhaps the Count merely sought to press a petition for assistance with the forthcoming wheat harvest?"

"If only wishing made it so, my Lord" Nal'gi smiled tightly. He sipped his drink. "The Commander left the Palace and returned immediately to Sar'kuc. Subsequently, the Kor'nai paid an impromptu visit to the Military Records Bureau, where he made enquiries concerning the official records of an old tribunal that convened twenty summers ago" Nal'gi continued.

General Az'nai's eyes narrowed suspiciously. "Let me hazard a guess. The Duty Clerk regretfully informed the Kor'nai that the records have inexplicably vanished?"

"I am afraid so, my Lord. According to my source, the Kor'nai seemed neither surprised, nor troubled, by the revelation" Nal'gi smiled tightly.

"The wily old bugger already knew it was a wild goose chase! Both the Kor'nai and the Crown Prince served as Jurists on the tribunal. I would wager heavily that both retain their case notes."

"They have obviously learned something, my Lord, but what? How in Hades name could they have made any such connection between an old case in the Military Records Bureau and a grisly double-murder in the Ironmongers District?" Nal'gi sighed.

"Ja'ghur has always been a liability!" Az'nai scowled. "He is a keen hunter, and an unflinching killer, precisely the qualities which single him out for this mission. He is a natural leader, as unfathomable as that may seem. Nonetheless, at heart, he is a mere brute. Little more refined than those savages we face in the plains" the General smiled grimly.

"Ja'ghur must have talked? Perhaps he taunted the men with a confession of guilt before he killed them? They all served together at the time, did they not?

"They did, old friend, and there was no love lost between them, you may rest assured of that!" the General shrugged ruefully.

"The brute made a point of making this personal!" Ny'azmi spat. "This gobshite gave free rein to his tongue, without first engaging his mind to the consequences!"

General Az'nai chuckled at the contemptuous rebuke. "A colossus Ja'ghur may be, yet sadly not in the realms of intellect! The man has shit for brains! It wouldn't surprise me in the least if he had confessed his guilt!" Az'nai growled.

"In any event, it would appear our elusive apprentice overheard everything?" ventured Ny'azmi.

"The Count must have discovered his whereabouts, however unlikely that prospect, and has questioned the boy and his family" the General mused bitterly. "Moreover, that shit-brain must have disclosed that the records had been destroyed! It is entirely possible that he may even have revealed my involvement. The man is quite incapable of bridling his base nature and is fast becoming a supreme liability!"

"What should we do, my Lord?" Ny'azmi asked softly.

"As luck would have it, I have some information of my own that may intrigue you. A ferry is now being prepared for imminent departure to Bu'khu. I have it on good authority that it will leave at dawn in three days' time" the General smiled mischievously.

"Princess Sychoria and Prince Voskar are returning from Archaeopolis so soon? That can only mean they have reached a favourable settlement in respect of the unions?" Nal'gi ventured.

"It also means their two little doves will be summoned south for the public celebration of their betrothals" General Az'nai smiled thinly.

"I had expected the negotiations to be protracted. Surely, we must move with haste, my Lord. The entire operation will have to be advanced?" Nal'gi insisted.

"I concur with you, old friend. With that in mind, I will despatch Ny'azmi east of the Wol'yi at first light to the Headquarters of General Til'koi. He will be able to change his steed on route, for everything has been arranged. He will liaise with Commander Zu'ki in three days' time, and they will then journey north, accompanied by a detachment of trusted men. All have sworn their allegiance to our cause."

"With due respect, but in light of what has transpired, I have grave doubts as to the competency of Ja'ghur and his ilk!" Nal'gi spoke evenly. "The man is injured, is he not? If we advance our plan at such short notice, we run a grave risk of compromising its success?"

The older General continued. "Sufficient flexibility is ingrained into the logistics of the scheme, for we always knew we may have to move at short notice."

Nal'gi drained his goblet and accepted a refill. He nods respectfully at Ny'azmi. "I have absolute faith in Ny'azmi, for that goes without saying. It is Ja'ghur and his men who give me sleepless nights?"

"Great care has been taken to ensure that sufficient horses are available. All things being equal, Ny'azmi and his adventurers should reach the farmstead in Zi'gursk in the early hours, five days from now."

"We would require at one days rest after such an arduous trek, my Lord. If everything is ready, we can strike that very night" Ny'azmi nodded his approval.

General Az'nai sipped his wodki. "We are in complete agreement, are we not? We will attack the village at first light of the following morning, seize the Princesses from their slumber, and spirit them swiftly to the farmstead. There they shall remain, at least until it is safe for them to be moved further east."

"The operation will take place in six days' time?" Nal'gi smiled thinly.

"That is correct, old friend. Now, we shall toast the health of our band of brothers, the souls of departed friends, and the future of our great race!" the General raised his goblet. The three men chink their cups and drain the wodki in a single gulp.

"What of the future of Ja'ghur and his merry band, my Lord?" Nal'gi smiled wryly.

"Once we have secured the little doves, they will be disposed of. In the interests of security, that was always our intention, was it not?" General Az'nai smiled tightly.

Eastern Plains of the Wol'yi, August 493 BC

Ny'azmi was a superb horseman, in the finest tradition of his people. He had learned to ride at the age of five and, even now, spent as much time in the saddle as possible. It was a glorious morning, a few hours after daybreak, with the sun rising fast in the east. He had spurred his horse to a canter, as soon as he cleared the outskirts of the settlements on the east bank of the Wol'yi and had now covered some twenty-five miles of golden fields and lush meadows, thronging with cattle and goats. Soon enough, the pasture and till gave way to dense woodland, and beyond, the barren and unforgiving plains, which stretched almost forever. This was the militarized zone. It was likely he would encounter regular patrols from the regional garrisons, yet he had a parchment bearing the seal of General Az'nai, a man respected by every serving soldier in the east, past and present. Ny'azmi slowed his horse to a canter, then a trot, as he dismounted on the banks of a large stream to allow his stallion to graze and water. A short while later, his horse refreshed, and fortified by a generous ration of wodki from his flagon, Ny'azmi gallops east, ever deeper into the barren plains, towards the great Uras'ka. Once he was safely across the river, it was a short rise to the *Opal*, the formidable fortress which lay at the centre of the Signet. If all went well, he should arrive before nightfall of the third day.

Sixteen

Mikhouri was standing in the corner of the scullery, busily cleaning shells of a newly laid batch of eggs from the hen coop, when her grandfather returned from his meeting at the Community Hall. "I see the travellers have left?" the Count remarked breezily. Things might quieten down now they had done so, yet in truth he wished them a safe and prosperous onward journey into the Nur'gat realms.

"They left in the mid-morning. My sister is deeply sad to see them go?" Mikhouri confessed.

"Alicharia is easily distracted, is she not? And besides, she has a new playmate to captivate her."

"She is forever fussing over little Nurialla. I cannot imagine what the poor girl's mother must think!" Mikhouri rolled her eyes.

The old Count chuckled. "Her mother has a shrewd insight into the ways of children, little rose. I suspect there is little your sister could do that would surprise her" the Count chuckled.

"Alicharia would like to teach her to ride, but she is far too young to be in the saddle, surely?" Mikhouri protested.

"The child is nearly four-years-old, is she not? There are those who would consider her to be the right age to learn the ways of the saddle?" the Count mused.

"Like the Sauromatae? All the traveller children learn to ride at the age of four. Is that truly the way of the barbarian?"

The Count furrowed his brow in puzzlement. "Do you think they were barbaric? You seemed to spend an awful lot of time with them, if their behaviour was so offensive?"

Mikhouri was startled. "They were not in the least offensive! I found them to be quite charming, and not at all brutish. Their clothes are beautiful, are they not?" the girl toyed with the neck-line of her new kurta. "They are certainly not the monsters that some in Mamy'eva would have us believe?"

"If that is true, my child, perhaps you should refrain from calling them barbarians, for they are no different from us, are they?" the Count smiled warmly.

"There is something that is quite peculiar" the child frowned. "Alicharia mentioned it, so I am not entirely sure it is to be trusted" the girl confessed.

"You think your sister's words are not to be trusted? What has she said that would encourage such a belief?" the Count probed.

"I am not saying Alicharia is dishonest, nor the travellers, for that matter. All I am saying is that they could be mistaken, that is all?" Mikhouri corrected.

The Count was intrigued. "What exactly did your sister say? Whatever the matter, it seems to be a source of some concern?"

"The travellers told Alicharia that we, the Orch'tai, are really Sauromatae!" the girl exclaimed in a disbelieving tone. "Our ancestors were no Scythia, unlike the Ur'gai and Nur'gat, and that the origins of the Argata are even more questionable. According to their folklore, our ancestors migrated from east of the Uras'ka and settled the Sama'zka Plains nearly two centuries ago, around the time of the rise of Nineveh. Over time, we became distinct in our language and habits. They said there are some who consider us *Barbarians*, for how *we* have chosen to *live*!"

The Count stifled a chuckle, for the child's face was a picture of disbelief. "And this revelation unsettles you, if it were to be proven true?"

"It is slander, is it not? We are Scythia, are we not?" Mikhouri protested.

"And yet, it is common knowledge that the Scythia are not originally from this region, is that not so? That our ancestors in the distant past were likely no different from the nomadic tribes of the east in a great many respects?" said the Count.

"The Scythia migrated from the west, did they not? That is not contested by anyone?" As for the Argata, they are more closely affiliated with us, are they not?" Mikhouri chirped.

"Does this trouble you so much because of your impending betrothal to Prince Disch'al? If that were so, I would not fret, little rose. We live in the present, not the past?" counselled the Count.

"If we our ancestors were Sauromatae, then it surely changes everything?" Mikhouri challenged.

The Count smiled wryly at the child. "I would venture that it changes everything and nothing, little dove? If our society were to embrace acceptance that our distant ancestors were once kin to the present-day communities living to the east of the Uras'ka perhaps we might look forward to a future of greater harmony and prosperity?"

"We would not need to raise and equip such a large army in the east, would we? Nor would we seek to garrison our southern frontier with the Argata, for we would be joined in a matrimonial union, would we not?" Mikhouri proposed.

"And what of our relations with the Ur'gai and the Nur'gat, little dove? How would you counsel your future husband in such matters?" the Count smiled wanly.

"We must remain friends, not enemies, for therein lies the keys to greater prosperity for all!"

The Count smiled warmly at the child. "You are wise beyond your years, Mikhouri. If only your sister could grow to be so perspicacious!"

"Alicharia wants to conquer the world! She wishes to bring peace by waging war."

"Your sister is young, and she has much to learn, little rose" the old man smiled warmly at his granddaughter. "War is a harbinger of pain and suffering, not peace and prosperity, and is no future for anyone!" the Count mused grimly.

"And so, we have peace?" Mikhouri quipped.

"And so, we have peace, little dove" the Count sighed contentedly. "With that peace, comes security and prosperity, both for us, and everyone else. Once upon a time, not that long ago, we used to have a military garrison not far along the river. We have no need for it now, not since the peace with the Nur'gat. And, in recent times, we have no need to fear a threat from the east."

"And so, we are safe? We have nothing to fear, from the north or the east?" Mikhouri ventured.

"You are perfectly safe, sweet child. You have nothing to fear, for there is none here who would ever harm you!" said the Count emphatically.

Zi'gursk, August 493 BC

The party of riders gallop north, through mile-after-mile of lush pasture and wheat-fields. Soon enough, they reach the crossroads at the hamlet of Zi'gursk, where the west road to Dobrin meets the east road from Nekh'tu. Ny'azmi, who had visited the region countless times before, pointed to the farmstead, which lay two miles due northwest. Zu'ki surveyed the land around the farmstead with an appreciative eye. "It is a pleasant little spot for a farm, is it not?"

"Good farmland, with excellent silts in the spring, not to mention exceptional hunting grounds" Ny'azmi indicated the dense forest immediately to the north, which seemed to stretch as far as the eye could see on the horizon.

"I cannot imagine our friend, Ja'ghur, as a natural farmer, can you?" Zu'ki grinned. "He does not have the necessary temperament, I would venture?"

"Fuck him!" Ny'azmi spat feelingly. "And the rest of his little band of poxed cunts! We will deal with them soon enough!"

Zu'ki eyed him steadily. "I would advise caution, my old friend, for perhaps it might be wiser to wait for our chaperones to arrive from the south. Once upon a time this was hostile country, was it not?"

Commander Hus'cha, who led a small force of ten Orch'tai cavalrymen, all sworn to the mission and the cause, reined in beside the pair. "A peaceful little spot, is it not? There has been little trouble from the Sauromatae in this region for decades, nor from the Nur'gat, not since the end of the last war. This should do splendidly" he sighed happily.

Zu'ki squinted in the glare of the sun and raised his right arm, pointing northwest. "It appears we have a welcoming party. With luck, they might even have a pot of mint tea on the go?"

"Fuck your tea! I could do with a drink, after this morning's ride!" spat Ny'azmi.

Hus'cha frowned at the naked disrespect shown to a senior serving officer. Zu'ki chuckled and turned towards him. "A small restorative draught of wodki might do wonders for the spirits, you would agree?"

"I it pleases you, my Lord. After all, there is little to fear here, is there?" Hus'cha smiled brightly.

Three riders, all heavily armed, trotted across the paddock to greet them. As they got closer, Zu'ki recognised them as Ja'ghur's trusted hands. They included the fugitives, Ba'chi and Mos'cal, and the boy, Na'kyr, eldest son of Vist'ari, departed rapist and murderer. "A fine day for a ride, is it not?" Zu'ki greeted them cheerily.

"It might be wise if we head inside, Sir. It looks like we might have a problem" Ba'chi said formally.

Zu'ki twisted in his saddle and gazed meaningfully at Ny'azmi. "I fear you may have spoken too soon, old man!"

The old Count knelt and outstretched his arms to embrace his Alicharia as she raced to him for a hug. The old man had been heading north along the trackway to the meadow to fetch the girls back home. They had spent the day riding in the meadow, with a brief repast at midday, returning in the afternoon. "Did you enjoy your ride, my little rose?" he asked.

"It was most agreeable. Though I suspect Silka grows tired of the meadow. She yearns for the trees, Grandpapa" Alicharia grinned slyly.

"You are eager to test your hunting skills, is that it? Now that you can ride and shoot a bow" the Count chuckled.

"Mikhouri told me that you took her to the forest two summers ago? I was forbidden to come, obviously!" the child scowled.

"You could not ride back then, my love" the old man chided. "I remember the day with great fondness, for it was most agreeable. You are quite right, my love. The horses enjoy a sojourn to the woodland, provided their riders are cautious" the old man sighed.

"I think that Silka would enjoy a trip to the woods. She has intimated, more than once, that she would like to visit that small copse at the end of the northeast meadow, where the river curves and breaks into smaller flows?" Alicharia smiled wryly.

"That stretch of the river can be treacherous, my love. The silts are very unstable and are prone to slipping and even sinking! I have seen many a man, and horse, devoured by the mud."

"You tease me, surely you do? There are no such things as mud-monsters and they certainly don't eat horses, or people!" Alicharia chided.

"Ah, but a child…? They have not had a taste of one of those for many a moon!"

"You must think me a rare sort of fool, Grandfather?" Alicharia snorted. "I am far too old to be terrified by tales of the mud-monsters of the Wol'yi, or Sauromatae ghouls with horns and tails, or anything else that will steal me from my bed in the middle of the night and carry me across the plains!"

The old Count laughed. "I suppose you are little rose! You are certainly old enough to learn of the dangers you may face in open country in a region as remote and sparsely populated as this."

"You promise to take us out to the woodland tomorrow?" Alicharia pressed.

"If that is what your sister desires, then I do not see why we should not! It will do me good to be back in the saddle?" the Count grinned.

"Mikhouri will surely say yes, for I will make her!" chirruped Alicharia.

The old man chuckled wryly. "I will make you a promise, little rose, for you are old enough to be taken at your word. We shall go to the woods on the morrow, leaving early in the morning, for that is when it is at its most glorious, if you agree to be a good girl and get yourself ready for supper? Why not wear one of your pretty new outfits you bought from the travellers?" the Count smiled warmly at the girl.

"Which one would you prefer?" Alicharia grinned.

"Why don't you surprise me?" the Count ruffled the child's hair affectionately.

"I will pick my favourite! And I shall sleep in it and wear it on the ride tomorrow!"

Zu'ki gazed piteously at the injured Ja'ghur, who lay sprawled on the bed, a thin smile playing at his lips. A succession of empty wodki flagons were arraigned in a neat row by the far wall. Following the incident at the Armourer's, Zu'ki could barely bring himself to be civil to the brute and had nodded in silent acknowledgement when he entered the room. Ja'ghur glowered at the Commander, who seemed amused by his predicament. "In case you were wondering, the leg is still attached to the rest of me!" the brute sneered insolently.

"I think you have me confused with someone who gives a Royal fuck!" Zu'ki spoke icily. The brute was momentarily startled, then his cheeks suffused an angry purple. The officer seemed bemused by the man's rancour. He turned to Mos'cal. "Tell me everything!" he clipped.

"We have had visitors, Sir. That is all I can tell you!" Mos'cal replied simply.

"Greeks bearing gifts, were they?" Zu'ki said acidly.

"They were Sauromatae, my Lord, judging by appearances. They were none too friendly!" said Ba'chi.

Zu'ki turned to Ny'azmi, who he considered to be something akin to a font of knowledge of the region and its inhabitants. "Is it possible that Sauromatae hunters would venture this far west?"

"Sauromatae caravans pass through the region every summer, Sir. The Thry'ga trail is the most ancient and well-travelled east-west passage in the Duchy" Ny'azmi replied.

"Was this a *caravan*?" Zu'ki could scarcely hide his distaste for this ancient way of life, nor its practitioners.

"We saw riders, Sir, not vehicles. They have congregated at the edge of the woodland, my Lord. About twenty of them, mounted on hardy steeds, every morning at dawn for the past three days" confessed Ba'chi.

"Was this rabble armed?" Zu'ki raised an eyebrow.

"They were carrying recurved bows, my Lord. They are most likely hunters, but they seemed to be taking an unusual interest in the farmstead" said Mos'cal.

"What do you think, Ny'azmi? Should we head into the woods and scour for these ghouls?" said Zu'ki.

"That might not be the worst idea I have ever heard, my Lord" Ny'azmi stroked his beard. "As the man has said, they could be outriders for a *caravan*, though it is rather late in the season to be journeying from the east. It could be a hunting party; in which case they might well have pissed off by now. It might be worth a look, merely to assess their strength."

"Is he up to a ride?" Zu'ki jerked a thumb at Ja'ghur, who had held his silent thus far.

"I can ride, boy! And I can speak!" Ja'ghur growled, wincing as he pulled himself to the edge of the bed.

"I am a Commander in His Majesty's Royal Guard, something you would do well to remember, Ja'ghur! I feel certain the Hangman in Mamy'eva will!" Zu'ki smiled thinly. He eyed the brute contemptuously, then turned on his heels and strode out of the room.

"Bastard!" Ja'ghur hissed, as he glowered malevolently at the back of the departing Officer.

"I would get my boots on and give my tongue a rest, if I were you!" Ny'azmi said icily. He turned away and followed Zu'ki out of the room.

"You are no fucking friend of mine, you miserable old cunt!" Ja'ghur cursed feelingly as he reached for his riding boots, which stood to the side of the bed.

A short while later, a party of fifteen riders ventured from the farmstead and trot towards edge of the woodland, a few miles to the northeast. The scouting party included the Commander Hus'cha, accompanied by ten of his men, together with Zu'ki, Ny'azmi, Mos'cal, and a visibly disgruntled Ja'ghur, who tottered unsteady in the saddle. The sun had reached its zenith and the heat was almost unbearable, especially to the men in armour, yet the horses amble happily across the meadow to plunge into the river. The river was lower than usual for the time of year yet was still sufficiently deep to submerge the riders to their calves. Once they reached the opposite bank, the ten cavalrymen fan into extended line, five on each side of the main party. The screen of the woodland was about a mile away, yet there was no sign of this elusive Sauromatae hunting party. Soon enough, the riders reach the woodland edge and plunge into the gloom.

Traces of the hunters were soon discovered in a small clearing, about a half-mile along a well-worn track, in the vicinity of a small stream. Across the stream was a steep escarpment, densely carpeted with trees. "A great site for a camp, and an even better place to lay an ambush, wouldn't you say?" Zu'ki grimaced. The remains of the camp, and the density of manure at its fringe, were consistent with a party of twenty riders. Strewed around the campfire were copious remains of wild game, rabbits, pheasants, and even a deer.

"Looks like they had a good time of it, if you ask me?" said Mos'cal.

"A hunting party, then?" said Zu'ki.

"They likely bagged a few deer and have taken the spoils back to their families" said Ny'azmi softly. "Maybe we don't have anything to worry about, after all?"

"Sauromatae scum!" Zu'ki spat contemptuously. "Why can't they hunt in their own territory?" He turns and gazes warily at the escarpment, his eyes narrowing as he scanned the trees for any signs of danger. Zu'ki idly kicked a rabbit skull and turned to his companions. "I think we have seen enough, don't you?"

"I think it might be wise if we move in staggered file, my Lord. I will take the lead, with five of my men. The rest can form a rear-guard" Hus'cha ventured softly.

Zu'ki blinked. He gestured towards the remains of the campfire. "I don't think we have anything to fear from this stinking filth! Very well, Commander Hus'cha, lead on!"

The scouting party mounted their steeds and headed back towards the southern edge of the woodland and the meadow. Unbeknown to them, as they did so, their progress is closely watched by a small group of heavily armed men, hidden in the dense screen of the escarpment on the opposite bank of the stream. "They should be all too easy to kill, the arrogant Orch'tai cunts!" spat Zorughul, a heavily scarred warrior, standing well over six feet tall. Zorughul and his band were all proud veterans of the last campaigns against the Orch'tai, some fifteen years earlier.

"Are you sure you are up to this, Ja'ghur?" asked Zu'ki.

"I told you that already, didn't I? I just need is a few slugs' of decent wodki and I shall be as fit as a flea!" the thug replied tersely.

"What about you, Ny'azmi? Are you convinced of the wisdom of our change of plan?"

Ny'azmi nodded his acquiescence. The group had convened around the dining table, Commander Zu'ki at the head, Ny'azmi at the far end, facing him. The table was set with bread, cheese, fresh fruit, and several flagons of watered wine. Ja'ghur sat three seats down from Zu'ki on his left. Their mutual hostility was keenly felt by every man present, including Commander Hus'cha, who seemed intrigued by their enmity. "The wisest course would be to hit the place after last light. That way, the villagers, including what few veterans are ready to hand, would be unwilling to come after us until dawn, especially if they believe this was a hostile incursion of Sauromatae raiders!" Ny'azmi declared.

"And you, Commander Hus'cha? Are you in agreement with our change of plans?" Zu'ki appraised the younger Commander searchingly.

"I am, my Lord. Considering this disturbing new development, I agree it would be better to strike tonight and then head east at first light" the Commander spoke evenly.

"You surely don't expect us to be attacked?" Zu'ki was incredulous.

"I said no such thing, my Lord! Nonetheless, I am a little disconcerted by the reports of a band of Sauromatae hunters taking such an interest in our affairs" Hus'cha said testily. He may have been younger, yet he was infinitely more experienced in the ways of the Sauromatae. "This is not typical behaviour of a hunting party deep into enemy territory. From my experience, such a band would seek to disguise, rather than advertise, their presence in hostile territory."

"You concur with that reasoning, Ny'azmi?" Zu'ki probed.

"I would defer to the judgement of the Commander, my Lord. It is many a moon since I have faced the Sauromatae. They are a most resourceful and dangerous foe."

"It is settled. We shall raid the Crown Prince's farmstead this night, secure the two maidens, and then return here. We can drug the girls and make our way south a few hours after first light."

"I will be glad to be away from this flea-pit!" Ja'ghur spat.

"Do you intend to head south, my Lord? Perhaps be wise to head east, at least for a day or more, and then tack south. It might dupe any pursuers that this was the work of a band of Sauromatae renegades?" ventured Hus'cha.

"What a capital idea! Does anyone have any issue with this?" Zu'ki appraised the reaction of the men before him with some interest.

"What of the Sauromatae, Sir! They have been spotted at first light every morning for the past three days. We would be taking an awful risk, would we not?" Mos'cal interjected.

"We have nothing to fear from those stinking heathens, you may rest assured of that!" Zu'ki said ebulliently.

"So, you say, Commander" Ja'ghur spoke softly.

"Indeed, I do, Ja'ghur. It is I, and not you, who command here. You will do well to remember that, as I have warned you before?" Zu'ki smiled tightly.

The raiding party comprised twelve men. All were garbed in dark cloaks to dun the sheen of their armour in the light of the moon, as they race west across the plain towards the river. They plan to hit their target fast and with a minimum of fuss, seizing their unsuspecting victims, and then completing their return journey without rest. If the Gods were smiling upon their endeavours, it would be late morning before their treason was discovered, by which time they hoped to be many miles away to the east, safe from the clutches of their pursuers. They broke into a canter, followed by a gentle trot, as they reach the edge of the plains and follow a narrow track which led to the ferry crossing at Ryg'nyk, ten miles north of the port of Ky'rovka. The ferryman was surprised to see a party of riders at such a late hour, but any suspicions were pacified by a silver coin and the assurance that the men were conveying an urgent despatch to the Crown Prince Sor'chir. "We intend to return within a few hours, my friend, for it is we must make haste back from whence we came" Zu'ki smiled grimly.

"It is always the way, my Lord, is it not?" the ferryman shrugged ruefully.
"That it is, my friend, for the King's business knows no hour!"

It took three crossings to get the twelve riders to the west bank, and a delay of some twenty minutes, yet this had been duly accounted for. Zu'ki thanked the ferryman and fished out a second silver coin. "We shall be returning with a valuable cargo, dear friend. Your discretion is greatly appreciated. You will earn the personal gratitude of the King. I shall see to it personally!"

The ferryman beamed back at him. "You shall have it, my Lord! We are loyal servants of King Tagar in these parts. You may rest assured of it!"

The riders trot west, following the winding course of an ancient trackway that snaked towards the northern outskirts of the village of Sar'kuc, historic fiefdom of the Crown Prince Sor'chir and his family. "If my memory serves, this track will take us all the way to the far north of the village" Zu'ki spoke softly to the men. "Thereafter, we cross the paddock and tack south along the west bank of the Illov'ya to approach the farmstead from the northeast."

"You are certain there is no guard detail?" asked Ja'ghur.
"Not when we were last here, and that was only a moon ago. The old Count's abode is set back from the village, encompassing the west bank of the Illov'ya" Zu'ki confirmed.
"There is no other location where we can cross the Wol'yi? Not without catching the ferry?" Ja'ghur muttered darkly.
"You worry too much, Ja'ghur. You can deal with the ferryman, in the usual way, once we are all safely across with our prize!"
"You are a ruthless man, Commander Zu'ki. I think I could grow to like you" Ja'ghur grinned.
"That is good to know, Ja'ghur, for we have a long journey ahead of us" Zu'ki smiled thinly.

The party continued west along the track, following the course of a small river, with lush gallery woodland on either bank. The track was unsuited to large, wheeled vehicles, and Zu'ki was reassured that they would not encounter any unwelcome fellow travellers at this hour. They reached the western margins of the coastal escarpment and followed the track down the gentle incline to the plains below. They now travelled through some of the richest land in the duchy, famed for its stables, and Zu'ki led his band northwest, following the course of a small stream. They would be strongly advised to avoid settlements, even at this late hour. An hour or so later, the band reach a junction with a large track, suited to conveying wagons and carriages, and crossed the bridge over the Illov'ya. Shortly thereafter, the ancient track veers south toward the northern outskirts of Sar'kuc. Zu'ki reined in and pointed towards a large, isolated dwelling to the south, close to the woodland fringe of the Illov'ya.

"Is this the place?" Ja'ghur whispered in disbelief.

"I take it you are not impressed with the Crown Prince's abode, my dear fellow?" Zu'ki chided.

"I expected the old bastard to live in a Khur'yi, surrounded by formidable walls. He is a Crown Prince, is he not? This place doesn't look any more splendorous than the dump we have been corralled in for the past week!" Ja'ghur sneered.

"If it were enclosed by formidable defences, it would be more onerous to breach and make good our escape, not without waking the entire village?" Zu'ki rebuked him gently. "Not too long ago, this was frontier territory. Only a fool would advertise his wealth to raiding parties from the north."

"Sauromatae scum! That is all they are, and all they ever will be! Not that the Nur'gat are any better, the heathen cunts!" Ja'ghur spat on the ground. "The Crown Prince is a rich bugger, or so it is said?" he grinned slyly.

"That depends upon your ideals of wealth" Zu'ki smiled wryly. The Count and Countess live a simple enough life, perhaps no more ostentatious than many villagers, yet their land is amongst the most fertile in the entire Duchy."

"I have heard it said that the Crown Prince has a fine set of stables. His horses rank among the most expensive in the duchy?" Ja'ghur asked interestedly.

"That is true, Ja'ghur. His horses are prized even by the King" Zu'ki smiled brightly.

"Is that why the King married his youngest filly to the old Count's hot-blooded stallion? The old bastard got a title, in exchange for a decent rider for a pure-blooded mare?" Ja'ghur grinned.

Zu'ki grimaced at the crudity of the analogy, yet the brute had a fair point. "You have a finer grasp of the subtleties of marriage than I would have hazarded, Ja'ghur. They have sired two delightful little doves, now fated to be joined in matrimonial union with the Argata Royal House" Zu'ki smiled ruefully. "I think it is time we were going, don't you?"

"That sits fine with me, Commander. I cannot wait to get back to Mamy'eva. I shall be a rich man, shall I not?" the brute grinned.

"Indeed, you shall, Ja'ghur. More wealth than you could ever have imagined" Zu'ki mused. He turned in the saddle and addressed the men. "The hour of deliverance is upon us. I warn you one last time, there is to be no unnecessary brutality!" Zu'ki glanced at Ja'ghur, who turned away and spat on the ground.

The riders approach the farmstead in single file, traversing a meadow to the north and splash gently through a stream. They soon reached the perimeter fence and chained gate. "This would be a good place to tether the horses, you agree. We don't want them wandering off and waking the villagers?" Zu'ki whispered to Ny'azmi. The plan devised by Zu'ki and Ny'azmi was simple, yet simplicity was a virtue, especially when its success hinged on the co-operation of a notorious band of witless cut-throats! Under Hai'mur's supervision, five of Ja'ghur's motley crew would remain at the gate with the horses, ready to deal with any unexpected surprises. The remaining seven, including Zu'ki himself, would enter the property and seize the Princesses from their slumber, preferably without undue violence. They had come prepared with sufficient hemp rope to bind the Count, the Countess, and the Princesses' Handmaiden. Just to be on the safe side, the three adults would be gagged. The Princesses would be enticed to drink a draught of wodki, laced with a few drops of *Belladonna*, which would send them into a deep and peaceful slumber. Thereafter, they would be bundled in hemp sacking and carried to the waiting horses. Zu'ki would take charge of the welfare of the Princess Mikhouri, whilst the fate of the Princess Alicharia had been wisely entrusted to of Ny'azmi.

The group of seven, equipped with bow, quiver, knives, and swords, move stealthily through the yard towards the back door of the property, which presumably led to the kitchen. All sported dark cloths wrapped around their lower faces and drew their hoods close to avoid recognition. Whilst the building was large, it was only single storey. Zu'ki had visited the Count for supper a few weeks earlier, where he had determined that the sleeping quarters were at the north end of the building. To his knowledge, the sisters were domiciled in adjacent chambers, along the corridor from the Count and Countess. Ba'chi and Mos'cal began to prize the door with a 'jimmy-bar', grunting and heaving, until, finally, the edge began to splinter. "Another few tugs should do the trick!" Mos'cal grinned inanely. Zu'ki nodded encouragement. There was a loud crack, followed by a second, and a gratifying splintering of wood. Ba'chi drew a dagger, pushed open the door, and slipped inside, closely followed by the others. Zu'ki closed the door and untied the straps on his knapsack. He fished out the candles and passed them to each man. Mos'cal laid a small bundle of kindling on the floor and began to draw a small saw blade against the side of a thin magnesium bar. Soon enough, he succeeded in generating a flame and lit his candle. This was passed around to light the others.

"Remember! No-one is to be killed, is that understood?" Zu'ki hissed, glancing meaningfully at Ny'azmi.

He led the way, candle in one hand, sword in the other, through a narrow passage to the kitchen and beyond.

The kitchen was deserted. The heat from the coals in the hearth confirmed that fuel had been added within the past few hours, sufficient to heat a kettle at first light the following morning and prepare a light breakfast. Zu'ki gently pushed an adjacent door open and stepped into the pantry, which had a large oak table in the centre and serving trestles at every wall. The Count and the Countess were evidently no strangers to Banqueting, yet there was no evidence of preparations for an imminent gathering. "Where are the servant's quarters?" Ja'ghur hissed in his ear.

"The staff all live in the village, for this is not the city. Even the Count's retainer lived off-site, for he was an important man. You remember him, of course?" Zu'ki could not resist a chance to needle the brute!

Ja'ghur was astounded. "That bastard Ais'ka, is that who you mean? You never told me he was the Count's retainer?" he hissed.

"Pay it no mind, for we have more important things to consider, do we not?"

The door on the opposite side was unlocked. The seven men, led by Zu'ki, enter the spacious Dining Room. The Dining Table was large enough to accommodate some fourteen guests at supper and was replete with bronze candlestick holders and exquisitely carved and chairs. "Worth more than a few pieces of silver, I would wager?" Ja'ghur grinned.

"Put the fucking thing down, friend? We are not here to rob the place, are we?" Ny'azmi hissed menacingly in his ear.

"Right you are, friend!" Ja'ghur muttered sullenly. Inwardly, he seethed at being spoken to in such a disrespectful tone in front of his men. He made a mental note to deal with this insolent prick, at a first convenient opportunity.

Zu'ki indicated the door at the far end. "If my memory serves, we have a corridor immediately beyond the door, with two rooms off the side, directly facing one another. One is a Reception Room and the other is the old Count's study."

"The bedchambers are beyond that?" Ny'azmi whispered.

"There is a corridor at the far end to the right, I cannot recall if there is a room on the left, but the bedchambers are on the north side of the right corridor, excepting the Master Bedchamber, which is at the end" Zu'ki confided.

"This should be a piece of piss, shouldn't it?" Ba'chi spoke softly.

"Who has the wine?" Zu'ki asked.

"I do, my Lord" replied Na'kyr. "Here it is?"

"Keep hold of it, good man. Right, now comes the difficult part" Zu'ki grimaced in expectation.

Zu'ki tried the door and was relieved to find it unlocked. He turned the handle and pulled the door ajar, careful to avoid making a noise. He was surprised to see that the passage was well lit by candles, but then remembered that young children are often terrified of the dark, and that the Princesses were accustomed to candlelight in the corridors of the Royal Palace at night "I don't think we need the candles, after all" he sighed happily. "Remember, we are not to kill anyone, are we all clear on that? The Count is much loved and respected, locally and further afield. We do not want every community in the region baying for our blood?" The men nodded and blew out their candles, slipping them into concealed pockets within their robes.

Zu'ki moved silently along the corridor, heading for the door on the right, which he knew as the old man's study. He tried the handle; the door was unlocked. He gingerly pushes the door ajar to peer inside, noting the neat and tidy habits of the Count, for everything was as it should be. Zu'ki gently closed the door, nodded to Ny'azmi, and added to the far end of the corridor to peer around the corner. He glanced left and saw a small stairwell. "Shit!" he cursed softly. Evidently, there was a second storey, but he had not taken note of it when he had visited those few weeks before. "We will have to check it, just to be on the safe side" he hissed to Mos'cal, who had morphed beside him at the corner of the wall. During his brief reproof, Zu'ki had completely forgotten about the Reception Room on the opposite side of the corridor, as Ny'azmi's fingers curl around the handle...

At first, Kal'gil thought he must be dreaming, yet the sound came again, just as before. He stepped away from the small brazier that stood in the centre of the small brick hut to reach for his recurved bow and quiver of arrows. Somewhere, not too far away to the north, a horse was whinnying. At night, sound travels further than in daylight. Kal'gil, the old Count's trusted shepherd, steps out into the cool of the night and edges towards the far wall of the hut. The noise came again; a soft, yet distinct, whinny of a mare. The Count kept his horses stabled well to the north of the village, so this must be visitors, but at this hour of night? Kal'gil reached for the quiver at his right shoulder and notched an arrow. There was something not right about this. It would be wise to investigate the matter further.

Ny'azmi turns the handle and pushes the door ajar. He gaped in dumbstruck horror at the sight of the Crown Prince, who sat perched in an armchair facing the doorway, perusing a papyrus manuscript in the light of a candle. The Crown Prince, it must be remarked, was equally astounded by the unwelcome intrusion, and quickly rose from his chair. Ba'chi morphed beside Ny'azmi, took aim with his bow, and fired. The old Count screams in agony as he slumps to the floor, upending the chair as he fell.

"He was not to be killed! No-one was to be killed!" Ny'azmi roared, his hand slipping to the dagger at his hip.

Ja'ghur moved his blade quickly to the older man's throat. "Don't even think about it, friend?" he hissed. "As for the old bastard, who cares? Let us snatch the two bitches and be gone from here!"

"What is Hades name is going on?" Zu'ki hissed, his eyes widening with horror as he gaped at the stricken body of the Count. "Did you do this?" he spoke evenly to Ba'chi.

"It doesn't fucking matter, does it? We need to grab the two whores and get out of here!" The brute practically manhandled the Officer out of the room and into the corridor.

"Who is that? Who is there? What is going on?" an authoritative voice, an older woman, clipped from along the corridor.

"Shit!" Mos'cal whispered. "It's the old boot! What should we do?"

"Kill her!" hissed Ja'ghur.

Zu'ki was appalled. "Have you lost your wits? You will hang for it, Ja'ghur! We all will!"

"Grab the whores. I will deal with the old bitch!" Ja'ghur paced menacingly to the end of the corridor.

"Don't do it, Ja'ghur!" Zu'ki commanded.

"Fuck you!" Ja'ghur spat. He turns the corner to face the countess, who stands framed in the doorway of the Master Bedchamber at the fare end of the corridor, attired in her morning cloak. The woman opened her mouth to scream and was cruelly shot through the throat by a sneering Ja'ghur. "Fuck you, you old cunt!" he cackled. He turned to Mos'cal. "Take Ba'chi and Na'kyr and check upstairs. Kill anyone who is not the Princesses! And leave the fucking wine!"

"I will see you hang for this, Ja'ghur!" Zu'ki spoke icily.

"Shut your fucking mouth! I have had enough of your orders for one day!" the brute seethed.

The three raiders, including the placid Na'kyr, who had been appalled by the murders of the Count and Countess, race up the stairs to the second storey. When they reached the top, they turn right into a small alcove, with two doors on the right, and one at the end, facing south. "This one first!" he grimaced, before booting the door ajar. It was a Bedchamber, clearly in use, yet empty. "They must be next door? Ah, well, here goes the neighbourhood!" and booted the door ajar. This too was a Bedchamber, also clearly in use, yet it too was empty.

"My turn, matey, if you please! Third time lucky, eh?" Mos'cal grinned, and kicked the door in.

In the far corner of the room, the two terrified princesses sit on their haunches with their backs against the wall, legs drawn tight to their chests. Mikhouri clasps an ancient sword in both hands "Get up, whores! You are coming with us!" Mos'cal hissed. Suddenly, there was an unholy scream of anguish! Mos'cal and Na'kyr turn to gape in horror at Ba'chi, and the sword point that protruded grotesquely through his belly. "What the fuck!" gasped Mos'cal. Before either he or Na'kyr could react, Asel'ya had grabbed Ba'chi's dagger and, stepping to her left, she plunged it wickedly in to Na'kyr's groin, severing the artery. The boy screamed like a stuck pig and slid down the wall as his legs buckled beneath him.

"Murdering little skank!" Mos'cal roars at Asel'ya, who glowers defiantly back at him, her eyes gleaming with hatred, the bloodied sword held tight in her right hand. He advances on the woman when, suddenly, Ja'ghur looms behind her. His left hand snaked around Asel'ya's neck to clamp across her mouth, as his right drew his dagger across her throat, severing the artery in a sickening spray. Asel'ya fell to the floor, blood venting in torrents from her ruined neck. The Princesses scream in terror and are suddenly silenced as the brute advances into the room. Ja'ghur swatted the sword contemptuously from Mikhouri's hands, slapped Alicharia hard across the face, and scooped her up.

"Grab the other whore!" Ja'ghur snarled. "I have this feral cunt!"

The Princess Alicharia was manhandled down the stairs by a laughing Ja'ghur, kicking and screaming like an Amazon. Her timid and ashen sister, who tottered unsteadily on her feet at the sight of the bodies, was led courteously downstairs without murmur. Both were forced to drink the tainted wine, then were bound, gagged, and bundled in the cloth sacking, before being carried outside. Back in the Reception Room, the Old Count lay on the floor, breathing wearily, as tears course down his cheeks.

They should have hanged that murderous bastard Ja'ghur all those years earlier!

Kal'gil edged north toward the old Count's farmstead, close to the edge of the gallery woodland of the Illov'ya. A sudden movement, some fifty yards to the west, catches his eye and he went quickly down on one knee, scanning the landscape for danger. He could see five figures loitering by the gate, yet there were at least a dozen horses close by. The silence was suddenly rent by an ear-piercing scream, which caused one of the men to curse feelingly.

"Shit! What the fuck is going on in there?" Hai'mur spoke softly to the man next to him.

"Fuck knows! We had better get the horses ready for the off. I wouldn't be in the least surprised if the entire fucking village heard that!" the man replied.

Kal'gil frowns. He knew he could take these men down, for he had the advantage of surprise. Yet, he had no idea how many more there were. One man alone could not save the old Count and his family. He would seek out old Ais'ka's nephew, Uh'gui, for the man was a soldier of some repute, was he not? As for the old Count, his wife, and the two Royal Princesses, there was little he could do for them now!

He went down on his hands and knees and crawled into the cover of the trees, edging south. Soon enough, he broke cover and raced west across the meadow towards the village.

An hour later, the remnants of the riding party reach the ferry crossing on the west bank of the Wol'yi. This was the most dangerous part of their escape, for it would take twenty minutes for the group to cross to the opposite bank. It would be several hours yet before first light, and some hours thereafter before the alarm was raised, yet the slaughter may have been already discovered. The two Princesses were safely ensconced in a drugged slumber, secured across the saddles of Zu'ki and Ny'azmi's steeds, cloaked by old hemp cloths. The ferryman was perched on the grass beside a small fire, upon which a kettle of mint tea had long since bubbled. "It is good to see you again, my Lord. I decided it would be wise to wait on this side, what with the urgency of your mission."

"I am in your gratitude, kind Sir, as is the King himself" Zu'ki spoke evenly.

"Well, my Lord, if you and your comrades would like to board, we can be on our way!" said the ferryman.

Ja'ghur grunted at the kettle. "Have you got anything stronger than tea?" he grunted.

"I might have on the other side, my Lord" the ferryman grinned.

"Then let's get going, shall we?" the brute said gruffly.

They were soon safely across the river without interference and the ferryman led the way up the track to his home, a small cabin, ample for him and his wife now that their children had flown the nest. "I have wodki and berry wine, if that will suffice, my Lord?" the kindly old man smiled warmly at Ja'ghur.

"I will take a flagon of both, old man" the brute replied. Zu'ki glanced quickly at the thug, his eyes burning with hatred. There would be a reckoning between them, of that he was certain.

The old man returned with two flagons, which he passed to Ja'ghur. The ruffian took a slug of wodki and passed the flagon to Hai'mur. The ferryman turned to Zu'ki, who remained in the saddle, and beamed expectantly at him. "You have the King's gratitude, my dear fellow!" Zu'ki tossed a silver coin to the ferryman, who gaped at it in wonder.

"I am at the King's service, my Lord. Anytime you require me!" the old man said dutifully.

"I think my comrade would like to thank you for your hospitality" Zu'ki smiled warmly.

The old man turned expectantly to Ja'ghur, who plunged the point of his sword deep into his neck, before twisting it free and wiping it clean on his thigh. "Can we please get going? I can't wait to get home to my bed!"

Uh'gui led a party of the old Count's retainers across the meadow, a hundred yards or south of the farmstead, angling north toward the gates where Kal'gil had seen riders and their mounts. A grim-faced Kal'gil strode beside him, armed with sword and shield, in addition tohis trusty recurved bow. When they reached the gates, the men and the horses were long gone, yet there were copious quantities of dung. "You said there were likely a dozen of the bastards, did you not?"

"I saw five or six men, my Lord. There were likely twice as many horses!"

"We had better head inside, my Lord!" Dal'vych growled.

"Once we get inside, pair up and stay close to one another. We have no idea what we will find, do we?" Uh'gui

The group made their way through the gate and across the yard to the door, which had clearly been forced and no longer closed. The Kitchen and Dining Room were quickly secured, followed by the pantry. The group made their way through the door, into the Dining Room, and down the corridor towards the old Count's study. There they discovered the body of the old man, lying motionless in the Reception Room across from his study, and that of the countess, lying dead in a pool of blood in the corridor outside the Master Bedroom. Both had been killed by arrow strikes. Uh'gui seethed with rage as he paced back along the corridor to address Kal'gil and Dal'vych. "The Princesses rooms are at the top of those stairs and along the corridor. That is likely where the scream came from."

"Secure this fucking corridor! Nobody touches those bodies until the Surgeon arrives" Dal'vych growled at one of the retainers, who nodded silently.

Uh'gui went first, stealthily padding up the steps. A veteran of the campaigns against the Sauromatae east of the Wol'yi, the sight of blood, and of the horrors inflicted upon human flesh and bone by weapons of war no longer shocked him. Yet, as he encountered the three blood-soaked bodies in the narrow corridor of the upstairs tower, he felt a visceral revulsion. He recognised two of the victims, Ba'chi and Na'kyr, both of whom had been presumably slain by the valiant Handmaiden, Asel'ya, who died protecting her Royal wards. Uh'gui raged in petulant fury. "Bastards! Bastards! Treasonous, murdering filth!" he seethed. Dal'vych and Kal'gil gaped incomprehensively at the officer.

"Do you know who is responsible for this outrage, my Lord?" Dal'vych spoke softly.

"I am certain of it!" Uh'gui grimaced. "And, when I find him, I will hang him myself!"

"There are three bodies upstairs, including the Handmaiden, Asel'ya. The Princesses have been abducted!" an ashen-faced Uh'gui who informed the men when he reached the corridor.

"This is treason!" hissed Ji'vyk, aged only a year or so older than Uh'gui.

"The nearest body of men is at Vy'khu, is it not?" Uh'gui pressed. "Is there a charter across the river at this hour?"

"There are always ways across the river, at any hour, my Lord" Dal'vych smiled wryly.

"There is something you need to see, my Lord. The old Count has left us a clue, perhaps even the identity of his assailants" Ji'vyk spoke softly.

"Show me!" Uh'gui clipped.

Ji'vyk led the officer into the Reception Room and pointed to a piece of papyrus parchment that lay to the far side of the old man's body, away from the blood beneath him. "Have you touched it?" Uh'gui pressed Ji'vyk.

"No, my Lord, I have not. There is something scrawled upon it. It was written in the Count's own blood!"

Uh'gui paced across the room and knelt beside the old man's body, blinking back the tears. The parchment was papyrus, a long since drafted note of harvest yields for the past three decades, written in neat ledger, with fine black ink. There was indeed a message, written by the Crown Prince himself, shortly before his breath abated. Just as Ji'vyk surmised, it was scrawled in the Count's blood, with the stylus held in his right hand. It was a single word: *JA'GHUR.*

"I will see you hang, you murderous, treasonous scum!" Uh'gui spat feelingly. He turned and addressed Dal'vych. "How fast can you ride? I need you to get word to the Commandant at Vy'khu. There is no time to waste!"

"As you wish, my Lord" Dal'vych turned on his heels and paced out of the room.

"The rest of you, come with me!" Uh'gui clipped. The filth who perpetrated this outrage also murdered my uncle. Even the Royal Army may be involved in this night's evil. We must take the young boy and his family into protective custody, for all our sakes."

Seventeen

Ri'kur hawked and spat on the ground. He grinned at Er'kru and gestured to the neat stack of bales against the far wall of the barn. "Another three bales should be enough. We have a long ride ahead of us."

Er'kru glances around to make sure they were alone. "I overheard the soldiers saying we were heading east. What the fuck is that about? We should be tacking south, surely?" he whispered.

"You know better than to listen to the idle chatter of soldiers, especially these gobshites!" Ri'kur grinned. "We will be following the course of the Tor'gu, initially at least. After a short ride east, we will tack south" Ri'kur replied confidently.

"I don't know about you, but I have a bad feeling about this. Nobody in their right mind would go east. That is frontier territory, isn't it? If the rumours in Mamy'eva are anything to go by, the fucking place is crawling with Sauromatae right now!" Er'kru sighed despondently.

Ri'kur chuckled. "Are you afraid we might run into that rabble of shit-kickers we encountered these past few mornings, is that it?"

"Has anyone checked to see if they are still there?" Er'kru was visibly uneasy.

"Fuck those snakes! From what I saw yesterday in the clearing, they will be long gone by now. I doubt we will be seeing them anytime soon" Ri'kur quipped. "Now, you can fetch three more bales. I will fill the trough with water from the well." He paced out of the barn, leaving Er'kru alone with his fears.

Er'kru strolled towards the far wall. He grabbed a bale of hay and carried it across to the small cart. "I do hope you are right, old friend, for everyone's sake!"

In the Kitchen, Dru'kan stands at the far side of the table, sawing loaves of bread bought at the bakery in Bai'vych the previous morning with a serrated blade. He gazes at the rising sun through the far window. They have little time left before they must leave. On the opposite side of the table, Vas'ghil liberally smears each portion of sliced with fresh honey and arranges them neatly on plates. "I hope those lazy twats have got the horses fed and watered? We need to get going!" Dru'kan mused sourly.

Vas'ghil glanced quickly around the room, leaned in close and spoke in barely a whisper. "Do you know what happened last night?"

Dru'kan simply shrugged. "I hear things, of course, but in my experience, it is not wise to ask too many questions."

"If what I heard is true, we will hang, for sure?" Vas'ghil hissed.

"I would not be too concerned about what you may have heard, friend?" a voice clipped icily from the doorway.

Commander Hus'cha stood in the doorway, attired in his uniform and weaponry, his helmet tucked under his left arm. He smiled thinly at the two blushing renegades, who averted his gaze. "Are those plates ready? Put four slices on a small plate and prepare a goblet of mint tea for the Princesses?"

"Yes, my Lord!" Vas'ghil quipped obediently.

"You will refer to me as Commander Hus'cha, do we understand one another?" the two men nodded silently. "I am the nominal Second-in-Command of our little party of adventurers. If anything happens to Commander Zu'ki, you will take your orders from me, is that clear?"

"Yes, Commander Hus'cha!" the pair chirruped.

Vas'ghil laid four slices of honeyed bread on a small plate. He removed the kettle from the stove and carefully filled a large ceramic jug with boiling mint tea. A ration was decanted into a ceramic goblet, which was laid beside the small plate on the table. Hus'cha fixed the man with a steely gaze. "You can follow me. Bring the plate and the goblet with you."

"If that is your heart's desire, lead on, Commander Hus'cha" Vas'ghil smiled wryly.

Hus'cha glowered at the man. "I have no need for comedians! You would be well advised to remember that!" He turned and paced down the corridor.

Vas'ghil picked up the plate and goblet from the table and followed the Commander out of the room. Mos'cal met him in the corridor just outside the door and stepped to the side to allow him to pass. He nods a silent greeting to Dru'kan as he enters, then turns away to peer along the corridor. "What did that prick want?"

"He wished to remind us of who exactly is in charge, nothing more sinister than that!" Dru'kan smiled wryly.

"Fuck that cunt!" Mos'cal spat feelingly.

⟳

Vy'khu, August 493 BC

As the darkness wanes and the first spears of light pierce the horizon in the east, the Duty Commander in the North Tower of the Fortress of Vy'khu gave the signal to the Senior Guard at the gates below. The Senior Guard barks his command, and the heavy wooden gates groan as they open. A detachment of one-hundred-and-twenty heavily-armed cavalry, seasoned veterans of the recent campaigns against the Argata in 'the lands between the seas', thundered through and made their way along the dusty track to the junction with the main west-east road. The first sixty riders turn left and gallop west towards the east bank of the Wol'yi to secure the Wharf of

464

Ky'rovka and other ferry crossings to the north and south. Sixty riders turn right at the junction and head east, until they reach a fork with the minor road that leads north to Bai'vych. Thirty riders veer north, as their comrades at the rear kick their heels to gallop east and secure the southern bend of the Tor'gu. If the raiders had succeeded in crossing to the east bank of the Wol'yi, which seemed unlikely, within a few hours every settlement in the region would learn of last night's outrage!

Mikhouri snaked her left arm around her sister's shoulder and leaned in close to whisper in her ear. "They won't kill us. If they wanted to do so, they would not have made us drink the wine" she smiled reassuringly.

"I don't trust them! They murdered Grandmama and Grandpapa!" Alicharia hissed. "I will see them executed for it, every last one of them!"

"They will be hanged. You may rest assured of that, little sister" Mikhouri quipped softly.

"Is that the cruellest fate you can imagine? They are far too wicked for hanging! I want them to suffer!" Alicharia mused bitterly.

The pair had been awake for several hours and now sat perched on the edge of the single bed they had spent the remainder of their drug-induced slumber. Neither had any idea where they were, nor of what fate had in store for them. Almost as soon as they had woken, they had wept solemnly over the deaths of their beloved Grandparents, yet had steeled their resolve to face their abductors, no matter the cost. "We are Princesses, no matter what they say" the older girl insisted. A knock came at the door. Alicharia scowled. Mikhouri reached out and clasped her hand. "You may enter!" The door was unlocked and opened by one of the Guards stationed immediately outside. Commander Hus'cha steps inside and ushers Vas'ghil through, carrying the plate of bread and goblet of tea.

"Leave them on the table and go straight back to the Kitchen" Hus'cha rapped. Vas'ghil nodded and left. Hus'cha closes the door and turns to face the sisters. "You must eat. We have little time before we leave?"

"Where are you taking us?" Mikhouri demanded icily.

"That is not a matter which you should concern yourself, sweet child?" Hus'cha clipped.

Alicharia wrinkled her nose with distaste. "Who are you, Commander?" she demanded. "You wear the King's uniform and carry yourself as though you are an officer. And yet, you are a man without honour! You are nothing but filth! No better than that other shit-pig!"

Mikhouri rolled her eyes. Hus'cha chuckles at the slight to Commander Zu'ki. "Who I am, and who I serve, is of no concern to you, young Lady" Hus'cha smiled tightly. "Now, you must eat! We have little time to waste and will be on the road within the hour."

"You murdered our Grandparents! They had never wronged you!" Mikhouri spat angrily.

"I murdered no-one, my Lady. I only learned of their killing once the party had returned from Sar'kuc. If it is any consolation, I regret their deaths and understand your desire for justice and vengeance" he turned away and opened the door.

"I do hope you enjoy your breakfast, Commander. If the Gods have any grace, it shall be your last!" Mikhouri said chillingly.

Tor'gu River, August 493 BC

The riders set off an hour after first light, tacking east across the grassy plain toward the river Tor'gu, a little over eight miles away. Zu'ki planned to follow the course of the river south to where it turned east, then northeast, deep into frontier territory, until they reached the isolated former outpost of Sy'vynka. The distance was a little over sixty miles of open country, and the party hoped to arrive at Sy'vynka before last light, if all went well. Leaving soon after dawn, they would then continue du northwest for a further fifty miles to reach the crossing at Ra'shykh by dusk. There would be a further day's trek east to Sa'vyza, and then, a final journey of some sixty-five-miles to reach the garrison stationed at Krasnoe, a crucial depot in the rear defensive line of the Signet, within striking distance of the Uras'ka. They had been assured by General Til'koi that the garrison had sworn allegiance to the cause, and they would be welcomed. There they could rest for several days prior to their foray across the Uras'ka. The journey was not for the faint hearted, as much of the trek would traverse sparsely inhabited plain haunted by the threat of marauding bands of Sauromatae renegades.

The party comprised twenty-one men, including Hus'cha and his ten regulars, Zu'ki, Ny'azmi, Ja'ghur and his seven hirelings, accompanied by the two Princesses. The girls rode on the back of a single horse and had barely spoken to their captors since they had ventured east, despite Zu'ki's efforts to engage them in pleasantry. The sun was rising fast, with not a cloud in the sky, and the promise was for another glorious day. It was a perfect day for a leisurely canter, covering mile after mile of picturesque scenery. Zu'ki gazed south, and reined in. He raised a hand to shield his eyes and warily scans the horizon. "Shit!" he swore viciously.

Commander Hus'cha reined in beside him and smiled grimly. "I would venture twenty to thirty men, judging by the size of the dust cloud."

"They are from the garrison at Vy'khu, I would wager?" Zu'ki mused sourly.

"We have riders on our tail, my Lord" Vas'ghil ventured in a bemused tone.

"What the blazes!" Hus'cha mused gloomily.

"They aren't pursuing us, my Lord" Mos'cal ventured. "It looks like they are heading for the junction with the main road at Bai'vych. They are at least five miles away. I doubt they have even seen us?"

Zu'ki twists in his saddle and looks meaningfully at Hus'cha. The younger man nodded his assent. The decision was made. "Those men riding south will piquet the southern margins of the Tor'gu. There is no other option, is there?"

"We are going to cross the river and head northwest?" Ja'ghur grinned. He seemed bemused by the scuppering of the soldiers' plans.

"That is exactly what we shall do. According to my intelligence, there is a ford five miles to the northeast. We will cross the Tor'gu and continue northeast, at least for the next few hours" Zu'ki said emphatically.

"We should reach the south bank of the Kuban in a mere few hours. It is twenty miles north-west of Sy'vynka, and fifty miles east of those bastards" Mos'cal jerked his thumb at the dust cloud of the riders to the south.

"The Kuban is the last place they would look for us. It is sparsely populated and far from the Wol'yi. From there, we will tack east and reach Ni'vah by late afternoon. We should be safe by then!" Zu'ki said breezily.

"Course we will, dickhead!" Dru'kan mused cynically.

Ryg'nyk, August 493 BC

A party of twenty cavalry slow to a gentle trot as they clear the woodland fringe, a half mile from the coast, and follow the dusty track towards the ferry at Ryg'nyk. The old ferryman, Ar'gahl, had operated the crossing for nearly forty years and was well regarded by all. Despite his advancing years, he welcomed all passengers with a cheery smile, no matter the hour or weather. To the great surprise of the cavalrymen, no Ar'gahl morphed to greet them, and the door of the Ferryman's Cottage was firmly closed. "This is strange? Not like old Ar'gahl at all!" Dy'gryn, the Senior Officer, mused airily.

Without instruction, one of the men trotted further along the track toward the ferry, which was visible from the clearing. The soldier, aged in his late twenties, was named Kar'grych, an expert hunter with a keen eye for the ground. It was on the ground that he made his fateful discovery. It was a large discolouration of earth, a short distance from the Ferryman's Cottage: blood! Kar'grych grimaced and twisted in the saddle. "You need to come and see this, Sir!"

"What is it?" Dy'gryn spoke warily.

"It looks like blood, Sir! At least a pailful of the stuff, I would venture!" Kar'grych mused sadly.

Dy'gryn raised a hand to steady his men and trotted forward to where Kar'grych had reined in and, even now, kept his gaze fixed firmly on the patch of earth next to his mare. The Senior Officer glanced at the ground, his eyes widening in horror. He turned back to the main body of men. "Check the cottage! Kick the fucking door in if you must!"

The nearest six cavalrymen dismounted agilely and raced to the door. They tried the handle; it was locked from the inside. "Ry'dai! Get your fat arse out of the saddle, now!" one of the men hollered. The rest of the party laughed raucously. At six-foot-three, Ry'dai was one of the tallest men in the Ur'gai Royal Army, a colossus of muscle and sinew, without a trace of fat on his entire frame. The brute scowled, dismounted his steed, and trooped across the clearing to the cottage. A swift and brutal kick sent the door almost off its hinges and, with a well-earned smirk of triumph, the colossus strode into the room. What he saw almost brought tears to his eyes. In the far corner of the room, the aged widow, Naemessa, cradled the body of her dead husband of five decades. The woman had whimpered when the door had been kicked in, yet now she gazed uncomprehendingly, her eyes betraying her terror and bewilderment. "I am sorry, my Lady, truly I am" Ry'dai spoke softly as he padded across to kneel beside the widow. "We are your protectors and we come as friends. I am sorry we could not come soon enough."

Dy'gryn appeared in the doorway and gazes pityingly at the distressed woman and her slain husband. He turns away and barks his orders. "I need five men to ride south immediately. We need to inform the men at Ky'rovka and the garrison at Vy'khu. Those bastards made it to this side of the river, after all!"

Du'byka, August 493 BC

Several hours after first light, as the temperature is beginning to rise, Uh'gui stands at the passenger Wharf at Du'byka. He is garbed in civilian attire and carries no weaponry. News of the previous night's atrocity had not reached the populace of this picturesque little peninsula, yet it would do so within a mere few hours. A young woman, slim and petite, with dark brown hair, accompanied by a boy of no more than seven and a younger girl, suddenly gasps in shock. Other passengers turn and point west, murmuring softly among themselves. Uh'gui turned to follow their gaze. A group of soldiers, mounted on thoroughbred steeds, amble along the main street toward the Wharf. The Senior Officer reined in and dismounted, then strolled along the path to where the passengers waited to board. "I am looking for Uh'gui!" he spoke evenly.

"You have found him, friend" Uh'gui replied softly.

"Follow me, my Lord" the Officer clipped.

Uh'gui followed the man a short distance from the passengers, where their conversation will not be overheard. "What is it?"

"The bastards crossed by ferry to the east bank last night, my Lord" the Officer spoke softly.

"Can we be certain of this?" Uh'gui whispered.

"We have come from the ferry crossing at Ryg'nyk, my Lord" the soldier confessed. The ferryman, old Ar'gahl has been murdered. His wife recalls a group of passengers arriving late last night. Ar'gahl ferried them across and waited on the west bank for their return."

"They will surely head east. We do not have the men to pursue them!" Uh'gui mused bitterly.

"We think they will tack south, sooner rather than later. The east is far too dangerous, for such a small party, encumbered by the two Princesses" the Officer ventured.

"Not if they were taken by Sauromatae? By the Gods! If they have fallen into the clutches of those brutes" Uh'gui lied smoothly. The old Count's retainers had been sworn to secrecy of the identity of the raiders.

"We will find their trail, my Lord, I promise you. It would be madness to go east for more than a day's ride. By the end of this day, we will have gathered as much intelligence as we can on the summer's caravans from the east."

"I will not be returning alone, you understand?" Uh'gui grimaced. He blanched at the prospect of informing the King that his beloved granddaughters had been abducted.

"Our army is second to none, is it not? We will find them soon enough, my Lord. They have nowhere to run."

"I can only pray you are right, my friend" Uh'gui sighed softly. "Every village in the plains must be informed of this outrage."

"It will be done, my Lord, you have my word on that" the Officer said emphatically.

Uh'gui watched the man stroll away and mount his steed. The cavalry trot west along the main street. He reached in his pocket and pulled out a plum, buffing the skin on the fabric of his light woollen cloak, before biting in to the soft, juicy, flesh. "By the Gods, you will suffer for this, Ja'ghur. I will see to it personally!"

The party of soldiers arrived at the isolated farmstead in the mid-morning, following a tip-off from the local baker in Bai'vych. Whilst nobody could be certain, a small party of visitors had been staying in the area for the past week and had regularly patronised the local baker and butcher, yet not the local hostelry, *The Pine Kernel*. This lack of courtesy had aroused suspicion, even resentment, among locals, for it was unusual for season labourers not to do so, the baker had ventured eagerly.

"These men were Sauromatae, were they?" Dy'gryn had probed.

The Baker could not hide his astonishment. "They were no Sauromatae, my Lord! I would not have served them had they been so. They hailed from the southern reaches of the Wol'yi, or so one of the men informed me" the man had ventured with a knowing look.

"They claimed to be farm labourers. And yet, we have spoken with the overseer of the Count of Kran'ye, who confirms they did not bring the men here. Surely, such news would have travelled beyond the walls of the Count's Khur'yi?" Dy'gryn smiled tightly.

The baker had chuckled, much to the Officer's chagrin. "The Count is not the only prosperous landowner in the immediate vicinity, my Lord. Count Ma'ghri has a large estate to the west, though his accommodation is decidedly more rustic" the baker smiled wryly.

"Rustic? What in Hades name do you mean by that?" the soldier had demanded.

"If you journey due east along the track, in the direction of the Tor'gu, you can't miss it" the baker confided breezily. "There is a large, fortified farmstead, not far north of the track, about nine miles away. Alas, the place has become a little run down these past few years, ever since the old Count's death. The present Count Ma'ghri is not as enchanted by the fruits of the soil, nor his duties to the community" the man shrugged ruefully.

"Where would I find this Count Ma'ghri, if I wished to speak with him?" Dy'gryn smiled tightly.

"You would have to venture far to the east, my dear fellow! He is a Senior Officer in the Royal Army, currently serving in the Signet, or so it is said" the baker confessed.

The farmstead was deserted when the soldiers arrived, yet it had evidently not been so a few hours earlier. Whoever had spent the previous few nights here, they had evidently left in a hurry. A cursory appraisal of the stable yard confirmed their worst fears, for copious mounds of fresh dung were piled in a heap in the far corner of the yard. To a learned eye, this confirmed a presence of a not inconsequential body of men.

"How many of the buggers do you think there are?" Dy'gryn demanded. He glanced quickly around the Kitchen, noting with some consternation that the place was remarkably clean.

"I would venture at least twenty, judging by the quantity of fresh dung, Sir! More to the point, they were likely fed and watered an hour or so before they left" Ry'dai spoke evenly.

"Which means they could spend most of the morning on the road, provided their horses have been rested these past few days" Dy'gryn mused darkly. "We will have piquet's covering every road south by now."

"If this is where they were staying, there are only two options open to them, surely?" Ry'dai smiled wryly. "They can ride north, which is madness, or else cross the Tor'gu and head east, which would be suicidal!"

"These are likely reckless men, Ry'dai, yet there is a distinct whiff of something sinister about this entire affair" the Officer mused grimly.

"I am not sure I follow your reasoning, Sir?" Ry'dai furrows his brow in consternation.

"What would you do, if you were in their position?" Dy'gryn challenged.

"That would depend on a number of issues. How many men do I have? Are they reliable and disciplined? What kind of weapons am I carrying?" Ry'dai quipped.

"You are thinking like a soldier, man!" the older man smiled sardonically.

Ry'dai gaped in astonishment. "Are you saying what I think you are saying, my Lord?"

Dy'gryn gazed around the spotless room. Beyond the horse dung, all trace of evidence that might have indicated their precise numbers and habits had been expunged. Even the privy pots had been emptied and cleaned. "Not your typical seasonal labourers, would you say?"

"Begging your pardon, Sir, but this is an area I have little practical experience of. I grew up in Mamy'eva. My father was a tanner, my mother a maid."

"I think we may be dealing with soldiers, old friend, and not crude hirelings from the bumpkins. If that is true, then a suicidal course may come naturally to them, you would agree?"

"According to the locals, there is a ford across the Tor'gu, eight- or nine-miles due northwest"

"That is where they would cross. After that, they would likely continue northwest, at least for the next few hours" Dy'gryn sighed lengthily.

"That would take them to the Kuban, Sir? They surely wouldn't venture farther north, for those lands are plagued with bands of Sauromatae hunters, or so I am told" Ry'dai mused grimly.

"A group of well-armed and disciplined veterans might fancy their chances against a band of witless Sauromatae cut-throats, old friend" Dy'gryn chuckled.

"More fool them, Sir! And bloody good luck to them, for the sake of the two little Princesses!"

Pry'ga, August 493 BC

Fury's Gate is the name given by the Orch'tai to a narrow pass which fords a minor river, some twelve miles northeast of the ford across the Tor'gu. It is flanked to the north by an ellipsoidal escarpment of darkly coloured rock. Ancient lore posits that the site was used by early Sauromatae settlers for ritual child sacrifices, yet Zu'ki was bemused by such quaint superstition. Ja'ghur was evidently not, and he frowned in puzzlement at the spectre of the plateau. "This is a bad place! It is cursed by the souls of a thousand murdered innocents!" he mused piously.

The party made had made good ground and were surely far away from their pursuers. Yet, they were not safe, for by now the local garrison at Vy'khu had surely discovered the dead ferryman. It would not take long to learn of their recent arrival in Bai'vych and, soon enough, of the farmstead at Zi'gursk. These were eventualities that had been carefully considered during the intricate planning stages of the mission, and there was nothing that could tie the soldiers to the farmstead, nor Count Ma'ghri himself, who had handed over a key with no questions asked. The key had been reported as missing, muddying the waters further. It was fast approaching mid-morning and the sun burned brightly in a cloudless sky. All things being well, they would reach the southern bank of the Kuban within a mere few hours. The group was now embarking upon the most dangerous part of their escape, for they were venturing ever closer to the northeast frontier of the Duchy, demarcated by two rivers, the Ka'myka to the north and the Uras'ka to the east. The lands north of the Ka'myka were claimed by no-one; Orch'tai, Nur'gat, or even the Sauromatae. There is an ancient Sauromatae lore; *one cannot tame land even the Gods have forsaken*!

Zu'ki kicked his heels and spurred away from Ja'ghur to speak with Hus'cha and his scouting party of five men, half a mile or so further west. Hus'cha raised a hand in greeting as Zu'ki approached. "A fine morning, Sir!" he smiled brightly.

"We should make the Kuban in an hour, you would agree?" Zu'ki ventured breezily.

"That would be as good a place as any to rest for a while" Hus'cha nodded at the two young girls, trotting north with Ja'ghur and his motley band.

"They will not leave Ny'azmi's sight, I assure you" Zu'ki smiled tightly.

"What shall we do when we reach the Kuban? It would make no sense to follow its course due southeast?"

"We shall cross the river and head east to Zhy'nyh. It would be a nice little spot for a few hours rest from the afternoon sun, provided we sedate the children" Zu'ki smiled brightly. "In the late afternoon, once the sun has begun to fade and the air has cooled, we could ride for Ma'laya. It would be a suitable place to camp for the night, you would agree?"

"It is the last place they would look for us, so close to the eastern frontier. There would not have been sufficient time to send word of our passage" Hus'cha smiled wryly. "The children seem docile enough, at least for now."

"Their morning tea was laced with poppy oil, was it not?" Zu'ki raised an eyebrow mockingly. Hus'cha laughed lightly. "They will be glad of the brief sleep by the time we reach Zhy'nyh, provided we lace their tea at the Kuban?"

Hus'cha turned away to gaze at the horizon to the north and east. He grimaces. "There are the obvious dangers, my Lord, for it goes without saying, does it not?"

Zu'ki eyed the younger man shrewdly. "I never pegged you for a superstitious man, Hus'cha?" he remarked acidly. "We have nothing to fear, you may rest assured of that!"

"I hope so, my Lord" Hus'cha sighed softly.

Sol'yka River, August 493 BC

Twenty riders, bound by blood and honour, cross to the east bank of the Sol'yka at its narrowest point, four miles south of the abandoned fortress at Me'lyva. These men had kept a respectful distance from their quarry for several hours and were now a little over eight miles to the southeast of Pry'ga. The men were Sauromatae, hailing from a settlement on the banks of the Upper Uras'ka, five hundred miles to the northeast, in the shadows of the Uruk Mountains. They had enjoyed a profitable few weeks' hunting in the forests, deep inside the frontier of their hated enemy, yet must now return, for winter would be soon upon them. The party planned to ride for Khy'kyva, on the banks of a large estuary, twenty-five miles due northeast, where they would spend the night. They had parked a wagon in the stable yard of *The Old Haybarn*, whose amiable owner, Kry'vyn, a native of the Sama'zka, turned a blind eye to their annual sojourn into Orch'tai territory, in exchange for a hearty share of their bounty. Over the course of a decade, their relationship had become mutually profitable, so much so that Kry'vyn converted an old outbuilding into a smoking shed for the considerable quantities fish procured by his guests. A separate building was converted into a salting shed for the deer and wild boar the men hunted and butchered. The tribute was sufficient to last several moons beyond the winter solstice.

The leader of the band was a heavily tattooed and terrifying colossus named Zorughul, scion of an ancient and noble line of Sauromatae chieftains. Standing six feet and seven inches tall, he was a scarred veteran of the last campaigns against the Orch'tai in the western plains of the Uras'ka, some twenty summers before. Now aged in his middling thirties, he had long since disavowed his thirst for war with his hated enemy, yet never his desire for vengeance. He could not have expected to encounter a small detachment of Orch'tai cavalry, accompanied by a band of irregulars, who had been stationed at an isolated and fortified farmstead these past few days. It was clear to the Sauromatae hunters that this rabble intended to head for the Kuban, where they might rest for an hour or so, for it would soon be midday. Zorughul glanced at the sun in the sky, and twisted in his saddle to his younger brother, Zai'lan. "They would make a fine series of scalps, would they not?"

"We are not supposed to be looking for trouble, brother!" Zai'lan chided.

"We did not have to look far, did we? And besides, these are not civilians. We would commit no crime against the locals, nothing that Kry'vyn could hold against us?" the older man mocked.

"What of the children? We cannot kill them, surely?" Zai'lan raised an eyebrow mockingly.

"Of course, we will not? Perhaps they would make fine slaves!" Zorughul grinned slyly.

"We have no idea who they are, do we?" Zai'lan shrugged.

"Whoever they are, they are travelling with an armed escort and may be of some importance, you would agree?" the heavily tattooed man ventured with a wry smile.

"We cannot take them with us to Ka'luga, or any further beyond, can we? The world beyond the Ka'myka is no place for children of that age?" Zai'lan mused.

"And what would our sisters make of that, little brother?" Zorughul laughed heartily. "I promise we will keep them alive! If they are of any importance, then we can always leave them at *The Old Haybarn*."

"You seem supremely confident of our success, brother? These are professional soldiers. You would do well to remember that!" Zai'lan smiled wryly. In truth, he had absolute confidence in his older brother, the heir to their fiefdom.

"These are not soldiers, little brother, these are dead men! They have yet to realise their fate!"

Zai'lan raises his right hand to his brow, his thumb tucked beneath outstretched fingers, to gaze northeast. "There is good cover from the woodland to the north of the Kuban."

"And that, little brother, will be the cause of their doom!" Zorughul smiled tightly.

The journey northeast to the southern bank of the Kuban, a trek of some nine miles, took less than an hour. Zu'ki dismounted, removed his helmet, and wiped the sweat from his brow. He gazed around the landscape, noting the gentle rise of the plain on the north bank of the river, and, beyond it, the dense thatch of woodland. To the south, lay an endless expanse of plain, untouched by the scythe and devoid of settlement. Regardless of his three-year stint at the Royal Palace in Mamy'eva, Zu'ki was a seasoned veteran of innumerable foot patrols east of the Signet, an unforgiving world where overconfidence was as sure a killer as a Sauromatae arrow strike. As he scanned the horizon to the west and south, he felt sure they had not been pursued. It might be another day before scouting parties were mobilised in sufficient strength to venture this far east of the Tor'gu.

"This would be as good a place as any for a few hours respite, you would agree?" Zu'ki smiled breezily at Hus'cha.

The young Officer blinked in astonishment. "I would not overstay my welcome, my Lord" he replied.

"Is there something I need to be aware of, Commander?" Zu'ki asked coldly.

"You must know of the training garrison at Ky'ovu, Sir!"

Zu'ki gaped at the man. "I thought that was long since abandoned? It was a nought more than a recruiting station in its last years!"

"It was resurrected in the last spring, before the first levies were raised. This is perfect country for training cavalry and infantry" Hus'cha smiled wryly.

"And you never thought to mention this?" Zu'ki bridled. Some of the nearby soldiers, who had dismounted to collect water from the river, were startled by the Senior Officer's chagrin.

"I thought you knew, Sir? Admittedly, it is little more than a recruiting station, albeit one of the largest in the Duchy!"

"How many men are we talking about?" Zu'ki whispered. His voice was edged with concern.

"About three thousand men, I would venture. Most of them can barely sit in a saddle with their equipment, I would wager, much less engage in a fight."

"They can form scouting parties, can't they? Hades aflame!" Zu'ki spat in a bewildered tone.

"We should be fine for the next few hours, Sir" Hus'cha smiled reassuringly. "The men deserve a rest, not to mention the little Princesses, for it has been a long ride. It will be equally arduous this afternoon."

A short time later, several fires were burning, and the soldiers were in a relaxed mood. Kettles of water had been filled at the river and steam gently as the men stir the mint leaves. Rations of bread, dried apricots, and flagons of wodki were passed around the clusters of men at each fire. A safe distance to the west, Ja'ghur and his band of adventurers sit at a fire, sipping wodki and chatting quietly. A few yards further south, Ny'azmi sits with the Princesses, as a kettle bubbles on a fire. Zu'ki accepted a steaming goblet of mint tea and scanned the horizon to the west, south, and east. He paid little attention to the north, for no threat lay there. Zu'ki sips his tea and smiles ruefully at the absurdity of the scenes being enacted before his eyes, for such innocent tranquillity belied the precariousness of their security and the scale of their treachery. If they were taken alive, every single one of them would hang! He was blissfully incognisant of the unseen party of Sauromatae hunters now concealed in the woodland on the north bank of the Kuban, a mere few hundred yards away.

At the edge of the treeline, cloaked in the deathly shadows of the undergrowth, a small group of hunters skulked in silence. Zorughul smiled grimly, as a group of soldiers teased one of their, a man not disposed to good humour. He watched as an Officer, perhaps the Commander of the party, strolls to a fire set to the south, where an older man and the girls sat. His intrigue had long been pricked by their presence, for they were unusual companions. Zorughul cackled as the younger girl went wild, attacking the Officer with clenched fists, hissing, and cursing, like an Amazon, much to the amusement of the irregulars a few yards away, who laughed heartily. As she was manhandled away by the elder girl, the child wrestled free and spat contemptuously in the Officer's face, to the evident delight of the rabble of ruffians.

"Laugh, my friends, for the talons of death shall fasten upon you!" Zorughul mused silently.

Mikhouri glanced up from the flames of the small fire and scowled as she espied Zu'ki approaching. Ny'azmi raised a hand in greeting. Alicharia seethed in silence. "I trust all is well?" Zu'ki announced cheerily.

"All will be well when you are dangling at the end of a rope, traitor!" Mikhouri hissed.

"I am sorry about what happened to your Grandparent's, truly I am. No-one was supposed to die, I swear it" Zu'ki beseeched.

"Where are you taking us?" Mikhouri spoke icily.

"We will be riding east, at least for a while, then we will venture south" Zu'ki confirmed. Ny'azmi shot him a warning glance, but the Commander simply ignored him. "You will be safe, I assure you. No harm will come to you!"

"Have you thrown your lot in with the Sauromatae, Commander? Do you plan to sell us for a princely sum in gold, is that it?" the girl spoke witheringly.

"You will not be sold, either of you" Zu'ki smiled sadly at the children. Alicharia could not even bring herself to look at him. She brooded silently; her gaze transfixed by a clutch of wildflowers at her feet.

"You will accompany us for the next few days. It will be arduous, I do not deny it, but if you behave, I am sure we can avoid any regrettable unpleasantries."

"You expect us to trust you, Commander, after what you have done?" Mikhouri glowered at the man. "You think we would trust that murderous snake, Ja'ghur, or the rest of his filthy tribe!"

Ny'azmi laughed softly. Zu'ki smiled wryly. "No, my Lady, I do not. Ny'azmi here will be your protector, until we meet up with our escort."

The two girls exchanged bewildered glances. "There are other soldiers involved in this treason! What mischief have you planned for the realm?" Mikhouri eyes gleam with hatred.

"That is of no concern of yours, young Lady. Nor of your sisters, despite her interest in military affairs! I promise you will be safely returned to your parents the moment our grievances have been addressed" Zu'ki replied evenly.

Alicharia sprang like a crazed animal, hissing and cursing, to attack the astonished Officer with clenched fists. "I hate you! I hate you! Treacherous, murderous cunt!" she raged. Ny'azmi rose to intervene. Ja'ghur and his men laughed raucously at the spectacle of the child's rancour.

Mikhouri rose and stepped around the fire. "Don't you dare lay one of your filthy fingers upon her!" she hissed at Ny'azmi. She seized the younger girl firmly by the shoulders and turned her around. "Stop it! He is not worth it! His time will come, I promise you."

"I am sorry for your Grandparents, truly I am!" Zu'ki spoke softly. Alicharia twisted away from her sister's grip and spat in the Officer's face. Mikhouri dragged her away. Zu'ki wiped spittle from his face and gazed icily at the children. "I would be advised to mind my manners, if I were you!" he hissed menacingly.

"Save your regrets for the Hangman, Commander, for rest assured that you shall hang!" the girl said icily.

Mikhouri turned to whisper something to her sister, and then turned back to Zu'ki and Ny'azmi. Suddenly, she frowned in puzzlement, blinking fast, as her eyes widen in terror. She began to chew her lip as her hands tremble. "If they don't get you first, that is!" the child gazed ominously north, all colour draining from her face. Zu'ki followed the girls gaze. *And saw death!*

A party of fifteen riders stream from the woodland in single column, to race across the plain toward the river. Unbeknown to the dumbstruck fugitives on the south bank of the river, all were expert killers, deadly in the saddle with a bow and arrow. Within seconds, three Orch'tai cavalrymen were down with arrows in their chests, as the air hissed with the incoming hail.

"Alicharia! This way?" Mikhouri screamed. She grabbed the younger girl and threw her on to the back of the horse, before leaping quickly into the saddle. She kicked her heels into the mare's flanks to spur her to the gallop. "Hold tight!" she yelled.

The mare spurs away across the plain, before splashing into the water and heading for the north bank and the safety of the woods, far away to the west. Mos'cal raced to his mount to retrieve his bow and quiver. He quickly notches an arrow to take aim at the fleeing children, but Zu'ki roared him to stop. By now, Hus'cha's cavalry had begun to engage their assailants with their own salvos, and two hunters fell from their saddles to immediately still. Ja'ghur and his band quickly concluded that this was not their fight and were already in the saddle, splashing into the water, cantering after the two fugitives. Neither Zu'ki, nor Ny'azmi, could prevent their flight. Ny'azmi vaults agilely into the saddle, kicks his heels, and spurs after the renegades, for he had sworn an oath to protect the lives of the Princesses. Zu'ki turns and races toward Hus'cha's beleaguered band. Before he reached his steed, he was struck twice in the chest and fell to the grass. The traitor twitched twice, and then stilled forever!

"Hold on tight!" Mikhouri spoke breathlessly as the mare thunders across the gentle uplands of the plain toward the safety of the trees. She glanced quickly behind and espied the pursuing raiders, led by Mos'cal, who had cleared the Kuban and were now pressing hard after them. As they reached the safety of the treeline, the mare slowed to a canter and ploughed into cover, hooves pounding a well-worn track that veers north-west into the gloom of the canopy.

"Where are we going?" Alicharia yelled.

"As far away as we can!" Mikhouri replied. An arrow flashed past to bury itself in a tree to their left. Alicharia screamed. "Be quiet!" Mikhouri scolded.

Another arrow flashes past, perilously close. Mikhouri kicks her heels, encouraging the mare to increase her pace. Without warning, the mare suddenly rears in terror, a spray of warm, arterial blood mists across the younger girl's face. A well-aimed arrow strike fired from the front has taken her cleanly through the throat. The mare collapsed instantly, venting blood in torrents from her mouth, as the two sisters are spilled into the ferns, miraculously unharmed. Mikhouri reacted instantly, grabbing her sister by the hand, and leading her into cover. "Are you hurt?" the older girl asked. Alicharia, who was weeping silently, shook her head. "Be quiet!" Mikhouri hissed. "We need to get far away! Let us go this way?" The two fugitives, wearing only in their sleeping gowns, race into the safety of the dense undergrowth.

The Sauromatae raising party had initially concentrated their efforts on the Orch'tai cavalry, yet they had witnessed the escape of the children, and the flight of their pursuers. Two of their number had taken careful aim from the saddle and despatched Er'kru and Hai'mur to the tender mercy of the ferryman, both felled from their saddles with a breath-taking contempt. Hus'cha's cavalrymen had rallied to stage a determined defence and slain three of their hated enemy. Despite their valour, they had been quickly slaughtered, for few on earth could match the agility and accuracy of Sauromatae bowmen.

They beat with the horse as they breathe with the bow!

Hus'cha and Zu'ki were dead. The surviving Sauromatae hunters plough through the Kuban to race across the plain in pursuit of Ja'ghur and his merry band.

It was a glorious day for the hunt!

Mos'cal was a superb horseman, having learned when he was younger than Alicharia. The youngest son of a tenant farmer in Zhu'ryk, a tiny hamlet one hundred miles southeast of Mamy'eva, he was a skilled hunter and expert bowman, as good as any Sauromatae, as he had proven in the Western Plains. It was his arrows, fired at the gallop, which had haunted the final moments of the two Princesses as they spurred into the cover trees, yet it was not his that had felled their mare. Mos'cal glanced nervously around, for, if he had not fired the fatal shot, then who had? Where in Hades name where the girls? The pursuers dismounted and began scouring the undergrowth, desperately seeking any sign of the young fugitives. A frowning Ny'azmi stood to the right of Ja'ghur, gazing at the arrow-shaft protruding from the mare's throat. *It had surely been fired from the front, and never from behind?*

"I see you have not lost your touch!" Ja'ghur grinned at the dead horse, the arrow protruding grotesquely from its throat.
"That isn't one of mine, Ja'ghur! I didn't kill anything!"
"Then who the fuck did?" Ja'ghur growled.

Before Mos'cal could reply, two arrows hiss through the air to strike Ny'azmi squarely in the chest, killing him instantly. In the space of a few terrifying seconds, a hail of arrows from the undergrowth to the northeast had downed five of the horses, as the remainder fled in terror! Ja'ghur and Mos'cal dive to the ground and scurry into the safety of the dense undergrowth.

"Keep your fucking heads down, you useless tits!" Ja'ghur growled.
"What about the Princesses? We won't find them now?" Mos'cal hissed.
"A pox on their bald cunts! Leave them to die!" Ja'ghur seethed.

"I don't fancy our chances against these murderous bastards, whoever they are?" Mos'cal whispered hoarsely.

"Let's get going. Keep your fucking heads down if you want to live! From now on, it's every man for himself, you understand?"

In a mere matter of moments, hunters have become quarry!

Zorughul and Zai'lan were adept stalkers. In the instant that their comrade had been downed, the fugitives had scattered like startled rabbits into the undergrowth. Zorughul grinned at his sibling. "Are you ready for the hunt, brother?" Zai'lan smiled tightly and nodded. The pair edge forward, weaving through the tangle of fern and bramble, bowstrings taut, arrows notched and ready. The rest of their tribe, including the newly arrived survivors from the plains, fan out in curved extended line and move stealthily towards the track, stalking the undergrowth with the confidence of seasoned predators.

Dru'kan dropped to one knee, his entire body shrouded by the dense canopy of ferns. He sucked his teeth and glanced to his rear. He was alone. Mos'cal and Ja'ghur had been with him earlier but must now have abandoned him to his fate. "Bloody typical" Dru'kan seethed silently. A twig snaps somewhere to his left, and Dru'kan edges his sword silently from its scabbard at his left hip. If he were fated to die this day, he would not go down without a fight. He shivered lightly, despite the day's heat, and waited patiently. No further sound came. Dru'kan sighs softly to himself and edges cautiously forward, the blade held tightly in his right hand, as his left hand gingerly moves the ferns out of his line of sight. He glanced quickly to his rear; there was no sight or sound of anyone else, friend or foe. Dru'kan smiled grimly and continued north. He did not get far!

There came an eerie sound, animal-like, to his right, and the canopy suddenly parted as the boar charged him at close range. It was a titanic creature; weighing over five-hundred pounds, with a shoulder height in excess of three-and-a-half feet, and a large, thick head with elongated lower canines, which could gore a man to death in a mere matter of moments. Dru'kan screams in terror as the animal collided with him with a sickening velocity. The sword was thrown from his hand to skitter helplessly into the ferns as he was sent hurtling to his back. Dru'kan screamed again as the boar gored his abdomen with its canines, as blood foams at his lips. The boar was now on top of him, savagely goring his face and neck, as his left-hand scrabbles for the dagger at his hip. The boar head-butted him and plunged its right canine into his neck, severing the artery and vein in an explosion of crimson. Dru'kan died. He was the not the first of Ja'ghur's merry ban to die this day. He would certainly not be the last!

A sudden snap of a twig, perilously close to their left, sends the sisters scurrying into the cover of a large bush. Mikhouri raised an index finger to her lips, imploring Alicharia to silence. Both girls shiver as a blood-curdling scream cuts the deathly silence like a honed razor. Alicharia whimpers. There is movement to the right, not far away, and the foreboding dread of lithe footfalls coming ever closer to their position. Mikhouri reached out and touched a finger to her sister's lips, eyes telegraphing her command. Whatever it was, animal or man, it soon slinked into the undergrowth. After what seemed like an eternity, Mikhouri decided it was safe to move. "We shall continue west, then head south towards the plain!" she whispers softly. The girls slip through the undergrowth, taking care so as not to make a sound or disturb any animal to flight.

Soon enough, they espied a small clearing, some twenty or so yards to their front. "I think we should go that way?" Mikhouri whispered softly and pointed south. Alicharia nodded. The pair skirted a large oak tree, keeping their profile low, when the younger girl suddenly turns and screams in terror! Mikhouri baulked! The body of a man was suspended from a large branch at the front of the oak, his back against the trunk, arms outstretched above him, and his wrists bound tightly by hemp-rope.

His ears have been removed, eyes brutally gouged, and his throat severed almost to the bone. The tongue had been cut and drawn through the gaping wound to hang upon his chest. *The ritual defilement of the Sauromatae!* It was Zafizal! Two arrows were lodged in his chest, as sure a death sentence as any, presumably inflicted before his mutilation. As the two girls gape in mortified terror, an arrow hisses and bites into a sapling to their left. The girls dive for cover, scurrying into the undergrowth, as further arrows taunt their flight.

Zafizal cursed silently. He was alone and isolated, surrounded by killers who would gut him with a smile on their faces, or a ballad on their tongue! He had been the farthest to the west when the arrows had taken Ny'azmi and the horses. Before the old man's body had hit the dirt, he had dived into cover and raced south until he had found a safe hiding place, certain that no-one would find him. From the safety of his covert, he had heard sounds of several men close to his position, edging west, with the lithe footfalls of seasoned hunters. He had even heard their dialect and had correctly placed its origins. These men were Sauromatae, hailing from the lands to the northwest Uras'ka. He had heard tale of their savagery, for they were a cruel and feral foe who delighted in inflicting barbarous insults upon the corpses of their enemies. He gritted his teeth in grim determination. What advice had that fucker Ja'ghur regaled to them, shortly before they had scattered like startled pheasants? *Keep your fucking heads down if you want to live! From now on, it is every man for himself!* An ear-piercing, blood-curdling scream of pure terror shrilled from the woodland somewhere to the east. Zafizal flinches and closes his eyes, praying silently to the Gods for salvation. He made his decision. He would tack west, for a brief while, long enough to throw these bastards off his trail, and then head south, straight across the small stream, some thirty yards to his left, for he could discern its tell-tale trickle. Once safely across, he would be home and dry, for the edge of the woodland was a mere hundred yards to the south. There was no time to waste, for this enemy was merciless. It was now, or never!

Zafizal edged cautiously through the ferns, keeping his profile low, his eyes scanning for danger. He dropped to one knee, as a twig snapped somewhere to his right. *How the former Orch'tai archer wished he had his trusty bow and quiver of arrows with him now!* He listened intently for any sound of approaching danger, yet there was only a deathly silence. The coast was clear; it was time to move! If he could make it a few more yards due west, he could then tack south, for his pursuers were presumably long gone. He let out a brief sigh of relief. An unseen hand slips around his neck to clamp his mouth. The point of a dagger, held firmly in the right hand of his assailant, is pressed into the right side of his throat. "Stand up, Orch'tai scum!" Zai'lan hissed. Zafizal was terrified, yet he knew it was wiser to obey the command. If he could lull his assailant into a false sense of confidence, there was a sliver of a chance of survival. It was hope born of sheer desperation, dashed by the fates in a heartbeat, as Zai'lan clicked his tongue. Two hunters rose from the undergrowth, seven yards to his left, with arrows notched. It was the twins, Jai'tu and Nai'da, aged in their early twenties. Zafizal blinked fast as two arrows struck him cleanly in the chest. His body convulsed, and then went limp.

Mikhouri espied a suitable hiding place and led her sister to safety. "They can't be far behind us! Whatever happens, no matter how awful, don't scream!" she beseeched. There came the sound of padding footfalls ever closer to their nest, converging from several directions. The closest stalker, a mere yard to their right, suddenly pauses to kneel in the dirt, his hand resting on the ground, a mere half-yard from Mikhouri's foot. There came a blood-curdling scream; a shrill of pure terror, from someone, somewhere, not far to the left. This was followed by sound of a struggle, just to the right, and Mikhouri saw the hand whip away, to be followed by a thud, as the body fell to the dirt. It was Mos'cal! Rather, it was what remained of him, for his head had been expertly scythed! She closes her eyes and blinks fast, stilling an urge to retch, as her hand snaked around Alicharia's neck to clamp her mouth to stay the terrified child from screaming. Mikhouri watched in morbid fascination as Mos'cal's lifeblood vents obscenely from the ruined arteries of his neck. Despite her terror, there was some meagre morsel of comfort.

Ja'ghur's band of traitors faced certain annihilation!

Vas'ghil and Ri'kur skulk silently in the dense undergrowth on the north bank of a small stream. They were certain their pursuers had slipped past and were now likely far to the west or north. Only then did they dare break cover. "These cunts are Sauromatae! We need to get as far away from here as we can" Vas'ghil whispered softly.

"Let's get back to the plains. There must be a couple of spare horses about?" Ri'kur whispered. "These pricks are too busy hunting us in the forest, aren't they?"

"You are right, old friend!" Vas'ghil grinned. "I'll be damned if I'm going to die here. This isn't even our fight!"

"You saw what they did to poor Zafizal! These people are fucking feral!" Ri'kur hissed. "I'm not going to die like that! Let's get the fuck out of here."

The two men emerged from cover and crossed the stream, scurrying up the south bank to move stealthily through the undergrowth, paying great heed to make as little noise as possible. They had to presume that everyone else, including the little whores, were surely dead. If that were true, there could be a dozen or so Sauromatae hunting them in these woods, and they would not rest until they had slaughtered them. Suddenly, a twig snaps, somewhere to the west, not far away. Vas'ghil dropped to one knee and scanned around. His right hand moved to the dagger at his left hip. There was only silence. The deathly silence was cruelly cleaved by an ear-piercing, scream of terror! It must be Mos'cal or Dru'kan, for both had crept by their covert on the bank of the stream a short while after their pursuers. "This place gives me the fucking creeps" Vas'ghil hissed. "It looks like they are heading north. We will be fine if we keep south!"

The men creep through the undergrowth, heading southwest, to where the track meets a small clearing. Somewhere in the distance, a horse whinnied. Ri'kur sighs with relief. "At least there is one horse. What are we waiting for?"

"Something's not right! I don't like it. Let us keep going this way" cautioned Vas'ghil

The men weave through the undergrowth, keeping their profiles low. Vas'ghil raised his left hand and went down on one knee, extending his left arm to point with his index finger. "Look? Over there! What the fuck is he doing?"

"It's Ja'ghur! The dozy bastard is sat on a log, without a care in the fucking world. What the fuck is he thinking?"
"Waiting for us, perhaps? Still, I don't like it! I have a bad feeling about this!" said Vas'ghil.

Ja'ghur was perched on a log on the near side of the clearing, seemingly immersed in his thoughts. A pair of horses loom into view at the far edge of the clearing and begin to graze, unperturbed by the brute's brooding presence. The two fugitives creep through the ferns, almost to the edge of the clearing, no more than half-a-dozen yards from the log where Ja'ghur sat with his back to them. "Ja'ghur!" Vas'ghil hissed. "Ja'ghur!" The brute did not reply. "The coast is clear, let's go!" hissed Vas'ghil. The two men race from cover to approach the seated figure. When they reach Ja'ghur, they stop dead in their tracks, their eyes widening and jaws sagging in horrified disbelief. Ja'ghur is dead! His eyes have been brutally gouged, his ears removed, and his tongue protruded through a gaping wound in his throat to hang grotesquely upon his chest! His abdomen has been expertly incised, and nearly all his innards; guts, heart, and lungs, are missing! The two fugitives turn to flee and are mercilessly cut down with arrows fired by the Sauromatae hunters on the opposite side of the clearing.

The shrill of abject terror that heralded Mos'cal's last rites came from none other than Ja'ghur himself! The pair were skulking in the undergrowth, side-by-side, their eyes scanning for danger, when Alicharia had screamed. "It's the whores!" Ja'ghur hissed. He tapped Mos'cal on the shoulder and pointed north. "You go that way, and I will head west. I couldn't give a fuck what the army wants with them. I want them silenced. If they survive, they will see us hanged!"

"I agree with you, Boss! A crying shame about the older girl, for she is a pretty wench and is old enough for a half-decent shafting!" Mos'cal sighed sadly.

"You don't have time to fuck her, dimwit! Not unless you run a blade in her bald cunt!" Ja'ghur glowered evilly. Mos'cal was a sick bastard, with a penchant for young flesh. If he had been graced with a younger sister, her virtue would have not survived long beyond her ninth birthday!

"I was thinking about doing that to the other bitch!"

"You are one sick fucker. Do you know that?" Ja'ghur grimaced. "Just knife the whores and be done with it. If we make it out of here alive, then you can fuck the first farm-girl we meet, no matter her age!"

Mos'cal grinned and set off north. Ja'ghur emerges from cover to head west, weaving around a sizable bush, before tacking south, through a small covert in the undergrowth. He did not see Mos'cal freeze, and stoop to one knee, left hand outstretched in the dirt, on the opposite side of the bush. Ja'ghur *sensed* something; there was no other word to describe his foreboding. He *sensed* something sinister, lurking close by. He scurried into cover and turned to face north, just in time to see a gore-smeared colossus, a giant of a man, taller than him, loom menacingly out of the undergrowth to close with his unsuspecting prey. Without a bow and arrow, he was powerless to save Mos'cal, yet he could surely have warned his comrade. Instead, he screamed; a blood-curdling, shiver-inducing, shrill of terror! As Zorughul's left hand clamped firmly around the mouth of his victim, and his sword point was driven deep into the right side of Mos'cal's throat, the entire undergrowth to the east blossomed with Sauromatae hunters, all armed with recurved bows, arrows notched and ready. Ja'ghur had never felt such fear in all his born days! He saw the bush shake violently, then the colossus rose, its face showered in his victim's blood, the bloodied sword in in his right hand, the severed head clutched by its hair in his left.

The nearest Sauromatae hunter clicked his tongue twice. Ja'ghur turned and crawled on his hands and knees, further along the narrow covert. He knew what he now had to do; there was no other option open to him. The brute rose from cover and ran as fast as he could, darting left and right, as a flurry of arrows flash harmlessly past. "Run, fatty, run!" his pursuers taunted, yet they were seemingly incapable of preventing his escape. Now was the time! Ja'ghur dived in to cover and scurried into a small patch of cleared ground. He could cross this easily and find a place to hide on the far side. *His pursuers would surely never expect that he would opt for such an obvious hiding place.* In rashness born of desperation, he completely missed the significance of the cleared ground. As he moved quickly across, the ground opened beneath him and he fell into the bear-trap to land on stake of finely-honed pine, buried deep in the earth. It went straight through his lower back and impaled him. Ja'ghur screamed in agony, over and over, as the bemused stalkers close around him!

The terrified sisters did not dare break cover until they were sure the coast was clear. They continue south, weaving through the dense canopy of ferns, heading for the safety of the plain. Their captors were being systematically hunted to extinction, yet surely no-one would fear two little girls. "We will, be fine, sweet sister, you must trust me" Mikhouri attempted to soothe a plainly terrified Alicharia. She too was scared, for they were being hunted by Sauromatae, and such folk were merciless. They soon reach a small stream and pause to slake their thirst. Neither child felt hungry, even though they had not eaten since first light. They plod across the stream, to scurry up the opposite bank and dive into cover. *They must surely reach the safety of the plains, by grace of the Gods themselves.*

Soon enough, they did. With every cautious footfall, the gloom was thinning as the trees became less thick and the plains beckoned. "Are you hurt?" Mikhouri whispered. Alicharia shook her head. "We don't have far to go now. Once we reach the top of this hill, we should be safe. See, there is a track?" she pointed encouragingly to a well-worn path which curves over the rise. The sisters move quickly, no longer caring about noise, for they were safe! As they scramble up the verge, they could clearly see the plain beyond. And yet, they were not safe! A lone figure stands silhouetted at the far end of the track, facing south. He was a giant; perhaps the tallest man they had ever seen in all their lives. Almost if he sensed their presence, perhaps even smelt them, the giant slowly turned north. The man was heavily tattooed and wielded a heavy sword in his right hand. His left held Mos'cal's severed head by a clutch of blood-matted hair! On either side of the track, a series of sinister figures morph from the undergrowth. The sisters scream!

Gods are merciless, just like the Sauromatae!